18th & M

by

Derek V. Brooks

Eloquent Books

Copyright 2009

All rights reserved – Derek V. Brooks

No part of this book may be reproduced or transmitted in any form or by any means, graphic, electronic, or mechanical, including photocopying, recording, taping, or by any information storage retrieval system, without the permission, in writing, from the publisher.

Eloquent Books
An imprint of Strategic Book Group
P.O. Box 333
Durham CT 06422
www.StrategicBookGroup.com

ISBN: 978-1-60911-060-4

Printed in the United States of America
All the characters in this novel are fictitious and created by the author's imagination. Any resemblance to actual persons living or dead is purely coincidental.

Book Design: SP

Dedication

This is dedicated to the memory of my father, Charles S. Brooks. Even though he is no longer here to share in my joy and accomplishments; I know he is somewhere looking down upon me with pride.

Table Of Contents

#	Page
1	9
2	13
3	27
4	33
5	39
6	53
7	57
8	73
9	81
10	99
11	111
12	119
13	127
14	137
15	141
16	151
17	153
18	157
19	165
20	173
21	181
22	185
23	195
24	201
25	205
26	211
27	221
28	237
29	245
30	251
31	263
32	293
33	301
34	303
35	313
36	321
37	323
38	345

He slipped up from behind and seized his victim before he knew he was there. "Shhh, let it happen," the man dressed in black whispered as he tightened his grip around his victim's neck and the chloroform filled his nostrils. His movements were as graceful and sure as a cheetah on the Serengeti Plains stalking its prey. The struggle was brief and he felt his victim relax as he involuntarily slipped into unconsciousness.

The cold filthy water of the Potomac River brought him back to reality as he awakened to a nightmare. His hands and feet were bound with rope and his arms and legs were bound together with duct tape. Water dripped from his soaked head. He was hanging upside down above the water. He tried to struggle, but it was futile. Besides, if he were to fall he would fall in the river with no way to right himself, he would surely drown.

The man in black, noticing that his victim was now awake, pulled him up over the rail that kept the visitors to the East Potomac Park from falling into the river. He dropped him on the sidewalk that ran the length of the park and all the way around Haines Point.

The young man on the ground pleaded with his captor, "What are you doing man? Who are you? What do you want?"

"I want you to suffer and die," the man in black said evenly.

"Why?"

"You know why motherfucker," he put duct tape over the man's mouth and wrapped it around his head several times before ripping it from the roll. "Now it's your time to suffer."

1

The talk was all around town. It was on the television news stations, in the print media, and on everybody's lips. Washington, D.C. was under the grip of a serial killer. The so-called serial predator is stalking and killing at a breakneck pace. Not since the D.C. Snipers has the region been under this type of siege. The latest victim, a twenty-three year old male from the Sirsum Corda housing projects, was shot multiple times in the legs and then had his head nearly severed from his body.

Fox 5 news anchor Holly Robertson reported, "An unidentified black male was found in the unit block of P Street Southwest D.C. by a woman out walking her dog in the early morning. Police say they did not receive any calls for sounds of gunshots and the homicide is under investigation."

Maria turned from the TV following Robertson's report and said to the patrons eating breakfast at the counter of Lucky's Diner, "I sure hope the cops do something to catch that sick bastard soon!"

Paul Smith, a burly forty-three year old Metro bus driver chimed in, "I don't know; it seems like the only people who are being killed are drug dealers and criminals. Maybe this guy is doing the city a big favor."

"Well, all killing is wrong no matter who's being killed," added Maria, a sexy Latino woman from Brazil with a body to die for. Her chest, thighs, and hips all hit on the right proportions. She has a caramel brown complexion with long, full, radiant hair. She is married to Manuel who owns the diner. They have been in business for nearly fourteen years and are a staple of the community. Maria works the counter while Manuel cooks. They are good people who believe in community and sharing. Once, a homeless guy from the New York Avenue shelter came into the diner and ordered breakfast. When he received the food, he said he did not have any money. Manuel, who donates time and services to several charitable organizations, fed the man for free.

The diner included a mix of city and federal government

employees on their way to work. Lucky's is a very popular diner where you can either sit in one of the comfortable vintage booths or carry your food out. Most people call in large orders for their entire office and send one person to pick it up. Metropolitan Police Department (MPD) officer's frequent Lucky's and engage the patrons in conversation. However, everyone was on edge on the subject of the possible serial killer. The police were at a loss for answers. There seemed to be no rhyme or reason to the killings. For the most part the victims did not seem connected, nor was there any apparent motive.

Officer Briscoe stopped in to have breakfast before he was due in court. He made it a point to stop in most mornings and have a light breakfast after his shift. He sat with two on-duty beat officers, Jones and Mathis.

Jones, a fifteen year veteran of the force said to Briscoe, "Damn, I can't believe you are out in the daylight, won't you burn up or something?" The vampire reference was often made to midnight shift officers.

Briscoe laughed and said, "Naw, I think I'm more like Blade, I can day walk." They all shared a laugh.

"Man roll call was a real motherfucker this morning," said Jones. "The watch commander is pressuring us to get out here and put everything that we have into finding whoever is committing these murders. He said to put feet up in some asses until we get answers. How are we supposed to put feet up in asses until we get answers? Answers to what? Even Homicide has no clue. Who the fuck am I, Sherlock Holmes?"

Briscoe and Mathis, a seven-year-veteran, just nodded their heads in agreement. Every cop on the force was feeling the pressure from within and from the public.

Briscoe excused himself from the diner and headed to court. He was catching the Metro rail from Florida Avenue to Judiciary Square where he would check into court liaison and proceed to court. It was easier to park his vehicle and ride the subway since finding parking downtown was a monumental task. Briscoe had a trial for a first degree sexual offense that involved a twelve year old girl. The defendant was the boyfriend of the girl's mother who has raped the girl repeatedly over a two year period. The girl is still in counseling and will probably be for quite a few years.

The defendant, Johnny Ray Simmons, had a lengthy arrest

record with a prior sexual offense, not to mention narcotics violations, aggravated assault, and numerous other violent crimes. This guy was bad news and a predator who should have never been allowed around a child or anybody who was vulnerable. Briscoe could not help but wonder what kind of mother would allow such a person around her children. The thing that makes you scratch your head and say 'hmm' is that this bum does not work. All he does is leach off the women who will have him. Go figure. Anyway, this is one deviant who will be off the streets for a long time to come. The evidence against him is overwhelming and the penalty for the crimes he committed against this child is life in prison. The thought of that comforted Briscoe and gave him hope that the system does sometimes provide justice for those who are victimized by the wolves in our society.

Once in court he was met by John Blaine, the Assistant United States Attorney (AUSA) trying the case against Simmons.

"Good morning Officer Briscoe. I have some good news for you. We reached a plea in the Simmons case, so there won't be a trial today. You can go home and get some rest."

Briscoe could barely contain his displeasure, "Good News! Good for who? That's rotten news! What kind of plea deal did you reach?" he asked with much consternation.

"In exchange for his guilty plea to a lesser offense, he will be placed on five years' supervised probation and must be placed on the sex offender registry." Blain tried convincing Briscoe that it was a good deal.

Briscoe just could not contain his emotion, "What about justice for the victim? Now she has to know that this piece of shit is lurking around the same streets that she has to walk every day."

"I understand what you are saying, but it would be hard on the girl if she had to endure a lengthy trial," Blaine tried to justify his position.

"Oh I see, it's easier for her to just see him on the street," he said sarcastically.

All Blaine could say was, "Well, it is what it is; there is nothing more that I can do. I'll sign you out if you don't have any other cases today officer."

Briscoe handed Blaine his court appearance form. *All he could think was 'weak motherfuckers . . . how dare they let a vicious predator back out onto the streets? This so called justice system is nothing like it should be.* In Briscoe's mind, justice for all means an eye for an eye. The system claims to serve the best interest of the public-at-large, but how could that be if they are releasing a confirmed molester into mainstream society? Briscoe tried to rationalize the situation by figuring *that it is not his to reason why, but to do. Isn't that what was told to him at the academy five years ago?*

Briscoe was raised as a military brat and his world was full of structure and discipline. In the places he was reared, there was a greater degree of law and order and people seemed to generally follow the rules of society. He could only image what he would have done if someone had molested his younger sister. Well, in Briscoe's mind, justice was not served and that just will not do.

By the time Briscoe made it home, it was nearly noon. He was tired since he went straight to court following his shift. Normally he went to the gym to burn off the overnight energy that was pent up inside and then he would be in bed by 10:00 a.m. Briscoe stripped out of his clothes and let them drop to the bedroom floor. He got into bed wearing only the birthday suit he was blessed with. His six-foot-two-inch muscular frame was tense from the night's activities and the disappointment of court. He was a lean 225 pounds of muscle, with tight abs and a tight ass to match. His caramel complexion and rugged good looks made him very appealing to the ladies. Briscoe could have any woman that he wanted . . . they always seemed to throw themselves at him. As he lay in bed looking at the ceiling, Briscoe thought about how to bring justice to a little girl whose only crime was having a mother who did not protect her from a rapist. In fact, her mother invited him in, fed him, clothed him, and sheltered him while he stole baby girl's innocence. The more Briscoe thought of this, the more enraged he became. Briscoe concluded that something had to be done. Yes, something will be done . . . he drifted off to sleep.

2

When the phone rang at 6:00 p.m., it startled Briscoe. For a moment he had no idea where he was; then realized, *Oh shit I forgot to turn off the ringer*. It felt like he only slept for an hour, and he was experiencing the groggy feeling one gets when they sleep into REM and are awakened prematurely.

He answered the phone, "Hello."

"Hey my sexy, chocolate lover," the voice on the phone was seductive and sweet.

"Hey baby, what's up?" Briscoe said in a raspy, sleep deprived voice.

The voice on the phone was that of Briscoe's girlfriend, Monica Turner. Monica is a twenty-eight year old entrepreneur who heads the non-profit organization, Sisters Healing Sisters. She created it to help women (mostly black women) transition from drug abuse and prostitution into a normal life. Monica is five-feet-ten-inches tall with a dark chocolate complexion. Her voluptuous body measures 38-26-40, with a traffic jam booty that just doesn't quit. Monica is a strong sista gurl who celebrates her successes and her blackness without reservation. Briscoe always admired her tenacity and was so very happy that she was his lady.

"Aw lover, did I wake you?" Monica asked in a sweet sympathetic tone.

"No it's okay, I had court this morning and was late getting to sleep, but I need to get up anyway."

He was still gathering his faculties when Monica said, "I called to see if you were watching the news. They arrested the person who has been doing all those killings around the area."

Briscoe sprung up from the bed and said, "What? Are you sure?"

"Yes baby, I know what I just saw," she said.

He reached for the remote control and turned the TV on. Fox 5 Evening News had gone off, but the News Edge at 6 just started. The News Edge is a half-hour-long program that covers in greater detail what the news station deems to be the most important stories from the regular hour long newscast.

Brad Boxer came on the air and said, "DC Police have their man. Arrested earlier today without incident was Marcus Langston III. With his arrest the area can breathe a sigh of relief."

Briscoe thought to himself, *Damn how could that be? Is this some kind of cover up, a trick, or a ploy to simply calm the public's fears? What did the department really know? Are they hoping that the killer will continue to operate freely and make a careless mistake, or figure that the police have someone else in their sights and quit while he is ahead, giving the police time to close in on the real killer?* Briscoe was so deep in thought he forgot that Monica was still on the phone.

"Antonio! Are you listening to me?" she asked.

"Sure baby, I was just listening to the story about the serial killer," he said.

"That should make you happy. It takes the pressure off you guys and makes everybody feel safer," Monica added.

"I guess you're right," he said.

"So, what time does my hot lover have to be at work tonight?" she asked seductively.

Briscoe could sense from the way Monica sounded that she wanted to come over and lay him down. But his mind was working overtime processing the information that he just received about the arrest of the killer.

"Ten thirty," he replied.

"I haven't seen you in almost three days, I miss my baby. I can come over and help get you ready for work," she said naughtily.

"That sounds so tempting, but I have to get up and get myself together now. I have a couple of things to take care of before I get to work tonight."

He really was feeling anxious and he thought how nice it would be to bust a hot nut off in Monica before he went to work. But he would not be able to fit that in tonight because there were far more pressing tasks to accomplish.

Monica was not going to let him get away with such a vague response, "What do you have to do?"

Briscoe, thinking quickly, said, "I have to see my parents and look over some insurance papers for them."

He hated lying to Monica but it was definitely necessary in this case. She would never understand the things that he must do to make things right.

"Okay baby, but tomorrow I am going to be with my man, regardless," she said firmly.

Briscoe smiled because he loved being her man and he loved hearing Monica acknowledge that fact even more. They said their goodbyes and hung up. Briscoe got up and immediately started to get ready for his night.

Meanwhile, at the Violent Crimes Unit (VCU) of the police department, Marcus Langston III was in the box about to be interviewed by veteran Homicide Detective Jamie Whitehead, who is the lead investigator on the serial predator case. Whitehead joined the department after he graduated college and has been a member for twenty-seven years, with sixteen of those years spent in homicide. He is the longest tenured detective on the squad and has closed many high profile cases. Whenever there is a case that needs solving quickly and effectively, they assign it to Whitehead. He is a big man, some six-feet-four-inches tall and weighing nearly 300 pounds. When he was younger, he was quite the athlete and has done a pretty good job of keeping himself in shape. But being over fifty it is hard to keep from getting a little extra padding around the midsection. He is twice-divorced with three children. He doesn't have much of a personal life now days, especially since the serial predator emerged.

He took a quick look at his case file before going into the box. He was given a tip that Marcus was possibly involved in the murder of a rival drug dealer, who was shot once in the back of the head. The decedent was Reynard Kelly, the third victim whose death was attributed to the serial predator. Reynard was a twenty-two year old high school drop out with a lengthy arrest record and was a suspect in a homicide case that is still under investigation. Reynard's hands were bound behind his back and he was shot point blank in the back of the head. Stuffed in his mouth was a large plastic bag containing several smaller baggies of crack cocaine with a street value of five hundred dollars. What kind of rival leaves that much product behind? It just didn't add up. To date there were nine homicides attributed to the serial predator. It all started in March and now it's July. The killer is working overtime.

"Marcus Tre' Langston the third, born April 16, 1985, address: 9712 M Street, Northeast. How am I doing so far? Is that you?"

He handed Marcus one of his previous arrest reports with all of his information and a photograph.

"Man what kind of Mickey Mouse shit ya'll try'na pull?" Marcus was agitated and did not want to cooperate. "Ya'll know damn well I ain't kill nobody, especially not that nigga," he was referring to Reynard.

"We have people who say otherwise," Whitehead bluffed.

"Who are they then?" Marcus asked angrily.

"Don't worry about that. Your concern should be how your dumb ass is not going to spend the rest of your life in a six-by-eight cell, trying not to get butt fucked every night by your cellie; unless you are into that kind of shit."

Whitehead got down onto a level that Marcus understood. This is how many seasoned detectives gain their street credibility and respect from the perpetrators that they must ultimately put away.

"Marcus we know that you had a beef with Reynard, and we know that you threatened to kill him."

Marcus interrupted, "That's some bullshit! We never beefed, I barely even knew that dude. This must be some kinda set up."

Whitehead continued questioning Marcus to find out anything he could about Reynard and any conflicts that he may have had with anybody in or around the community. Whitehead discovered that there was no shortage of people who wanted to see Reynard dead. But it was becoming more and more apparent that Marcus had nothing to do with his death and nothing led him to believe that he had any knowledge or involvement in the other eight homicides. Following the interview, Marcus was transported to the Central Cell Block for processing. He was being held on an outstanding narcotics warrant.

The media had their facts wrong; and this isn't the first time they were wrong. They jumped the gun and assumed because Marcus was interviewed that he was the suspect in the serial killings. They just rushed to be first with the story; because they know that sensationalism sells. It serves them right to have to go back and eat crow. They will just play it off on the police and say that was the information they received from officials or a confidential source, even though none of that is the truth.

Briscoe left his house in Temple Hills and got into his black

Dodge Charger with dark tinted windows. He was dressed in black jeans, black tee shirt, and carried a black backpack. He hooked his iPod into the onboard docking station and started playing tunes from his library. The sounds of Bob James and Kirk Whalum's "Joined at The Hip," one of the best collaboration CDs ever, was cascading out of the speakers with a melodious thump that a true jazz aficionado could appreciate. Jazz was Briscoe's passion. He rarely missed a jazz festival that came through or near the DC area. Briscoe would take leave from work to attend jazz festivals and concerts. That is where he met Monica and is one of the passions they share.

He navigated the always treacherous Branch Avenue where people believe they can drive eighty miles per hour between traffic lights. He was headed to VCU, which is located on Branch Avenue, just minutes from his home. He planned to snoop around and gather as much information about the case as he could. He needed to know where the investigation was headed, and what connection Marcus Langston had to it.

When Briscoe arrived at the VCU Homicide division, he went in and talked to Detective Willis Sanford. He and Sanford served together in the Fifth Precinct and were good friends. They would go out occasionally and have drinks, catch a Redskin's game, attend jazz festivals, or barbecue at one or the other's home. Sanford has been a member of the department since 1994 and has been a detective for ten years with two of those years in Homicide. He was an intelligent man, whose greatest attribute was his doggedness. He did not give up on anything. Even if it appeared hopeless to others, Sanford would keep going until he found a solution. He is the father of two daughters and recently divorced their mother, so right now his whole life seems to be his case load.

"What up dog?" Briscoe exclaimed as they gave each other dap. That is one of the rituals that the black culture has maintained for generations . . . the hand shake with a little something extra.

"Ain't nut'n but some killin," he replied.

"Tell me bout it," Briscoe said in agreement.

Sanford looked at his watch then at Briscoe and said, "Damn playa it's early. What brings you through at this time?"

"I was on my way into work early to type up a couple of warrant affidavits. I thought I could stop by and get some information on the serial predator case. Since there were three of them near my beat I figured that if I knew more details I could start pressing some of my contacts for information. You know that nothing goes down around there without somebody knowing something and they trust me in those neighborhoods. They would normally tell me anything."

"Dude, I wish all the officers in patrol thought like you. Then we could close a hell of a lot more cases than we do."

Sanford trusted Briscoe like a brother and loved him like one. He felt that Briscoe was a really tough dude with a stellar past and a very bright future with the department.

"Have a seat and I'll see what Whitehead or his partner has and how much I can disclose. You know how they get when it comes to information going out from an open case."

"Thanks brother, I appreciate anything I can get to be of help," Briscoe said.

When Sanford returned, he told Briscoe the case is still a blank slate. He told him about the dead-end Marcus Langston provided. He mentioned how in every instance nobody heard anything, saw anything, or knew of any victims' whereabouts prior to their demise. Briscoe soaked in all the information, then said his goodbyes and departed.

As Briscoe walked to his car, he thought about how Sanford thought of him as a rising star in the department. He knew that most of his peers felt he was too intelligent to remain where he was in patrol. They all believed he would participate in the promotion process and move quickly up the ranks. But for Briscoe there was nothing like being in the trenches and having a direct impact on the people that needed him most.

Briscoe, as he prefers to be called, is a highly intelligent overachiever. He was born Antonio Lawrence Briscoe on March 1, 1977, to Anthony Briscoe and Alexis Payne-Briscoe. He is the oldest of three military brats. He attended elementary school in Wurzburg, Germany. When he was in the fifth grade, his father was reassigned to the 10th Mountain Division in Fort Drum, New York, where Antonio and his siblings, Alicia and Andrew, attended elementary, middle, and high schools. Then his father was reassigned to Fort Campbell, Kentucky, where Antonio finished high school Suma Cum

Laude. Following his high school graduation, Antonio attended one semester of college and realized it just wasn't for him at the time. He needed a bigger challenge and more excitement. So he did the one thing that he knew and that was to join the military. Briscoe signed up to be an Airborne Ranger. He received a signing bonus, which he thought was awesome. *Hey, they are going to pay me to have fun, and adventure . . . how cool is that?* Briscoe excelled during his Ranger training in Ft. Benning, Georgia and was assigned to the 3rd Battalion 75th Ranger Regiment at Ft. Benning. After his promotion to sergeant in just three short years, Briscoe attended the Special Forces qualification course, where he set a record in the seventy-five meter swim. Once his training was complete, Briscoe was assigned to the 7th Special Forces Group in Ft. Bragg, North Carolina. His three years as a Weapons Specialist on an A team took Briscoe all around the world. He still possesses a Top Secret Security Clearance and some of the missions that he participated in are still classified. He has done things that he could never share with anyone. That is not only because of the sensitive nature of the unit's mission, but also because he has buried the horrific images of the evil he did deep inside his subconscious. He does not want to awaken those demons.

    Briscoe got into his car and immediately reached for a case folder that was in his backpack. The case was that of Johnny Ray Simmons, the child molester who was basically set free earlier in the day. Briscoe looked at the addresses of Simmons' mother, his known associates, and his known hangouts. He thought it would be a good idea to keep tabs on Simmons and know where he was at all times. One thing that Briscoe considered was what if the girl's mother let Simmons back into the home? He knew that some women would allow a man like that back around their children. Just the mere thought made Briscoe shudder with disgust. But curiosity got the better of him and he decided to start by driving over to the girl's house just to see if Simmons was there.
    He drove to the 1200 block of 18th Street and parked in an obscure spot where he could clearly see the home that the little girl shared with her mother. Briscoe was due at work in a couple of hours, so he did not have very long to just sit and watch the house.
    While sitting there he noticed that the block was quiet compared

to many other blocks in the neighborhood. However, something caught his eye. He observed a lot of traffic in and out of the little girl's house. There were all types of people, white, black, male, female, young, old, and they occupied vehicles with Maryland tags, and Virginia tags; and some came on foot. This sort of behavior is indicative of drug dealing, and Briscoe was well aware of this. To say his curiosity was piqued is an understatement; his radar was fully extended and tracking.

He stayed there videotaping the activity of the people coming and going for about an hour. Just as he was about to pack up his camera and depart, he saw a man come around the corner. It was none other than Johnny Simmons. He videotaped as Simmons went to the front door and used a key to enter.

Briscoe said out loud, "I'll be damned! I cannot believe this bullshit!"

Oh well, since he was planning to hunt him down, now he does not have to. Simmons has saved Briscoe a trip around the city. It was now 9:15 p.m. and Briscoe was due at work in a little more than an hour. He decided that he had enough information right now and would follow up later. His mind was racing and he was feeling anxious about what he just saw. What should be his first course of action? Should he involve the Vice Unit? Should he contact the Youth Division? Maybe the United States Attorney's Office. *Oh yeah, that's right, they were the ones that let Simmons back out onto the street today.* This situation is delicate and it will require some detailed investigation to determine who the perpetrators are, and more importantly to Briscoe, who the victims are.

As Briscoe was packed up his Sony Handycam with the thirty gigabit hard drive, and forty-times optical zoom, he thought was an awesome a piece of equipment the camera was. It had the ability to capture up close and clear video and photos in the darkness. There could be no disputing what he witnessed because of the crystal clarity provided by the camera.

"Smash!" A loud crash of breaking glass startled Briscoe. He whipped his head around in the direction of the noise and saw a woman lying crumpled on the ground just beneath a shattered window of an apartment about twenty feet from where he sat. Suddenly, a very large shirtless man emerged from the house and yelled at the woman,

"I told you about your shit bitch! I said I wasn't going to put up with it anymore. Now look at your dumb ass!"

The woman was lying motionless; possibly lifeless, Briscoe thought.

He did not hesitate, he sprung into action, exiting his vehicle and rushing to where the man was standing over the woman yelling obscenities. The man looked up as Briscoe approached, and stood in a defensive position sneering,

"Get the fuck away from here and mind your own business!" he screamed.

When Briscoe reached the man, he did not utter a word, he immediately executed a perfect roundhouse kick that struck the big man on the left side of his neck impacting his jugular vein and sending him crashing to the ground like a meteorite. As the big man clambered to his feet, Briscoe punched him with so much force to the solar plexus, he was sure that he inflicted internal damage. The final blow that Briscoe delivered was the one that put his lights out. It was a right hook directly to the temple, which connected with such force that Briscoe thought he heard the behemoth's brain impact his skull. The big man never knew what hit him. Briscoe looked at him and knew that his injuries were very serious, but it did not faze him one bit. He could have no compassion for a man who would inflict such pain on a woman.

His attention then turned to the woman. He assessed her injuries and discovered that she suffered multiple cuts to her head, face, and body as a result of being thrown through the first floor living room window. He could also smell a strong odor of alcohol on her breath. The woman started to come around. It was apparent to Briscoe that her injuries were not life threatening as long she receives medical attention soon. Briscoe reached into his pocket and pulled out his Motorola Razor and dialed 911. He identified himself as a police officer and requested the police and two ambulances.

The woman stirred and became more coherent as Briscoe asked, "What happened?"

"He keep on accusing me of chea'n. I told him that he was trip'n. Just cuz I go out and drink don't mean I'm chea'n," she explained. Her face was bloody and bruised and there was blood pooled in one of her eyes.

"How did you end up out here?" he had to ask, even though he was sure that he knew the answer.

"That piece a shit threw me out the window after he punch me in my face. That's all he know how to do is beat on women. I shoulda left his ass a long time ago." She started to cry, and then asked, "Is my face messed up?"

He did not know exactly what to say, "No it's not too bad, you'll be back to normal in no time." He knew that was a lie but wanted her to be comforted, "Just lie still and try not to move, help is on the way."

Throughout all of this, Briscoe did not initially pay close attention to the crowd that formed to view the spectacle of someone else's misery. There were about fifteen people who assembled to gawk at the victim and her crumpled assailant, and they all knew well what he was doing to this woman, and nobody in the community had the guts to step up and try to help. One person in the crowd caught Briscoe's attention immediately. It was the little girl who Simmons had victimized repeatedly. She looked at Briscoe and their eyes met. The pain in her eyes looked deep into his soul, as though to say; *I know how she hurts, and I wish you would have killed him. He hurt her so bad, and his pain should be worse than hers.*

Briscoe scanned the rest of the crowd to see if Simmons was amongst them, but he wasn't. That was good for Simmons, because he was feeling vengeful and his adrenaline was high. Only God knows what he would have done if Simmons was standing there in a place where he did not belong.

The sirens were blaring in the distance and closing fast. Briscoe contemplated, *What can I tell the units responding about why I was on this street?* He had to think fast and come up with something that would not tie him to the little girl, her family, or Simmons. Then he got pissed, as he looked at the heap of the man that was lying on the ground nearby. *Why in the hell did you have to do this right here, right now? How can he explain himself without raising the curiosity of the units, and more importantly that of the detective, who will surely be called to the scene?* The sirens were very close now, and his mind was speeding, as he kicked himself for not having a contingency plan for a situation such as this.

Suddenly, Briscoe sprang to his feet and ran to his car, started the engine, pulled from the parking space and turned the car around to face in the opposite direction. He moved the car forward and angled it in such a manner as though he exited in a hurry without pulling all the way to the curb. He got out and left the engine running with the headlights on, and returned to the spot where the woman and man were still lying on the ground.

The first MPD unit turned into the block just as Briscoe made it back to the couple. Officer Smith was in service as a single unit, when he jumped from his cruiser and ran up and surveyed the scene.

"Are you okay?" he asked.

"I'm fine, but these two are going to need the Board." The police department refers to the Fire and EMS as the Board.

"Daaamn, what happened to them?" Smith asked astounded as he pointed to the two bodies mangled on the ground.

Briscoe began to recite the story that he just quickly concocted in his mind, "I was driving down M Street on my way to work, when all of a sudden a young black female dashed out in front of me. When I stopped, she said call the police a woman just fell out of a window. I turned up the street and drove here and saw this guy standing over the lady yelling obscenities at her. Man I thought she was dead. As I approached and identified myself as a police officer, the dude became combative and threatened to kick my ass. So I had to get him under control to help her."

"Under control?" Smith repeated with a slight grin on his face, "It looks like you tried to put him under ground. What did you hit him with?"

"Just my hands," Briscoe said.

"Wow! Is he under arrest?"

"Yeah," replied Briscoe.

"Why didn't you handcuff him?"

"I don't have any. And besides I don't think he will be moving anywhere on his own for a while."

"True that," agreed Smith.

As more units arrived, and the Board collected the couple, Sergeant Stenner arrived on scene and directed the actions of the officers. He asked Briscoe what happened and Briscoe told him the same story that he told Smith. The sergeant decided to send two officers to the hospital with the suspect and one unit to the hospital with the victim to ensure that her injuries are not serious enough to notify VCU. Because the man will be charged with a domestic violence felony, a detective must be notified.

Detective Brown was notified and that was all the involvement that he needed since the case was closed with an arrest. The detective gets credit for closing a case without having to do a thing. Briscoe thought a win-win for the both of them. With the way that many of the domestic cases in the area go, the woman will not even show up in court on the day of trial. When asked about the whereabouts of the young girl who flagged him down, Briscoe dismissed it by saying he doesn't know where she went. Nobody ever asked about it again.

Briscoe left 18th Street, turned right onto M, then right onto 17th, and finally right onto Bladensburg Road. The station was just a couple of miles further. When he arrived at the station, he went into the locker room to change into his uniform. From there he stopped by the sergeants' office to inform them that he was going to be upstairs processing an arrest and would not make it to roll call. Once Briscoe finished processing the arrest, he decided to use this opportunity to find out who the people were that visited the little girl's home. He also decided to find out everything that he could about the girl's mother. Since the sergeants knew that he was processing an arrest, they would not be inclined to question why he wasn't on his beat.

As Briscoe ran tag after tag, he realized that these people had nothing in common, and their only connection was the house on 18th Street. So he looked into the background of the little girl's mother.

Her name is Janice Russell, and as Briscoe soon discovered, she was not the caring mother that she portrayed herself to be during the period following Simmons' arrest and up to the trial that didn't happen. Janice was a convicted felon with a record damn near as long as Simmons'. In 1996, when her daughter was just a year old, she went to prison where she stayed for eight years. It appears that while involved in the narcotics trade, she shot an undercover cop. She set the UC up to be robbed not knowing he was a cop. When it all went down, she produced a hand gun and shot him in the leg. She is lucky that she wasn't killed.

Briscoe thought, *Damn, the AUSA and the detectives knew this information. Why didn't somebody do something to challenge this pathetic excuse of a mother, to see if she was fit for parenting?* He also discovered that Janice had a past case with Child and Family Services, concerning neglect of her daughter. Briscoe was starting to feel that the system was just one big joke. The only ones to benefit are the violators who prey on the innocent. After learning more about the mother, Briscoe felt like the little girl has a narrow chance to escape the future that is being laid down before her. She would have to leave that environment soon so as not to become tainted by its ills. It is a damnable thing to see a young mind and body ravaged by the examples, molding, and constant imaging of negative, unhealthy, and undesirable wretches in the home and community. To stand by and do nothing to change it is unacceptable in Briscoe's mind. He gathered all of his paperwork, placed it into his backpack and hit the street to begin his patrol.

3

Johnny Simmons left Janice Russell's home on 18th Street at 1:30 a.m. He told Janice he was going to the 24-hour store and would be back in about thirty minutes. As Simmons made his way down the dark alley leading from the back of the home, he put the earphones of his MP3 player into his ears and cranked up the volume and began to rap along with Nas. He was so wrapped up in his music that he never noticed the tall lean, muscular male standing in the shadows at the mouth of the alley near the Arboretum. Just as Simmons reached the male, he looked up just in time to catch a straight right fist in the throat. The blow was so devastating that it cut off his ability to speak or scream. As Simmons dropped to his knees clutching his throat, the shadowy figure quickly bound Simmons' hands behind his back with flex cuffs, which resemble twist ties.

The man pulled the earphones from Simmons' ears and said, "Don't make a sound, or I will blow your head clean off your fucking body. And stop struggling or I will cut your nuts off right here."

The man reached down and grabbed Simmons' crotch and showed him a large serrated knife, similar to one carried by Commandos. Simmons stopped struggling, and the man taped his mouth with duct tape, and put a black sack over his head drawing the string securely around his neck. He then lifted Simmons and carried him over his shoulder to an awaiting vehicle and placed him in the trunk.

The man took a look around and was sure that nobody was out and there were no witnesses. He then got into the vehicle and drove off. He went to the rear of Phelps Junior High School, which is boarded up and has not been used in many years. There were very few people out this time of the night and nothing about the man would draw any unusual attention. He was not out of the ordinary in the least.

Upon reaching the back of the school and nestling into his favorite hiding spot, the man opened the trunk and pulled Simmons out dropping him hard to the ground.

"Sit up," he ordered while helping Simmons into a seated position.

The man then removed the hood from Simmons' head. Simmons' eyes grew wider than two silver dollars when he saw the face of the man who had him captive.

"Now it's time for you to pay for the dirt that you have done."

At that moment, the police radio called out, "Officer Briscoe, are you monitoring the air?"

Briscoe reached into the car and picked up the radio mike. "Yes ma'am."

"I have a run for you," the dispatcher stated.

"Is it a priority ma'am?" Briscoe asked.

"No. Is there a problem?"

"No ma'am; I was just about to ask you for a personal at the station, it's kind of urgent," he lied.

The dispatcher knew that this was a nice way to say I have to use the bathroom, now.

"It's just an attempt to locate the auto on your beat; I'll hold it."

"Thanks ma'am." Briscoe said.

He then turned his attention back to Simmons. The adrenaline was coursing through his veins, yet he was calm and business like as he proceeded to prepare the rapist for his rendezvous with destiny.

"You thought it was over when you got that plea deal. Well, you were wrong. You think you can just continue living around that child like nothing is wrong. You and that sick bitch mother of hers are out of your fucking minds if you thought the universe would allow that shit."

Briscoe was wearing a hooded wet suit with rubber boots, and chemical resistant gloves. The only exposed portion of his body was his face. The trunk of the patrol car was lined with plastic, and everything was now in place to make Simmons his number ten. Simmons' eyes were pleading for his life, and if his mouth was not taped, he would probably be screaming at the top of his lungs like the little bitch that he is.

"There is nothing you can do to change your fate. Think about how much the girl cried and begged you not to put your dirty hands on her. It didn't stop you, so your bitch ass whining won't stop me."

Briscoe lined the ground with plastic and then laid Simmons

flat on his back with his legs spread apart; he tied his ankles with flex cuffs snuggly to the rail that leads to the basement of the school. He then tied a rope around Simmons' neck, ran it through the flex cuffs that bound his hands and secured it to the rail opposite of the one that his feet were tied. Briscoe then pulled Simmons' pants to his knees exposing his genitals. Simmons was really trying to move his body at this point, but with every movement, the rope tightened around his neck.

"Don't try to fight it now bitch, you should have kept that little thing to yourself. I thought you like taking it out. I just thought I would help you take it out one last time."

Briscoe grabbed the head of his penis with a pair of pliers and squeezed so hard that Simmons' body convulsed from the pain. He then used the pliers to clamp down on a testicle until it popped. He then applied the pliers and his powerful grip to the other testicle, and twisted and squeezed until that one also exploded in the sack. The pain that Simmons was experiencing was beyond anything that words could describe. It was more than excruciating. However, Briscoe was not going to let him pass out. He placed ammonium capsules under his nose to bring him around whenever he thought he was losing him. Briscoe felt there was no way Simmons was not going to feel all the pain of his punishment before he meets the sweet release of death.

"How does that feel? Is it good for you? I didn't think so." He wanted Simmons to feel the pain for an eternity.

"Now to fix the hands that caused so much pain to a child. You have been dancing to his tune for years. Now it's time to pay the piper," he said, as he produced a Cuban Crafters Cigar Cutter with stainless steel self-sharpening double blades.

He then grabbed Simmons' right hand and slid the cigar cutter over his index finger and severed it with nearly one motion. His agony was great, and the moans and muffled screams grew louder. With a hammer motion and a closed fist, Briscoe came down with violent force on his throat in an attempt to silence him. The tape came loose from his mouth, and the blood and sputum came rushing out. Simmons was gagging and coughing trying to clear his throat so he could scream for help or plead for his life. Just then Briscoe retrieved a sledge hammer from the trunk, and while Simmons was writhing on the ground, he brought the sledge hammer crashing down on his face. Blood spouted from the spot where his nose used to be.

And then again the sledge hammer crashed down on his forehead, sinking his skull nearly an inch into his brain. Simmons stopped moving and his lifeless body went limp.

Damn it! He had more suffering to do, thought Briscoe. *How could he let him get away without more pain?* But he knew that he had no choice. If someone heard his cries, they would start to notice things that they would not normally notice. Briscoe figured that he has come too far to be careless now. Okay, at least he will no longer victimize good people, or steal the innocence from defenseless children.

Briscoe cut the flex cuffs from the rail that secured Simmons' ankles, and he cut the rope from the opposite rail that bound his hands and neck. He then wrapped Simmons, his detached index finger, the rope, flex cuffs, and everything that was used to serve justice, in the plastic. He dragged the body and all the evidence of his work down the steps and into the basement of the building. Once inside Briscoe turned on his flashlight and located a room that was approximately twenty-five feet from the entrance on the right side of the hallway. As he made it to the room, he discovered that it was the boiler room. Once inside Briscoe cut the flex cuffs from Simmons' hands and ankles, and the rope from around his neck. He carefully placed the items in a black, leaf and lawn trash bag. Briscoe then rolled Simmons' body off the plastic and onto the floor of what was once a very warm room that provided heat for children as they studied to be the next generation of business and political leaders. They were preparing their minds to be, and some are now, doctors who heal, and lawyers and judges in the criminal justice system who are tasked with keeping shit like Simmons out of mainstream society. Briscoe put the sledge hammer, cigar cutter, pliers, and plastic into the trash bag. He then walked back out the way he went in, closed the door, and put the board back in place that he removed earlier before he picked up Simmons. As Briscoe made it back to the car, he scrutinized the crime scene, ensuring that there was nothing left behind. He then peeled off the wet suit, gloves, and boots and placed them in the bag, then put the bag and its contents into the trunk of the patrol car.

Once behind the wheel of the vehicle, Briscoe picked up the radio mike and said, "5 Baker 44."

"5 Baker 44 go ahead," the dispatcher replied.

"Ma'am I'm clear the personal and ready for the assignment."

"Disregard 5 Baker 44; 5 Baker 41 handled it."
Briscoe said, "Thank you 5 Baker 41. I'm 10-8, ma'am."
"Copy," she responded.

He drove from the rear of the school, looking around to ensure that nobody was paying him more attention than normal. He often would go behind the school to take a break out of the eye of the public. Besides, there was nothing unusual about a police officer checking on abandoned city property. Occasionally car thieves would bring stolen vehicles to the location and torch them so the neighboring community was used to seeing a patrol car on the premises.

He drove from the school directly to the rear of the police station. He wrapped the trash bag inside of the plastic that lined the trunk. He then placed everything into an Army duffle bag, and locked it in the trunk of his Charger. Once he disposes of that bag, Simmons will be a distant memory.

As Briscoe drove back out on patrol, he allowed himself to think about the justice he served in the rear of Phelps Junior High School. It was so befitting to punish Simmons at the very place that his young victim would have attended school, had it been open. He thought about the possibility that rats would consume the corpse as it decomposes in the unused boiler room of a forgotten educational landmark that once educated so many Washingtonians. Briscoe felt good about his mission and wished he could share it with his friends and colleagues. But he knew that no one would understand. Until there is dramatic change in the criminal justice system, he would just have to keep his self-directed crusade to himself. He didn't come into his line of work to serve as executioner, it just happened that way. After seeing victims suffer and victimizers smile their shit-eating-grin when they are acquitted, triggered something inside of Briscoe that set him slam the fuck off. He is on a mission to serve the justice the system refuses to serve.

4

Janice Russell was lying in bed on her left side facing the bedroom door. She opened her eyes and blinked as she focused on LCD display of a small battery operated clock situated on the tattered nightstand beside the bed. The time was 7:25 a.m. She reached behind her and felt the empty spot that was normally occupied by Johnny Simmons. When she did not feel him, she slowly rose up on her elbow and looked over her shoulder. There was no sign in the room that he returned home last night. After a brief pause, a chill went up Janice's spine. *Oh shit, what if he's in the bed with Shauna? I told him not to fuck with her right now.* She got out of bed and hurried to Shauna's room, slowly pushing open the door.

The little girl was still asleep, and there was no sign of Simmons. Janice then thought, *Where could he be? He doesn't have anywhere else to go. Everybody else has thrown him out and will no longer let him stay in their homes. He said he was going to the store, but he didn't come back. Sometimes he would run into some of his street friends and hang with them for a while, but they wouldn't stay out all night.* Janice had an uneasy feeling inside that something was wrong. Back inside her bedroom, she sat on the edge of the bed and retrieved a cigarette from the pack of Newports that were on the nightstand. As she inhaled the calming sensation of the nicotine, she thought that maybe Simmons did something to get locked up. But what? He was so happy to be free of the charges that Shauna put on him; it would be a while before he crossed the law again.

She then picked up the cordless telephone from the base station and dialed Simmons' mother.

"Hi Miss Simmons, is Johnny there?"

"Child, why are you calling me so early in the morning? You know damn well that nigga ain't coming up in here. Maybe he found another skank to freeload off," Ms. Simmons spoke vehemently with malice directed toward Janice.

"Well I don't know, but he left here at one thirty in the morning and was supposed to be going to the store and back. He didn't come back and I'm worried something might've happened to him."

"You would be the only one! Don't call here no more looking for that bum. If you want to worry about somebody, worry about your daughter!" Ms. Simmons slammed the phone into the cradle ending the call.

Janice placed the phone back in the base station and realized there was nobody she could call. She can't call the police because Simmons was not supposed to come around her home or her daughter ever again. All the people who loved him at some point in life were now fed up with his selfish and deceitful ways and couldn't care less if they ever heard from him again. She could only continue to hope that he was okay and would be home soon. She will never have that wish fulfilled. She sat on the edge of the bed and began to sob quietly.

Briscoe left work on time, and since he got Smith to respond to the U.S. Attorney's office to walk the paperwork through the system on the man who threw his woman out of the window, he was free to get breakfast and then hit the gym. The light breakfast at Lucky's was great and the workout at the gym was phenomenal. He had so much energy to work off, that he stayed in the gym doing cardio endurance and strength training for two-and-a-half hours. Wow! It was invigorating and his whole body and spirit were now relieved and ready for a long sleep.

Upon arrival at home, he took the duffle bag from the trunk of his car and walked around the outside of his house to the back yard. He went into his storage shed and retrieved a five gallon gasoline can that he uses to fill his lawn mower. He walked to where a large fifty-five gallon barrel was standing in the yard not far from the shed. He opened the duffle bag and dropped it in the barrel. He then poured gasoline inside of the duffle bag and along the sides, and then threw in a match. Whoosh! The flames sprung up from the barrel and then slowly settled into a very intense fire. The bag and all its contents were transformed from solid matter to unrecognizable ash. Everything burned completely except the head of the sledge hammer and the pliers; however, he had plans for their disposal.

Briscoe finished his work in the back yard and went into the house to shower and retire to his bedroom for some much anticipated sleep. It was ninety degrees and humid outside and he got into bed the way that he did every day . . . completely naked. The silk sheets felt good next to his smooth skin and the cool breeze of the air conditioner relaxed his muscles and helped him fall fast asleep.

While Briscoe slept, the region continued to ponder the identity of the so called serial predator. The media was starting to allude to the possibility of vigilante justice as the motive for the slayings. With the overnight slaying of two people in the city, and no official word from the police department, the media speculated that they were possibly the latest victims of the serial predator.

The mood at the daily COMSTAT meeting at police headquarters was somber. The Patrol Precinct Commanders of the two precincts where the killings took place knew that the Deputy Chief of Police (DCOP) would be in a very foul mood. Once all the Bureau Chiefs, Precinct and Division Commanders, and specialized personnel were assembled and ready for the meeting, the DCOP and the Chief of Police entered the large high tech briefing room. The Chief took his seat near the door, which he did often without speaking directly to anyone. The DCOP, whose job it is to run the day-to-day crime fighting operations within the department, stood in the center of the room in a position to command. It was his job to ensure that all strategies and courses of action were carried out according to directives from the Office of the Chief of Police.

Prior to the COMSTAT meeting, the Chief of Police and the DCOP had completed a conference call with the Mayor and the City Council Chairman. Both had expressed their displeasure with the police department's handling of the serial predator case so far. They were also displeased with the rise in the homicide rate and were demanding to be briefed on the department's strategy to reduce the number of homicides and the strategy for catching the predator.

"Holy shit, are we doing anything to catch this guy?" the DCOP asked the Superintendant of Detectives, who had responsibility for the Homicide Division.

"Yes sir, we are working around the clock on the case and we have put other cases in holding patterns and reassigned several detectives to the case," the superintendant said humbly. "I will let Captain Johnson brief you in detail sir."

"Well, what are you waiting for Captain? Am I going to get some answers now, or do I have to dial the psychic hotline?" the DCOP said rancorously.

"Chief, to begin, neither of last night's homicides were the work of the predator. The 3rd Precinct homicide was the result of a robbery gone bad. We have witnesses who said the victim resisted and tried to subdue the robber.

The 6th Precinct homicide is possibly domestic related. We are still investigating, but nothing about that case point to the predator," the Captain paused.

"That still doesn't tell me what you are doing to catch the predator," the DCOP interrupted.

"Yes sir, I just wanted to bring you up on the two homicides from overnight. Well, in the serial predator case, it is a cold path. The only thing that has tied the cases together is the weapon. Ballistics has confirmed that every victim was shot with the same .45 caliber handgun. The other oddity is in the way that each victim was killed. In some cases, they were partially mutilated and tortured. So we are certain all the killings linked to him, are his doing. He moves about with stealth and anonymity, because apparently nobody has ever seen or heard anything related to the homicides. There just doesn't appear to be a clear motive for the killings. Each one on its own is a complete mystery, but combined it looks like a vigilante has decided to rid the world of certain members of the criminal element."

The DCOP interrupted, "Are you telling me that a vigilante is out there killing criminals?"

"Well sir, I'm not saying that for sure, but it is a strong theory. All of the victims were ex-cons with multiple charges for violent crimes and drug distribution. We have been working to see if there is a common link between them all, an affiliate, a rival, a girlfriend, anything that could tie them all together and give us something to work with," Captain Johnson was optimistic.

"Since you have identified the class of victim, what is your strategy for keeping them safe and catching the predator?" the DCOP asked with genuine concern.

"We plan to assemble a task force consisting of three detectives from each of the seven patrol precincts. Their job will be to do surveillance on some of the more notorious offenders in the city. They will see what they are up to and see if anybody else is watching them. In addition we have the hotline staffed 24/7 with a detective, who is ready to follow up on any tip at anytime." The Captain hoped this was sufficient for now.

"You will have to hold up on the task force until we can

determine if we have the manpower," said the DCOP.

"Yes sir, I understand."

"Okay Captain, I want updates daily on your progress and I expect results sooner than later," the DCOP snarled.

Throughout the remainder of the meeting, the command staff discussed other crime and community issues. The serial predator was the main concern echoed by the communities at the various town hall meetings held by the police department. Everybody was fearful and the men and women sitting in the COMSTAT meeting knew that the burden rested with them to apprehend the killer and bring him to justice.

5

Monica entered the home quietly with her key and slipped out of her clothes in the living room. As she reached the bedroom, she stood and admired her man's beautiful body as he slept peacefully. His rock hard abs were moving with every breath as he slept on his back on top of the sheets. His legs were slightly apart with his left hand resting on his left thigh, the other hand was by his side. Monica approached the bed from the foot. She started to rub his right thigh with her left hand, while her right hand massaged his stomach and then worked its way to his large muscular chest. Briscoe started to moan and move slightly, as Monica licked her fingers and then caressed his nipples. His manhood stood up and begged for the sensation of her touch. Both of Monica's hands moved down to massage his massive cock. As she stroked it gently, she licked his balls, and then softly sucked them. Briscoe could now feel the throbbing of his dick. Monica licked the shaft all the way to the head, where she engulfed it with her sexy lips and luscious wet mouth. She sucked his big dick until he was on the brink of busting his load. Just then, Monica climbed onto the bed and straddled him like a cowgirl mounting a stallion and guided his rock hard cock to the warmest place on earth. She faced away from him, letting him see her round sexy ass as she went slowly up and down, taking every inch of that sweet stick inside. Briscoe rubbed her ass and massaged her beautiful breasts as she rode. With every motion, he became more and more aroused as the grinding of their bodies intensified. Monica was slapping her butt cheeks on his pelvis with force and vigor as he gripped her hips and forced his dick deeper and deeper with each forceful thrust. Monica screamed out in pleasure.

"Oh my god, fuck me baby! Fuck me like you own me! It's your pussy daddy! Fuck it good!"

Briscoe's only words were, "Ride me baby."

As Monica continued to take all of him deep inside of her wetness, they moaned, screamed, and expressed animal desire for one another. The heat of her pussy intensified to the point that

Briscoe could tell that she was cumin.

"I feel you cumin', baby," he said.

"Oh yeah daddy, I'm cumin all over your fat dick. Give it to me lover. Bust your nut inside of me," Monica begged for his cum.

The heat of her pussy was so intense that he could no longer hold back the cum that was raging inside of him like hot lava in a volcano.

"I'm cum'in!" Briscoe screamed as his whole body became rigid.

Just then, Monica lifted her pussy up and off his dick and wrapped her lips tightly around that pretty shaft and sucked like a Hoover vacuum. The cum exploded from the head of his penis straight into Monica's mouth. She sucked and sucked and once all of his juice was in her mouth, she swallowed.

Briscoe laid back in the bed and reveled in the feeling of bliss that Monica just created for him. Boy was he glad that he gave her a key. She stayed down by his manhood and gently kissed it from the head to the balls as she massaged his thighs. She then laid her head on his stomach and massaged his beautiful tool as she looked at it. He stroked her head and ran his fingers through her hair.

"Antonio, I love your pretty dick," Monica said in a low sexy tone.

"What about the rest of me?" Briscoe asked with a chuckle.

"You know that I love the man that he is attached to even more," she said sincerely.

He smiled and thought how great a lover Monica was. *She has a freaky side to her that he just finds so damn intriguing. To look at her, you would think that this highly educated entrepreneur would be your typical missionary lover with inhibitions and hang-ups, but she could not be further from that. Monica loves to try new things in bed, and she is always up for sex in public places. Her sexual appetite is one of the many things about her composition that makes Briscoe love her so deeply.*

He looked at the clock and realized it was just a few minutes past 8:00 p.m., and he still had more than an hour before he needed to get ready for work. Monica was looking very luscious as she stroked him. His nature started to rise and he thought, *What the hell; I'm going to ride my baby for the next hour.* He put all of himself—mind, body, and soul—into loving the woman of his dreams. They loved and embraced in unconventional ways until he had to get ready for work.

Briscoe parked the white Ford Crown Victoria, outfitted with police lights and markings, at the end of Janice Russell's block and pulled out his camera. It was 11:30 p.m. and the traffic was still steady in and out of Janice's home. He decided to observe the people coming and going, and then he would move in to get a closer look.

A white Cadillac Escalade with twenty-two-inch chrome rims and hip hop music blaring, pulled to the curb and a white female laced in Prada and Gucci got out of the front passenger seat and walked to Janice's house and knocked on the door. The woman was carrying a large black bag; one that was too big to be a purse and too small to be a suitcase. The door opened and she went inside.

While the white woman was inside Janice's home, Briscoe decided to approach the vehicle and identify the driver. He pulled his vehicle to the rear of the Cadillac, offset to the driver's side and shined his vehicles spotlight into the Cadillac. He exited the cruiser and approached with his flashlight in his left hand, while peering into the rear of the vehicle. As he walked, he cleared the vehicle and determined that the driver was the only occupant.

"Good evening," he said. "It's pretty late in the night for you to be playing your music so loud."

Briscoe was just establishing a reason for the contact.

"I didn't realize it was so loud officer. I'll turn it down."

Briscoe took a close look at the driver and realized who he was. It was Marvin 'Brick' Jackson, a notorious drug dealer with alleged ties to organized crime. He and his so-called organization, no more than a ruthless street gang, are connected to multiple drug related homicides in and around the city. If he is somehow connected to Janice Russell, then Briscoe knew she was up to no damn good.

"Let me see your license and vehicle registration," Briscoe requested.

"Is there a problem officer?"

"No sir. I'm just going to check you out and make sure everything is in order. It won't take long." While Brick was fishing around for his license and registration, Briscoe asked, "What are you doing sitting here?"

"I'm waiting on my girl," Brick said without hesitation.

"Does she live around here?"

"No; she's visiting her friend over there," Brick pointed at Janice's house, as he handed his papers to Briscoe.

Briscoe looked at the license and said, "Okay Mister Jackson, remain in your vehicle. I'll be with you in a few moments."

Briscoe went back to his vehicle and entered Brick's information into the mobile data terminal, to run an NCIC inquiry to see if there were any outstanding warrants. He then entered Brick's information in his notebook. He did not know for sure how the two were connected, but he had a good idea and was determined to find it. Briscoe knew if he searched Brick's vehicle he would likely find a gun and possibly drugs, because there is no way a thug like Brick is that cordial and cooperative with a cop. But he did not want to spook him, or cause him to change his habits as they pertained to Janice Russell.

Briscoe finished writing and returned to Brick's vehicle, "Okay sir, everything is cool. Enjoy the rest of your night, sorry for the delay."

Brick was just relieved that his vehicle was not searched, because he did not want to deal with another charge, "Thanks officer. I should only be a few more minutes."

"That's okay, take your time. Just try to keep the music down," Briscoe stated as he turned and proceeded back to his vehicle. He entered his vehicle and drove off past Brick and out of the block.

Inside of Janice's house, the white woman, Christine Sherman, who was every bit of five-feet-ten-inches tall with curves that are not so prevalent on white chicks, was unpacking the bag. Christine is what one would call "smokin' hot" with sexy pouty lips, long auburn hair, and a body like a sistah. She is always draped in designer fashion and iced with expensive bling. She is the main squeeze of the most notorious drug dealer in the region; is there any other way she should roll?

"Hey girl, what's up witchu?" she asked as she gave Janice a hug. "You look down, like somebody kicked your cat," she winked and laughed.

"I am so confused I don't know what to do," Janice said in a solemn tone.

"What's the matter sweetie?"

"It's Johnny; I haven't heard from him in a couple days. He left here in the middle of the night to go to the 24-hour store and ain't come back."

"Maybe he got into something or somebody and just decided to hang out for a while," Christine was trying to be supportive for her friend, but she really didn't think his absence was a big deal.

"But it's just not like him to do that. He would have at least called. All of his stuff is still here. Something bad happened to him, I can feel it," Janice started to weep softly.

Christine embraced her and said, "J, don't cry sweetie, it's gonna be alright. I'm sure he is okay; you'll see."

She gently wiped a tear from Janice's face with her left hand and kissed her gently on the cheek as she ran her right hand through Janice hair lightly touching her face. Janice hugged Christine tightly and buried her face in her chest as she allowed herself to sob from deep within. Christine embraced her for what felt like five minutes. Then she placed both hands on Janice face, looked into her eyes and kissed her gently on the lips. Janice opened her mouth and let her tongue explore the wetness of Christine's lips and tongue.

Christine pulled her head back and kissed Janice on the forehead, the cheek, and then whispered in her ear, "I'm here for you sweetie; don't worry, everything will be alright."

Janice could feel a throbbing inside her loins that she has not felt for some time for her friend.

"Chris, make love to me."

"I would love to J, but my man is waiting for me. I'll come back later okay?"

"I hope so, cause I miss feeling you," Janice was in need of love and that kiss reminded her of how great the loving was with Christine.

The two of them met when they were locked up together in Lorton, the D.C. prison that was located in Northern Virginia. They were cell mates for nearly two years and they shared more than space. They bonded in more ways than one and have remained very close since. They vowed to look out for each other when they returned to the streets and that is what they have always done.

"J, do you have the money for Brick?" Christine asked.

"Yeah, let me see the bag."

Christine handed Janice the bag. She went into a small safe inside of the hallway closet and took out two stacks of money and placed it in the bag and then handed the bag to Christine.

"It's all there."

"I know girl, I trust you with my life. Now stop worrying about Johnny and be happy with all this money we're making," they both laughed.

Janice walked Christine to the door where they embraced again and kissed goodbye.

Janice looked at the two kilos of cocaine that Christine dropped off and decided to wait until later to process it. She sat on the sofa and hugged a pillow as she thought about Johnny, Shauna, and Christine. She really was lost without Johnny guiding her and helping make the tough decisions. That's why it wasn't hard for her to accept when Johnny started having sex with Shauna. She told the child to let it go because it was how he showed his love for her. But deep down she knew that it tore Shauna up inside to have Johnny touching her and putting his penis inside of her. When Janice told Johnny that she would do anything for him, he tested that and Janice was true to her word. She delivered her daughter's innocence to a low life knuckle-dragger whose only love for her was the fact that she would do anything for him.

When Christine got back into the Escalade she playfully said, "Did you miss me baby?"

"I was about to come in there to see what was taking you so long. I was sitting here and some punk-ass cop came out of nowhere and ran up on me. He scared the shit out of me."

"Who, you? Brick Jackson, who said he ain't scared of no cop, and would drop their ass in a New York minute," she laughed.

"Naw man, he surprised me. I'm holding all this product up in here and my gun is under the seat, I would be looking at some real time. But all he wanted me to do was turn down my music."

"Well baby it's all good and he's gone. Now check out all these ends J laced us wit," she opened the bag exposing the money stacks.

"Man your girl be rollin. You said she was like that. She bring in more paper than any of the other joints. I'm diggin her flow," Brick was pleased with Janice's ability to sell drugs and keep track of the money with no problems. Christine kissed him on the lips and they drove off.

Briscoe was now certain that Janice was slinging dope from her house. All he needed was some concrete evidence. He also believed that something else was going on in that house, and it was not all good, especially for the little girl. He decided to venture closer to the source and get all the intelligence he could gather without arousing suspicion.

He sat in the report writing room on the computer and started by pulling all the information he could on Marvin Jackson from the various crime databases; Motor Vehicle Administration records and court services records. He compiled a list of Jackson's address, previous addresses, hangouts, employment history, known associates, and their addresses. He also listed every vehicle registered to Jackson. If Jackson was not in his sight, he wanted to know where to find him at all times. Also, he needed to know who that long tall white broad was. Is she just a friend of Janice or is she something more? He would have to turn to one of his snitches to help him with some inside information on Janice and her dealings.

Briscoe knew exactly who to contact. He would pull up Connie Little, AKA 'Golden Head', a well known crack ho that seems to know everybody in the neighborhood. Connie has hung out with or fucked every drug user in the neighborhood. If there is anything going on in that house she would know.

He logged off the computer, gathered his notes and printouts and went to his vehicle to get back on patrol. This time he was not only patrolling the streets looking for crime, he was also looking for Connie. She normally worked West Virginia Avenue, and would occasionally venture up to New York Avenue, where all the prostitutes found their ready and willing Johns. If she is out here, he will find her.

While traversing the streets of Washington, DC he began to think of all the various issues that people face daily in a city that should be an oasis, if you will. It's the nation's capital. All the resources should be there to ensure a low crime rate, high employment levels with great paying jobs, and clean streets. But instead, you have one of the highest HIV/AIDS rates in the nation, high rates of unemployment, and a crime rate that is off the charts. How could this be the seat of the United States Government and there be so many human issues that destroy and decay block after block. The education system in the city is dysfunctional to the point that high school graduates are reading on a 9th grade level, and the parents who have school aged children do not place much value in education, because they too are the product (or should I say victims) of the DC public school system.

A lot has to be done to fix the ills that plague this great city. There must be a cleansing, and it has to take place in the areas that are most affected by the destructive forces that move throughout the city everyday victimizing good law abiding people. They, the law abiding, are people who want what every other red blooded American wants; a safe environment to raise their children, a job that pays a livable wage, and quiet enjoyment of their lives without fear. The destructive ones are just the opposite; they are selfish, lazy, hard hearted, evildoers. The only thing that matters to them is themselves. They would never make a sacrifice for their fellow man. If they are denied anything they whine and complain. If that doesn't help, they just victimize someone who is just as bad off as they are and take what they want. These people live hand-to-mouth and refuse to see past the moment. They will stand out on the streets all night selling drugs and pussy, and making all sorts of ruckus. When the good people, who must get up early for work complain, they threaten them with physical harm. These are the people who Briscoe felt he needed to rid the communities of. They are blight on all humanity and should be extinguished from this realm of existence.

"5 Baker 44," the dispatcher's voice came over the radio.

"5 Baker 44" Briscoe replied.

"Take the aggravated assault in progress, the alley rear 1200 block West Virginia Avenue. The caller states two men are beating a male with sticks at the location; 5 Baker 44."

"5 Baker 44 I copy ma'am. Is there a lookout?" he asked.

"Lookout for two black males, both wearing white tee shirts and blue jeans; nothing further. 5 Baker 42, back the unit on West Virginia."

"5 Baker 42, I copy; responding."

"Make your status code one and advise when you arrive on scene," the dispatcher said.

Code one is lights and siren, making the vehicle a full-fledged emergency vehicle.

Briscoe had to put Connie out of his mind for now and prepare himself to deal with the issue at hand. When he was about eight blocks from the location, he cut off his emergency equipment and radioed 5 Baker 42 to do the same. They coordinated to enter the alley from two different directions; just in case the bandits run they will box them in.

5 Baker 42 was the first to enter the alley. He saw the two bandits going through the pockets of a man, who was motionless on the ground. When they saw the police car they fled in the direction that Briscoe was coming.

"5 Baker 42, I have two running. They are heading north in the alley toward you 5 Baker 44."

"I'm entering the alley and waiting on them," Briscoe said in a calm voice.

He angled the vehicle to prevent someone from getting past it without climbing over the hood or trunk. He then exited the vehicle and stood off in the shadows about twenty feet ahead of the vehicle. He removed his Glock 17 service pistol from his holster and held it ready. As the two bandits made their way down the alley they realized the cop that entered the alley where they were was not chasing them. They slowed down figuring that he stopped to help the victim.

As they reached Briscoe, he stepped from the shadows with his gun raised, and said, "Stop! Or I will blow your fuckin' heads off!"

They looked at the weapon pointed directly in their faces and stopped in their tracks. They instantly put their hands in the air and said, "We give up; don't shoot."

"Get on the ground. Now!" Briscoe commanded.

They dropped to the ground on their stomachs with their hands outstretched.

The whole time they pleaded. Briscoe told them, "Just shut the fuck up before I shoot you in the mouth."

He quickly patted them down for weapons, but did not find any.

"What did you do with the sticks you beat that dude with?"

"We didn't beat nobody," one of the bandits said.

Briscoe stood over top of him and punched him in the side of his face.

"Ouch! Shit man, you can't do that!" the young bandit screamed.

"I am going to kill both of you in this dirty ass alley in one minute. I don't give a fuck and nobody will ever know what happened here. Now where the fuck are the sticks?"

Briscoe then kicked them both in the ribs. They cried out in pain, but did not disclose the location of the sticks, so Briscoe took his ASP baton off his belt and opened it with a loud crack. That sound sends chills up the spine of bad guys who have been hit with one in the past. The two bandits knew exactly what it was and they started talking,

"We threw them in a yard down the alley."

"What side of the alley?"

"The left side," one of them said.

Briscoe radioed that he had two apprehensions and requested assistance with the crime scene. 5 Baker 42 advised that the victim was in grave condition, unconscious with a very weak pulse, and the Paramedics were working on him. He requested the homicide unit respond.

Briscoe handcuffed the two bandits and began to search them thoroughly. He found property on them that likely belonged to the victim.

"Do you know the guy you just beat?" he inquired.

"Yeah, he owes me money and I was just trying to get it when he punched me in the face," the bandit said.

Sure he did, Briscoe thought. They always have a justification for what they do. These two fools are about to face a murder beef and they have no idea. Briscoe decided not to question them any further because he did not want to taint the homicide investigation or jeopardize the case by violating their Fifth Amendment rights.

Other units arrived on scene and supervisors were en route. This was shaping up to be a big deal, and these two were going to face the ultimate charge. The victim was identified as Kenneth Johnson, a local eighteen year old black male who sold drugs in the Trinidad neighborhood. He was ultimately taken to Washington Hospital Center's MedStar Trauma Center where he was pronounced dead. It is official, the two bandits are now being charged with first degree murder.

Briscoe felt pretty good about getting two killers off the street. He was happy that they were able to catch them on the spot and close the case as soon as it opened. The VCU detectives were equally as happy. They love it when their job is made this easy. Since he was the officer given the assignment, he would be the one handling the arrest, along with the assigned homicide detective. While Briscoe was still on the scene with the Mobile Crime Lab as they processed, and patrol officers canvassed for witnesses, Detective Sanford arrived. He came over to Briscoe, and they embraced.

"What up dog?" Sanford greeted.

"We closed it for you with two arrests," Briscoe said.

"Out fucking standing! I told you that you are the man!" exclaimed Sanford.

"It was nothing. We caught them in the act and just reacted," Briscoe was being modest.

"Where are they now B?"

"We have them in two separate transports waiting to take them to your office whenever you're ready for them."

"Go ahead and send them over. Somebody is there now and they'll put them in the box. I'm just going to interview the caller and any other potential witnesses. You can do the arrest paperwork at VCU since you have to make a statement anyway."

"That sounds like a winner to me," Briscoe agreed.

The two of them were on another case together again, like old times, and it felt great. Now it gives Briscoe an opportunity to stay close to the investigation of the serial predator. He did not want any surprises from the department. If they even had an inkling of a thought that the perpetrator was a cop, he would have to change his methods.

He had to stay a step ahead of them at all times.

Briscoe gathered information from both bandits for his report. Their names sent a red flag up in his mind. Earlier, when he ran Brick Jackson's information, the two of them were listed as known associates. They are members of his crew and they both live in the community. David 'Red' Abernathy was a lanky nineteen year old light-skinned black male with freckles. He has a juvenile record longer than Briscoe's arm and he had an adult gun and drug charge recently. He is starting off his adult life of crime right where his juvenile life left off. He lives in the 1600 block of Trinidad Avenue with his mother and four siblings. The other bandit is nineteen year old Antoine 'Ant' Lakeland. He also lives in the 1600 block Trinidad Avenue, where he and Red grew up and have embarked on a life of crime together since elementary school.

They have been friends since they attended kindergarten at Webb Elementary School. When they were in the 6th grade, they would jump other kids and take their lunch money, video games, and anything else they wanted. Their reputation followed them to Brown Middle School, where they stepped up to using weapons and causing severe pain to many. They were ultimately kicked out of all the public schools in the District and ended up serving time in the Oak Grove Youth Detention Facility for violent felonies. They were bad news from the start and this deadly union has now culminated in a homicide. Anyone who knows them and has eyes could see that it was only a matter of time before they killed somebody. And that time is now.

Briscoe could not understand why the courts cannot see this.

You ask any cop on the beat who dealt with either of them and they would probably say it was no surprise they killed a man. It was bound to happen. Once again Briscoe felt that the system just does not do enough to prevent these animals from destroying other lives in the wake of their madness. Since Briscoe will be off for the next two days he decided, *Fuck it! I'm going to step up my game and clean this shit off the streets!*

It was now 2:10 a.m. and Briscoe was on his way to VCU to process the prisoners and make his statement to the homicide investigators. He decided to spend the next two days dropping bodies around the city like Johnny Appleseed planting a grove. The nights will belong to him and the criminals will cringe with fear. It's time to take the city back and hand it over to those who can appreciate it and care for it. The good people who hung in here for generations, through good times, the Mayor's drug fiasco, and the really bad crack epidemic, and they did not flee to the suburbs. They kept a tax base and the city moving forward in spite of the crumbling school system and the burdensome crime rate. It is time to get it on and send the message straight to the bottom-feeders of the District that they either ride or die.

He arrived at VCU, where he completed the arrest paperwork and made a statement to Sanford's partner. Since this case is a homicide, Sanford will go down in the morning and walk the paperwork through the U.S. Attorney's Office. Briscoe could check off on time and go home.

By the time everything at VCU was completed, it was 5:50 a.m. and almost time for Briscoe's shift to end. On the way back to the District, he drove through West Virginia Avenue and New York Avenue once again searching for Connie. He went past the 24-hour store on Mount Olivet Road and the various diners that catered to prostitutes, crack hos, and the like. He did not run across Connie and decided to go in for relief. He'll try to catch up to her when he returns to work in a few days. He knows Connie's address, but decided against going to her home. He had to be very careful in his approach and careful not put Connie's life in danger. He had plans to use Connie, as an unwitting participant in his crusade to rid the city of the sagging pants vermin that plagued its streets.

When he checked off from his shift, he changed clothes and headed for the parking lot. When he got to his car, Officer White was waiting for him. Officer Karen White was a six-year veteran who had a thing for Briscoe. While working together one night, she told him that she would suck his dick in the scout car.

He thought she was joking, but she said, "I'm not laughing. I want you that bad."

Briscoe felt that having relations at work was a bad idea, so he declined. However, she still has a crush and still lets him know that she is available and ready to love him down.

"Hi big guy," she greeted him. "Where are you off to?"

"I'm on my way to the gym and then home to bed. What's up?" he said warmly.

"I was wondering if you wanted to grab breakfast with me this morning?" she smiled.

"That sounds good Karen, but I really can't today. I have to get to bed so that I can get up early. I have a pretty full schedule later today."

He had to keep his distance from Karen because she is very tempting. Her body is a perfect ten and she has the cutest dimples he has ever seen. If she were not a cop, he would have jumped all over her. But being on the job, she was in his book as off limits. Many of the other guys on the department were trying to get at her, and the way he heard it, many of them got her. She is a very attractive lady with her cocoa butter complexion, and teardrop onion, but she was just not what he needed at this point in his life.

"I thought you said you were going to the gym?" she said as though she caught him in a lie.

"I am, but immediately afterwards I am getting in the bed so I can get up early."

"You can miss the gym for one day," she said while looking at him with a puppy dog expression.

"I really can't Karen; I have to burn off this overnight energy that is pent up inside of me like a lion trapped inside a cage."

"I can help you get rid of that energy and release that beast," she said with a wink and a smile while rubbing on his abdomen and looking at his crotch.

"We can't do that Karen; you know better," he was very polite.

"Well you can't blame a sister for trying. I was just feeling a little down and I wanted some company. You don't have to give that dick up or anything . . . right now. I just didn't want to eat alone." She really wanted to get him alone, to try and change his mind.

"Maybe another day, but I can't today, okay?"

He knew that being alone with her would cause him to slip so he just would not put himself in a compromising position.

"Okay baby boy, but if you change your mind about breakfast . . . or anything else, I'm always available. You have my number just use it when you get ready."

"I'll keep that in mind Karen," he said.

She leaned in and kissed him on the cheek and said, "Sleep tight beautiful."

She turned and walked to her car.

Briscoe watched that sexy tight ass as she walked away. *Daaammn, I would rock that ass like nobody has ever rocked it before. But some things are just not meant to be, and that's one of them.* He smiled at her and waved goodbye as she drove past.

6

When Briscoe awakened it was 7:25 p.m. He felt reinvigorated and ready to get started with his night. He planned to leave an indelible mark on the face of the city and make a statement that the underbelly will not be able to ignore. It was a Friday night in July. The streets would be pregnant with many possibilities for him to shock the conscious.

There was still close to two hours of daylight left. Briscoe would use that time to prepare his equipment and finalize the plans he has prepared for many months. This is not a spur of the moment move on his part. He has planned this operation for the past three months and now is the time to execute . . . no pun intended. He loaded his black backpack with flex cuffs, rope, duct tape, and ammunition for the Sig Sauer P245, semi-automatic .45 caliber handgun he acquired by less-than-legal means. There is nothing about the gun or the attached HK Evolution 45 sound suppressor that could possibly be connected to Briscoe. He made sure to bring everything that he would need and the items necessary if he needed to move to his contingency plan. In addition he packed a first aid kit, his police radio, night vision goggles, and a change of clothing. He was ready to get dressed and hit the streets.

He emerged dressed in all black clothing carrying his concealed .45 caliber handgun in a belt holster, his .25 caliber gun in his ankle holster, just in case, and his Special Forces bowie knife. All the other items were in the backpack. As always, once he entered his vehicle he docked his iPod and decided to jam Phil Collins "In the Air Tonight." The music set the mood for him and sent him driving into the night with a purpose.

It was now 9:30 p.m. and time for justice to be served scorching hot with a vengeance. He would start in southwest; because it would not be too difficult to capture someone in a small enough group for him to work with. Then he will move to the other three quadrants of the city, making northwest the last because it would be too busy there until after 3 a.m.

He drove to the unit block of M Street and parked his vehicle at the mouth of an alley in a position where he could see the group of men on the corner at the end of the block. He took out his night vision binoculars, and just as he figured, his first target was in sight. These mouth-breathing, knuckle-dragging, bottom-feeders are so predictable. They are truly creatures of habit with nothing positive to contribute to society or their community. The only thing they contribute is destruction and despair. The disheartening fact is they destroy the very communities in which they live.

Briscoe was determined not to let a few of them breathe another breath after tonight. The rest would know that a change was on the horizon, and either straighten up and fly right, or suffer the same fate.

His target is Miles Holloman, aka "Stink." He is long past time for removal from the streets. Stink is a thirty year old OG who has been out here for a long time and has left a path of misery just as long as his years. It appears to Briscoe that nothing the criminal justice system is doing will put Stink away or stop the pain that he causes to non-aggressive people who are just trying to live their lives. His rap sheet contains violent crimes, drug trafficking, and gang activity. His reputation in the community is that of violence and intimidation. It seems that everybody fears his wrath and nobody will oppose him.

A woman, who was new to the community, denied him and his drug gang access to the building in which she resided, when they were fleeing the police. Stink attacked her and her thirteen year old daughter stabbing them multiple times. They both had extensive surgeries and rehabilitation, and were moved from the neighborhood under police protection. The case is ongoing, because they are just getting to the point where they can talk again, but they are deathly afraid and thus reluctant to testify against him.

Stink came to Briscoe's attention six months ago when he beat an elderly woman for bumping into him and knocking a bag from his hand. The offense took place at the flea market on Benning Road one Saturday afternoon. The place was crowded and people would often bump into one another. Normal people would apologize and continue shopping. Well, this low form of existence is not quite what you would call normal. A seventy year old lady bumps into this piece of shit, knocking his bag from his grasp. She immediately apologizes and starts to bend down to pick up the bag.

Then Stink says, "You stupid old bitch; look at what the fuck you've done!"

The lady once again, very fearful said, "I'm sorry."

Stink, being the shit bag that he is, punched her in the mouth with a closed fist, knocking her to the ground. He then jumped on top of her and started beating her in the face. All of the men in the market saw and none of them tried to stop him.

A young woman in her early twenties started yelling for help and jumped on Stink's back to stop him. Then he commenced beating her, but she was doing all she could to fight back. Three security guards arrived and knocked Stink to the ground and restrained him. Briscoe was the MPD officer who arrived on scene and arrested him. The elderly woman suffered a concussion, lacerations, and swelling to her face. The case went to court and was lowered to a misdemeanor, and all Stink received was twelve months probation. *What a travesty?* Briscoe thought at the time. He knew he would revisit this with Stink somewhere in the future and the future is now.

Briscoe exited his vehicle and took a long look at his surroundings. He searched the windows, doorways, porches, parked cars, and every square foot of the block. He needed to be sure of all he was up against and what his environment had to offer. There were a handful of people sitting on the front of one building on the south side of the street and a couple was sitting in a parked car, five spaces up from where Briscoe was parked.

He pulled his black baseball cap lower over his face and proceeded to the alley. He moved quickly but stealthily to get closer to the group of men on the corner. He was now slightly crouched in a very good over-watch position where he could hear their conversation and clearly see their faces. His next moves would have to be decisive, quick, and violent. There were now just three left standing on the corner; Stink and two of his flunkies. Briscoe pulled out his silencer-equipped Sig Saur and stood straight up and proceeded with a brisk pace directly toward the three men.

Before they could turn in his direction, Briscoe raised the gun and shot two of them in their heads in rapid succession. Before they hit the ground, he holstered the gun and grabbed hold of his razor sharp bowie knife. Since there was no signature from the gun, Stink had no idea why his boys fell to the ground.

He looked down and said, "What the fuck y'all doing?"

Just then he looked up and into the eyes of Briscoe, who reached out and slashed his throat with the knife. The gurgling sound of blood coming from Stink's open throat and him clutching his mortal wound were the only sounds heard on the corner. As Stink started to stumble around, Briscoe kicked downward as hard as he could on his knee cap breaking it and forcing him to the ground. He then stabbed him twice in the heart.

Briscoe took a quick look around and realized that everybody was still going on with their activity and did not see a thing. He reached down and grabbed Stink by the leg and dragged his limp, lifeless body into the alley like a rag doll. He searched Stink's pockets and removed the contents. He found a few bags of crack and a large amount of money. He then made the hole in Stinks throat larger, and placed the money and drugs inside. He left the rest of his belongings on his chest. He wiped the blood from the knife on Stink's shirt and returned it to the sheath as he stood and casually walked back to his vehicle. He pulled into the opposite alley, drove through to the next block and headed for the southeast quadrant of the city to rendezvous the next shit bag with his destiny.

7

About five minutes after Briscoe finished his deed to society, a crack ho named Mindy was in search of a fix when she discovered the two bodies on the corner. Briscoe heard the call go out over the police radio. When the units arrived, they called for the Board and a Homicide unit. They said there were two down on the corner and one in the alley. When the police canvassed for witnesses, everyone they spoke to said they were outside for hours and did not see or hear anything. How is it possible for two people to be shot multiple times and nobody hears anything? "Maybe they were dumped there," one officer speculated.

No, because several witnesses said one moment they saw them standing on the corner and when they looked again, they were not there. A few moments later, they heard the girl screaming for help. When the Homicide detectives arrived and saw the condition of Stink, they knew it was the work of the serial predator, and immediately called Detective Whitehead.

"Detective Whitehead speaking," he said as he flipped open his cell phone.
"Jamie, it's Doug. I have some bad news, dude," Doug Hendricks, a fellow homicide detective informed.
"Let me guess, it's another one?" Whitehead said.
"You must be psychic," Doug confirmed.
"Damn. I was really hoping this guy would slow his roll. I haven't even had a chance to get an angle on him. He is all over the place; uptown, downtown, in the projects, even in Georgetown. What does the scene look like?"
Normally he wouldn't ask, but Doug is a homicide detective so maybe he could give him something to think about while he was en route to the scene.
"There are three victims."

"What the . . ." Whitehead interjected.

"Yeah man, there are two shot in the head on the corner and one who had a slice job done on him in the alley. The dude is split open like a piñata. And check this, his product and cash was stuffed inside his wound," Doug paused.

"That's similar to the one that had the product stuffed in his mouth," Whitehead said.

"Exactly, that's why I called you. The only thing different about this is he took down two other people at the same time. I have to tell you Jamie, this guy is like a phantom or something, because these dudes were shot at least twice in the head and nobody saw or heard a thing."

"Hum, is it that they 'didn't see anything', or they really didn't see anything?" Whitehead asked, because he knows the code of the street.

"They really didn't see or hear anything. That is what's so creepy," Doug said.

"What's the address, Doug?"

"It's the unit block of M Street Southwest"

"Thanks, Doug, I'm getting dressed now, and I should be there in about thirty minutes. You all know what to do. I'll hit my partner Jake and get him rolling that way also."

"Cool, I'll see you when you get here; Peace," Doug hung up the phone.

Little did they know their night was just beginning.

Briscoe arrived at his next destination in southeast and drove through the target location looking for his subject. There were many people outside, including children. It was after 10:00 p.m. He thought, *That's why children become victims. What kind of parent allows their elementary aged child to play outside this late? Damn. What could be done to change a culture that does everything they can to kick against any beneficial change? The people living in these neighborhoods have been through so much; the brutality of the criminal justice system, the broken promises of the legislative system, and the outright raping at the hands of the social services system. They have had the proverbial carrot dangled before them with no hope of ever getting a taste.*

Briscoe was reminded of a time during one of his military deployments to a third world nation; someone said they were okay with their poor living conditions because they did not know any different. But they pointed out that in America we're shown expensive things and glamorous, lofty lifestyles that many could never have. These are the dynamics that fuel the flames of hate, jealousy, envy, anger, and crime. Briscoe could see the wisdom in that and it helped him better understand the people that he dealt with daily.

His target would be somewhere in the 2500 block of Elvans Road, but he did not see him when he drove through. So he decided to park his vehicle on Stanton Road, far enough away to not arouse suspicion, but close enough to see the block and the obvious drug activity that was taking place. He shut the engine off and pulled out his binoculars. Since the windows of his vehicle had a heavy dark tint and it was nighttime, he did not worry if he was being watched. However, he took a 360 degree assessment of his position and determined that he was safe, and nobody was watching him.

Now that he was settling in, Briscoe allowed himself to think about the subject that he came to send to the upper room. Damon Mason was, and still is, one bad news bear that no one should ever have to deal with. He is forty-two years old and has spent most of his life behind bars. That is part of the problem. He should have spent all of his life behind bars. He was convicted of second degree murder, and manslaughter, and somehow is still permitted to walk the streets of the District. When he was seventeen, he killed a boy for his leather jacket. He was somehow tried as a juvenile and subsequently released when he reached the age of twenty-one. The manslaughter conviction came when he was twenty-four years old. He claimed self defense, arguing that the victim attacked him first. The fact was Damon found out that the victim was banging his woman while he was locked up in the D.C. Jail awaiting trial for an armed carjacking, which somehow he beat. Damon beat the guy with a solid four-foot metal pipe, two-inches thick, transforming his face into ground sausage. There was so much damage, his funeral was closed-casket. Damon spent ten years behind bars for that. Once he returned to society he picked right up where he left off. For the past eight years, he has committed armed carjacking, armed robbery, burglary, theft, aggravated assault, and is a suspect in two murders. He is somewhat of a lone wolf who shows no loyalty to anybody. He seems to do his dirt by himself, but it is just as destructive as being associated with a gang.

Briscoe chose him because of his violent behavior, the system's inability to keep him off the streets, and his obvious unwillingness to stop victimizing innocent people. Damon is five-feet-seven-inches tall and weighs every bit of 140 pounds soaking wet. He preys on his victims with the element of surprise and a heart blackened to the point that he kills without hesitation or remorse. Tonight Briscoe will give him a taste of his own medicine.

"Where is that little cock sucker?" Briscoe said to himself. "Every time I came through here checking, his ass was always sitting out there on the front running his mouth."

He decided to give him fifteen minutes to come out. If he doesn't, Briscoe would be on his way to the northeast quadrant and would have to come back later for Damon.

The time went by with no sign of Damon, so Briscoe started his vehicle and drove off. Just as he reached the intersection, Damon emerged from the doorway of the apartment building adjacent to and facing the intersection of Elvans Road and Stanton Road. He was wearing a silk shirt, slacks, and a fedora, with gold chains draped around his neck, and both wrists iced with a gold watch and bracelets. It appears his target is stepping out tonight.

Briscoe paused at the intersection long enough to see Damon enter the front passenger seat of a burgundy Chevy Tahoe. Briscoe proceeded through the stop sign and drove slowly toward Suitland Parkway while staring in his mirror. As luck would have it, the Chevy turned right and was heading toward the Parkway also. As they reached the traffic light at the intersection of the Parkway and Stanton Road, Briscoe waited to see which way the Chevy was going before he signaled. The Chevy was making a left turn that would send them toward Maryland. Briscoe activated his left turn signal and waited for the light to turn green. He wished he could see inside the vehicle but the headlights were all he could see in his mirror. Maybe when they turn he will get a glimpse inside of the vehicle and see what he was up against.

The light turned and both vehicles turned left onto Suitland Parkway. Briscoe moved to the right lane and the Chevy got into the left lane and passed him. As the vehicle passed, he tried to get a look inside, but the windows were tinted all the way around and he could not see who or how many occupants were inside.

They continued straight on the Parkway into Maryland. They passed Naylor Road, Silver Hill Road, and then Suitland Road still proceeding east on the Parkway.

Where could they possibly be heading? Briscoe wondered. They made it all the way to the end of the parkway where it intersects with Pennsylvania Avenue and made a right turn. He continued to follow the vehicle. After a mile on Pennsylvania Avenue they turned right onto Dower House Road. The Chevy drove until they came to a mobile home park at the end of the road. As the Chevy drove into the trailer park, Briscoe turned in the opposite direction and pulled to the shoulder of the road. He looked over his shoulder and watched as the Chevy turned left in between a row of mobile homes. He U-turned and followed the road the Chevy took, turning his lights off as he crept into the trailer park.

Since the mobile home community was very small, he decided to park near the entrance and walk through the community to get an up-close view of the occupants of the Chevy and their destination. He grabbed his binoculars and exited the vehicle. He moved about the complex with stealth and quickness, carefully observing his surroundings and listening for any signs of danger.

The Chevy slowed and then stopped in front of a white mobile home with green shutters. Then it backed into the driveway that was covered by a green and white carport that matched the home. The driver turned off the lights, but sat for about ten minutes with the engine running. Briscoe could now see into the vehicle, although not clearly, but he could see that the driver of the vehicle was a woman. It appeared that she and Damon were the only occupants.

What the hell are they doing here? There doesn't seem to be anybody home at the trailer, because it is dark and there are no cars parked outside. Then it hit him like a light bulb turning on to illuminate a room clothed in darkness. *The woman lives here, and she is bringing Damon over as her guest*

Since he didn't expect to go so far into Maryland, he would have to modify his plan in order to send his intended message. It is a minor detail and does not deter Briscoe from his mission at hand. In the meantime, he watched as Damon and the female embraced and kissed in the front seat of the vehicle. They were enthralled in a passionate make out session that Briscoe felt was way too long. It was actually only ten minutes, but it seemed more like thirty when you are waiting for something.

Finally the engine went dead and both doors opened. Out stepped Damon from the passenger seat, and the driver, who was about six feet tall, wearing a short black mini skirt displaying her long thick legs that went all the way up to her tight well shaped ass, exited from the driver's side. She had a flat stomach and large breasts that were spilling out of her burgundy silk top. From where Briscoe was standing, this chick was sizzling.

How does a narrow ass piece of shit like Damon pull a fine hottie like that? Briscoe could never understand how the thugs, with no prospect of a future, or the ability to support a woman into her golden years, got fine, gorgeous, well-to-do females. It must be something about that bad boy image that some sisters just love to be around.

The two of them made their way to the front door of the trailer. The woman unlocked the door and they both entered. Briscoe could see a light come on just before the door was closed. Now it was time for him to go to work. It was well after 11:00 p.m. and quickly approaching midnight. If he didn't step it up, the clock would start to work against him.

He went back to his vehicle and moved it to a spot just outside of the trailer park near the auto auction lot, really no more than a vehicle junk yard. He gathered the equipment he would need to complete his mission, and then proceeded fifty yards on foot to the trailer that housed Damon and his conquest. Briscoe went to the windows to see if he could see into the trailer before making entry. The light was left on in the living room, but no one was in there. He looked into every window along the trailer in an attempt to locate where they were inside. He also looked for signs of a dog. If there was a dog he would more than likely have to abort, because the dog would alert them to his presence long before he wanted them to be aware.

Thank God there was no dog. While peering into the bedroom window he could not see anything, but he could hear the voices of two people wrapped up in ecstasy. He could hear moans and whispers of a man and woman making love. Excellent! This was the perfect time for him to enter the home and get at his target. So Briscoe hastened to the front door and used his tools to pick the lock. He pulled his ski mask over his face, with only his eyes visible, and quickly but quietly entered the home. He scanned the room and realized they undressed in the living room and all the way down the hallway leading to the bedroom. He stood and listened to their moans of pleasure and readied himself for what he was about to do. *I hope he enjoys his nut, because it will be his last.*

Briscoe moved quietly down the hallway clearing the other small rooms as he passed them to ensure that no one else was in the small trailer home. As he made his way to the bedroom, where the door was wide open, he stopped in his tracks as he looked at the reflection in the mirror that was situated just inside of the bedroom. He could not believe his eyes. There was Damon on his knees, with his hands wrapped around his date's buttocks and his mouth wrapped around his date's dick.

What the fuck? Briscoe was stunned. He had to look again wondering where the woman was that came into the house with Damon. *Oh shit, that is the woman.* This man was a transsexual who looked just like a woman. It freaked Briscoe out for a moment, but it was not enough to keep him from the task at hand. He pulled out his Sig and stepped into the room. Damon was so busy sucking dick and the shemale had her eyes closed so engulfed with pleasure that neither one realized they had company.

"Take that dick out of your mouth faggot," Briscoe said as he pointed the gun at both of them.

The shemale opened her eyes and said, "Oh no please don't shoot," as she pulled away from Damon and cowered against the wall next to the bed in the tiny room.

"Just shut the fuck up and you won't get hurt," Briscoe ordered.

"What do you want man?" Damon asked still on his knees afraid to move.

"I want you to take these and put them on your bitch," Briscoe said as he handed Damon a pair of flex cuffs.

"Lay face down on the bed, bitch," Briscoe ordered the shemale.

"Now tie his hands behind his back," he directed. Damon complied, putting the flex cuffs snuggly on the shemale's wrists.

"Now you lay face down on the floor," Briscoe directed Damon, who did exactly as he was told.

Briscoe took out a second pair of flex cuffs and placed them on Damon's wrists. He put away his gun and then duct taped the shemale's mouth, wrists, and legs. He then ripped a piece of clothing that was on the floor and tied it around the shemale's face covering her eyes and secured it with duct tape.

"What do you want? I will give you anything, just don't hurt us," Damon pleaded.

"Shut the fuck up before I cut your head off and leave it under the bed."

Once Briscoe finished securely taping the shemale, he laid him on his side in the bed, to avoid positional asphyxiation, and he cut away the flex cuffs and placed them in the cargo pocket of his pants. He did not want to harm the shemale because he did not know her or any of her deeds. He was there for Damon and that is who is going with him.

"You have a debt to pay, you dick-sucking little fucker. And I am here to collect," Briscoe said to Damon.

"Who do I owe? I'll pay anything, please just don't hurt us?"

"Stop begging you little bitch and show some heart. Your debt is to all the victims you left in the wake of your destruction."

"Come on man please," Damon started to whimper.

Briscoe grabbed him underneath his chin, and wrapped the duct tape around his head and over his mouth several times, ensuring that it was tight. He then rolled Damon onto his back where he wrapped duct tape around his thighs, below his knees and around his ankles. Then he grabbed a sheet from a bed in the second bedroom and wrapped it around Damon's still-naked body, from his feet all the way up and over his head. He used the duct tape to secure it tightly. He picked Damon up and put him over his shoulder.

Once he reached the front door of the trailer home, he dropped Damon on the floor. Briscoe then picked up the keys to the Chevy off the counter and went outside to open the vehicle. As he emerged from the home, he scanned the mobile home park to be sure nobody was watching him. He then opened the driver's door, got into the seat and disabled the dome lights. He pulled the latch releasing the rear cargo door, which opened slightly. He exited the vehicle and went to the rear where he opened the door wide, looked inside to make sure there would be room enough for Damon. He moved quickly inside and picked Damon up from the floor and carried him to the rear of the vehicle, placed him inside, and closed the hatch. Then he went back inside to check the scene for anything that would give the cops a lead.

Once he checked everything, he went to the shemale and said, "This has nothing to do with you, so let's keep it that way. All you know is a couple of dudes came in here and said Damon owes them money and they took him out of here. Do you understand?"

The shemale nodded her head.

"I would hate to have to come back here and kill you right there where you are laying. You didn't see my face or any part of my skin, so as far as you know I could be a white man with a limp. Just keep your story simple. But the safest thing for you is not to even call the cops. I would hate for you to suffer the same fate as Damon."

Briscoe took all of Damon's belongings and left the trailer, locking the door behind him. He got into the Chevy and drove it to where his vehicle was parked. He exited the Chevy and retrieved his backpack and a metal pipe from his vehicle and then got back into the Chevy. He looked around studying the landscape to ensure that his vehicle being parked on the street near the auto lot was not going to warrant any undue attention. He also checked that no one was around watching him work. He was satisfied that everything was in order and nothing looked out of place. There were several cars parked on the street next to the auto lot and his blended in. He then drove off in the direction of Washington, DC.

He was taking Damon back to his neighborhood in southeast, where he would exact his punishment. Just as he started to think of the task at hand, his cell phone rang.

Damn, I thought I silenced the ringer. I'm glad it didn't ring just as I entered that house. He despised mistakes like that, because little details like the phone ringing at the wrong time could get him killed or captured. He looked at the caller ID and saw that it was Monica and prepared himself before answering the phone.

"Hello."

"Hey sexy, where are you?" Monica sounded cheerful.

"I'm out with a couple of my boys having drinks," he hated lying to her, but he had no choice.

"Where at? I can come and meet you there."

"We are out in Maryland somewhere; I just stepped outside to get something out of my car when you called," he was trying to think fast on his feet.

"Is it far from your house?" she really wanted to be with him.

"It's a place near Fort Meade called the Eagle's Nest. It's just a bunch of guys. We are shooting pool and talking a bunch of shit about nothing."

"You sound like you don't want my company," she feigned disappointment.

"No, that's not it. I'm here with a bunch of dudes and there are only a handful of women in the place and I don't need them fools gawking over you." He was playing it off, because he really kind of liked the way men stared at her when she was with him.

"Okay, okay I know you just want to play with the boys tonight. Well, I have dibs on tomorrow anyway."

"You don't have to wait all the way until tomorrow; you can be in my bed tonight when I get there," Briscoe was getting aroused by the tone of her voice.

"I'm way ahead of you; I have been lying in your bed watching TV for the past hour," she giggled.

"Well, don't wait up for me. I'll be more than happy to wake you when I get there."

"I love you Antonio, please come to me and then cum inside of me baby," she was really being mischievous and it was turning Briscoe on like nobody's business.

"Umm, you are so tempting, you little hot tamale. I can't wait to get inside of you," his nature was starting to rise.

"Just hurry home lover and it will be hot and ready just for you and your big friend," Monica knew how to get him excited.

"Alright Moni, now you got me so hot I can't go back inside the bar. I have to think about baseball or something," they both laughed. "I'll be home later baby; you know how these guys do. I have to hang until everybody is ready because I'm a passenger. I left my car at my boy's house," he was all the way into his lie and just played it out.

"Okay sweetie, be safe and I'll be laying here with my panties on the floor and all of my nah-nah open for you."

"I love you, Moni."

They gave each other telephone smooches and hung up.

Damn I wish I didn't have to lie to her. But what else can I do? At least I'm not cheating on her.

He turned his thoughts back to Damon and the work he was going to do on his no good ass. He pulled the vehicle along side of Moten Elementary School at the top of Stanton Road, just a few blocks from Damon's home. He drove around the school and the surrounding area to be sure that nobody was on school property or near enough to see or hear him. He also tuned his police radio to the 7th Precinct zone and monitored their activity. He wanted to be sure that nobody, including the police, was anywhere in the area. He was satisfied, and determined that it was safe to leave the vehicle on Pomeroy Road, and walk the 200 yards to the rear of the school;

but he would not be able to carry Damon that far without attracting attention.

He decided to drop Damon in the tree line adjacent to the school approximately fifty yards from Stanton Road. He stopped the vehicle, turned off the lights, and quickly pulled Damon from the back hatch of the vehicle. When he dropped him on the ground, Damon started to wiggle.

Briscoe kicked him in the stomach, "Stop moving before I put a bullet in your head. If you want to survive this, you better stay still and listen to me."

Damon stopped moving and did exactly as he was told. Briscoe wedged him in between a dead stump and a large pine tree. There was no room for Damon to wiggle and it would only be a few minutes before Briscoe would return to him. He quickly retrieved all of Damon's belongings from the vehicle, placed them on the ground beside him, and then went back to the vehicle and drove it to Pomeroy Road. He parked the Chevy as inconspicuously as possible amongst the other vehicles. He grabbed his pack and placed it on his back, then reached in and seized the metal pipe. He closed the door and used the keyless remote to activate the lock. He thought how devastating it would be for him if the vehicle was stolen while he was taking care of business.

He walked the short distance, which was mostly uphill, to where he left Damon. Just before he crested the hill of the small street that parallels Stanton Road, a police cruiser drove up and turned onto the drive leading to the rear of the school, passing the location where Briscoe left Damon. He turned his face away from the police car but continued to walk uphill. He knew not to do anything to cause the officer to become suspicious. It would be very difficult to explain to a fellow officer why he is in southeast dressed the way he is carrying a metal pipe. Besides, it could be someone that he knows, since he was acquainted with a few officers from the 7th Precinct, who patrolled the area. As soon as the car passed and was out of sight, Briscoe stepped into the woods and walked deep enough to be concealed from view. He reached into his backpack and pulled out an earpiece and plugged one end into his police radio and the other in his ear. Now he could maintain constant surveillance of the channel without emitting audible sound that could possibly be heard. He could reach Damon from where he is by walking through the thick patch of woods. The quarter moon and illumination of the street lights provided enough light for him to accomplish his mission without a flashlight. However, he used a pair of night vision goggles to get his bearing. Just about twenty-five yards ahead through the thick foliage is where he left Damon.

He started to walk briskly through the brush because the goggles allowed him to see everything as if it were daylight. When he got within ten yards of Damon, he stopped and took a close look at him and the surrounding area before taking off the goggles.

Damn, where is the unit that went by? I hope he is just making a check of the property and not going back there to take a nap. He needed to get a visual on the cop or get him out of the area. Briscoe had a plan to get the officer out of the area, but he wanted to get a closer look to see what exactly he was doing first. So Briscoe walked up and checked to see that Damon was still secure. Then he went up to the road where he could see the cruiser sitting behind the school. It was near the playground with his parking lights on and the dome light on inside. It appeared the officer was completing paperwork. Briscoe looked at his watch and realized it was 12:40 a.m., and the cop has only been on shift for about an hour so chances are he was just fucking off.

Briscoe does not have time to wait him out, so he must take matters into his own hands to get him out of the area. He went back to where he left Damon and went through his belongings and retrieved a cell phone.

He dialed 911 and said, "It's a big fight at Good Hope Road and MLK Avenue, and somebody has been shot. There is blood everywhere and they are down on the sidewalk not moving. The crowd is very large and people are still fighting. They all just came out of the bar that's right there."

"Sir, can you tell me how many people are fighting?" The 911 operator was trying to gather more information for the responding units.

"Man I don't know the exact number, but it's more than ten. Please get some help here before that guy dies and more people get hurt," he hung up the phone.

The alert tones went out within thirty seconds from the time Briscoe hung up the phone. The dispatcher sent all available units to the priority call that he just made. The officer sitting behind the school turned off the dome light, activated his emergency equipment, and expedited from his spot to the bogus fight. Briscoe quickly collected

Damon and his belongings and dragged him to the location he had picked out in the rear of the school. Even if the cop comes back, Briscoe is out of his sight and will be able to do his business without interruption.

When Damon was dumped hard on the ground, he started to wiggle more than he had before. Briscoe took out his Bowie knife and cut the sheet open, exposing Damon, who was blinking, trying to focus his eyes in the darkness, to see what was happening to him. Briscoe rolled him off the sheet and threw it onto the pile with the rest of his clothing. Once Damon's eyes were focused, the fear was undeniably emblazoned within. His heart was racing and he could sense the end was near. His thoughts were running wild, *Why me? What did I do, and to who?* He was truly a coward of a man, with a big mouth and an evil streak that showed no mercy to his victims.

"Damon, you have brought nothing but pain, suffering, and heartache to the world that we live in. I am here to send you to another world where your dirty deeds can be judged," Briscoe looked into Damon's eyes as he was lying naked and bound on his side on the hard concrete of the grease trap used by the school's cafeteria.

Damon's eyes were pleading for mercy, but he will find none in the heart of his slayer tonight. Briscoe raised the pipe and brought it crashing down onto Damon's knee cap with a tremendous amount of force, like a jack hammer breaking away dense concrete. The knee cap buckled under the pressure and dislodged. The pain was excruciating, and his body moved violently under the pain delivered by the pipe. His eyes watered and the tears flowed freely. The muffled sounds of his screams told the entire story of his agony. WHAM! The pipe came crashing down on the other knee cap. WHAM! A blow to his exposed stomach, and then the chest. CRACK! Was the audible sound of his collar bone breaking like a brittle rotted twig on a brisk fall morning. Briscoe punished him with well placed blows from the pipe. His pain was so intense, his bowels released, and he pissed and shit all over the place.

"Oh you nasty motherfucker, can't you hold your shit? Didn't that fag pack your shit in for you? Well, don't sweat it, because I planned to knock the shit out of you anyway," Briscoe laughed at his own words.

Once again the pipe crashed down breaking his ankle, and then again, breaking the other one. It was amazing to Briscoe that Damon did not pass out from the agonizing pain that was inflicted upon him. His body was moving involuntarily from the pain, which beat upon him like an ocean wave crashing violently upon the rocks. Briscoe kicked him in the throat, the face, and the groin. He was trying to inflict as much suffering as possible before he released Damon into death. He wanted him to feel the pain of all his victims who were unable to collect restitution, have justice served, or exact punishment. The time was running short, and he had other people to visit, so it was time to put Damon away . . . for good.

"Goodbye Damon; say hello to Satan when you get there and tell him I have more coming."

He then raised the pipe like a lumberjack readying his ax for a precision strike to a tree. With a powerful crashing swing, the pipe contacted Damon's forehead with so much force his head bent backward so far that Briscoe thought it would detach from his body. Again and again, he pounded his face with the metal pipe until there was nothing visible but bloody flesh. One could not distinguish his nose from his eyes. His face was literally beaten off. Somewhere during the violent beating his heart stopped and his body ceased to move. The only movement was caused by the metal pipe as it was transforming Damon into something that resembled a creature from a horror movie.

"Now you've paid your debt," Biscoe said as he cut the flex cuffs and duct tape from his body.

He then laid the sheet out flat on the ground and placed the duct tape and Damon's clothes on top and then gathered up the sheet and tied it closed. He placed the flex cuffs in the backpack and placed Damon flat on his back and laid his wallet and other contents from his pockets on his torso. He placed Damon's cell phone in his pocket because he was going to need it again, and decided to use it for the rest of the night.

Throughout his session with Damon, Briscoe monitored the radio, and was listening when the units arrived at the bogus call and found that there was no fight. It was time now for him to return to the Chevy and continue his night. He moved slowly from his concealed location carefully watching for any signs of movement. He listened for approaching vehicles, and was pleased that there were none, and there were no pedestrians out either. He reached the Chevy and opened the rear hatch with the keyless remote entry and tossed the sheet inside. He then got into the driver's seat and placed his backpack on the front passenger seat and the pipe on the floor.

He needed to make a decision, but he did not want to sit there while he contemplated. So he started the engine and drove off.

It was now after 1:00 a.m. and the clock was ticking loudly. If he were to take the Chevy back and retrieve his vehicle it would take forty-five minutes round trip and he was not sure that would be enough time to get to his last two clients . . . and he desperately wanted to take care of both of them tonight. If he kept the Chevy what would be the risks? The shemale could get free and call the police; they would put out a BOLO for the vehicle and he would have a serious problem. The evidence is still in the vehicle and it would tie him to Damon. But the shim (a term by which many cops refer to transsexual males) is not going to get loose until somebody lets him loose and it did not appear that anybody else lived there.

I should be safe at least until daylight, Briscoe thought. It would be a small risk so he decided to use the SUV to complete his mission. In some way it seems like a blessing, because he doesn't have to worry so much about people seeing the vehicle or remembering that it was in the neighborhood. So off to the northeast quadrant he went.

8

He reached into his pocket and retrieved Damon's cell phone, dialed *67 then 911 blocking the phone number.

"911, what is your emergency?" the call taker asked.

Briscoe distorted his voice, in an attempt to disguise it, "There is a dead body behind Moten Elementary School on the concrete pad."

When the call taker started to ask questions, Briscoe hung up. He knows the number will be discovered later and the investigators will know Damon's phone was used to place the calls. He only blocked the number to keep the dispatchers from calling him back tonight. He continued to monitor the 7th Precinct radio zone to be sure that the call would be dispatched. About four minutes later the call came over the radio for one unit to check the location for the report of a man down. The dispatcher did not broadcast it as a priority or with any urgency. Ten minutes passed before the unit marked on scene. After a brief canvass, he came over the air asking for a supervisor, VCU and the Board. Briscoe then switched his radio to the 6th Precinct zone where his next subject resides and eats at the heart of the community, like a progressively advancing cancer. he blackens and devours everything that is clean and wholesome.

Briscoe took the Hayes Street exit from Interstate 295 and proceeded to the stop sign. He began to look around closely at his surroundings. All the while, he was monitoring the police radio. It appeared there was a shooting on Clay Terrace, which stretched the 6th Precinct's resources thin. Their Board was growing increasingly long with radio runs stacking up and no one to answer the calls for service. This was an excellent scenario for Briscoe, because the cops would now be too busy to concentrate on proactive police measures. So he is less likely to be singled out as a suspicious person. Now he can do his work without a great deal of concern that the cops were lurking about.

He drove forward slowly to the next stop sign looking from the rooftops to the ground and from the front doors to the street. He was gathering intelligence on every person and type who was out at this late hour. Even though his target is around the corner and several blocks down the street, he needed to know the situation on the approach. He knows that several MPD officers live in the community and he did not want a confrontation with one of his comrades. It was always Briscoe's policy to be careful and thorough and it has served him well for many years. He turned right and proceeded toward the block, where his target would be hanging.

Briscoe drove through. Sometimes he sat in a covert position to observe the target and his crew. So he knew that over the past three weeks, including three Fridays, the crew was there doing their business. The latest that Briscoe checked on them was 1:00 a.m., so he was hoping they were still there.

The community is a large gated apartment complex. Hayes Street runs around the perimeter like a race track, with one way traffic only, in a clockwise direction. There are parking lots on the right hand side of the street that accommodate the residents. On the left hand side is a wooded area that connects to Kenilworth Park. There are no streets that run through the community, so all traffic has to come out of the respective parking lots and get on Hayes Street to exit. If you were to miss your parking lot, you would have to drive all the way around, 360 degrees, to get back.

Briscoe pulled into a parking lot in the 8700 block and parked the Chevy next to a dumpster. He grabbed his backpack and the pole that he used on Damon and exited the vehicle. He walked through the breezeway (an enclosed walkway that joins two buildings) and emerged on an interior portion of the complex. From there he went to building 8744 and walked the steps to the top. He produced a key and entered a door marked Do Not Enter/Off Limits, then locked it behind him. This was the maintenance entrance to the rooftop. Briscoe procured the key a few weeks ago and had used the roof for surveillance during the intelligence gathering phase of his operation. He made his way to the edge where he could acquire his subject. He stooped low so that if anybody looked up, they would not see his silhouette. Just like the predictability of an ocean's tide, the shit bags were there, feeling content to fuck up a nice neighborhood, and raise enough ruckus to keep others from enjoying the very thing that they worked hard for.

His target was one DeShawn Jones, aka "Black." He, like the others who Briscoe sent on to the next realm, is a real piece of work who needed to be wiped from the earth's canvass. He started committing crimes the day he came from his mother's womb, or at least that's what it seems like. His rap sheet dates back to his eighth birthday and contains some thirty-two arrests, and he is only twenty-five years old. This character has committed more than a lifetime of crimes. If he has been arrested thirty-two times, imagine all the crime that he got away with before being caught. The thought should make any decent person shutter. In Briscoe's mind Black was beyond rehabilitation, because the dude just didn't have any remorse for anything that he did. His mindset is that only the strong survive, and if nobody can stop him, then he is going to continue.

He once told a cop who arrested him on a drug distribution charge, "I'm not new to this, and I'm true to this."

He has always been defiant, with no concern for anybody or anything that did not benefit him. His father is serving a life sentence in a federal prison for murder and his mother can be found strolling Minnesota Avenue selling her decrepit goodies for a hit of the crack pipe. Briscoe did not sympathize with people who say their lives were tough and who could not help the way they turned out. He knew there were people who came along to lend a helping hand, but met with resistance and animosity from the very people they were trying to help. There was no excuse as far as Briscoe was concerned; justice will be served and notice sent to all the others who choose a lifestyle that victimizes others.

Black was introduced to the criminal justice system on his eighth birthday, when he did not get any presents and went berserk. The little shit went outside with a kitchen knife and stabbed a neighbor's son and took his new bike. The child suffered a deep puncture to his lower abdomen and was hospitalized for a short period. When asked why he did such a thing, Black said he wanted the bike and the boy wouldn't give it to him. He fully understood what he had done. What's worse is he did not feel bad about it. The psychologist at the time said Black was a very unstable boy and should be intensely counseled or institutionalized. The courts declined to prosecute him because of his age, but they did send him for psychological counseling. A lot of good that did. Seventeen years later he is still victimizing people, and he has thirty-one other documented cases of the 'I'm never gonna change blues.' He and his crew are responsible for the murder of at least four rival crew members and he was investigated for the rape and murder of a Howard University student. That case is three years old and still open, but they have not charged him with anything yet. He actually has four prior rape arrests, but for some reason he never goes to jail for longer than a couple of months.

In one case the victim, who Black met on the Metrorail, said he seemed like a nice guy and she agreed to go have a drink with him. They got off the train at Union Station and went to the Amex Grill, had drinks and wonderful conversation. When they were leaving the restaurant, Black got her to agree to a ride to her vehicle. He told her they could get off the train at the Minnesota Avenue station, where he parked his car, and he would give her a ride to her car, which was parked at the Largo station in Maryland.

When they got off the train and into Black's car, he told her he needed to make a quick stop to pick something up from a friend. Black pulled up to a green dilapidated house that sat inauspiciously in the middle of a rundown block. He told her to sit tight and he would be right back. He went into the home, which was very poorly lit, and remained for just a few minutes. Then he came back to the vehicle and told her to come in and meet his friend, who was his best friend from childhood. When he saw her reluctance, he said his friend's wife just had a baby and he wanted her to meet the wife and see the baby. Well, this unsuspecting, naive girl from a very nice neighborhood in Maryland had no idea what was in store for her. When they stepped inside she could see that the house looked abandoned and somewhat like a club house or hangout for heroin addicts.

She asked, "Where is the baby?"

Black said, "I'm the baby, and I want some milk from your big jugs."

She tried to leave but he would not let her. She tried to resist but all that brought was punishing blows to her head and face. He choked her nearly unconscious, then violently ripped her pants and panties off. This aroused and excited him.

While he was having his way with her, two of his crew members came through the door. He looked up and said, "What took ya'll so long? This bitch got some good pussy, ya'll better jump in."

His two boys took turns violating her. She started out crying in pain that slowly turned to sobs and then barely audible whimpers, as she lay unable to resist and nearly unconscious. Her face was a bloody mess and her body was beaten and bruised. All three men assaulted her in the most heinous way imaginable. When they were done, they all stood and urinated on her. She suffered like nobody ever should just because she thought Black was a nice guy. He deceived her and tricked her into trusting him. Then he tortured this beautiful young woman simply for his power and pleasure.

She pursued the case but Black's attorney argued that the sex was voluntary. As far as the physical abuse, he said that was a part of the rough sex that they always enjoyed together. Black's attorney had the court subpoena the waitress and bartender from the Amex Grill, who testified that the two of them were there having drinks, laughing, and enjoying each other's company. The young woman victim could only sit there and be victimized again . . . this time in open court. She was portrayed as a whore because they never did determine who the other two perpetrators were, but analysis determined that two other people deposited semen inside of her. Black's attorney insinuated that she had other lovers besides Black.

It was a terrible time for the victim and Black walked away from that crime scot free. But that trusting, ignorant young woman has to pay for it the rest of her life. All the therapy in the world will not be able to erase the memories of what happened to her. Briscoe was sure she struggles with the thought that these dirty dogs live and breathe the same air that she breaths and fears they are probably doing it to other women. She could not easily love or trust another man. Even then there are fears, nightmares, and scars (both physical and emotional) that she must bear for a lifetime. Well, no deed, good or bad, goes unnoticed or unpunished. Briscoe is the punisher who is here to dish out the pain.

He looked around at the other buildings that faced the courtyard where Black and four of his crew members were sitting around boisterously drinking beer and smoking blunts. They were so loud that Briscoe could hear them from the roof. His scan of the area revealed that the coast was clear of pedestrians. He could not be completely sure about people looking out of their windows. He monitored them for about ten minutes and decided to strike quickly while the coast was clear. He was not so concerned about anybody seeing him from their window, because he planned to be in and out swiftly. Before they could reach the courtyard, he would be gone.

He packed the night vision goggles and started down from the roof. He secured the door and walked down the three flights of stairs to the front door. He cracked the door open and looked to make sure they were still in their previous location. All five were still sitting and talking loudly, barely paying attention to anything around them. They were thirty to thirty-five yards away from the front door. Briscoe readied himself for his business at hand.

He rolled his mask onto his head so that he could pull it down over his face quickly with one hand. The pole was secured between his back and the backpack. He placed the .45 in his right hand and held it down behind his right leg. It's time to go to work and Briscoe is focused and poised to rain down on them with furious vengeance. He pushed the door open fully and walked briskly toward the group. He took a last quick look around, making sure there were no pedestrians in the area. Then his eyes then locked on the group, as he closed the last twenty yards very quickly. When he was within five yards of the group he pulled the mask over his face, and in one motion, raised the .45 and steadied it with is left hand. His steely grip was steady and sure as he fired the weapon striking one after another in rapid succession. There was yelling and screaming as the pain raced through their bodies. One tried to turn and run but Briscoe was too good to allow that. He pulled the trigger, sending a hot lead injection into the rear of his dome, dropping him instantly. Briscoe then walked to each of the men and methodically fired one round into each of their heads. Thump, thump, thump was the muffled sound of the .45 caliber as it performed the deadly deed it was designed for.

He then stood over Black who looked at him and said, "Fuck you! Do it nigga!"

Briscoe shot him in both legs, then kicked him in the mouth. Black was spitting blood, but he was still defiant. Briscoe pulled his bowie knife from the sheath on his belt and cut Black's pants off. He was now wracked with pain and his defiance was waning. Briscoe holstered the .45, returned the knife to its sheath, and retrieved the pipe from behind his back. He kicked Black several times in the stomach and throat, causing him to convulse and try to move his bullet riddled body. Just as he tried to protect his stomach, Briscoe beat him violently in his lower back dislodging his spinal cord.

"This is for everybody you ever fucked. Now it's your turn to be fucked. Enjoy it bitch!" Briscoe said as he shoved the pipe into Black's rectum.

He started pushing it in just a little to get it started.

Black screamed out in pain, begging, "No, no, no! Please no."

Briscoe jammed the pipe violently into his rectum, pushing

with much force and violence. He continued to push until there was not a sound made or movement from Black. The pipe was now so far inside of him that only about a foot was hanging out. Briscoe stopped pushing and stood up, taking a look around to see if anybody was approaching. He pulled the .45 from its holster and fired one round into Black's heart for good measure and holstered the gun. He made sure that he dropped nothing on the scene that he didn't want to leave there. Once he was sure the scene was exactly like he wanted to leave it, he ran to his vehicle as fast as he could. Once inside he drove slowly to the end of the parking lot with his lights off. When he reached Hayes Street he pulled out of the lot and turned on his lights. He was pretty sure that nobody saw him, but he could not be sure since there were so many apartments. He was sure of one thing: nobody saw his face. However, he did not want the vehicle to be associated with the homicides because every cop within one hundred miles of the city would be looking for the vehicle and he would have no choice but to ditch it right now.

He continued to monitor the 6th Precinct radio zone as he pulled out Damon's cell phone and dialed *67 911.

Once again he disguised his voice and said, "Now check the 8700 block of Hayes Street. You will find five men down. I think they were shot." He hung up abruptly.

It was now 2:10 a.m., and he was back on track. The last one is due to fall into his trap at 3:00 a.m. when the bar closes. He headed toward the northwest quadrant of the city. It will take him about thirty-five minutes to get to where he has to meet the next subject and send him to his meeting with the Man.

9

Briscoe thought about Black and his crew as he drove. He wondered if any of the assholes that he took down, were the two who raped the woman from Largo. He hoped they were, but either way, they all got what they deserved. He also knew that the phone calls to 911 would be traced to Damon's cell and the connection would lead them to the conclusion that they were connected by the serial predator. That is exactly what he hoped for. He wanted the media to start getting the word out that a killer was stalking the stalkers of the community and preying on the predators. His purpose this night was to make a visual statement to everybody, especially the wolves who do harm to the lambs of society. If you are going to do dirt, you are going to get dirt. They all better stop their selfish, destructive ways, or suffer the consequences. For, the wage of oppression is death; and they will never see it coming. He put the Hayes Street business behind him and started to focus on his next wolf.

He pulled the vehicle into the unit block of P Street and looked at the glow of the digital LED display in the vehicle's dash. It was 2:35 a.m. and he was only blocks away from his objective. Briscoe knew precisely what time to expect his victim wolf, because he, like the others, was also predictable. But unlike the others, he was not a street level predator. He chose his victims from the most vulnerable amongst us. You see, Briscoe was going into the DuPont Circle neighborhood—which is well known for the gay community that resides there. They frequent the many bars and bath houses—and he was to serve the former Father Sebastian Weaver.

Weaver was a community leader and a polarizing figure on the political landscape of the city. This one sickened Briscoe the most. He was a man who had the trust of his parish, the community, and the children. This ungodly piece of dung decided the feel of his filthy dick inside of a five year old boy was more important than trying to deliver souls from damnation. He operated for many years from an elevated platform with supercilious, high minded ideals of his righteousness. All the while, he was molesting boys, in some cases violently.

Now, Weaver is by no account a small man. He is six-foot-three-inches and weighs close to 300 pounds. Although it's mostly belly, he is still an imposing figure. Imagine if you were an eight year old child and a man that size, who speaks from a position of authority and power every week, and people listen to what he says as though he is God, as he talks about hell fire and judgment, touches you inappropriately. What would you . . . or could you do? Ponder that for a moment. Here is the representative of God rubbing on your penis. Then he tells you not to say anything to anybody or they will be sent to hell to burn for an eternity . . . and you with them. Now this is just one example of the mental and emotional anguish the good Father put so many boys through over the years. Briscoe first came to know about Weaver's dealings when he saw a news story about a priest who was accused of molesting children. He did a little more snooping and discovered that the evidence against Weaver was overwhelming. Many boys, some of whom are now men, came forward to tell their stories of how Father Weaver had his way with them. The final tally was forty-seven over a fourteen year period.

Briscoe was just as pissed off at the system as he was at the lying devil in angel's robe, for allowing him to walk free. The church has dished out so much money to quash the cases against the priests responsible for instances of abuse, especially of a sexual nature. But money doesn't erase memories. Nor does it stop the feelings of shame, embarrassment, or betrayal. How hard has it been for these boys to go through life knowing that a man, someone of the same sex, has had sexual intercourse with them? In nearly all cases, it happened before they had sex with a girl. The innocence that was stolen from them could never be returned. The difficult lives that many of them led over the years were a direct result of Weaver's lust for their young virile flesh. One particularly disturbing incident involved a five year old boy who was left in his care for the weekend.

Weaver would sponsor weekend retreats where he would take boys between the ages of six and twelve (elementary-aged) to a campground in Virginia. The retreats, as he called them, allowed the boys to forge lasting friendships and learn spiritual-based lessons of teamwork and problem solving. He would often say he was doing his part to set the children out on the right path for their future. He would normally take no more than fifteen boys at a time. He never took chaperones or additional adults to help him with what appeared to be a noble endeavor. No parent ever questioned the practice of the priest taking the boys alone for the weekend.

One weekend, he asked a parent if he could take her five year old son along on his weekend retreat. The mother was a bit reluctant because of the child's age, but Weaver assured her that it would be good for the boy. He would keep him close by his side and guarantee his safety. Since the boy lacked a father figure in his life, the mother agreed and sent him off with Weaver. He was infatuated with the child and had developed an obsession that he could barely hide. Weaver had masturbated to the thought of the boy on several occasions. He plotted and planned a way to get the boy alone since he first laid eyes on him weeks earlier. His mother was new to the church and was a devoted Christian who trusted the church and its pastor. While at the cabin, the other boys slept in the open bay area, where there were two rows of bunk beds and wall lockers. Weaver slept in a private room at the end of the bay with the five year old boy. Weaver sucked on the little boy's private part and had him do the same to him. He kissed the boy in the mouth and fondled him, gaining his trust by promising him fantasies and treats. He continued to molest the child the entire weekend. The child had no idea what was happening to him, but he knew he didn't like it because he cried out. But Weaver was not having that, so he beat the boy and made sure he understood to just accept it without bickering.

He smacked the child in the face and grabbed him by his tiny testicles and said, "You listen to me; if you don't stop your crying I will never let you go home again to see your mother."

The entire weekend was one mental strain on the boy after another. It seemed that Weaver was setting the boy up for long term sexual abuse and everything was going according to his plan. But little did he know this little boy would be the linchpin of the gate to his demise. Weaver was so enamored with this child that he could not stop from forcing himself inside of him. When he first entered, the boy screamed so loudly that Weaver's covering of his mouth with his hand could not contain it, so he punched the boy in the head. His little body went limp, but Weaver's sick ass continued to penetrate him until he climaxed. When he finished, he got a wash cloth, soaked it in cold water and applied it to the boy's face. He shook the boy and rung the wash cloth over his face forcing cold water to stream. Finally, the boy came around. Weaver held him in his arms rocking back and forth, relieved that he did not seriously injure the boy. This took place Sunday morning, and it was nearly time to go back to DC, so Weaver used the wash cloth to wipe in between the boy's legs and the crack of his anus. Then he and the other kids loaded the bus and returned to the city.

When the little boy's mother picked him up from the church, she could sense something different about him. She asked him numerous times what happened, but he would just say, "Nothing."

Later in the evening when it was time for the child to take a bath, his mother noticed blood stains in his underwear. She pulled him close and examined his anus and could see bruising. She looked him in the eyes and could see the pain as the tears welled within. He told her how Weaver touched him and put his thing inside of his butt and how he kissed him in the mouth. His mother had to stop him, because she could not stop herself from crying. She did not want to cry in front of him, because she wanted him to see her as being very strong, because she was going to need him to be strong.

She called MPD. When the officers arrived, they summoned a Youth Division Detective who headed the case against Weaver. The young boy did a fine job of relaying the details of the abuse, and once others saw the strength and courage the little boy displayed, thanks to his mother, they followed suit and came forward to tell their stories. Weaver's case was presented to the U.S. Attorney's Office, who for whatever reason decided it was too traumatic—or political suicide for someone—to move forward with a case against the good Father. They claimed the identities of the young victims could be compromised and there could be more unnecessary suffering for them. The church settled, financially with many of the victim's families. Briscoe was sure Weaver had enough dirt on people in high places that his punishment would not be worse than what the church imposed. The church, by the way, did impose severe penalty. They excommunicated the father. They sent him packing, with a severance package of course, and told him never to set foot into any of their churches again.

Ever since this happened, about one year ago, the former Father has been hanging in gay bars picking up men from time to time. He goes for the really young, or young-looking men, but he will settle for whoever he can get. He has always obsessed over boys and very young men, perhaps due to their vulnerability, or his ability to assert his will. He is still spending the money from his severance and the new church that he pastors in Alexandria, Virginia.

Yes, he has started his own church and has a sizeable congregation of followers who say they believe in the man. Go figure. Some people will stand for nothing, but fall for all kinds of bullshit. Briscoe could only wonder how many boys he has molested in the new church. How is it that people know what he has done, while they still listen to his preaching on how to live a moral life and do right in the sight of God? In Briscoe's mind, he represents the pinnacle of hypocrisy and deception; which are two of the devil's most distinct traits. How can you go to heaven if you are willingly led by the devil here on earth? Some people believe they can live like hell here, and then be welcomed into heaven with open arms. Some Christians baffle the hell out of Briscoe and he strains to understand. But it does no good because they continue to do the very things that seem to be contrary to God's word. Well, it won't matter much after tonight, because Weaver will be no more. If he is in God's graces, then he will be welcomed, but if not, he will go to were his other master resides . . . the master who he serves when he is stealing innocence from a defenseless child, or wrecking the foundation of a promising young mind. Briscoe was prepared to wreck his foundation with pain and anguish like none that he has ever felt. He was, for all intent and purposes and lack of a more descriptive term, planning to get medieval on his monkey ass. It's going to suck to be Father Sebastian Weaver. In a short, it is going to be hell on earth for the man.

Parking was always a bitch in the city; it could frustrate the most patient person. Briscoe had to circle the block several times until a spot opened up for him to park the Chevy.

This is ree goddamn diculous, all of these people still out at fifteen minutes till three, he thought, as he pulled up and backed into the spot.

He was going to a joint called Mister Raze near the intersection of Connecticut Avenue and P Street. That's where Weaver could always be found indulging in liquid spirits trying to get his swerve on. Briscoe placed his backpack on the floor behind the front passenger seat and made sure the vehicle was ready for Weaver to get into the front seat. He got out of the vehicle, removed his gloves and put them in his pocket. He looked around at the environment, studying the people and the vehicles, scanning faces and paying close attention to everyone's actions. He did not want to make an impression on anybody. He knew that a hot July night brought people into the streets and kept them there until the wee hours of the morning when all the bars closed. However, he did have one thing in his favor . . . alcohol. Most of the people he saw outside had spent the greater part of the night partaking in libations. They could not have been any less interested in him, and would never remember if they saw him.

He was confident in his approach as he walked toward Mister Raze. He went inside and surveyed the clientele as he made his way to the bar area. The lounge was nearly empty. The only people who appeared to still be there were the staff and two guys sitting on a sofa engaged in a heated make out session. When he reached the bar, he saw Weaver sitting alone nursing a drink and talking with the bartender.

Briscoe stood for a moment, as the bartender turned and said, "The bar is closed; we had last call about twenty minutes ago."

"Aw man, I thought I would be able to get a quick one before I make the long drive home," Briscoe said.

"I'm sorry, you should've come earlier, the place was lively then," the bartender smiled, as he looked at Briscoe sincerely.

"Oh well, I guess I'll just have to wait till I get home, thanks."

Before he turned to leave, he gave Weaver a smile and a sly wink. This excited Weaver and he said, "You can share my drink."

"Oh, no thanks, maybe some other time," Briscoe did not want to be seen talking with Weaver or leaving the bar with him.

"Well, I'm here all the time, so the next time you stop in you can have a drink on me." Weaver offered.

"Thanks, I'll remember that," he then turned and left the bar.

The stage was set and the actors were just off in the shadows awaiting the curtain call. Briscoe went back to the Chevy, put his gloves on, got back inside, and watched Mister Raze waiting for Weaver to emerge. The place is closed and it is only a matter of time before he would come out to walk the three short blocks to his home. Briscoe watched as the two lovers who were kissing on the sofa came out of Mister Raze and walked arm in arm up the street. They walked directly past Briscoe's vehicle never noticing that he was sitting inside. The number of people out was greatly diminishing and the streets were starting to look bare. He was starting to get anxious because it was taking Weaver a while to exit the lounge. If he took too much longer, Briscoe would be the only vehicle left on that end of the block.

What the hell is he doing in there? Briscoe asked himself. He didn't see anybody else inside, so unless Weaver was hooking up with the bartender, he should be coming out alone and walking home. The lounge closed at 3:00 a.m. which was shortly after Briscoe walked back to the Chevy. It is now 3:15 a.m. and still no Weaver. Briscoe was committed to his mission and decided he didn't care how long it takes. He would put Weaver down before the sun comes up.

Meanwhile, Detective Whitehead was on the scene of the homicides Briscoe committed on Hayes Street. His partner, Jake Sutton, was still investigating the killing of Damon Mason behind Moten Elementary School. The two were together on the scene of Damon's murder, when the call came out for the five bodies on Hayes Street. Once the on-duty VCU detectives arrived on scene and saw Black's condition, they called Whitehead. He was checking the bodies as the Mobile Crime Technicians were processing the scene.

"Jamie, I think your boy is trying to send us a message," Detective Hendricks said, referring to the onslaught of killings committed by the serial predator overnight.

"Uh-huh, but I don't know if he is sending the message to us or them," Whitehead said as he looked down at the five bodies still laid out in the positions they died, "I know all of these guys. Each of them was suspect in some of my other cases. This crew has been running together for years. I recognize all of them."

Whitehead knew that the serial predator singled them out for some reason. He also recognized that Black was the main target. It seemed to be a pattern with the predator. He put the non-targets down quickly with gunshots, and reserved the torture for the main target. His theory of a vigilante was now confirmed. Each of tonight's victims was a career criminal with very violent pasts. For the first time, Whitehead considered calling in an FBI profiler to assist him with a composite profile of the serial predator. Maybe they could review all that he has and help him narrow the scope of his search to a specific type of person. Before he could do that he would need approval from his Captain.

"Damn Jamie, I'm sorry that you caught so much work tonight. I almost feel bad because we didn't catch one case all tour. But if you need help with anything let me know, I'm here for you." Hendricks was sincere about helping in any way. He was equally happy about not catching a new homicide case overnight, although there was a shooting in the Sixth Precinct. It was non-life threatening, thank God.

"Hey Doug I appreciate that. If you could compile the notes from the first responding officers and then get their statements back at the office, it would be a big help."

"No problem big guy, I'll handle that for you."

Whitehead normally tried to keep all of his case material away from other detectives and he rarely accepted help. He figured the fewer people sticking their hands into his cases, the better its investigatory integrity. But in this case, he was just overwhelmed, and needed the additional help.

While looking at the condition of Black's body he realized the pipe stuck in his anus was symbolic of something. He thought about all of the victims since the killings began a few months ago. The way their bodies were left has something to do with the reason they were killed. If he were to closely scrutinize Black's life, perhaps the way he died will give some insight into the mind of the serial predator. It has already been a very long night for Whitehead and Sutton and the day will be even longer. Neither one will be able to rest until they have exhausted every lead. They will have to dedicate the first eighteen hours to each case without ceasing. But deep down inside, Whitehead knew there were no leads to pursue. The serial predator was very careful. He seemed to be a ghost who never left finger prints or DNA evidence.

"Some day in some way this guy is going to slip up, and I'll be there to slam his ass," Whitehead said to Hendricks.

Finally, the fat piece of dookie came bopping out of that fudge-packing plant they call a lounge. It is time for Briscoe to get to work. Weaver stepped out onto the sidewalk and began his familiar journey toward home. He had several cocktails over the five hours he spent in the lounge and the full effects hit him just as he stood up from the barstool. He stepped cautiously as he negotiated the slight incline from the front door of Mister Raze to where Briscoe was sitting in the vehicle.

Just as he made his way gingerly, Briscoe lowered the front passenger window and said, "Hey big man, where are you trying to go?"

Weaver looked at the vehicle and then moved closer to get a

better look.

"Oh it's you; I'm going anywhere you want to take me," he said flirtatiously, excited about the possibilities with the fine young black man who showed an interest in him.

"Well, why don't you hop in and let's see where the night takes us," Briscoe patted the seat as to say sit right here.

Weaver opened the door and slid his big ass into the passenger seat. He then turned to Briscoe and said, "I've never seen you around here. Do you live in the area?"

"No, I live in Maryland. I came to check out a few bars in hopes of meeting a nice guy. Are you a nice guy?"

Briscoe was playing it up, trying to get Weaver comfortable enough to invite him into his home.

"Oh yes honey, I'm a very nice man. I would take good care of you and feed you breakfast in the morning," Weaver said with a big smile and a sly chuckle.

"I like the sound of that. Do you have anything to drink at home?"

"Most definitely!" he was getting excited by the thought of sex with Briscoe and could feel a chubby well up in his pants.

"Well, I'm game if you are. Just tell me which way to go."

Briscoe started the vehicle, put it in gear and proceeded to drive off.

He knew it would be easy to get into Weaver's home with the prospect of sex. The irony of his lust opening wide the doorway to his death nearly made Briscoe laugh out loud. As they drove the three blocks to Weaver's home, they introduced themselves, with Briscoe telling him that his name was Mike. He kept asking which turns to make on the way to the house, even though he knew exactly how to get there. When they arrived there were no parking spots in front of the house, so Briscoe told him to get out and go into the house and he would park and come right back. He did this because he did not want anybody to see him with Weaver. There could be no tying him to the man in any way. Before he exited the vehicle, Weaver pointed out his house and said he would turn on the porch light once he got inside.

Briscoe drove the Chevy around the corner and parked alongside an alley. He grabbed his backpack and got out. As he walked back toward Weaver's house, he studied the entire route, surveying every home from the roof to the ground. He looked at windows, porches, and the small parcels of land they call a front yard. The neighborhood is a row house community where all the homes are smashed together with neighbors to the left and right, with the only exceptions being the end units. The row houses in Weaver's community are vintage, made of stone and brick. The walls are thick and well-constructed, build with privacy in mind. So your neighbor's business remained their business. There were not very many noise complaints called into the police department from the community, and that was directly attributed to the thick walls.

Briscoe reached the front door of the house and was fairly confident that nobody saw him. The screen door was shut but the main door was wide open. He could see a dim light from a room just off to the left of the foyer. He opened the door and went inside. He closed the main door and turned off the porch light. He observed light at the top of the staircase that was on the right hand side as he entered the front door.

He called out to Weaver, "I'm back."

"Make yourself comfortable, there is beer in the fridge, and liquor in the kitchen cabinet above the sink."

Briscoe was sure they were alone, but he had to ask, "Are we alone?"

"Yes sweetie, it's just the two of us. So feel free to do whatever pleases you. I'll be down in a few minutes."

Briscoe heard water running in the upstairs bathroom and assumed Weaver was freshening up for him. He stepped into the room with the dim light, which was a small sitting area. He took a look around the room and got the impression that a female decorated the place. It had a feminine appeal, but everything within was Weavers', from his undergraduate diploma to his seminary diploma and the many accolades hanging on the walls. He also noticed a magazine that bordered on child pornography lying on the sofa. It is a monthly rag called *Barely Legal.* They try to get models who are just at the age of eighteen. but who look like they are twelve. Seeing that magazine infuriated Briscoe and confirmed for him that nothing has changed with Weaver. For all he knew, there were already victims at the new church.

Briscoe dug into his backpack and pulled out a pair of flex cuffs, a roll of duct tape, and a six foot length of rope and laid them on the floor. He stood in the entrance of the sitting room, facing the steps that lead from upstairs. He pulled the Sig Saur from its holster and held it behind his back. The upstairs light went out and he could hear the footsteps as Weaver made his way down the vintage hardwood staircase, where he came face to face with Briscoe. Weaver was wearing a silk half robe that came down just below his butt cheeks, partially exposing his genitalia. The robe was tied just above his hips and his chest was mostly exposed. The only other thing he was wearing was perfume. It was the distinct aroma of Glow, which was Monica's favorite scent. Briscoe nearly laughed at the sight of this big fat queen trying to turn him on. He really is a sick bastard.

"Wow baby, you are standing there in that black looking all sexy and mysterious," Weaver said as he started to close the short distance from the steps to where Briscoe stood.

Just as he got within five feet, Briscoe raised the gun and pointed it directly in Weaver's shocked face.

"Oh dear lord! Please, you don't have to do this," he pleaded.

"Shut your fat mouth and get over here," Briscoe motioned with the gun for Weaver to move into the sitting room.

"Please, I won't say anything. I have money, just take whatever you want."

"I have what I want. Now get on your knees."

Weaver tried to turn around and plead.

"I said get on your fuckin' knees!" Briscoe yelled as he kicked the back of his right knee forcing him to drop down to the floor on that one knee. "Now put the other one on the floor," Briscoe ordered.

Once he was on his knees Briscoe cuffed his hands behind his back and then duct taped his feet together. The entire time Weaver continued to plead for his life, offering his worldly possessions in exchange.

Briscoe then stood in front of him and said in a tone similar to that of a judge handing down a sentence to a convicted felon, "Father Sebastian Weaver; for the theft of innocence, the brutal assaults, the terrorist threats, and the mental anguish that you forced on more than forty-seven young boys, you are sentenced to death."

"Oh my god, please don't do this. I beg of you. Jesus begs of you."

With that said, Briscoe punched him in the mouth as hard as he could, causing blood to explode from his lips. He even dislodged a couple of teeth.

"Shut the fuck up! What does a lying piece of blubbery whale shit like you know about Jesus? You didn't think of that when you were committing your crimes against the children that you vowed to guide and care for."

Weaver was now crying and sniffling, "Please don't hurt me," he said with a trembling voice.

Briscoe picked up the duct tape and wrapped it around Weaver's head, completely covering his mouth.

"I've heard enough of your shit. There is nothing you can do or say to change the outcome of this situation. Your fate is sealed, and your destiny has been determined."

Briscoe then went to the fireplace that was in a corner of the room between the front window and a side window, where he retrieved a poker from the stand, and thought, *It really is a beautiful home, but too bad something this ugly has to take place inside.*

He went to the kitchen and ignited two burners on the stove and placed the poker on top. While it was heating, he went back to the sitting room to get started on Weaver. He once again reached into his backpack, and this time retrieved a cigarette lighter and a small self-contained acetylene torch.

"Now for a preview of your final destination," he said as he lit the torch.

Once he adjusted the flame, Briscoe put the torch to the bottom of Weaver's left foot. He immediately began flopping around trying to avoid the pain of the searing hot blue flame.

"Damn, stay still! Shit, this ain't gonna work," Briscoe grumbled and extinguished the torch.

He picked up the rope and tied it around Weaver's neck and looped it through the hand cuffs on the way to the duct tape around his ankles. He had Weaver cinched up like steer that has been roped in a rodeo. His back was bowed and he could not move left or right as he lay on his side on the hardwood floor in his sitting room.

Briscoe took the cigarette lighter from his pocket, ignited it and held the flame to Weaver's left forearm. He was screaming beneath the tape, but no one could hear his cries, and he could not move.

"Perfect, now you are going to know what pain feels like."

Once again, Briscoe lit the torch, and held it to one foot until the smell of burning flesh overwhelmed the room. The pain was excruciating for Weaver, but there was nothing he could do to stop it. Briscoe then moved the torch to the other foot and burned that one until it blistered. He noticed that Weaver's body was not as tense as it was moments earlier. When he checked, he discovered that he had passed out. Briscoe then extinguished the torch and retrieved ammonium capsules from his bag. He popped one and placed it under Weaver's nose, causing a reaction as he came around.

"You're not getting off that easy," he said smiling looking at the anguish in his eyes, as his body was engulfed in pain. When Briscoe stood up he kicked Weaver in the face, attempting to knock out his teeth. The pain Weaver was feeling became evident when he involuntarily urinated on himself. Briscoe watched as the yellow fluid streamed down his legs.

"Oh, you can't hold your piss?" He again ignited the torch. "I'll see what I can do about helping you with that," he said, as he placed the business end of the torch directly on his penis.

Weaver's body tightened like a knot in a rope as the pain ran completely through him like a bolt of lightning. Briscoe placed the flame on his scrotum, causing unimaginable pain and suffering. He continued to burn the most sensitive parts of Weaver's body, and punching him in others. Every time he tried to pass out, Briscoe revived him with the ammonium tablets and cold water. He just had to endure a little more pain on this earth, and then he could be released to his eternal punishment.

Briscoe went to the kitchen and removed the fireplace poker from the stove; the portions that were directly in the fire were cherry red. He stood over Weaver and said, "Now for the eyes that lust for small boys," and then laid the poker directly on his eye. The screams of pain were nearly ripping through the duct tape. The eye was almost instantly cauterized, and his sight was gone in an instant.

"I'll leave you with sight in the other eye so you will see your way into hell," Briscoe said as he hit him in the cheek with the still hot poker.

He stood and positioned Weaver's body so one of his hands was on the floor. He then stepped on his wrist to steady the hand with the palm facing upward. He raised the poker to chest level, holding it in both hands with the pointed end facing downward. With as much force as he could muster, Briscoe drove the poker into Weaver's hand, putting his weight on the end forcing it as deep as it would go. He pierced a whole the width of the poker, almost completely through his hand. He then repositioned his body and did the same thing to the other hand. Briscoe checked the time; it was 4:10 a.m. He has been punishing Weaver for nearly forty minutes. He figured each moment of severe pain must have felt like an hour. Now it is time to put an end to Father Weaver.

Briscoe reignited the torch and set Weaver's thick auburn and grey hair on fire, burning it quickly down to his scalp. The flesh of his scalp was melting right before Briscoe's eyes. Weaver was in more pain than humanly imaginable. He screamed beneath the tape, cried, and tried feverishly to move, but was unable. The muffled screams of a tortured soul is an eerie sound that could soften the heart of the hardest person, but it was nothing new to Briscoe. He felt nothing but justice as he continued. He directed the torch to the bottom of Weaver's robe and set it ablaze. The silk robe melted onto his body, burning pubic hair and flesh. *Such agonizing pain, and he deserves it all.* As soon as the flames died down, Briscoe positioned Weaver's head so he could get to his mouth. He then placed his left foot on his forehead. Weaver looked up at him with the one functional eye, still pleading for mercy . . . there would be none. Briscoe raised the poker once again to chest level, and this time he drove it violently into his mouth, forcing it through the tape and as far as he possibly could to the back of his head. He put nearly his entire 225 pounds of lean muscle on the poker and Weaver died with the one eye open.

Briscoe rolled him over and cut the flex cuffs from his wrists. He then rolled him onto his back and left him bound with the tape and the rope, with the poker protruding from his mouth. He then placed the flex cuffs and all the items he brought with him inside the backpack. He picked up the copy of *Barely Legal* and dropped it on Weaver's chest. The entire house smelled of charred flesh. That was a smell that Briscoe could never get used to. Even when he was in the Special Forces operating in Bosnia and had walked knee deep through the burnt remains of a village of unfortunate souls who happened to belong to the wrong ethnic group. It was just something that shocked the conscious. A normal, well-adjusted person could never get used to the smell of human suffering.

He left the house, leaving the front door open, but closing the screen door. He made it to the vehicle and drove off.

Wow, tonight was a success. He was pleased with the work he accomplished, by putting all of his targets down. But there was still one thing left to do.

He pulled Damon's phone from his pocket, dialed 911, disguised his voice, and told them Weaver was dead inside of his home. He thought about how his last target was once revered and considered a model citizen. He was a man who was esteemed as a symbol of morality with the highest degree of integrity. And yet, he was fucking children literally and fucking them over. He destroyed more lives than he could ever pay for here on earth. Briscoe felt good about his ability to serve justice for those hurt deeply by the monster cloaked in the lamb's goodness.

Come tomorrow, everybody will know of his death. There will be some who breathe a sigh of relief and others who feel a sense of joy that he died so violently. Briscoe felt completely justified in what he had done; and he felt a calling to continue with his very important mission.

He drove out of the city directly to where he left his car. It was now 5:00 a.m. and the sun would start to rise in less than an hour. He drove past his vehicle checking to see that it was still there and intact. He looked around the area to make sure there were no cops or anybody else snooping around. Once he was satisfied that everything was in order, he drove the Chevy about a quarter mile down the road to a clearing that was just beyond a patch of woods on the other side of the auto lot. Once there he turned the engine off, leaving the keys in the ignition, with the windows partially down. He removed his backpack from the vehicle and placed it on his back. He broke a branch from a tree tied a rag that was in the vehicle to it, and dipped it in the gas tank. He removed the dripping wet rag and wiped it across the front seat that he occupied, ensuring that he put gasoline on the steering column, console, and floor. He dipped the rag several times to get a substantial amount of gasoline into the vehicle. He then dropped the rag on the floor just beneath the seat. He retrieved another rag from the vehicle, and did the same thing in the compartment that he transported Damon. Briscoe opened the sheet containing Damon's clothes and the duct tape used to bind him, spread it across the back seat, and used Damon's clothes to soak up gasoline. Then he put the gasoline-soaked clothes on top of the sheet. Now the vehicle was ready to be sanitized.

He removed the extra set of clothes from the backpack and stripped out of the black clothes he had worn all night. He changed into new clothes and put the old ones inside the backpack. He used his lighter to set the rag on the floor in the front, the sheet, and clothing, and the rag in the rear on fire. As the flames grew and the heat intensified, he closed the doors and walked off.

He walked the quarter mile to his vehicle without incident. No vehicles were on the road, all was quiet. He reached his car, put his backpack in the trunk and got into the driver's seat. He drove off with a warm and fuzzy feeling inside, but he was still hyped. He shuffled through the music library on his iPod and cranked up the sultry sounds of Goapele. Her brand of soul was just what he needed to soothe him as the adrenaline was still coursing through his body.

When he pulled up to his house and saw Monica's car in the driveway, a rush of excitement came over him. He could feel his penis rise at the thought of playing inside of her moist, inviting playground. The disposal of the evidence from the night would have to wait until later in the day; he wanted very bad to be inside of Monica.

He parked his car in the driveway next to hers, got out, and locked the doors. Once he got into the house, he walked to the bedroom. The TV was on an infomercial about getting rich in the real estate market. He saw that Monica had a pretty nice time waiting up for him, evident by the wine glass with the residue of Merlot. There was a finger nail polish kit on the night stand and a partial plate of cheese. It looks like girlfriend had wine and cheese while she watched TV and pampered herself. He looked at her lying there in her Victoria's Secret that she planned to share with him. Her body was slamming with her sexy ass turned to the side and her picture perfect breasts protruding from the Secret that unsuccessfully tried to contain them. Briscoe thought about how tasty she looked sprawled out on the bed. He considered taking a shower first, but the urge rising between his legs was too overwhelming. He stripped out of his clothes and left them in a pile, as he climbed in the bed and reached across Monica for the remote. She stirred just as he picked up the remote. He kissed her lightly on the cheek while turning off the TV.

"Hey baby," she said as she opened her eyes.

Wow, she looked so damn good looking at him with her beautiful brown eyes.

He leaned in and kissed her lips long and deep. She started to moan, and move in closer to him, groping his arms, his chest, and his back as she pulled him closer. Their breathing was getting heavier and her moans sexier as their tongues collided with passion and sheer delight. When her hand moved down his solid muscular chest, to his chiseled abs both their moans and passion intensified. When she wrapped her hand around his thick, hard dick, she pulled and stroked it until he could no longer control himself. He rolled

Monica onto her back and, in one motion, he was deep inside of her pussy. He fucked her like a caged beast, with pent up rage. The animal in him tore through her pussy like it was made of Teflon. There was nothing smooth about his loving. It was raw animal rage and he beat her pussy up like it owed him money.

She screamed out, "Oh my god!! Oh it hurts so fucking good! Fuck me, fuck me daddy!"

He could not say a word. His only sounds were animalistic groans from way down deep inside. His penis was harder than he had ever known it to be and Monica was sensing the animal in him and fucking him with frenzied passion. He pounded and pounded and beat her tight pussy with his sledge hammer dick until he could no longer take the heat of her juice as she busted her nut like a waterfall. He reached the pinnacle of his sensation and the raging inferno inside of his massive cock was about to explode into the sensational abyss that is Monica's now throbbing pussy.

"Aahh!" his scream was so loud, as he released the cum that flowed from way down deep in his loins, it felt as though he shook the house. He wrapped himself around Monica so tightly that she thought he would squeeze the life right out of her. He held on tight as the orgasm rocked his body and the sperm flowed freely into her hot vagina. He collapsed on top of her and they silently embraced for a moment. When his weight got to be too much for her, he rolled off and laid beside her while they shared the same air and held hands. They fell asleep without saying a word.

10

Detectives Whitehead and Sutton were spent by the time they made it to the Weaver murder scene. The two of them worked the day tour yesterday. But before they could get in bed last night, the first murder occurred. They were too tired to put in eighteen straight hours on Weaver's case. The canvass of the neighborhood turned up nothing. It's like the killer just appeared inside of the home, did his business and then poof . . . disappeared into thin air. No one heard a sound or saw a thing. And just like all the other killings, there is no forensic evidence to collect. This guy seems to know what not to leave on the scene.

Well, regardless of how many hours they spend working this case today, Whitehead was determined not to miss the pool party at Sanford's house later in the evening. Everybody has been talking about how much fun it will be and he is in bad need of some fun. The serial predator has already ruined his Friday night. He hopes he doesn't ruin his Saturday as well.

"Goddamn it, what kind of sick bastard does something like this to a person?" Sutton asked as he looked at the extensive damage done to Weaver.

"I guess somebody that is pissed way off," Whitehead said.

"What do you make of the burns and the fireplace poker shoved down his throat? And why is just one eye poked out?" Sutton made note of the condition of Weaver's body as he spoke.

"I guarantee when we check into this guys life, it will all make sense." Whitehead had a clear understanding of the message the serial predator was sending. It was directed at a certain class of people.

"Detective Whitehead, the media is out front asking for a statement," a patrol officer interrupted.

"Tell them we will make an official statement later today. PIO (Public Information Office) will contact them with a time for a news conference."

"Okay will do," the officer went out to relay the message to the media, who had swarmed the area.

All local and some national news agencies spent the night following the multiple murders. They were already reporting that the so-called serial predator was on a rampage.

"Jamie, what should we do about the media? We both know that we have a killer out there who is targeting the worst criminal offenders in the city. The department is going to have to come clean and notify the public in a way that doesn't panic them," Sutton spoke in a tone just audible for the two of them to hear.

"I know, you're right, but we have people above us who make those determinations. All we can do is present the facts to them and recommend that we get the word out." Whitehead felt that his case could use all the help it could get.

Maybe somebody has heard the killer sitting around bragging about some of his killings. Or maybe somebody has noticed a change in their loved one and that kind of break could be all they need to solve this thing. When a Mobile Crime technician brought the decedent's identification to Whitehead, he looked at it and handed it to Sutton.

"I'll be damned," Sutton said. "This is the priest who was in the news last year for molesting young boys. We might have a lead on this one because there were a lot of people pissed off at him."

"There were a lot of people pissed at the others also and we still have nothing," Whitehead hated to sound so pessimistic, but it has been one dead end after the next.

They knew the investigation into Weaver's death would have to go through the Youth Division, where the investigation into his sexual abuse was conducted. This serial predator case was shaping up to be a long hard task, and the detectives knew that it was time to bump it up to task force level.

"Heads up; Captain Johnson just arrived on scene," the same patrol officer advised.

The Detective Captain walked into the house and looked around at the scene. He was greeted by Whitehead who immediately started to brief him about the overnight killings that were all tied to the serial predator.

"Captain, counting this decedent, ten people were killed by our guy overnight. The initial investigation leads us nowhere."

"Whitehead, are you telling me that there isn't one piece of evidence that stands out as something we could use to lead us to the killer?" The captain was feeling the same frustrations as the detectives.

"Sir, that is exactly what I'm telling you. We are going to need the media's help with this, and we should bump this up to a task force. The workload is becoming burdensome."

"Damn Whitehead, if you are saying this, then it must be necessary, because as long as I've known you, I have never heard you ask for help."

"Well, there is a first time for everything, and this guy is way too good. I don't see him slipping anytime soon."

"Okay, I'll run it by the Superintendant and let him convince the Chiefs. They are planning an 11:00 a.m. press briefing. The Superintendent and I have to go downtown at 10:00 a.m. to brief them. I would like you to come with us. At that time you can present your theories and ask for the task force and the use of the media."

"Thanks Captain, I appreciate your support with this. I'll be there." Just as the captain was about to walk out the front door, Whitehead called out, "Oh, Captain I almost forgot. I would like to use the FBI to help with a psychological profile of the killer."

"Okay, just bring it up when you come in for the briefing," the captain said just as he walked out the door.

The mobile crime resources were stretched so thin overnight, they had to call several technicians in on their days off to assist. The Weaver crime scene was going to be active well into the evening. So Whitehead and Sutton decided to split up and follow different leads. It was now 7:00 a.m. and they agreed to meet back at their office at 9:00 a.m.

Briscoe slept like a rock. He barely moved a muscle the entire time. He awakened to the aroma of bacon sizzling in the kitchen. It was 11:00 a.m., and even though he had only slept for about five hours, he felt great. His spirit was renewed and his body was completely relaxed. Wow, his beautiful girlfriend fucked him like a warrior, putting him to sleep and now she is in the kitchen fixing breakfast. What a wonderful thing he has with her. She is by far the best thing happening in his life. He was starting to think seriously about making her an honest woman by putting a ring on her finger. They have been together for a while and she has never pressed him about the issue of commitment. He liked her understanding and independence. *Their marriage,* he thought, *would be a blessed union that could only get better.* But as his thoughts drifted to his mission to rid the city of the undesirables, he realized that marriage would throw a monkey wrench into his plans, and complicate everything. So for right now he decided to just enjoy Monica the way they were. While he was lying there basking in his thoughts, Monica walked into the bedroom with the widest, brightest smile that he has ever seen on her face.

"Good morning tiger, grrrr," she said as she made a motion with her hand like a cat's paw scratching.

"Wow, look at you in your Victoria Secret fixing breakfast for your man. I must have been a good boy."

"Oh you were better than good, you were an animal. My pussy was sore as hell when I woke up, but damn, the sensation feels good."

"I don't know what came over me; I just couldn't stop myself from ravishing you. I love you, Moni."

When he said that, she climbed on the bed and crawled on all fours up to where he was laying.

"Baby, you can ravish me anytime you want. My stuff is wide open for you and only you," she kissed his lips softly, then with a little more vigor.

His eyes were closed as he was savoring the taste of Monica. She stopped abruptly and pulled her head away from his. He was still laying there with his eyes closed and his lips puckered.

Just as he opened his eyes, she said, "I have more of that for you later; right now I have to get the bacon before it burns. I got the newspaper from the porch and I'll serve it with your breakfast right there where you are laying. So relax and enjoy."

She hurried to the kitchen to keep her morning surprise from burning. Briscoe got up and went into the bathroom that was a part of his master bedroom suite. He needed to relieve himself, and wash up a bit before his wonderful girlfriend serves him breakfast in bed.

He finished his business and got back in the bed, where he cleared his mind and only focused on beautiful things; the types of things that soothe the spirit. He even fantasized about a life with Monica that had children and a home with constant happiness and joy. He did this to block out the thoughts of what he had done overnight—and the many more things that he planned to do. Today is reserved for Monica, his family, and friends. That other shit will have to take a back seat.

"Okay Antonio, close your eyes," she paused, "are they closed?"

she asked from the hallway.

"Yea baby they're closed," he replied.

"Now don't open them till I tell you to," she peeked into the room to make sure his eyes were closed and then she entered with a large tray. It was fully laid out like room service from a four-star hotel, complete with coffee and juice.

She stood beside the bed and said, "Okay, now you can open them . . . Surprise!" She was elated that she was serving her man in bed.

"Wow Moni, this is beautiful. You cooked all this food for me. You are so special."

"I would do anything for you Antonio. I love you from way down deep inside of me."

They shared a kiss, and Monica got into the bed next to him. They both dug into the food and talked.

"Oh, I forgot the newspaper," she said jumping up to retrieve it from the living room. When she returned she got back into bed and handed the paper to Briscoe. He unfolded the paper, and right there on the front page was the blaring headline, "Serial Predator kills 9."

Monica got a glimpse of the article and said, "Oh my god, he killed nine people in one night. That dude is a beast. You all are gonna have do something to get that crazy lunatic off the streets."

Her words tore at his heart.

"Why do you think he's crazy?"

"Who could kill that many people if they weren't crazy?"

She had a look of sympathy on her face for the victims. She took the article from Briscoe and started to read it, out loud in some places.

Then she said, "He tortured some of them. Now you tell me that isn't some sick stuff."

"It's possible he was punishing them for something," he ventured.

"That's what the courts are for, right?" she asked as she continued to read the article.

"Well, the courts don't always serve justice and bad people are released back into society to inflict more pain on the innocent."

"Oh, so you agree with the killing of another human being?" The question floored Briscoe, hitting him like a jackhammer driving a rivet into steel.

How is he supposed to answer that question? If he answers truthfully about the way he feels, Monica will think the man she loves is a monster. She is all into helping others and caring for those who cannot care for themselves. She does not understand the justice system and all its shortcomings and blatant miscarriages of justice. He never did tell Monica about his past in the military and the lives that he ended in the name of democracy and freedom. *Now he realizes he never will.*

"Well baby, sometimes a life is taken to save a life. Some people are so inherently evil that they will not stop a violent behavior until they are stopped by an outside force," he felt that his answer was a good one.

"I don't think it's ever okay to take the life of another, regardless of what they have done. Only God should mete out that kind of judgment. This serial predator person should suffer the same fate as the people he is killing if it is like you believe, because he is just as bad as the people he killed."

Monica was adamant in her position and it nearly ripped Briscoe's heart out of his chest. He knew how Monica felt about crime and its victims, but he did not anticipate that her convictions were so strong about punishment. It was now official in his mind; he could never let Monica know that he was the man responsible for cleansing the streets of the District.

"Wow, I didn't know my baby was such a good Christian girlie," he said jokingly as he tickled her waist.

She started to laugh and said, "I'll show you a good Christian girl," as she moved the tray to the floor and climbed on top of him.

Whew, I'm glad we got away from that conversation, he thought as they hugged and kissed and told each other how much they were in love.

The 10:00 a.m. briefing of the Chiefs went well. Whitehead was given all the resources and support that he requested. He felt good about the department's position and their willingness to go all out to catch the predator. The meeting ran over so they rescheduled the press conference for noon.

All the local news outlets and several national media entities were set up on the steps in front of Police Headquarters. The Chief of Police came forward to the podium and addressed the public.

"There were ten homicides over night. We are not completely certain they were committed by one person; however, there are similarities. The victims were all male and they were killed in each of the four quadrants of the city. At this time we do not have a motive or a suspect. If anybody has any information about any of the homicides overnight or any of the other homicides that have taken place over the past three months, please call our twenty-four hour anonymous tip line on 777-TIPS. Thank you. I'll now take a few questions."

"Chief, is it true that there is a serial killer loose in the city?"

"Well, I don't want to say a serial killer, but there are similarities in many of the homicides."

"Chief, what are you doing to catch the non serial killer?" one of the local reports asked in a sarcastic manner.

"We are assembling a task force that will consist of veteran detectives, uniform patrol officers, and other local and federal agencies."

"I don't know chief, but that sounds like a serial killer to me. Should the public be worried?"

"It doesn't appear that the public is at risk, just a certain type of person," the Chief said he would disclose that information only if asked, he was not going to give it voluntarily.

"Chief, what type of person should be concerned about the serial killer?"

"It appears that the victims are career criminals for the most part."

"A minute ago you said there is no serial killer." the same sarcastic reporter fired.

"I did not say that, I said I didn't want to say that. The fact is we are following the evidence and chasing down leads. If they lead to one or multiple people so be it."

"Chief who is the lead investigator on the case?"

"Detective Jamie Whitehead will continue to lead the investigation and he will head the task force. He is a seasoned veteran with many high profile closures. I think most of you know him."

"Chief, can you tell us anything about the suspect? His race, age, anything?"

"I wish I could, but we have nothing. That's why we are asking for the public's help," he looked directly into a camera, "If anybody thinks they saw anything that looked suspicious anywhere last night; a person, a vehicle or anything, please contact us on 777-TIPS."

He turned his attention back to the reporters, "That's all the time I have, thank you for your attention." He turned and walked back inside the building to a chorus of questions from the media who were still gathered around the podium which was now behind him. The TV reporters began to talk into their respective cameras giving a recap of the press conference to their viewers, as the Chief walked away from the podium.

Monica and Briscoe were now up cleaning his house so they could go out for the day. They had plans to go to his parent's home in Fort Washington, Maryland for a cookout. His sister Alicia Graduated from Howard University a month ago with her Master's Degree, and the family was celebrating. There was going to be family in from out of town and Alicia had a bunch of her friends attending. His brother Andrew was also coming in with his family from Pennsylvania.

Monica turned on the TV in the bedroom and sat on the end of the bed changing channels.

"That doesn't look like work to me," Briscoe said playfully, as he tossed a pillow lightly hitting Monica in the back."

"I have to check the weather, so I'll know what to wear," she said with a smile.

She turned to Fox 5 just as they announced breaking news, and she paused on the channel. It was the news conference in front of police headquarters. Briscoe listened intently to the conference. He noted that there was a task force being assembled. That meant around the clock investigation so he will have to be very careful from now on.

Damn, how can I get on that task force? The closer he can get to the investigation the better. He also realized that it would only be a matter of time before they try to compose a psycho profile of the predator. So he knew it was imperative for him to keep his personal views to himself, because when they start to look for the person that the profiler describes, he wants to be all the way on the other end of the spectrum.

"Aaw sookie, sookie now, it looks like they are about to get his ass good," Monica said in a satisfied manner. She turned the TV off after the Chief finished talking, and said, "I don't need to see the weather, it looks gorgeous outside."

"And you look gorgeous inside," Briscoe said.

He decided to put the thought of the killings, and the department's strategy to catch him, out of his mind for the day. He did not want to see another news brief or anything associated with dying or justice.

He was going to enjoy himself today at his parent's house and later tonight at Sanford's pool party.

"What time are we going to your parents?" Monica asked.

"I guess around three. Why, what's up?"

"I wanted to go for a run." She liked to exercise because it kept her gorgeous body firm and gave her energy.

"I was going to the gym to workout, are you down with me?" he asked.

"Hell yeah; I've never gone to the gym with you, that should be fun. I'll even drive."

They finished picking up around the house and left for the gym. They both got in a good workout at the gym and got back with plenty of time to get ready for the cookout.

Monica stepped into the bedroom where Briscoe was standing in front of a full length mirror without a shirt, considering his physique.

She touched his chest as she said, "Oh my god, your chest is so firm."

Then she started to rub his chest and abs. It felt nice having her touch him while he stood shirtless looking at their reflections in the mirror. She started to rub his shoulders and neck, and he told her how good it felt. His muscles were still tight from the workout. Her voice lowered to a very frisky level with a soft and seductive tone,

"Take off your shorts baby and I'll start the shower." He wrapped his arms around her and held her for a moment while he enjoyed the beauty of their union. Their lips touched softly, as they exchanged sweet saliva and their tongues wrapped around each other in a warm embrace as they met time and time again inside of their mouths.

"Oh Antonio, your tight body feels so good next to mine."

"It's all yours, Moni; do anything you want with it." He watched her hot, gorgeous ass, as she walked into the bathroom to turn on the shower. The shape of her hips in the spandex shorts that she wore excited his cock. It started to rise as the thought of riding her danced around his mind. He heard the water come on, and let his shorts and underwear drop to the floor. Just as he looked up, Monica was standing at the bathroom door wearing only a smile. Her beautiful black body glistening in the light of the dimly lit bathroom, and it was calling his name.

"Wow, you are so fuckin' HOT!" he said.

He wanted to ravish her sexy frame right there in the doorway, but she held out her hand, and he reached out and grasped it gently. She led him to the shower, and he watched as she stepped in and moved underneath the water flow, allowing it to cascade through her hair and down her body. He stepped in and stood near, but not too close yet...he wanted to admire the sexiness of her supple breasts, the curve of her sensuous hips, and the tightness of her perfectly shaped ass. He picked up the liquid soap and lathered the bath bonnet. He started by washing her back, slow and gentle, lathering every part. He moved his focus lower, to her very sexy ass, where he soaped it, rubbed it and caressed it like a fine delicate sculpture. His hands moved down her legs, rubbing the inside of her thighs and finding his way into her tight crack, where he gently washed her sweet wet pussy, and tight asshole. He wanted it to be clean enough to eat. He then sat the bonnet aside and massaged the soap into her soft tender shoulders with his bare hands. He let his hands rub the soap all around her back, beautiful ass and thick luscious thighs. He was digging the relaxation she was experiencing. His cock was hard enough to break stone. She could feel it pressing into her back as he was soaping her sexy breasts from behind. She looked down at his hands as they were soaping her, and she guided them down to her precious hot love box, where his fingers started to tickle and massage her clit. Her chest heaved with every breath, which grew deeper with every stroke of her sensitive, delectable, and very moist clit. Oh she felt so good, and her body responded to every touch of his large powerful, but gentle hands.

 She turned around to face him and said, "Oh my god baby, your dick is so hard and fat. It's throbbing and the veins are pulsating. It's calling my name."

 She then took it in her hands and started to stroke it. She pulled it back and forth, and then put soap on it and rubbed until it was so hard that she could feel his pulse beating through it. She started to soap his chest and nipples and he started moaning. He could feel a fire raging inside. He was burning for her love. He switched places with her and had the water from the shower head beating on his back. He picked her up, placing her back against the shower wall, and then slid his long hard dick deep inside of her dripping wet cave. Umm! Ooh, the tightness engulfed his rock hard dick as he slid in and out feeling the heat. She was wrapped around him with her hands around his broad shoulders, as her pussy was enjoying the feel of all his manhood deep inside.

She was saying, "Yes baby."

He screamed out her name, "Monica, Monica, Oh god you are so damn hot baby."

They stroked, and stroked in the warm shower and he could feel her pussy tighten around his dick, and the heat intensify as she let herself bust off.

"I'm CUMMING!" she screamed, as she grabbed him tight and dug her fingers deep into his back.

He could feel the very hot, intense heat of her cum as it ran down over his still throbbing dick. She sucked very hard on his neck while her pussy was releasing sweet sticky juice that went all the way down to his balls. She started biting and licking his neck and that drove him wild. He started to thrust deeper, and harder into her smoking hot cunt. She kept sucking on his neck until he let out a loud scream as the cum burst from the head of his thick robust cock. He held her tightly as he kept thrusting in and out, deeper and deeper into the softness of her effervescent vagina.

"I love you Moni!" he said, moaning loudly while the cum continued to flow from deep inside of his immense penis.

They held on tight to each other while her back rested against the shower wall and he held her up on top of his dick. Their embrace seemed to last for hours. They kissed deeply and lovingly. Finally they had to clean each other and get out of the tub, but his heart was feeling her so tenderly that he didn't want them to be apart, so they lay in the bed together and just caressed for the next half hour.

"Wow Antonio, we are so good together. I love the way you let me express myself when we make love. I am making a vow to you right here, right now. Nobody else will ever taste my goodies, they are only for you and you alone."

"Moni, are you sure that I am enough for you?" he said light heartedly.

"Boy, I'm being serious. I am so in love with you and I don't ever see living my life without you."

Her words soothed his soul, because he felt the same way about her. Life truly was good. He was dancing on cloud nine.

"I know you are, Moni, because I feel the exact same way, and whether you know it or not, I have been committed to you from the beginning."

Following his words, she squeezed him a little tighter, "Baby, we'd better get up and get ready to go to your people's house."

She didn't want to move from their current position of bliss, but she knew they had to go. They got up and got dressed.

They walked outside and Monica asked, "Do you have your keys?"

Oh shit! He thought. He did not dispose of the evidence in his backpack; neither did he sterilize his vehicle's interior. He knew that he transferred blood and dirt from his clothing onto parts of his interior. He planned to detail the car and dispose of the evidence today, but Monica side tracked him.

"I thought we were taking the Beemer. I was hoping to ride in style today," he said playfully; but he seriously wanted to take her car.

"Okay, but you're driving," she said as she dug in her purse for the keys to her BMW 745i.

Briscoe really did enjoy driving the high performance sports sedan, and today he had good reason.

The first thing tomorrow I am going to detail my car and burn the contents of my backpack, he thought. They drove to his parent's home in Fort Washington, stopping at a liquor store along the way to pick up a one liter bottle of Hennessy for his father. He figured that was a pretty decent contribution to the cookout. Monica was looking luscious as ever, the sun was out with the temperature in the mid-80s with low humidity, he could not have asked for a more perfect day.

As they drove the back roads to Fort Washington, he thought about his family and how they felt about Monica. His mother thought the world of Monica and she always asked him when he was going to settle down. If things were different right now, he would definitely marry Monica. She was the one and only true love in his life, he could not imagine being with another woman. His unconditional sweetness was uncompromised for her. He would just never, ever stop loving her. Every aspect of his life, professionally, socially, economically, and emotionally was firing on all cylinders and he could not have been happier. Now it's off to the parent's house where he can relax his guard, and love with no limit, because all the people there will be good people.

11

"Detective Sutton, this is Detective Bainbridge from the Prince George's (PG) County Police Department," the voice on the other end of the phone said.

"Yes this is Sutton, how can I help you?"

"You released a BOLO earlier today in reference to a red Chevy Tahoe, possibly connected to an overnight homicide?"

Detective Sutton, while investigating Damon's murder discovered that he left with a male-to-female transgendered person in a red Chevy with Maryland tags. So he created a BOLO seeking information and assistance with locating a red Chevy that is possibly operated by a transgendered female from surrounding jurisdictions, especially Maryland.

"Yes, I sure did. Did you guys locate it?" he asked with a glimmer of hope.

"Yes we did and we have a witness that I think you might want to talk with ASAP."

Sutton's heart was dancing with excitement. He could not believe their first real break in the case, the predator has slipped and left a witness. He wanted to yell out to the entire squad room.

"Where is the witness now?" he asked.

"In her trailer home at 75344 Dower House Road. I'm on the scene; I'll wait here for you."

"Okay I'll grab my partner and we will be on our way. We should be there in twenty minutes," he said and hung up the phone.

Sutton could barely contain his enthusiasm as he yelled out, "Jamie, we caught a break!"

"What's up partner?" Whitehead asked as he noted the excitement in Sutton.

"PG County has a witness in connection with Damon Mason's homicide. They are holding her at the scene in Maryland. Grab your hat and let's roll," Sutton was ecstatic.

"Alright, Jake. Man I haven't seen you this excited since that time you thought you won the Powerball lottery," Whitehead said as he laughed at Sutton's exhilaration.

"Jamie this is the first real break we've gotten since this thing started. Hopefully this witness can put a finger on our guy; then we can put an end to all of this."

"True that partner, true that," Whitehead said.

It was now 2:00 p.m. and both detectives were running on adrenaline. The news of the witness gave them a boost of energy and partially recharged their investigatory batteries. The day tour detectives in the squad room said, "Go get 'em, fellas." As they all cheered them on and gave them words of hope and encouragement as they departed the station for their meeting with the PG County police detective and the witness.

The entire VCU was pulling for the two of them to solve the most high profile case in the District and one of the most infamous in the city's history. They were comforted to know that they had the support of their colleagues.

As they drove to the witness's location, they compared notes, and devised an interview strategy to be sure that they extracted as much information about the predator as they could.

When they arrived, they were greeted by a uniformed patrol officer, "You gentlemen must be the DC detectives."

They acknowledged his observation and he called Detective Bainbridge over the radio. Seconds later a white male, with more wrinkles across his face than anyone his age should have, and a receding hair line that was catching up to the bald spot in the middle of his head, emerged from the home. He was an eighteen year veteran of the force and has had many long sleepless nights working a never ending case load that showed on his seasoned face. He wore a blue sports coat with brown slacks and brown shoes, but the thing that jumps out at you is the bright red tie around his neck.

He approached the two detectives, and as he got near extended his right hand and said, "Hello detectives; Detective Dan Bainbridge Major Crimes Unit."

They introduced themselves and Bainbridge began to explain the details of what he had,

"An officer responded to a call of a vehicle fire along with the Board earlier this morning. Once the vehicle was extinguished, the officer ran the tags and went to the address to speak with the owner, but he got no answer at the door so he left. Once your BOLO hit, the officer thought about the burned vehicle and he, along with his supervisor, decided to do a forced entry on this place. Once inside they found the owner of the vehicle bound and gagged on the bed in the back bedroom. They called me to the scene, and once I saw what we had, I called you."

"Did anybody touch anything inside?" Whitehead asked.

"I would have to say yes. I don't know to what extent, but there have been at least six officers in and out of the location, and naturally they released the victim from her bonds," Bainbridge said honestly.

"Well, I think we will still have our Mobile Crime Unit come out and process the scene, just in case. We can always exclude your officers with DNA samples if it comes down to it," Whitehead said.

"How is the witness? Does she seem cooperative?" Sutton asked.

"I really didn't ask very many questions, but she does seem somewhat shaken. I think you guys have your work cut out for you."

"Do you have all of her information?" Whitehead asked.

"I sure do. Would you like to copy it now or when you finish?" Bainbridge inquired.

"We'll get it from her, but I would want to match it to what you have to ensure accuracy." Whitehead said.

"I'm tracking. Good idea," Bainbridge said as he realized the simple technique used to qualify the truthfulness of certain witnesses.

"Thanks detective. We will need some time alone with the witness inside. I appreciate your assistance with everything," Whitehead said as he shook Bainbridge's hand again before proceeding to the entrance of the home.

Sutton was already on his cell phone placing the call to request the Mobile Crime Unit. He moved the phone to his left hand and shook Bainbridge's hand also.

"Thanks a lot man. Good work," he said as he followed Whitehead into the home.

When they entered they were greeted by a uniformed officer who was standing in the living room listening to the witness speak about something unrelated to the case. The officer was standing by so as not to lose positive control of the residence. Once the police made entry they can stay in without the need of further probable cause, but if they were to leave and it turned out that the witness was a suspect, they would need a warrant to get back in. The detectives told the officer they would let him know when they were done. He said okay and walked outside.

The witness, whose name is Tanisha Goodall, was sitting on the sofa drinking water and looking rattled. Sutton looked at her and thought, *Damn! I thought they said it was a shemale; this is a woman, and damn she's fine.* He needed a moment to compose himself and get back on his game.

Whitehead did not seem fazed by her beauty, nor could he care less if one could not easily discern whether it was a man or a woman, because he was focused and about his work. However, they both treated her like she was a natural woman throughout the interview.

"Ma'am, I'm Detective Whitehead and this is Detective Sutton," he motioned, "from the Metropolitan Police Department. We would like to ask you a few questions about what happened to you last night."

"Okay," Tanisha said as she took a sip of water.

"First, how did you come to know Damon Mason?"

"I met him in club Odyssey where I perform."

"What kind of performance?" Sutton interrupted.

"I dance and sing, kind of like a sexy review. Some men are turned on by girls like me, so they come in to check out the performances," she said.

"How long have you known him?" Whitehead asked.

"About six months."

"Do you know if anybody was out to do him harm? Or did he ever speak about anybody that he was beefing with?" he inquired.

"No. Damon never spoke about anything like that. He seemed to be cool with everybody."

"What happened last night?" Whitehead decided to let her just tell him from start to finish what took place and he would interrupt her with questions.

"Well, I picked up Damon from his house in Southeast and we drove straight here."

Whitehead interrupted, "What time did you pick him up?"

"It was around 11:00 p.m.," she said. Whitehead nodded and she continued to talk. "We came in the house, and while we were in the bedroom, this dude came in and made Damon tie me up and then he tied up Damon and took him out of the room." She looked very worried and afraid while recounting the incident.

"What did he look like?" Whitehead asked.

"I don't know. He was wearing all black clothes and a black mask with just his eyes showing. It was dark in the room and as soon as I saw the gun he made me lay face down on the bed."

"How tall was he?"

Whitehead realized that he would have to take this one little baby step at a time.

"He was taller than me. And I'm six feet tall. He was about this much taller," she said as she held her hand above her head as to show his height in comparison to hers.

"What color was he?"

"I don't know I couldn't see his face or any skin. He was completely covered."

"I understand that, but could you tell from his voice what his ethnicity was?"

Whitehead knew that he couldn't stake the farm on it, but he was willing to take whatever he could get, because he knew that the race of the vast majority of people could be determined from their speech.

"Not really, he just sounded serious."

"I know you must have been frightened, any lady would have been. But try hard to think about how he sounded," Sutton said in a very calming, empathetic manner.

"I thought about it all night while I was tied up in there and I just could not tell one way or the other," she said in her most sincere voice.

To tell the truth, she is scared shitless. *The killer told her not to say anything or he will be back to kill her and if he could get in the first time unnoticed, he could do it again. She was only going to tell them enough to get them out of her house.*

"Did he say why he was here?" Whitehead asked.

"He said he came to get Damon; that he owed a debt. He also said it had nothing to do with me."

"Has Damon ever mentioned that he owed money to anybody?"

"Not to me. He has never asked me for money."

"Is there anything you can tell us about this guy that stands out in your mind?" Sutton asked.

"The only thing I can tell you is he had a gun and he was serious."

"Okay ma'am, thanks for your help. We are going to have a

crew come in and process your home for evidence since it is a crime scene. Sorry for the inconvenience," Whitehead said with not much genuine regret.

"What happened to Damon?" Tanisha asked with hope in her eyes.

"He was beaten to death overnight. I guess the guy that took him from here collected on his debt," Whitehead said with absolutely no compassion.

"Oh my God, no! Oh no! Why would somebody do that to him?" she was now crying with both arms wrapped around her body holding herself.

"I'm sorry," Sutton said sincerely as he handed her a handkerchief.

"You can help us catch the man that did this to your friend, if you could just recall the details of last night," Whitehead said, playing on her sorrow.

"I can't think of anything else," she sobbed.

Once she learned that Damon was dead, she knew for a fact there was nothing more she would say to cause the killer to come back for her.

"Well if anything comes to mind later, give us a call anytime day or night," Whitehead said handing her a business card.

Sutton also gave her his card. She tried to hand him his handkerchief but he refused,

"You keep it sweetheart. I'm sorry for your loss."

"Thank you; you are so sweet," she said looking longingly into his eyes, feeling a connection.

Detective Whitehead obtained her personal data to compare with what Detective Bainbridge had, and they departed the house. Outside, Whitehead told the uniformed officer they were finished, and advised him that the MPD Mobile Crime Unit was coming out to process the scene. They compared Tanisha's information with that obtained by Bainbridge and were confident that it was accurate.

During the ride back to their office Whitehead said, "That bitch is holding back. I don't know why, but she is holding back."

"She might be afraid," Sutton said.

"Well I don't know if that's the case, but we have to find out. And since you act like you want to fuck her, you should be able to get the information easily," he said as he looked at Sutton.

"What? I don't want to fuck that," Sutton said defensively.

"Well you sure were Mister Compassionate back there. 'Oh you keep the handkerchief, sweetie,'" Whitehead said mockingly as he laughed.

"Aw go ahead with that, man," Sutton said.

"She was feeling you Jake. You might have to use that to our advantage. Give her a couple of days and then call . . . that's if she doesn't call you first," Whitehead was only thinking of the case.

"What makes you think she will call me?"

"Because I know people and I could clearly see is attracted to you. She thinks that you may have connected with her. Just take this one for the team," he laughed out loud.

"Whatever," Sutton said. But he was secretly hoping to see Tanisha again. He was not gay, but there was something about her that intrigued him. It aroused a curiosity like nothing he ever experienced before.

"Hell, that sexy motherfucker looks so damn good, I would almost fuck it. So if you hit it I won't tell anybody," Whitehead was now laughing from his belly.

"Man you are crazy," Sutton said as he laughed along with Whitehead.

12

Briscoe turned into a beautifully maintained and well-designed subdivision of luxury estates in Fort Washington. He maneuvered Monica's midnight blue 745i onto the cul-de-sac at the western end of the community. They pulled to the curb and parked in front of a large two story brick colonial, with a two car garage and drive way large enough to accommodate six vehicles. The yard was impeccably manicured, with a lush green lawn, exotic flowers, and shrubs. There were balloons with congratulatory slogans tied to the mailbox, a vintage light post, and several other locations around the yard leading to the back of the house. The strong aroma of meat cooking on a grill filled the air and the faint sound of music billowed from the rear of the house.

"Why don't you park in the driveway?" Monica asked.

"I don't want to be blocked in. We're going to Willis' pool party tonight and I think everybody will be here till late into the night."

"You are the man, let me step back," she said as she pat him on his crotch and smiled.

"See baby, I'm always thinking ahead," he said with an exaggerated Buckwheat smile.

"What did you say about some head?" she said with a devilish smile.

"Girl, don't tempt me," he grinned as they exited the car and walked to the front door of the house. There was a sign on the door that instructed all guests to come around back. The rear of the house was separated by a six-foot-high beautifully constructed black wrought iron fence. The gate was an elegant design that gave the home the appeal of a mini-mansion. When the development was under construction, it was marketed as a Luxury Estate Community and elegance was the theme.

Once they passed through the gate and made their way to the rear corner of the house, the yard opened up to a landscape that could easily grace the cover of Better Homes and Gardens. There was a waterfall with the appeal of an Asian garden, similar to something from a Japanese movie. A huge two-story deck coming off the back of the house landed onto a twelve by fifteen foot brick patio. There was deck furniture on both levels of the deck, with chairs also on the patio and a picnic table on the lawn. There were more balloons throughout the yard and citronella torches burning to ward off mosquitoes.

Someone called out "Antonio!" then others started to speak as he and Monica made their way to the deck.

His sister Alicia met them at the steps to the deck and gave Monica a hug and said, "Girl you look good! And you look great too big bruh," as she hugged him also.

"Congratulations Alicia," they both said to her in unison.

"Where is everybody? I know you have more people than this coming," Briscoe asked.

"Hell yeah, I have a rack coming and we are going to party hard. But you know how Negroes are; everybody wants to make an entrance."

"I know that's right child," Monica said high-fiving Alicia.

Monica and Alicia then went inside to speak to Briscoe's mother, Alexis, and see what they could do to help out. Briscoe went to where his father, Anthony, was cooking on the grill and talking to a couple of his buddies.

"Hey Dad," he said as he gave him a hug, and shook hands with the other two men who were there.

They are the neighbors to the left and right of his father. The men were standing around talking and drinking beer while the man of the house was grilling.

"So what have you been up to son? I haven't talked to you in a week, you must be very busy," Anthony Briscoe didn't expect to hear from his son every day, but he did like for him to speak with his mother, if not every day, close to it.

"Yeah, things have been hectic lately and we are doing a lot of overtime."

Briscoe was just too busy over the past week planning his big night out that he couldn't drop by like he tried to do frequently. Briscoe admired his father and loved him dearly. His father was, and still is, his hero. He taught him about responsibility, integrity, and courage of convictions, and to never quit or give up on himself. He knew that the strength of his father is what molded him into the man that he is today. Briscoe remembered a time when two bullies picked on his best friend and he went to his father for advice about how to help his friend. His father told him that friendship is sacred, and to be a true friend one must stand beside, behind, or in front of them, and endure the risk of harm to protect them. Briscoe contemplated the meaning of friendship all night. The next day, he was with his best friend and the bullies came along and started picking on him.

He said, "Why don't you just leave him alone?"

The two then turned their attention to Briscoe. At the time he was fifteen years old in the 9th grade. The bullies were in the 12th grade and slightly bigger. What they didn't know was that Briscoe had a black belt in Taekwondo and had practiced karate since he was four years old. He beat the two of them so badly that he was suspended from school for fighting. His mother was ready to come down on him with both feet, but his father stood by him through it all. He even went to the Principal of the school and informed him about the way the two boys had terrorized other students and when they messed with his boy, they got what they deserved. Briscoe was admitted back into school with the promise that he would not fight again. His father was very proud of him for standing up to the bullies and being a true friend. His mother was not as happy; but what else could you expect from a female?

"Dad, the yard looks great, and that smells good," he gestured to the grill.

"There are some hot dogs, burgers, and I think a couple of steaks already done on that table over there," Anthony motioned to a long table at the end of the patio.

"Nah, I'm alright for now, but I'll take one of those beers," he said as he reached into a nearby cooler and retrieved a Heineken.

"So, how are things at work? I see ya'll still haven't caught that predator," one of the men said.

"We're working on it," he really didn't want to have this conversation.

"I think ya'll should leave him alone. Shit, it looks like he is doing a good thing ridding the city of those shit bags," the man said.

"As long as he sticks to them, I don't see a problem," the other said.

What? Am I hearing this correctly? Briscoe thought.

He asked, "So you guys think what he is doing is okay?"

"Well I wouldn't say okay, but I would say it provides a service that nobody wants to admit the area needs," the man clarified.

"I don't know what ya'll are talking about, but there is something called a criminal justice system, and it was designed to give people due process before punishing them. This guy is just out there doing the job of the judge, jury, and executioner," Anthony said.

Briscoe did not want to respond yet, because he was not sure how his father actually felt about the killings, and more importantly for him; how he felt about the person doing them.

"What criminal justice system? The only people who get justice it seems are the criminals. The system is broke and too many of these shitheads get put right back into society where they continue to terrorize good hard working folk. I for one, feel a lot better knowing that somebody is taking them off the streets."

Briscoe liked the sound of that. He could only wish his father felt the same.

"I agree," the other man said. Anthony did not offer up an opinion, but Briscoe was very curious what his father thought.

"What about the person that's doing it? What kind of person do you think he is?" Briscoe asked hoping his father would answer.

Instead, one of the men said, "I think he's a goddamn saint. If we knew who he was we should give him a medal."

"Yeah, and a paycheck, and let him do it as a full time job," they all laughed.

"What do you think dad?" Briscoe asked.

"I don't know. On one hand, I think the people deserve what they get, but on the other I think no man should make himself God and decide to dish out the ultimate punishment. By doing so, this killer has placed himself on a level with the heavenly father and that is never right."

Damn! His father thinks like his girlfriend does. It is becoming increasingly clear to Briscoe that he will not be able to share his mission with anybody. His father was the one person that he thought might understand.

"Well somebody on this earth needs to do it and it sure as hell isn't the justice system," one of the men said.

"How do we know this isn't sanctioned by the hand of God and the killer is merely doing as God directs? His Angel of Death, if you will," the other added.

"I don't know about that, I think the bible says God will take care of all the vengeance. I don't remember seeing anything in there about a man on earth," Anthony said.

Briscoe just stood by and listened to the debate waged by his father and the other two men, when he suddenly caught the eye of a tall, light-skinned woman with light green eyes. She must be six feet tall with very crisp features. Her face is that of a model, but her body is banging like the average girl from a rap video, with curves from top to bottom. And speaking of bottom, she has a very nice apple bottom. Her eyes seductively said hello as she and Briscoe exchanged a smile from across the yard.

Anthony noticed the exchange and commented, "Boy, you better take your mind off that before Monica comes out here and kick both ya'll asses."

The men laughed. "Man she is a fine ass thing," one of them said.

"Yeah, but Antonio has a dime piece in the house and he don't need that kind of trouble over there," Anthony said referring to the female.

"Who is she?" Briscoe asked his father.

"That's one of your sister's friends. She lives in her apartment complex. Why?" Anthony asked.

"I was just curious."

"Well, don't be curious, because all that will lead to is trouble. Trust me when I tell you."

His father really liked Monica and he didn't want Briscoe to mess things up with her.

"I hear you Dad."

"I hope you are listening as well," he said.

The rest of the time Briscoe was at the grill talking to his father he tried not to look at the woman, but she was stunning. He found it difficult not to sneak a peek at her from time to time, and to his delight, she was peeking back.

Monica, Alexis, and Alicia emerged from the house and joined the guests, who grew in number. Alexis came over to Briscoe and he hugged her and kissed her on the cheek.

"Hey baby, you didn't want to come in to say hello to your mother?" she asked.

"No ma'am, I got caught up out here with Dad, but I was on my way in just as you were coming out," he said with a smile.

"Yeah right, tell me anything," she said as she nudged him.

Monica gave Anthony a hug, and he introduced her to the two

neighbors.

"Hey daughter-in-law, how have you been? I haven't seen you in a while. How is business?" Anthony said as he gave Briscoe a look of, 'did you hear me call her daughter-in-law?'

"I've been well and business couldn't be better. How about you?" she asked happily.

"I'm hanging in there enjoying every day that the Lord blesses me with."

Anthony was not a religious man, but he did yield to a higher power. Alexis on the other hand is a Christian woman who is active in the Baptist church where she is a member. She raised all three of her children in the church and has always preached do unto others as you would have others do unto you. Briscoe knew, when he started his mission to cut the cancer out of society, his mother would never approve. If she knew what he was doing, she would probably die of a broken heart, because she thinks her baby is the sweetest gentlest person in the world and would never hurt any living creature.

Monica enjoyed the time mixing with the family and Briscoe felt proud to have her by his side as he introduced her to aunts, uncles, cousins, and family friends who didn't already know her. Everyone liked her immediately and made her feel welcome. They mingled, ate, drank, and had a great time. It was now getting dark, nearing 9:00 p.m. and Briscoe was ready to leave for the pool party. They said their goodbyes and departed.

They were driving on the beltway when Monica said, "Somebody has an admirer."

"Who?" Briscoe asked innocently.

"You do. That red bitch was all up in your sauce. She couldn't keep her eyes off you. I thought about going over and scratching them out. But I ain't want to get all ghetto up in there," Monica never showed this side before.

"Really? I didn't notice," he lied.

"Yeah right; I bet you like that kind of thing don't you?"

"What kind of thing?"

"An Amazon hoochie like the one that eye-fucked you all evening in your parent's yard and disrespected me," she was genuinely jealous.

"Moni I didn't even notice, but I am not into anybody but you. I'm only excited by you and I don't want anybody but you," he reached over and took her hand in his.

"I'm sure everybody in that yard could see how that bitch was swooning over you. I should have told her to reel her fucking eyes back in before I put them out permanently. Disrespecting me like that," Monica was letting it out.

"Moni, I've never seen you like this. You don't have to ever worry about me stepping out on you. If I had known she was eye-fucking me, as you say, I would have told her not to disrespect my future wife."

When he said that, she looked at him and said, "Your what?"

"Yes baby, you are the only woman I'll ever need. I don't plan to let anybody into this beautiful love that we share."

With that said, she relaxed a little in her seat and continued to hold his hand. She realized that Briscoe was feeling a lifelong commitment for her. That warmed her soul and took away any insecurities that she might have felt over the past few hours.

Wow, I have never seen Moni get that worked up over another woman before, he thought. His father was right about that chick being a problem. *It's a good thing he didn't go over and strike up a conversation with her like he had initially planned. Can you imagine the night he and Monica would have after that?* He figured that Monica could sense some sort of a mutual attraction, because he definitely was attracted to the woman. It was just something about her that made him curious and somewhat desirous. They are gone, and the woman is a thing of the past, so Monica does not have anything to worry about and neither does he.

They drove into Sanford's block looking for a place to park, but the pool party was in full swing, and there was no parking in sight. They ended up parking one street over and walking back to the house amidst a chorus of barking dogs, in what seemed like every yard they passed. Monica clung tightly to Briscoe's arm and walked on the curb side of the sidewalk. She felt safe and protected by him and loved the way it felt walking arm and arm. Her man could do no wrong and she admired his quiet strength and introspective nature. She had been with men who constantly talked about how great they were and what they had, but Briscoe was nothing like that. He listened closely, reflected on matters of the heart, and issues surrounding honor, loyalty, and community. He never came across with pomp and circumstance or looked down on others. With all he has, and all he could have, he is a very humble person. She was always proud to be in his company and knew that other women envied her for having him. Until the redbone tonight, she never felt threatened by any. But she feels that Briscoe is very loyal and she can trust him when he says he will never cheat on her.

When they made it to the party, the music was jumping inside and out. There were people in bathing suits in the front yard, in the house, out back around the pool, and just about everywhere you looked. It was off the chain, and they stripped out of their clothes down to the bathing suits underneath. The temperature had crested at ninety-three degrees earlier, and it was still in the mid-eighties; but with all the alcohol flowing, people would not have noticed if it was below freezing.

While at the party Briscoe got to talk with Whitehead and put in a bid for a position on the serial predator task force. He convinced Sanford to talk him up to Whitehead and get him to request him for the task force from the 5th Precinct when they start pulling uniformed officers. Whitehead knew Briscoe, but not as well as Sanford did, and he agreed to ask for him by name. That made Briscoe happy because he wanted to be as close as possible to the investigation. Coming to the party was a good move he thought, and he and Monica stayed and partied until 2:00 a.m.

13

"Adams." "Here" "Bailey." "Here" "Briscoe." "Here" The sergeant continued the roll call till the last name, "Williams." "Here."

When he finished he announced the VCU task force for the serial predator and told all who were interested to sign up on the sheet posted outside the roll call room. He informed them that each shift would have a chance to sign up, and the commander, based on recommendations from the supervisors, will choose the four officers who will be detailed. Briscoe felt like his chances were good. As long as Whitehead asks for him by name, he will be in there. Following roll call, he went directly to the board and signed up. He noticed there that ten names were already on the list.

He left the station and reflected on his weekend and the wonderful time he had with Monica and his family. But now, it was time to get down to some serious work. His two days off were eventful; he made a searing statement to the underbelly of the city. But he still had a lot of work to do. His main objective tonight is going to be finding Connie Little and pick up where he left off on Thursday night. It shouldn't be hard to find her. Sunday nights are usually slow for tricks so crack hos spend more time outside waiting to be picked up. He felt the odds of finding her on the street were greatly improved. He also thought about Brick Jackson and his connection with Janice Russell. He thought about Janice's daughter, who is still in the house where she was violated and her mother who is still up to no good. His thought of the little girl becoming corrupt because she was in an environment with no hope of achieving success. The longer she is there, the more damage is done to her self-esteem and self-worth. She could easily fall into a life identical to the one that her mother carved out for herself. These thoughts motivated him to continue to save those that he could—and rid the world of the ones who perpetuate the problems.

Once he was in the cruiser and in service, he drove straight to West Virginia Avenue to search for Connie. He went south to the

1300 block where he saw her leaning into the passenger window of a silver Jeep Cherokee that was stopped on the corner at Owen Place. Briscoe could not see the attraction any man would have for Connie. Her teeth protruded from her mouth, were crooked, and appeared razor-sharp like a reptile. But she claims to be called 'Golden head' because of the great way she performs fellatio. However, her mouth is scary looking. You would think she would hurt your private part instead of giving pleasure. In addition to her wrecked grill, she is skinny as a rail, and looks like she is suffering from AIDS. Her eyes are always yellow or red, and the dark skin on her face is covered with bumps. *Go figure,* he thought as he made a u-turn and pulled in behind the Cherokee.

Some men have a beautiful woman at home and they come out here and mess with something like Connie . . . unbelievable, he reasoned. When he pulled in behind the Cherokee the driver took his foot off the brake and applied it to the accelerator and slowly drove off.

Briscoe pulled up to Connie and spoke to her in a friendly manner, "Look at you girl. Out here doing wrong."

"Aw Officer Briscoe, you know how I do."

"I know Connie. I need your help with something. Get in and let's go somewhere where we can talk."

She opened the passenger door and got in. He drove off in the direction of Mount Olivet Road.

"How are you Connie?" he asked with genuine concern.

"I'm good, just doin what I do."

"I know that's right," he said. They were exchanging pleasantries as Connie slouched down in the seat and looked around trying to make sure nobody saw her in the car as he steered the cruiser to the rear of Webb Elementary School. He often went there to get out of the view of the public and complete paperwork. It was completely closed off from the public view, and nobody would or should, be back there. Once in the rear of the school, Connie relaxed and not as fearful of being seen.

"Wow Officer Briscoe you bring me back here like one of them tricks, are you gonna try to fuck me?" she laughed.

"That's funny, but no. I want to talk to you about something that we are working on," he said as he studied her body language and facial expression. He had to do this right, because a trick like Connie could cause his demise.

"You've been good to me and you always treat me like I'm somebody. So I'll try to do whatever I can for you."

Connie was referring to how Briscoe went out of his way on more than one occasion to help her with personal problems and how he allows her to work the streets without harassing her or locking her up. Briscoe is a veteran who knows how to use street people to his benefit. Besides, he tries to treat everybody with the respect that all humans deserve.

"I wanted to start by getting some information about somebody," he said.

"Okay, that's cool. Who?" she sat up and prepared to listen.

"Do you know Janice Russell?"

"That live on 18th Street?" she asked.

"Yeah," he said.

"Yeah I know her. What about her?"

"Well first off, what is she slinging from her house?" He was going to keep the initial conversation on drug related issues, then work his way into what he really wanted to know.

"She deal'n crack. The only one in the area too, cause that nigga she deal'n for made sure a' dat."

He knew the answer to the next question but wanted to confirm it with Connie, "Who is she working for?"

"Brick and his crew; and they won't let nobody else sell nut'n out here."

"How long has she been working for him?"

"It been a minute since that white girl got her hooked up wit him," she was referring to the white woman who Briscoe watched go into Janice's house when he pulled up on Brick.

"Do you know the white girl's name?" he asked.

"It's Christine."

"Do you know her last name?"

"I think Shepherd or Sherman or sumt'n like that, I know it start wit a S," she said as she strained trying to recall Christine's last name.

"That's cool Connie, I can find it. What do you mean Brick won't let anybody else sell drugs around here?"

"No, not all drugs, just crack. He said if he catch anybody else round here sell'n crack he gonna fuck em up. He said if anybody buy from em and he see it, he gonna fuck em up too," she said with a tinge of anger in her voice.

"So everybody has to go all the way to 18th Street to get their crack?" he asked slightly surprised that Brick would attempt to regulate in such a manner.

"They better, or dem niggas gonna do to em what they did to that dude in the alley last week."

"You mean Kenneth Johnson?" he asked, recalling that he was the young man killed on Thursday night, before his two nights off.

"Yeah, that's him, Kenny. He was sell'n crack up on Montello Avenue when dem two boys from Brick crew seen him and chased him into da alley. They said they beat him to death wit a baseball bat. Now nobody try'na sell nut'n cause they scared."

"How well do you know Janice?" he was now ready to move the conversation to Janice's other activities.

"We jive ah'ight. I used to hang wit her sometime, but she got some issues."

"What kind of issues?" he could see it was going to take a little prodding to get everything he wanted out of Connie. For some reason her tone changed when he got down to her relationship with Janice.

"That punk ass nigga she got livin' up in there for one," she was referring to Johnny Simmons. "He is just a creepy dude and I don't like the way he use her," she said with a frown on her face like she smelled something rotten.

"How does he treat her?" Briscoe was very interested in the answer.

"He always bummin' money off her and then he fuck other women in the house wit her right there. He tell her if she really love him she a join in and fuck em too."

"Does she?" he asked.

"Yeah sometimes. I went over there one night and he was eat'n this girl's pussy right on the sofa. Janice daughter was in the house. She was the one dat answered the door and let me in."

"Damn!" Briscoe exclaimed, "where was Janice?"

"She was right there let'n the girl eat her pussy while dat punk was doin da girl," she said.

"And her daughter was just in there in the middle of all that?" he was starting to feel disturbed thinking about what else that little girl has had to endure.

"Dat was nut'n compared to other things Janice let that girl see. It's a rumor round here that Janice was pimpin' her. Men were comin' to her house and sleepin' wit dat girl for money."

That news really pissed Briscoe off. He had to use every bit of restraint inside of him not to show his emotions.

"Have you ever seen this yourself?" he asked.

"No, but I think it's true. Cause Janice be havin' sex wit women and men in front of her and you know Johnny been fuckin her for a while."

Connie might be a crack ho, but she is honest and seems to have her ear to the street.

"Is that an old rumor?" he asked.

"No, they was talkin' bout that the other day after Johnny went to court and didn't get no time."

Briscoe was fuming inside. He wondered how early in that child's life was she exposed to the madness of this world.

"What kind of person is Janice's daughter?" he was somewhat afraid to hear the answer, but he had to know.

"Oh Shauna is a good girl. She sweet, and one of da few kids nowadays who call you Ma'am. I like her."

He was happy to hear that, because to him that meant there was still hope for her.

"What about Janice's family? Does she get along with them?" he wanted to know that somebody could take care of the little girl if it came down to it.

"I don't think she get along wit none of em. But her moms love Shauna and always threaten to take Janice to court to get custody."

That was good news to Briscoe because it let him know that somebody would care for the girl and try to raise her right.

"Will you talk to Janice anytime soon?" he asked, even though he figured she would see her soon because Connie smokes crack every day.

"Yeah; I told you she was the only place to get crack from," she laughed out loud.

Briscoe laughed along with her and said, "Connie you are so crazy." Then he fallaciously said, "Don't let her know that I have been asking about her okay? We are setting up an operation to take down Brick. Janice will probably be given a deal as long as she cooperates."

"Shiiit, you don't have to worry bout me sayin' a damn thing. If they knew I talked to you, I wouldn't be round to tell you bout it. Dem niggas would kill me for sure."

He trusted Connie with that, because he was well aware of the code in the street about talking to the police.

"I might need you to do a couple of things for me; I'll make sure you get compensated," he said, trying to sound official.

"What kind a things?" she cocked her head and eagerly listened.

"Well, I want you to go over to Janice's house and get some names for me. The names of the people coming through there having sex with the little girl and the names of the people that help her with the drugs," he was looking intently at Connie while making this request.

"What kinda compensation are you talk'n bout?"

There it is, the business side of the crack ho coming out. He knew it would be a matter of economics to get her on board.

"I have to see what the Lieutenant is willing to pay, but I will fight to make sure it is worth your while," he impressed himself with how official it all sounded.

"Okay, when do you want me to start?"

He wanted to say right now, but he already told her that he has to see how much the department was willing to pay.

"Well, you could start now if you want to, but I won't know until the morning how much they are willing to pay."

"Okay, I'll start goin' over there tomorrow. I'll get the information and you can pay me when they agree."

That was music to his ears.

"Thanks Connie, you are going to be a big help," he had plans for her and this was just the beginning.

"Now do you want a discount blow job? SIKE!" she laughed. She enjoyed watching him squirm.

"Maybe in another life," he said laughing along with her.

He then gave her his cell phone number and told her to call him anytime day or night.

"Thanks Officer Briscoe, I'll call you tomorrow. I'm a get out right here and walk back to West Virginia so give me some time before you pull off," she wanted to be sure that nobody sees her leave the school at the same time as a cop.

"Okay, I'll wait. Be safe and have a good night. Thanks a lot Connie."

"You welcome, I don't mind doin it for you," she was sincere, and was already thinking about the money she was going make.

Briscoe went into service and answered a few radio runs, while patrolling his beat. As things slowed down and it got to be near 1:00 a.m. he went over to 18th Street to do surveillance on Janice Russell's house. He pulled his cruiser into the familiar spot that he always used—close enough to see, yet far enough away so as not to spook anybody. He intended to just sit there and watch the people who came and went, but after about fifteen minutes he noticed a few people go up and knock on the door but receive no answer. He could see lights on in the house, but thought perhaps Janice was asleep. The crack fiends will have to make it until tomorrow or find somewhere else to get up. Since he was parked, he decided to complete the family disturbance report he had from the previous radio run on L Street. It involved a brother and sister arguing over the TV. How stupid was it for him to have to write a report for something so trivial, but the directives were clear. Anytime there was any type of domestic dispute a report had to be generated. So he turned on the map light in the cruiser and began filling in the report form. Periodically he looked up from the report and studied his surroundings to ensure that no one was approaching him or violating the law. He looked up on one occasion and watched as a white male emerged from Janice's home. The man was about six feet tall and wore a suit. *It's a little late for a business call from an insurance agent,* he thought. The thick framed glasses he wore looked somehow familiar to Briscoe. He could not hear what was said at the door, but Janice stood and watched as he got into his Mercedes 500 SL and drove off. Briscoe turned off the map light and followed the vehicle.

When he caught up to the Mercedes, he realized from the license plate the person driving was in some way connected to the city government. He either worked in a high level position or had a close contact in a high level position. Tags, like the one on the Mercedes, were reserved for city council members, high ranking city management officials, Mayoral cabinet members, judges, prosecutors, and other people high up on the city's food chain. Briscoe wrote the tag number down. He decided to run the information on the computer in the station where he didn't have to put in his access code. He did not want his name to be associated with a tag check on the vehicle. *The man looks very familiar to him. When he runs the tag and gets his name he can pinpoint who he is and where he knows him from.* Briscoe followed the Mercedes out to Bladensburg Road, and then broke off for the station to run the information in the DMV database.

He arrived at the station and parked around back near the downstairs entrance. As he exited his vehicle officer White came out the station.
"Hi Antonio, what's up?"
"Oh nothing much, just came in to check some email," he lied.
"I saw you at the party Saturday night," she said.
"Oh yeah? Why didn't you speak?"
"You had your girlfriend with you and I didn't want to cause no problems."
"It wouldn't have been a problem."
"Oh yes it would have. Women can sense those sorts of things about each other," she winked.
He thought about her statement, and figured she was right, especially after the way Monica acted with the tall redbone at his parent's home.
"I guess you're right. You women seem to have a sixth sense when it comes to your men."
"I just wish you were my man. You looked so damn good in your swimming trunks. I wanted to give myself to you. Hell, I want to right now," she licked her lips.
"Karen you know that can't happen."
"Why not Antonio? You always say that, but I don't understand why we can't be together," she stood looking into his eyes expecting an answer.
"I told you a long time ago that I don't believe in workplace romances. I feel that colleagues should remain professional and leave all that other stuff at home."
"That's what I'm saying also Antonio. We will be professional at work and lovers at home," she said seriously.
"Come on Karen, you know what I'm saying. The only thing that comes out of situations like that is hurt feelings. When it's over we wouldn't even be able to work together anymore."
"Who said it would ever be over?"
"All things have an ending Karen and we would also."
"So you and that girlfriend of yours are going to be over someday?"

"I hope not. I hope to marry her and have children when the time is right."

"I like you so fucking much that I stroke my pussy to the thought of you and you don't even care! You can just tell me how much you love her," the tone of her voice made Briscoe a little uncomfortable. He almost gave into her before he met Monica and boy, is he glad he didn't.

"Karen I can't help the situation we are in. Being co-workers puts us off limits as a couple, but we will always be friends."

"I have enough friends Antonio; I want you as my man; I want to feel you inside of me in every way imaginable," her eyes were fixed on his . . . pleading.

"That's flattering, but it just could never be. So does that mean you no longer want to be friends?" he asked, putting her on the spot.

She looked at him and he held her gaze without either of them speaking a word for a few seconds that felt like a moment of silence for the dearly departed.

"Damn Antonio! Why can't you just give me a chance? I'm not like the other women around here."

"You didn't answer my question," he said still staring into her eyes.

"Damn it boy, you know I'm gonna still be your friend. I just don't know what you do to me that I can't stop thinking about you," she said disappointedly. "Well, if that girl do you wrong and you need somebody to run to, I'll be here. I'm yours whenever you want me," she was sincere.

Karen was sought after by many guys on the department, but she didn't want to go down as an easy mark so she wouldn't date any of them. Briscoe's kind and encouraging demeanor, and the fact he never hit on her or any of the other female officers, attracted her to him. Female officers could feel completely comfortable around him because he treated them as officers first and women second. They were truly his equal. In a male-dominated field it was refreshing to have a man as dedicated and successful at his craft as Briscoe treat them like professional police officers.

"Cool, because I don't want to lose your friendship over our personal lives. We can meet at the Dunkin Donuts for coffee and hang like we used to if you want," he smiled at her.

She said, "Okay, we can hook up around 4:30 a.m. if we ain't tied up on anything."

"That's my girl," he said as he gave her a hug.

Briscoe continued into the building and Karen got into the car with her partner, Officer Shaniqua Williams.

"Girl, are you still trying to get that sexy ass brother? Give it up, he got a woman," Williams smirked.

"I'm just gonna play it cool but I'm gonna get that."

"I heard him say it's not going to happen."

"That's what his mouth is saying right now, but I'll get it. I know he want me too, and besides, I got skills like that," White said laughing and holding up her hand for a high five.

"Go for it ho," Williams said as she slapped her five.

Briscoe thought about Karen as he walked up the stairs to the main station where the computer was. He knew that if Karen ever got him alone somewhere she would get what she has been begging for. He would not be able to contain himself because the girl is so damn hot. The way her body is calling out to him, it would be too hard to resist. Lately, it seems that she is stepping up her game. Every time she sees him, alone she puts a move on him. Maybe her woman's intuition is telling her that if she gets him alone, it's only a matter of time before he gives in. He asked her to meet for coffee near the end of the shift because he may be able to show her that he will never be interested in her the way she desires. As long as he stays out of her house and keep her out of his, things should not get out of control.

He stepped up to the computer terminal that sat on the counter adjacent to the entrance to the cellblock. As he figured, it was already logged on with the station's generic access code. Nothing that he runs will come back to his name if an audit was conducted. He brought up the DMV database and entered the two digits from the tag. When the name came up on the screen, his jaw dropped nearly to the floor. *Phillip Danielson! He is the AUSA in charge of sex crimes.* It hit Briscoe like a bucket of ice water on a cold December morning and it explained the case against Johnny Simmons. What kind of dirt did Simmons have on him to maintain his freedom? The thoughts were racing through his mind. He wondered how deep the corruption went. Well, it is too late for him to seek an investigation, because when bodies start dropping there would be too many eyes on the common denominator. Danielson will just have to suffer the consequences of his actions. He jotted down Danielson's home address on a piece of paper, put it in his wallet and went out on patrol.

14

"Locked up they won't let me out. I'm locked up they won't let me out," went the sound of Briscoe's cell phone with the Akon ringtone.

"Hello."

"Hi Officer Briscoe, its Connie, did I wake you up?"

"No, don't worry about it, it's cool. What's up?" he tried clearing the cob webs of sleep and focus on the voice on the other end of the phone.

"I was at Janice house and I got some stuff to tell you."

"Okay, do you want to tell me now or do you want to meet later tonight?"

"Uh, what did your people say?" she asked in reference to the money.

"They said to start you with twenty dollars and raise it up with the level of information you provide," he hoped that would be enough to get her started.

He didn't want to go too high, but he didn't want to underestimate her intelligence either. Some confidential informants are paid very well by the department. He wasn't sure if Connie had knowledge of any of them and what they were paid. Knowing Connie's affinity for crack, twenty dollars sounded good. She might have to blow two johns to get that much.

"Okay, I can work wit dat," she said enthusiastically, "but I don't have a lot a minutes on my cell phone, can we meet tonight?" she asked.

"Sure, I can pick you up at the same spot on West Virginia Avenue," he offered.

"How bout I just meet chu in back of da school?" she offered.

"Okay, if that works best for you. I'll be there at 11;15 p.m."

"That's a bet, I'll see you then," she said and hung up the phone.

It was 1:00 p.m. and Briscoe had only slept for about three hours. He normally turned the ringers off on his house and cell phones, but since he was expecting to hear from Connie he left the cell phone on. He knew that he would have to get in the habit of leaving that one on because Connie was going to be working for him. She would need to have access to him 24/7. He started to think about the people he killed over the past few months. Normally, when they started to creep into his thoughts, he would bury them deeper and think of more pleasant times. He tried to shake their screams and cries, but it was more difficult than normal. He struggled internally to gain control over his thoughts until he fell asleep.

"5 Baker 44 investigate the suspicious person standing in front of Brown Middle School," the call came from the dispatcher. When he arrived on scene there was a shadowy figure standing on the front steps. His clothes were tattered and he looked a bloody mess. His features were distorted and his body looked bent and broken. Briscoe stopped the scout car at the base of the steps, about forty-five feet from the subject. When he got out of the car and started to approach, the person turned and walked into the school.

Briscoe called out, "Hey you, stop right there!"

But the subject continued into the dark school. When Briscoe reached the door he held his flashlight in his left hand and filled his right hand with his Glock 9mm service pistol. When he stepped inside, an eerie feeling crept into his soul. The building felt cold and the odor that permeated the air was similar to that of the morgue. He focused his eyes and readied himself for whatever he might have to deal with.

Now, which way did that dude go? He looked down at a trail of bloody footprints that led down a corridor to the left. He followed the prints to where they ended at the cafeteria. He stepped inside and scanned the large room with his flash light. There was no sign of the person. The footprints mysteriously ended in the middle of the room. While Briscoe was looking down at the last foot print, he felt someone or something's, hot breath on his neck. When he turned around, there standing face to face with him was Johnny Simmons. His face was badly beaten and it looked as though something had eaten most of it away. Johnny grabbed him around the neck with one hand and squeezed. His grip was so tight that Briscoe could not break it by striking hard on Johnny's forearm. He struggled to break free from his grip, but it was like a vise that was being wound tighter, clamping his trachea and blocking the flow of oxygen to his brain. Johnny lifted him off the floor with just the one hand that was still tightly clamped around his neck and looked into his eyes with blackened eyes that appeared void of a soul.

Just then Briscoe raised his gun and fired three rounds directly into Johnny's morose face. Johnny barely flinched, but he released his grip from Briscoe's neck, dropping him to the floor. He quickly jumped to his feet and fired several rounds into Johnny but none of them seemed to affect him.

"Why the fuck won't you die?" he screamed.

But Johnny did not speak. He just stood looking with lifeless eyes directly into Briscoe. The next thing that Briscoe knew, he was being pulled from behind. He fell to the floor as the panic and fear coursed through his body like the rush of the wind during a category five hurricane. He whipped his head around to look at the badly burned Sebastian Weaver pulling him toward a room with a red hue emanating from within. He fired a shot from his service weapon into the back of Weaver's head but it had no affect and he continued to drag him toward the room. As he struggled to break free from Weaver's grip he noticed that there were many other people standing and looking down at him with lifeless eyes. He recognized all of them.

"I killed you, and you, and you too."

Then he fired his weapon into Weaver's back until it was empty, causing him to release his grip. He scuffled to his feet, just to be knocked back to the floor. This time several of the ghoulish men in the cafeteria grabbed him and raised him above their heads and walked toward the red room. The closer they got to the room, the hotter it became. The heat was intense, and a rush of sadness and doom fell over Briscoe as he screamed out to Jesus for help. When they reached the door the men dropped him to the floor and began to bite him all over his body. They were ripping the flesh from his body with their teeth. Briscoe screamed out in agony as the pain shot through his body like lightning from above. He was powerless to stop them. Just then someone opened the door that held back the redness within, to reveal a raging fire. A beast with the face of a man, teeth of a lion, and hooves where feet should be, emerged carrying a scepter. The hair that covered his head and most of his body was coarse, with insects crawling throughout. The beast spoke,

"You are coming to meet your destiny. I am your master, and I am taking you to your reward for getting all of them off the streets. Ha Ha Ha," he laughed with a deep guttural voice.

"Noooo!" Briscoe screamed.

"It's too late, you are all mine," the creature said laughing from the depths of his loins.

He picked Briscoe up like a rag doll and carried him into the flames of the red room.

Briscoe woke in a pool of sweat. His heart was beating as if it was trying to escape his chest. He was trembling; his mind was trying to process where he was and what just happened. He looked around the room and noted that it was his bedroom. He looked at the clock, which read 5:45 p.m.

I had a nightmare, but it seemed so real. He laid there staring at the ceiling thinking about what the dream meant. *Could it be that God is trying to tell him something? Or maybe the devil is playing with his mind.* It was so frightening that he rolled out of the bed onto his knees and started to pray to God, seeking strength and protection from the devil and all harm. He trembled the entire twenty minutes he remained in prayer.

Afterwards, he got to his feet and started to move about the house, but his thoughts were fixed on the nightmare that jolted him awake. He eventually shook the thoughts and buried them in the back of his mind. He went on the Internet to do research on AUSA Danielson and the Sex Crimes Division of the Unites States Attorney's Office for Washington, DC. He wanted to know how long Danielson has been an AUSA and how long he has been in charge of the sex crimes division. He was trying to learn where he grew up and where he went to school. He is ultimately going to learn what circles he run in and what his home situation is.

But first he has to confirm what he was doing coming out of Janice Russell's house at 1:00 a.m. Briscoe was sure it had nothing to do with court business. He had an idea, but he had to know the facts. If the man has a drug problem, he can figure a way to anonymously expose him, get him disbarred, and removed from the criminal justice process.

Hypocrisy has no place anywhere in the criminal justice system, especially in the high court, where the fate of the guilty is apportioned and the making whole of victims is pondered. How many deals has this guy made because of his habit? Are there other offenders that he let walk because they knew about his propensity for crack? Mister Danielson has to be held to a higher standard than the others. Maybe he shouldn't die for what he has done, but he definitely has to pay.

15

When Briscoe arrived at work, he was greeted in the parking lot by Officer Keyes, who said, "Congratulations big boy."

"Congratulations for what?" Briscoe asked dumbfounded.

"You're on the VCU task force. They posted the list earlier this evening."

"Damn that was quick," he was genuinely surprised. He didn't think it would be determined for at least a few more days or even a couple of weeks.

"Yeah man, they want to get started soon because the predator is the Chief's number one priority," Keyes said.

"That's cool with me; I'm ready to do what I can. Thanks Keyes."

"No problem, just catch that motherfucker so things can get back to normal."

Briscoe went into the locker room, changed into his uniform and went into roll call. On the way into the roll call room he looked at his name on the VCU detail memo and noted the other names listed. To his surprise Karen White was on the list along with Officers Leroy James and Mark Mathis from the day shift. The memo said they are to report Wednesday at 1000 hours to VCU headquarters in plain clothes. Since it is Monday night and he works the midnight tour, this will be his last night on the street in the 5th Precinct for a while. He wondered what his assignment and duties would be. Whatever it is, it will keep him close to the case allowing him inside knowledge of the progress being made.

Once roll call was concluded he relieved the car and went to Dunkin Donuts for a cup of coffee prior to meeting with Connie.

Karen came into Dunkin Donuts, gave him a warm embrace and said, "Baby, we are going to be working together on a high profile case. How bout that?"

"Yeah that is something," he said with little enthusiasm.

He wondered if she would be a problem for him when he is trying to do his mission with VCU, *Is she going to be a pest? How will I distance myself from her when it is time to do what I do?*

"I'm so hyped about this. I was surprised they picked me. It's going to be great working closely with you again," she said smiling.

"Yeah, me too. Well, I have to get out of here. I have some business to take care of before we get busy. I'll see you later," he said and left.

He decided that he couldn't worry about Karen right now. If she became a nuisance he would just have to deal with it.

He pulled to the back of Webb Elementary School and turned off his lights. It was 11:10 p.m. and Connie should be on her way. He took twenty dollars from his wallet and put it in his left shirt pocket. He did not want Connie to see him reach into his wallet and take the money out. She may wonder why he would pay her from his own stash. Everything had to appear to come from the Metropolitan Police Department, not Officer Briscoe personally. He looked at the time on the car's dash and thought how slow five minutes pass when you were waiting for something. He did not expect her to be on time, so he concocted a lie for his sergeant that gave him time before he went in service. If she shows before 11:30 p.m., it will be a miracle. Just as he was thinking about how long it will take, she walked around the corner, up to the vehicle and got in.

"Hey Officer Briscoe," she said cheerfully.

"Hey Connie, look at you, all on time and everything," he said playfully.

"I'm about my word baby boy," she said, grinning that raggedy, bucktooth smile.

"What do you have for me?" he asked.

"You know I said dudes be buying Shauna?"

"Yes."

"Well, I went over there today and this dude came in while I was sit'n on the sofa. He went down the hall wit Janice and then she called Shauna down there. The next thing I know Janice came back in the livin room wit me, and the dude and Shauna stayed down the hall in the back bedroom."

"Who is the dude?"

"His name is Sonny Garfield," she said proudly, knowing she earned her money.

"Is he any kin to Janice?"

"No, I don't think so. I know him from round here and I'm

almost sure he ain't no kin to her."

"How old is he?"

"He about forty, I think."

Briscoe's blood started to boil. *What the fuck do these old ass niggas want with babies?* "Where does he live?" Briscoe asked.

"He live over on D Street somewhere. I got his tag number if you want it."

Briscoe looked at her with a big smile on his face, "Connie I could kiss you. That was good thinking baby."

"I figured that would be what you want me to do," she said proudly.

"You did great Connie. Is there anything else?"

"I think he paid her money for Shauna," she continued, "cause when she came back in the livin room she was put'n somethin' down her bra. The only thing I put in there besides my titties is money. And they was back there for a long time. When he finished and left, Shauna went into the bathroom for a long time."

Connie had a sad expression on her face while relaying that bit of information.

"Okay Connie, thanks a lot," he said as he reached into his pocket and handed her the twenty dollars. She took the money and handed him a piece of paper with Sonny's license plate number written on it.

"So, how bout that kiss?" she asked laughing.

He laughed along with her and said, "Girl you are so crazy. But you are the bomb. Keep up the good work."

She got out of the car and disappeared into the darkness. *He was now convinced the rumor was true about Janice selling her daughter to dirty old men. How could Janice accept that grown men were violating her daughter for money? How could she allow Shauna's innocence and dignity to be cast to the wolves so early in her development? She is not giving her a chance to choose her own path; instead she has chosen a destructive one for her.* Briscoe could only hope that the damage done to the girl so far isn't beyond repair.

He needed to find Sonny Garfield and pay him a visit. If he can't stop Janice right now, he could at least try to keep the dirty dicks away from the girl. He entered the tag number Connie gave him into his cruiser's computer, and it came back to Sonny, with an address of 7820 D Street. Briscoe decided to take a ride over and see how Mister Garfield is living.

When he drove into the block, the dope boys started to walk off because they thought he was coming to get them for selling drugs. Briscoe located Sonny's car in front of his row house. He saw a light on inside. He surveyed the street and the climate. It was a typical inner city block, complete with all the problems. There would always be somebody up or out on that block. If he is going to move on Sonny it will have to be away from his home. But right now, he just needed some better intelligence on the man. So he parked the car on the corner and walked up to Sonny's front door and rang the bell.

"Yes, who is it?" a voice inside inquired.

"It's the police," Briscoe answered.

"The police? Hold on one second," Briscoe could hear fumbling while somebody was trying to undo several locks.

When the door opened, a pudgy, potbellied man about five-feet-eight-inches tall was standing there in a wife-beater and shorts. The hair on top of his head was gone, but the sides were full and well maintained. He had a long thick mustache and beard that put you in mind of Fu Manchu.

"Yes officer, how can I help you?" Sonny asked.

"We got a call for a domestic violence assault at this location," Briscoe lied.

"Are you sure you got the right address? I'm the only one here," Sonny said.

"This is 7820 D Street right?" Briscoe asked.

"Yes, but I live alone and I haven't had any company all night." Sonny looked puzzled.

"This is the address I was given. The call came in from a concerned neighbor. I just have to come in and check to make sure nobody is injured inside," he recited police protocol.

"Officer I told you I've been here all night alone, but if you must, come on in," he stepped aside and allowed Briscoe in.

Sonny closed the door and said, "Where do you want to start?"

"You can show me the basement and then we will work our way up."

They went down the narrow staircase to the low-ceilinged basement. From there they went to the main floor, where Briscoe came in on and he checked to ensure that nobody was there. They then went to the top floor where there were three small bedrooms and a bathroom in the hallway. Briscoe was confident nobody was there. From the looks of the place, nobody was ever there besides Sonny.

"What kind of work do you do sir?" Briscoe asked.

"I'm a plumber by trade, but right now I'm out on workman comp. I was injured on a contract job my company was doing for the city."

"Do you have kids?" Briscoe asked.

"Yeah, I have a son and a daughter who live with my ex-wife."

"How old are they?"

Sonny started to feel a little uncomfortable with the line of questions and asked, "Why are you asking me these questions?"

"I just wonder how you would feel if a forty year old man was fucking your twelve year old daughter," Briscoe said as he looked raptly into Sonny's eyes.

A bead of sweat appeared above Sonny's brow.

"Why are you sweating Sonny?"

Now he was sweating profusely and his heart was racing faster than his thoughts. 'How does this cop know my name? What else does he know?'

"Calm down Sonny, I'm just going to ask you some questions. Based on your answers I will decide if you are going to jail for a very long time or if you are going to go on with life as usual. Do you understand me?"

"Not really; I don't have any idea what you are talking about," he said nervously with a cracking voice.

"So you want to play it that way. We both know you have been fucking that little girl on 18th Street with her mother's sick ass pimping her to you. Now what part of that don't you understand?" Briscoe barked at him.

"I . . . ," he started but was interrupted by Briscoe.

"Shut the fuck up with your lies. I'm inclined to lock your ass up right now and let them deal with you in prison. I'm here trying to give you a chance to redeem yourself and save your family the embarrassment and heartache. Now do you understand?" Briscoe's ire stirred.

"Yes sir," Sonny said sheepishly.

"I'm not here to build a case against you. I'm here to find out some facts so we can remove that girl from the house and put her in a safer environment. Now, if you prefer I can lock you up and you can get an attorney and then you can deal with the consequences of that. Or you can cooperate, keep your mouth shut and nobody will know anything about you. It's your move, what do you want to do?" Briscoe stared him down.

"I don't want to go to jail. My kids would be destroyed if any of this got out. What do you want me to do?" he asked despairingly.

"First I want you to stay away from that little girl. Never go to Janice's house again. Do you understand me?"

"Yes sir. I'll never step foot in there again," he said in agreement.

"Secondly, you don't speak a word of this to anybody. You don't let Janice or anybody else know the police are watching her house."

"I won't say a word," he vigorously agreed.

Briscoe needed time to check Sonny's record before he decided what to do with him. He also wasn't sure that he could trust him to keep his mouth shut and that alone dictates what he must do with Sonny.

"I need a phone number for you Sonny, because I want you to meet me at my office later tonight."

"I thought you said I wasn't going to be arrested," Sonny said panicked.

"You're not going to be arrested; I just want to get some information from you. I don't have the time right now. I promise you that when this investigation is completed your name will not be anywhere in it. I give you my word on that, as long as you cooperate and don't yank my chain." Briscoe was very convincing.

"Okay sir, I won't jerk you around. I'll cooperate and do anything you want. I just can't go to jail again. I'm sorry. The best number to reach me on is 689-9064," his voice trembled more than his hands.

"I'll call you in about an hour or so and you can come to my office. If not, we can do it tomorrow. But it has to be soon because we are trying to move on this matter quickly," Briscoe had to get things set up for Sonny.

"Yes sir I understand and I'll answer no matter what time you call."

"I'll be in touch," Briscoe said as he departed the house.

Sonny locked the door behind him, went to the kitchen cabinet, and poured himself a straight shot of Crown Royal to steady his nerves, and his trembling hands.

Briscoe reluctantly went into service, knowing that he would have to answer radio runs, but he knew that he could not justify being out of service too much longer. True to the nature of the job, he was dispatched on a run to investigate an alarm sounding. He perked up a bit because he knew that most of those calls were accidental and only took a few minutes to complete. He quickly responded to the call, and just as he thought, the homeowner set the alarm off accidently by coming downstairs after it was set and did not enter the code to disable it in time. He held the run for awhile and went to the station to run Sonny's criminal history on the computer. He learned that Sonny spent a period of time in prison for first degree child sexual abuse and he was also on the sex offense registry. He also had other charges with various levels of child molestation. It became clear to Briscoe that Sonny was not going to stop himself from messing with children so he would have to stop him.

He logged off the computer and went back into service, clearing the alarm call with the dispatcher. He would deal with Sonny tonight before he has a chance to open his big yap. He could not run the risk of being compromised by the only person he has ever approached openly and allowed to live. He decided how he was going to deal with Sonny Garfield and drove to the pay phones in front of the Safeway Food store in Hechinger Mall. He called Sonny and said, "Mr. Garfield, this is the officer who was there earlier."

"Yes sir?" Sonny shakily replied.

"I need you to meet me at 21st & M Streets down the end near the Arboretum. I'm involved in something and I'll meet you there in about ten minutes," Briscoe ordered.

"I thought you wanted me to come to your office?" he questioned.

"I got tied up on something else and my supervisor came out and gave me a list of questions to ask you and some photographs for you to look at. He told me to get this done now, but I can't make it back to your house because of what we have going on over here," Briscoe hoped he sounded convincing.

"Photographs of what?" Sonny became even more apprehensive.

"Of other people we think might be paying Janice for sex with her daughter.

"Okay, I can be there in a few minutes," Sonny said defeated.

"Just park down at the end of the block next to the Arboretum and I'll be there. Once we finish you never have to hear from us again. I hope you learned something from this."

"I sure did and you won't have to worry about me. I will never do anything like that again," he said relieved.

Briscoe thought, *Yeah right you won't do it again.*

A guy like Sonny could never stop himself from abusing young girls because that is what turns him on. As long as he is able to get an erection he will mess with them. In this case he was right; he will never do it again. As a matter of fact, he will never do anything again. Briscoe wondered if Sonny had molested his own daughter. *Is that why she doesn't live with him?* But he knew that in most cases, guys like Sonny would never do those things to his own children. It was something that he didn't quite understand completely, but he knew that people who committed such crimes were evil and needed to be taken out of mainstream society permanently.

Briscoe drove by the substation and checked to see if anybody was there. He got out of the car and walked inside where the security guard was and he spoke to him as he went to the restroom. He spent about five minutes making small talk with the guard before returning to his cruiser. He called the dispatcher and requested a personal at the substation. She granted him the personal and he drove over to where he was to meet Sonny.

He drove around the area checking to see who was out and what the traffic situation was like. It was well after midnight and there were only a few people out on the streets in the residential neighborhood. He checked the immediate area as he approached Sonny's vehicle which was parked on M Street along the Arboretum's fence. There were apartment buildings in the distance to the front and open space behind. It was as secluded as he was going to get without alerting Sonny that something was not quite right. He approached from the front and pulled alongside Sonny's vehicle where the two drivers could talk with nothing between them.

"Turn your vehicle off," he said to Sonny. Sonny shut the engine off and looked at Briscoe.

"Are you ready?" Briscoe asked him.

"Yes sir, I'm ready."

Briscoe reached into his backpack and pulled out his faithful, silenced Sig Saur.

"I want to know if you recognize this," Briscoe said as he lifted the powerful firearm and pointed it directly into the surprised eyes of his prey.

Before Sonny could utter a word, he fired two quick shots into his stunned face, ripping bone, cartilage, and brain matter. The force of the impact sent his head and torso to the right, as he fell over onto the seat, and blood splattered. Briscoe slowly drove off placing the gun back into his bag.

He picked up the radio and cleared his personal, "5 Baker 44, clear me from the personal, I'm 10-8," he voiced calmly.

"I copy 5 Baker 44, you're clear," the dispatcher acknowledged.

He went back into service without a second thought. He was there with Sonny for less than a minute, so if anybody saw his vehicle, they would barely be able to recall that he stopped.

16

When Briscoe completed his shift in the morning, he gave in and had breakfast with Officer White at Lucky's Diner. They were joined by Officer Mathis once he got out of roll call. They talked about their excitement to be on the serial predator task force and reminisced about some of the experiences they shared on the streets.

Mathis said, "Briscoe are you still dating that fine-ass CEO I saw you with at Sanford's party?" Karen frowned when he asked the question. The disappointment was written all over her face.

"Yeah man, that's my baby," Briscoe said beaming.

"She is so fine. Does she have any friends?" Mathis asked grinning.

"Fool, your ass is married. You better take care of home," Karen smirked.

"Hell, I might be married, but I'm not dead and out of the game yet."

"Why can't you married men just be happy with your wives? Ya'll always want more. One day you're gonna get one of those crazy bitches that's gonna come to your house and tear that motherfucker down," she said as though she was kicking some science to him.

"Well, I'm not the one that's married, my wife is," he joked.

Briscoe joined in with the laughter and Karen looked narrowly at him,

"Well Antonio I hope when you get married you will treat your wife with more respect."

"I was just laughing. How did I get dragged into it?"

"Because you are a man," she said with her best black sistah expression.

They ate and continued to talk until the alert tones went off on Mathis' radio. He was dispatched on a priority call for a man down at 21st & M Streets, who is bleeding in a parked car and appears to have been shot.

"Well, I got to go; this is my last day out here until after the task force. I'll see you guys at VCU tomorrow morning," Mathis said as he ran from Lucky's to respond to the call.

Briscoe asked Karen if she had her radio with her. She pulled it from her purse.

"Let's listen to that run, it sounds like a possible homicide," he said.

They listened as Mathis marked on scene along with other units, and then requested VCU, and a few moments later the Medical Examiner.

"Damn, the Board must have left dude on the scene," Karen said.

Briscoe was somewhat relieved that his body was not found until after his shift because he would have probably been the officer tasked with doing the report. He thought about the shell casings, and knew that they would be found. But even if they are not, the ballistics done on the slugs in his face will be matched to his gun, and they will know that Sonny was a victim of the predator. That will take a couple of days unless the detectives request a rush. But it doesn't matter because they don't know who they are looking for and there are still no witnesses.

"I'm glad dude didn't get killed during our shift because I sure didn't want to be held over today. I was ready to go home right after I found out that I was chosen for the task force," Karen said.

"Yeah I know. I started to take the last two hours off just to make sure I got out on time," he said.

They finished breakfast, gave each other a hug, and went their separate ways.

17

The FBI profiler came to VCU and met with Whitehead and Sutton. They gave her all the information they had on every one of the serial predator's crime scenes. They spent hours going over each victim, his criminal history, and the details of his death. They looked at crime scene photographs, the type of weapons used, and the time of death. The profiler made copies of various documents and photographs, and she noted the times of the killings. She told them that it would take her about a week to put something together, but she was positive that she could come up with a suspect profile that should give them some direction. They were pleased that she was eager to help.

It was not easy getting the Chief to agree. He personally felt that psychological profiling was no more than voodoo science and was merely a guessing game. He said they might as well get Miss Cleo to tell them who they are looking for. Whitehead, on the other hand, was convinced that there was some merit to the practice of psychological profiling. He had seen cases where it actually was effective. It couldn't do any harm, and at this point in his investigation, he was ready to consult Miss Cleo. This was by far his toughest case. Here is a guy who has seemingly no motive for killing his victims and that is what makes this case so difficult. Most homicides are rooted in a motive and the killer is always somehow connected to the victim. But in this case it is a person whom it appears had no personal contact with his victims until he introduced them to their end. *Someday he will slip and leave a witness or a piece of evidence that point directly to his identity. But how far down the road is that, and how many more dead thugs?*

"Agent Bell, we appreciate your help, and if you couldn't tell, I am at my wits end with this one," Whitehead said.

"Detective, I know how frustrating it can be. I am happy to lend a hand."

Special Agent Doctor Deborah Bell is a graduate of Howard University with a PhD in Clinical Psychology. She has been an FBI agent for fifteen years. She was recruited by the agency because of her undergraduate degree in psychology and her work in psychiatric hospital wards with the criminally insane. She has twenty years of experience in the field of psychology including previous, very accurate profiles of killers. She is one of the best the FBI has working in the field today. Her personal life is a whole different story. She is getting close to fifty and has never married or had children. She deals with a lot of regrets in her personal life; one being her unwillingness to put her career ambitions on hold to start a family. Now she feels she is past her prime and nobody would want to settle down with an old hag. But contrary to the way she views herself, she is a stunning woman. She looks younger than her years and her body is well-toned, thanks to the five hours she dedicates each week to the gym. She is sophisticated and intelligent, with a very warm personality and inviting demeanor. As a matter of fact, Whitehead liked her from the moment she stepped into the building. He thought about asking her out, but he was a professional first, and did not want to do anything to slow his case. Agent Bell could sense that he liked her a little bit more than professionally.

"Call me Jamie. I appreciate anything you can provide; it is very nice of you to help us with this," Whitehead said.

"Anytime Jamie; and you can call me Deborah. Here is my card, I'll put my cell number on here and you can reach me anytime you like," she was very suggestive, because she too was feeling Whitehead. And she noticed that he did not have a wedding ring on his finger.

He gave her his business card with his private cell number and said, "You can call me as soon as you have something and I will meet with you to go over it."

"That sounds like a winner to me. Take care Jamie and good luck with the case," she said as she gathered her belongings to depart.

Whitehead and Sutton walked her outside and said their goodbyes. They stood in front of the building and watched as she got into her car and drove from the parking lot.

"You want that pussy don't you playa?" Sutton suggested laughingly.

"Aw man go ahead with that," now it was Whitehead on the defensive.

"I can see it partner. You were drooling all over her. But she might be out of your league."

"Shiiiit, ain't nothing out of my league. I could have her if I want," Whitehead said confidently.

"I don't know partner, she looks like it might take a lot of maintenance to keep up."

"I doubt it; she is a woman like any other, and she needs loving too. Besides I couldn't get caught up in that right now anyway. But I can tell that she wouldn't mind going out with me."

"Oh-oh, here it goes. Alright professor, kick the ballistics. Where did you pick up on that? I was here the whole time and I didn't get that at all," Sutton said as he crossed his arms awaiting an answer.

"See young Skywalker (A Star Wars reference), there is where you must learn the intricate workings of the female psyche. When she gave me her personal cell number and told me to call anytime, that was an invitation into her personal space. She almost forgot that you were in the room. She focused most of her attention on me because she knew that I was digging her on more than a professional level," he spoke like a teacher to a student.

"Okay, I have to hand that one to you. But when will you have time to pursue all of that serious woman?"

"That's why I didn't ask her out. I wouldn't have time to pursue her like I really would want to."

Sutton did an exaggerated bow toward Whitehead grinning and said, "I'm sorry for doubting your skills Master Yoda; you the man, you the man."

They shared a laugh as they walked back inside and got back to putting together packets for the briefing of the task force that was convening tomorrow. They stopped putting together the packets for the three hours it took them to brief Agent Bell.

Each packet contains a brief synopsis of the victim and information about each crime scene. While they were in the conference room putting together the packets, Detective Feldman, the day shift on duty Detective, who caught the homicide on 21st & M Street, came in from the homicide scene.

"Hey fellas what's happening?" he said speaking as he passed by the conference room.

"Hey Feldman!" Sutton called out as he passed.

He stopped and stuck his head in the room and said, "What's up?"

"The case you caught this morning; what's up with it?" Sutton asked.

"A dude got popped sitting in his car. It looks like somebody walked or drove up and shot him in the face."

"So, it doesn't look like our boy does it?" Sutton asked.

"Not on the surface, but we did recover two .45 caliber shell casings. I'm about to run the decedent's history and then go from there. Nobody out there saw or heard a thing, but what else is new?" he asked sarcastically.

Whitehead and Sutton looked at each other when they heard .45 caliber and nobody heard anything.

"When will you get the ballistics back on the slugs?" Whitehead asked.

"I requested Mobile Crime to put a rush on that for me, so a couple a days."

"Well, good luck with it dude," Sutton expressed.

"Thanks," Feldman said as he continued down the hall.

Once Whitehead and Sutton finished with the packets, they finalized the strategy for the task force and left for the day. It was nearly 6:00 p.m. They decided to go to Union Station to have a drink at the Centre Café because they could unwind and check out all the honeys passing through on their way home from work.

18

It was after 9:00 a.m. when Whitehead and Sutton arrived at VCU to set up the roll call room for the arrival of the newly assembled task force. It would consist of twenty-eight uniform patrol officers and seven detectives from the patrol precincts. They laid out thirty-five information packets and set up a table with coffee, bagels, and pastries from Dunkin Donuts. Sutton set up a computer and projector to aid with the briefing. The first officer arrived at 9:45 a.m. Sutton told him to help himself to the refreshments that were provided. Over the next fifteen minutes the remainder of the newly-commissioned team arrived. Some officers knew others from the different precincts so this provided an atmosphere of familiarity and camaraderie.

Whitehead stood in front of the room and began by welcoming everybody and thanking them for volunteering to help with the case. As he delved deeper into the progress made thus far, Briscoe listened intently and took copious notes. If he was going to be this close, he would gather all the information he could to remain several steps ahead of the investigation. The briefing was detailed and very intense. Whitehead decided not to hold too much back from the task force. Perhaps there is a minuscule detail that would trigger something in one of the officers that leads his thoughts to a potential suspect. Everything there was to know about the investigation was being briefed at this moment. Whitehead then mentioned that he enlisted the help of the FBI's most prominent psychologist, who was working up a psychological profile on the serial predator.

Upon hearing that news, Briscoe's heart started to race and a thin layer of sweat formed on his forehead. This was not good news for him, because he knew how accurate many of these profiles were in the past with other serial cases. What would the profile reveal? How much will it resemble him? Will he have to change the method of his mission?

Damn, I was hoping they wouldn't use a profiler, he thought. The possibility was there, but he was sure the department would be against help from the FBI. He could only hope Whitehead would share the profile with the entire task force. The first portion of the briefing lasted about ninety minutes.

"Alright guys, let's take a break before we get into our strategy for catching the predator and your assignments. Take fifteen and we'll start back up say 11:45 a.m.," Whitehead said.

Karen, sitting next to Briscoe and said, "This is so exciting. I hope we are partners if that's how it's set up."

"Yeah," was Briscoe's non-enthusiastic response.

He stood up and went outside for a breath of fresh air while Karen was pulled aside by an officer she knew from the 6th Precinct. Briscoe stood in front of the building with a few of the smokers, and engaged in conversation, mostly about the case. His cell phone rang and he answered,

"Hello."

"Hey Officer Briscoe; it's Connie."

"Hi Connie, what's up?"

"I don't know if you heard, but they found Sonny dead yestaday."

"Yeah, I heard about that but I wasn't sure if that was the same dude. I didn't get a chance to check up on the person you gave me," Briscoe lied.

"It's him; he was found in his car shot."

"Do you know why somebody would want to hurt him?" Briscoe asked just to throw Connie off.

"I don't know, cause I don't know him like dat. But I never heard nobody say nut'n bout him like dat."

"I'm in a meeting right now. I don't know too much about that right now, but when I find something out I will let you know if you can help," he had to speak in a way as not to give rise to Connie's suspicion.

"I'll let you know if I hear anything on da street," Connie was really getting into her role of informant.

"Thanks dear. Do you have any news on Janice?" he might as well ask since he has her on the phone.

"Naw, I didn't go over there yestaday, but I'm goin' over later today and I'll let chu know if I hear somethin'."

"Thanks Connie. I guess I'll talk to you later then. Take care," he hung up the phone and proceeded back inside to the roll call room for the remainder of the briefing.

"Somebody had to go outside to talk to that lucky-ass girlfriend of his," Karen sneered.

"Yeah, something like that," Briscoe said as he focused his attention on the front of the room where Whitehead was starting to speak.

"Okay, let's dive right back into this thing. What we have done is divided you all into three shifts of ten individuals. You will be assigned a target and your job will be to follow him for eight hours doing counter surveillance. You will see who is watching him. I know many of you have not had this type of training, so starting tomorrow there is a three day class being held exclusively for us. Everybody is to report here tomorrow morning at 0800 hours. The class should run until 1600 hours daily through Saturday. We begin our assignments on Monday morning."

Detective Sutton took over, "Based on the previous victims, we compiled a list of the ten most likely victims of the predator. These are the most violent criminals with lengthy records and not a lot of incarceration time. They are also involved in criminal organizations and sexual abuse. Each of you will work alone for your tour of duty. You will be assigned a take-home rental car, which means you will not have emergency vehicle capabilities and nothing about the vehicle will identify you as a cop. We will have the windows tinted, offering a little bit of concealment. Your job is not to engage the targets, but to watch them. If they commit crimes, just let it go, and I cannot emphasize enough that you are not to take police action against them for law violations. Just make a note of it and pass it along at the end of your shift. If they commit a murder or a crime of violence, then naturally do what you have to. All of you will be issued departmental cell phones and a credit card to fuel the rental car. If your target travels out of the area, follow him for fifty miles, then turn around and go to his residence and wait there. Inform your relief and they also will set up at the target's residence and await their return. You will keep your police radio with you but out of sight. Monitor the police channel in whatever precinct that you are in, but do not get involved in anything that will alert the target, or potentially the predator to your presence. We set your schedule up for three shifts; day work 0600-1400, evening 1400-2200, and midnight shift 2200-0600. We tried to keep you on whatever shift you currently work, but that wasn't possible in every case. Your days off are Sunday and Monday. I'm sorry but this is the best we can do until we convince the Chief to give us more people. Following the briefing, check the board on the wall to your rear for your shift assignment. Also, look on the table to my left where there is a folder with three of your names on it. That is your target information. The three of you are assigned to him on the three different shifts. You will report all the details from one shift to the next and each morning the day work officer will fire off a twenty-four hour report and have it delivered to Whitehead or me. If, for whatever reason, you cannot make it in to relieve the prior shift, contact Detective Whitehead or me as soon as possible. Are there any questions?"

"Yes, I have a question. You said there were three shifts of ten, but there are thirty-five of us here. What about the five additional people?" Detective Brown from the 5th Precinct asked.

"Five of the detectives are going to be used to run down leads and close some loops in the investigation," Sutton informed.

"Who do we report to?" an officer from the 2nd Precinct asked.

"Nobody. Everything that happens here stays here. That goes for all of you. I want you to report significant information to Whitehead or me, and nobody else; not even the Chief's office. It is imperative that we keep all the information coming into this investigation confidential. When your shift is due to begin, be on time to relieve your partner. When your shift ends, you are free to do whatever. There is no roll call or check off and there is no need to call anybody to let them know that you are working. You are all on your own. It is up to you to do the very best job you can, because what you are doing is very important to this investigation and your service is greatly appreciated," Sutton spoke like a coach motivating his team before a big game.

An officer from the 1st Precinct raised his hand and when called upon asked, "For how long will we follow the targets?"

"That's a good question," Sutton said. "We will start out with this strategy and follow them for at least a month. If it doesn't get any results, then we will have to regroup and move to the second phase of our task force strategy."

The same officer asked, "And what is that?"

"I'm not at liberty to say right now, but if it comes to that, you will be the first to know."

"When do we get the car, cell phone, and credit card?" a voice from the back of the room boomed.

"This week during the training. We will pull you out individually to issue the things that you need. Alright, are there anymore questions?" he paused and looked around the room.

Briscoe really wanted to know if they were going to share the results of the psychological profile, but he didn't want to be the one to ask. It seemed that nobody else was even thinking about it.

"Okay, since there are no more questions I will see everybody back here tomorrow morning at 0800 hours for the first day of the counter-surveillance training," Sutton said.

They stood up, gathered their belongings, checked the board for their shifts, and the table for their assignments. It turned out that Briscoe and Karen were working the midnight shift, but she was assigned to a different person. Briscoe was on the team with Mathis and Officer Michael Seth of the 7th Precinct. The three of them did as all of the other teams did; they took the folder containing the information on their target and discussed it.

Briscoe's team was assigned to Sherman Edwards, a callous thirty-two year old drug dealer from the Clay Terrace projects. He has seventeen adult arrests for crimes ranging from distribution of PCP to murder. He has never been convicted of the more serious charges. On the three murder arrests, the witnesses always turned up dead. He has a reputation of fear and intimidation and it is nearly impossible to get anyone to testify against him. He has moved up in the world, with his drug activities and gang affiliations. He moved to Georgetown to a vintage brownstone that costs somewhere around $800,000. His illegal activities are masked by a legitimate urban clothing and music business located on Minnesota Avenue in southeast DC.

"He definitely fits into the category of a person the serial predator would like to take out," Mathis said.

"Damn, I'm surprised the predator hadn't already torn into his ass. You mean to tell me there are worse people than this piece of work out there? Damn, maybe we need an army of predators," Seth said causing everybody to laugh.

"Yeah, there are some bad motherfuckers out there, but nobody has the right to go around wiping them out like the Angel of Death," Mathis said seriously. They all nodded in agreement.

Since Mathis would be the one to start off the surveillance on Tuesday, he was also the one tasked with completing the twenty-four hour report. They thought it just natural for him to hold on to the folder. Briscoe took a look at the list of ten targets and to his disappointment he saw Marvin 'Brick' Jackson's name on the list. To make matters worse, Karen's team was assigned to him. That poses a bit of an obstacle for his mission, but it isn't anything that he cannot figure his way around. He plans to dismantle Brick's operation one member at a time until the only person left is Brick. Then he will reduce him to ashes.

It wasn't quite 1:00 p.m. and they were done for the day, so Briscoe decided to follow up on AUSA Phillip Danielson to see what his connection was to Janice Russell. He drove to the U.S. Attorney's Office and went inside to the 12th floor, where he stopped at the desk and talked with the receptionist. He told her that he was a part-time student at a local college and is doing research on sex offenses for a term paper that was due by the end of the summer semester. He asked if there was some way for him to see the cases that were presented to the US Attorney's Office over the past five years and their disposition. She advised him that it would be no problem. As a police officer he could see all the data, not just the redacted versions. She led him to a room with boxes upon boxes of case folders. There was a photocopier against the wall directly across from a long table with two computers and a shared printer on top. The receptionist explained that the room was where they stored all the case folders for their division for three years; after that, they are archived. She explained the filing system and logged Briscoe into the electronic catalog on the computer. She also explained that the printer and copier were for his convenience. He thanked her and sat down at one of the computers.

He had it all mapped out. Through his digging, he discovered that Danielson has been an AUSA for twelve years with the last three being the AUSA in charge of the Sex Crimes Division. He learned that Danielson was a local boy who attended Georgetown University Law School and appears to be from a very good family.

Briscoe decided to look at all the cases presented to the U.S. Attorney's Office over the three years that Danielson has been in charge and at all the cases that Danielson himself has prosecuted. He started with the first case on the first day that Danielson took over. The division handles about 1600 cases per year. Many of the cases are domestic related or the victim knew the perpetrator. Briscoe was a little taken aback by the number of incest cases. He could not believe how difficult it must be for a girl to grow up and keep her innocence from all the men who were trying to defile her. Such things are hard to fathom for one who does not have those ill intentions floating about their heart and mind. But for the evil, sneaky, wicked ones, it is just something to do and they feel no remorse for it.

Briscoe did not initially see anything that was out of the ordinary. It appeared that cases were prosecuted and convictions made. There were also plea deals and dismissals. But when he searched by perpetrator, he noticed that Johnny Simmons had come before Danielson on four different occasions. Each time he was not prosecuted or a plea was entered. He then ran Sonny Garfield and he also was given a plea in one case and a declination to prosecute in another. Briscoe pulled the most recent case files from the boxes and read the details of each case. There was no reason that either of them should have been given a plea or a declination to prosecute.

"What the heck is up with that?" Briscoe asked himself. He was now convinced that Danielson was up to no good. It was going to take a closer look at the man and his dealings before Briscoe could move on him. He replaced the case files and logged off the computer. He stopped at the desk, thanked the receptionist and took the elevator to the main lobby, exited the building and headed for his vehicle.

19

Janice opened the front door and let the tall lean man inside. He bent down and kissed her softly on the neck. It felt good to Janice to be touched in such a sensual manner. She embraced him and he allowed his hands to slip from her back to her round supple buttocks. He massaged them gently, then a little more vigorously while embracing her and kissing her neck passionately with wet, warm kisses.

"That feels so good Phil," Janice said.

"Where is Shauna?" he asked.

"She outside; do you want me to call her in?"

"Not yet. I want to spend time with you for a while," Phillip Danielson felt a fire kindle in his loins that he wanted Janice to stoke.

The thought of having a black woman in this way tantalized every beta-receptor in his body. As his kisses moved to her lips, his hands moved to her shirt, where he started with the top button and undid them all the way down to the last. He reached down to massage her now exposed breasts as his tongue explored the inside of her mouth. She let out a moan and her desire for him intensified.

He unzipped her jeans, revealing her powder blue panties. He then ran his hand down her chest, over her stomach and into those panties, where he felt the warmth and wetness of her vagina. He reached down with both hands and pulled her jeans and panties down to her ankles and she stepped out of them. He kissed the top of her foot and started to kiss and lick his way up to her moist vagina. As she held on to his shoulders to steady herself, he licked and sucked her with such passion and vigor that she screamed out. At that moment Shauna walked in the house and looked at the two of them in the middle of the living room with Danielson on his knees and his tongue inside of her mother.

They both looked at Shauna, and Danielson said, "Come here Shauna."

She closed the door and walked to where they were. Danielson stood and took Shauna by the hand and pulled her close to him, wrapping his arms around her in an embrace that she did not return. He bent down and kissed her lips, forcing the tongue that just came out of her mother inside her mouth. She unwillingly opened her mouth and accepted his fishy tongue.

"I want both of you together," he said looking toward Janice.

Janice unbuttoned Shauna's pants while Danielson pulled her tee shirt over her head exposing her still developing breasts. He became very excited and the bulge of his penis beating on the front of his slacks told Janice that he wanted Shauna in the worst way. He quickly undressed down to his socks, and he and Janice touched, kissed, and fondled Shauna, who was motionless and just did what she had always done in these situations; thought of something pleasant, while they did the things to her body that she had to keep secret from everybody in the world.

Danielson was overly excited by Shauna; even though this wasn't his first time with her. It was his first threesome with her and having it with Janice mesmerized him and made him feel something inexplicable about this forbidden love.

Shauna fought back the tears as the pain turned to numbness and she struggled to remain detached. When Danielson reached his climax, he screamed out so loud Shauna thought the windows rattled. Suddenly there was a noise of the front door shutting, and all three of them looked up. There was nobody there, and they looked at each other. Janice stood up and went to the door where she saw it was unlocked. She looked out the front window where she saw Connie scurrying down the sidewalk leading away from the front door.

"What was that? Was that somebody?" Danielson asked.

"It was nothing. I didn't see anybody," Janice lied.

She did not want to make Danielson nervous, because he pays her good money for sex with Shauna and she does not want to lose that because he is afraid somebody will find out.

She went back to where they were seated on the floor and joined them. Danielson told them that he wanted to have the two of them again and he wanted Shauna to have an orgasm. Shauna just looked dumbfounded because she had no idea what that was or what it meant to have one. She has just been used by the men that Janice received money from to satisfy their sick desire to have sex with a child. They would mainly have her suck their penis and they would fondle her body and occasionally someone would enter inside of her. She never had any feelings for any of the men. She just did what her mother told her they needed to do to survive. She did not want to live on the streets and she surely did not want anybody to hurt her mother.

"Can I go to the bathroom now?" Shauna asked.

"Sure baby," Janice answered.

"Give me a kiss before you go," Danielson said as he pulled her close.

She disgustedly leaned in and he kissed her with a deep wet kiss. She stood up, gathered her clothes, and went to the bathroom where she closed the door and sat on the toilet and cried profusely. She was hurting inside emotionally and physically. She wrapped her arms around her body and held herself tightly as she leaned over and fought back the overwhelming desire to vomit. She felt hopeless and humiliated and could not get herself together enough to take a shower.

When she did stand to her feet, she could not hold back the vomit as it escaped her petite body and went mostly in the toilet. She fell to her knees and cried silently so that her mother would not hear. Her pain was deep and nearly unbearable. She cried out for a father that she never knew, feeling that if he was there none of this would be happening.

Shauna's father was killed a few months before she was born. He was involved in the drug game, and it claimed his life late one rainy spring night. But that doesn't stop a child in pain from crying out for the one that she believes would have protected her.

Janice and Danielson got dressed. He gave her $200.00, a hug, and a kiss goodbye. Janice closed the door and thought about Connie and what she might have seen. She had to approach Connie and find out what she saw and then decide what to do with her. She couldn't believe that her door was unlocked during that whole thing. She picked up her cell phone and scrolled through to Connie's name and pushed the send button.

"Hello," Connie answered.

"Hey Connie, its Janice."

"I just left from around there a little while ago but you didn't answer your door," Connie said.

"What chu need?" Janice asked cautiously.

"Girl you know what I need," Connie said.

"You gonna come back?" Janice asked.

"Yeah, I'll be there in a few minutes."

They hung up the phone. Moments later Connie knocked at the front door and it was immediately opened by Janice, who invited her in and closed the door.

"So, what's up Connie?" Janice asked.

"I wanna get a twenty," she replied, reaching into her pocket and retrieving a twenty dollar bill.

"Are you sure that's all you want?" Janice asked, staring into her yellow eyes.

"Yeah, that was it. What's up witchu?" Connie asked.

Janice could not tell if Connie had walked in and saw them having sex on the living room floor or if she really didn't come in or see anything. Connie carried on like normal, as if she saw nothing. But Janice wanted to be sure, so she asked,

"Did you come inside when you came here earlier?"

"No, I just knocked on the door and waited for a while, but nobody answered so I left."

Janice looked intently at Connie but was not able to determine if she was telling the truth. She reasoned that if Connie did see something so what. She is an old crack-head trick who wouldn't say anything to anybody. And if she did, who would believe her? She reached out and took the money from Connie and handed her a small plastic baggie containing the white rock that Connie loved so much. They made small talk for a few more moments then Connie left.

Shauna was still in the bathroom trying to scrub the filth of Phillip Danielson from her body and mind. She was sobbing when Janice walked into the bathroom and looked at the heap of her daughter sitting in the bathtub in tears scrubbing herself. Janice walked over to the tub and sat on the edge. She reached for the wash cloth, removing it from Shauna's hand and then she picked up the soap and began to lather the cloth.

"Shauna, I know you don't like doing things with Mister Phillip, but I need you to hang in there with me baby," she said as she rubbed soap on Shauna's back and shoulders. "You are such a pretty young girl and the men are always gonna want to give you things if you treat them right. All you have to do is have sex with them and let them make you feel good, and you can have anything you want—even love."

"I don't feel any love," Shauna complained through her tears.

"Do you love Mommy?"

Shauna did not answer.

"If you love me, then do it for me. We will be homeless and starve if we can't get money from Mister Phillip and the others. You don't want us to live in a shelter or on the street do you?"

The sadness was tearing through the fabric of Shauna's being. All she could do was cry. Janice leaned in and kissed her on the lips while washing her young body.

"Are you ready to get out?" Janice asked her softly.

Shauna nodded yes and stood up. Janice caressed her and wrapped a towel around her. Once she dried off, Janice led her to the bedroom and laid her on the bed. She grabbed a bottle of baby lotion and rubbed lotion on her young body.

"Shauna, Mommy loves you so much. I only try to do what's best for you. I want you to know that you made me feel really good tonight and I am gonna teach you how to feel just as good. Relax right here and I'll be right back."

Janice made sure the house was secure before turning off the lights and heading back into her room with Shauna. Janice removed her clothes and got in the bed with Shauna. She did things to her daughter that she never felt before and then held her close until they fell asleep.

Connie was so pumped about what she saw, she could barely contain herself. She called Briscoe to relay the news.

"Officer Briscoe! It's Connie."

"Hey Connie what's up, It's almost midnight," he said as he collected his faculties.

"I just came from Janice house and you ain't gonna believe what I seen," she said enthusiastically.

"What?" Briscoe asked in anticipation.

"Janice and Shauna was fuckin a white man on the livin room floor."

Briscoe could feel his blood boil, "What? They were doing what?" he could hardly believe what he was hearing.

"Yeah, I walked in cause nobody answered the door. I stood there for a few minutes and they didn't even see me. Shauna was eat'n Janice pussy and the man was fucking Shauna."

Briscoe had a vision of the scene and the thought of it nearly sickened him.

"Do you know who the man was?" he asked.

"No, but I seen his car round there before."

"What kind of car?"

"It's a green Mercedes," Connie said.

Briscoe knew immediately who it was. So that is why Simmons and Garfield beat their charges. They probably knew that Danielson was fucking the little girl also. Briscoe could barely contain the rage. He could feel his emotions were belying his exterior and perhaps Connie could hear it in his voice. So he composed himself and asked,

"Did you get his license plate number?"

"No, but I can when I see it around there again."

"That will work. I'll get up with you tomorrow and give you a little something for this information."

That sounded good to Connie, and she asked, "What time do you want to meet?"

"I'm in training all day tomorrow. But I'll call you when I have a break and then we can meet someplace."

"Okay; I'll holla at chu tomorrow, good night," she said.

Briscoe lay in his bed staring at the ceiling wondering how confusing and hurtful it must be for Shauna to have sex with her mother. Just thinking about it makes him want to run over to the house and beat Janice to death. He never imagined that Janice would take her daughter to that level of disgust. It is one thing to allow dirty old men to penetrate your daughter, but it is an abomination for a parent to engage their child in sex. He thought that he should go over and cut Janice's head off and stick it up Danielson's ass. He was seething with anger and wondered why justice could never be served publicly on people like them. Why the two of them can't be hanged in the public square like they used to do in medieval times and early western civilization. Briscoe could not help but feel the pain that Shauna was probably feeling from the sickening act that her mother put her through.

Shauna woke a few hours later and looked at her mother lying naked next to her, sleeping peacefully. She was having a difficult time processing what took place between herself and her mother. The excitement her body felt as her mother touched her in ways that she had never felt before and the conflict of her heart and mind was so confusing to her. It was as though a war was raging inside of her and she knew that the things done to her last night was not right. But she loves her mother. She does not want anything bad to happen to her, and she does not want to be taken away from her. She thought about Johnny Simmons and how he used to touch her and do things to her body. She never did like it and she often wished that he would just go away or die. She told her mother that she didn't want Johnny to go to jail, but secretly she wanted him and all the other men not only to go to jail, but to Hell also. In her young unlearned, underdeveloped mind, her mother is a victim of the evils of the world and she needs Shauna to help them both survive. She believes that her mother loves her and only wants the very best for her. But the truth is her mother is a sick, selfish, evil woman, who tells Shauna that people will hurt her if she doesn't give them money each week. She manipulates her daughter through fear of losing her and the safety and security of home.

Janice started pimping Shauna when Johnny Simmons came into her life and he convinced her that people would pay good money for sex with her. Janice never did fight it. She figured since Johnny loved her she should do anything to make him happy. Janice never did have a father figure in her life and felt abused and unloved by her mother. She reached out to the streets and the decadence that dwelled there. She would have thrown Shauna away long ago had it not been for her mother forcing her to raise Shauna and be a responsible adult. Every time Janice stumbles her mother is there threatening to take Shauna away from her. But the fact is Janice's mother really does not want to take Shauna from her, she wants Janice to raise her right. She has no idea what is going on in the house of horrors that Janice has made for Shauna. But the love a child has for their parent is something that is not easily broken as long as the parent gives love back to the child. In the case of Janice and Shauna, showing love has taken on a whole new meaning.

Shauna stared at the ceiling overhead and wondered if any of her girlfriends experience the same things that she does. She wondered if their mother or father touched them and licked on them in the same ways that her mother did to her. She knew that most of the girls were still virgins and they would sometimes talk about boys and the idea of giving up their bodies to them. Shauna had to harbor the terrible secret of the many men who have been inside of her and how she lost her virginity at the age of nine. All of these thoughts rushed through her mind like a tsunami, bringing pain and eventually the flood gates opened and the tears flowed from the young eyes that have witnessed evil far beyond their tender age.

She grabbed her pillow clutching it tightly to her body as she trembled and sobbed deeply asking, "Oh God why?"

20

Briscoe was so furious with the knowledge of Danielson having sex with Shauna it made him want to destroy his world before he takes his life. He wanted to humiliate him and take away the good reputation that he hypocritically hides behind. He knows that if he does, it would have to be something that wouldn't tie Danielson to the little girl, because Whitehead is too smart not to begin to make connections. Once the connections are made, all eyes will be on her and everybody surrounding her. He must put some real thought into how he will deal with AUSA Danielson. And to think, he figured the man had a drug problem, when all along it was something much worse.

Here is a man, who is the head of the sex crimes division responsible for ridding society of the sexual predators and deviants who prey on the innocence of our most vulnerable members, committing the same heinous acts. These thoughts compelled Briscoe to sit down at his computer and compose the following letter:

Mr. Danielson,

I know what you have been doing. I am watching you when you don't think you are being watched. The disgusting things that you like to do with children will not remain your little secret. Soon the entire world will know that you are a sick demented hypocrite and they will judge you accordingly.

The best thing that you can do right now is stop having sex with children and hope that I change my mind about exposing you. I don't seek anything from you; I am only concerned about the young lives affected by your wicked desires.

If you know what's best for you, you will keep your little wiener where it belongs, in your pants. I am watching you. If I see any more of your sick-ass behavior, I will show the world exactly what you are. The next letter goes to your wife! Cease and desist, you fucking baby raper!!

Briscoe looked over the letter three times to ensure it conveyed the right message to Danielson; and that message is he better stop sleeping with that little girl. Briscoe did not plan to do anything to Danielson right now, but he did want to stop him from having sex with the girl. He will deal with him at the appropriate time, but he has to do something to keep him away from her. Briscoe wished he could stop every man from touching her, but at this point he knows the only way to accomplish that is to get her away from her mother. But in the meantime, he can slow down Danielson by letting him know that his secret is no longer just his secret, it belongs to another.

He saved the letter on a two megabyte thumb drive and powered down his desktop computer. He grabbed his backpack slinging it across his left shoulder as he grabbed his car keys from the kitchen counter. He left his house, got into his Charger and headed for the public library on Iverson Street in Capitol Heights, Maryland. There, he removed a pair of tweezers from his backpack and exited the vehicle.

He walked into the library and signed up for a computer using a false name. The librarian instructed him to use the one in the corner near the window that overlooks the parking lot. He sat down and inserted the thumb drive into the USB port in the front of the CPU. The window opened and he selected the letter that he wrote to Danielson. Once the letter was opened on screen Briscoe did one more proof reading. Satisfied the letter was exactly what he wanted to send, he clicked on the print button. He shut down all programs, removed his thumb drive, and hurried to retrieve the printed letter at the library staff desk. He paid the librarian for the print copy and the copy he was going to make on the copier. The librarian handed him the letter and he took it to the copier near the entrance to the library. He placed the letter on the copier glass and printed one copy. When the copy came out he took the original from the glass and folded it over the copy so not to touch the paper with his bare hands. He brought the tweezers to pick up the paper, but there were too many people in there, and he did not want to look suspicious picking up paper with a pair of tweezers.

He walked from the library to his vehicle, reached into his backpack, pulled out a pair of latex gloves and put them on. He reached in and pulled out a box of envelopes, retrieved a single envelope from the middle, folded copied letter, and stuffed it into the envelope. He took a red pen from the console and addressed the letter to Danielson at his office. He carefully peeled a stamp from the book of twenty and put it on the envelope. Briscoe took extra care to ensure that he left no finger print or DNA evidence on the letter or inside the envelope.

He held the envelope in his left hand as he drove to the post office where he deposited the letter in the drive up mailbox. It's done. The letter is on its way to Danielson. That should keep him away from the little girl. Receiving the letter at work will let him know the writer knows more about him than just his personal activities. Briscoe was also careful not to threaten bodily harm in the letter, because he did not want Danielson to go to the police fearing the serial predator was on his case. He is calculating that Danielson will read the letter and hide or destroy it, then stay away from the girl for fear he will be exposed.

It's now after 7:00 p.m. and there is only one day left in the counter surveillance training. Briscoe has to report to VCU early tomorrow morning to pick up his rental car, cell phone, and credit card. He has not had the opportunity to hook up with Connie since they talked on the phone two nights ago when she informed him of the abominations committed by Janice and Danielson. He decided to hook up with her and give her some money and see if she has any more information that he could use.

"Hey Connie, what's up?" he asked when she answered her cell phone.

"I'm chillin, what up wit chu Officer Briscoe?"

"I wanted to hook up and hit you off with a little something and talk for a minute," he explained.

"That's cool wit me, when?"

"Now if you can get away," he was not too far from her and decided now was as good a time as any.

"In the daytime?" she was surprised and apprehensive.

"Yeah, but don't worry, I'm not on duty. I'm in civilian clothes and driving my personal car."

"Is it anything on it dat let people know you five oh?" she was very concerned about being seen talking to him.

"No Connie, its black with tinted windows and nothing on it says anything about the police. If you want, we can meet somewhere and then you can jump in and we will drive away from the area. Stop worrying, it'll be dark in about an hour anyway."

Connie's fear of being seen talking to the police was real, but it would have to take a backseat to her need for the money.

"Okay, where do you wanna meet?" she asked.

"I'll pick you up in front of the newspaper warehouse on West Virginia Avenue in twenty minutes. I'm driving a black Dodge Charger with tinted windows and Maryland tags."

"Okay, I'll be there," she said and hung up the phone.

Briscoe was driving on West Virginia Avenue toward the warehouse when he saw Connie walking in that direction, about five blocks out. He considered driving to the warehouse and waiting for her to walk the distance, but he quickly changed his mind and pulled to the curb beside her. He pushed the button letting down the front passenger window.

"Connie!" his voice bellowed. She turned and looked into the vehicle and approached cautiously.

"Oh, Officer Briscoe; I had to make sure that was you," she reached for the door handle and got in. He put the window up and drove off.

"How are you Connie?"

"I'm good. How bout you?" she countered.

"I'm doing well dear," he said reaching out and handing Connie forty dollars.

She accepted the money and said, "Thanks, this is cool."

Briscoe figured as soon as she gets out of the vehicle she will run to Janice and spend every penny on crack. He decided to ride instead of looking for a place to park and talk.

"What else has been going on lately?" he queried.

"Red and Ant got outta jail. They back on the block fuckin' wit people."

Briscoe was surprised they were released on bail. He was going to start taking down Brick's network so he might as well start with those two. But why were they granted bail when they are facing a murder charge? And how could they afford the bail, which was surely very high? There could be some real shenanigans afoot and he was going to find out what they were.

"Where have they been hanging out?" he asked.

"They be on Montello a lot," she said.

"Cool, thanks for that Connie. You have been a big help to me since we started this. We are building cases against several people and thanks to you we are able to identify the players. The best thing is you don't have to worry about testifying, because as a confidential informant your identity is protected." Briscoe was hoping that Connie would never piece things together and realize the people she tells him about turn up dead.

"I like helping you," she said proudly, showing her crooked teeth.

Once again Briscoe could not help wonder how men trusted her enough to put their penis in that scary mouth.

"Have you been to Janice's house since we talked the other night?" he was curious if there was anything else of interest going on there.

"Yeah, but I didn't hang around, I just went there to pick something up."

"I bet I know what that was," he grinned and continued. "Alrighty then, where do you want me to drop you off?" he was ready to get back home and prepare for the weekend ahead.

"West Virginia Avenue will be cool."

She would not have to work the johns so hard tonight, because of the money she got from Briscoe.

He drove her back to where he picked her up. They said their goodbyes and Connie got out of the car. As he drove off he thought about Connie and wondered if he would have to kill her later. He does not want to kill her, but if the situation dictates, he would. If she starts to put things together she must be dealt with.

Briscoe went to the 5th Precinct police station to use the computer to check on Red and Ant's conditions of release. He entered the station and made small talk with a few of the officers there, then went to the computer on the counter where he ran information on both of them. He was surprised to see that they were released on some sheer bullshit. The U.S. Attorney's Office decided to drop the case without prejudice and release the two of them. This infuriated Briscoe. *How the fuck could they drop the case against these two shit birds? This is some horse shit, and it reeks of Philip Danielson, or God knows who that might be corrupt in the U.S. Attorney's Office.* He left the station and once inside his vehicle called Willis Sanford.

"Hello."

"Will, its Briscoe."

"What up dog," Sanford said happy to hear from him.

"What's up with that case we made on those two dudes from the alley the other day? Somebody told me they are out on bail," Briscoe lied not to let on that he was following the case.

"Naw dog not bail. The U.S. Attorney DWIPed (Dropped Without Prejudice) the case. Said we don't have sufficient evidence to prosecute," Sanford sounded disappointed.

"Damn, I thought that was going to be an open and shut case," Briscoe said.

"Me too. For all intent and purposes it should've been. I don't know what more we could do or what evidence we need to collect. We have the murder weapon with their finger prints and your partner saw them going through the victim's pockets. The prosecutor claims that he will hold the case and give time for an eye witness to come forward or we track one down. I think it's some crap, but the department counts the case as being closed with an arrest and they don't give a damn about the U.S. Attorney's Office stalling the prosecution," he explained.

"Well, I guess there isn't anything we can do about it. We have to think of it as job security. We put them in jail; the prosecutor's job is to keep them there. If they don't then it is on their conscience. At least we have done our jobs," Briscoe had to talk this way because he did not want to give Sanford an inkling of how he really felt inside.

He plans to deal with the two young bandits in his way. Their case was dropped; now they will be dropped from earth . . . at least the top side of it.

Briscoe changed the subject to something different and talked for about thirty minutes until he arrived at home. He was pleased to find Monica there. Sometimes she came over, let herself in and waited for him. He was always happy to see that she was at his house; he often thought about the two of them moving in together. That idea was always squashed when he thought about the mission that he is on. There were times when he did not come home for hours or want to account for his whereabouts. Living with Monica would mean he would have to tell her where he had been and where he was going. He was not ready to do that yet, so he suppressed the idea of asking her to move in right now.

He went inside and kissed her hello. They talked while he

prepared for the next day. They took a shower together and then made love over and over again until they fell asleep in each other's arms.

21

There was not very much traffic out on the streets at 6:30 a.m. Saturday. Briscoe always liked that atmosphere. It was as though the city was asleep trying to recover from a hectic week of hustle and hurt. It was resting, trying to heal the wounds inflicted upon it during the week, and the wildness that it endured Friday night when the inhabitants took to its streets and caused each other pain and heart ache. With all the turmoil, inhumanity, and even death that occurs during the week it is hard to imagine any of it on a peaceful early Saturday morning when the sun is just rising and all is calm. Briscoe and Monica were heading to VCU to pick up his rental vehicle and the other items he will need for his new assignment.

Monica looked over at him and said, "I am so proud of you Antonio."

"Wow, where did that come from?" he smiled.

"From my heart," she said seriously. "You are doing a great thing by volunteering to try and catch that fool. It shows just how honorable you are."

Her words did not comfort him; instead, they made him feel uncomfortable. His girlfriend has no idea he is the man who he is supposed to catch. He is the fool she despises and wishes would be caught and punished. The thought of being caught sometimes crossed his mind. But his biggest fear is not punishment; it is the disappointment and pain it would cause Monica and his mother. They are the two people in his life who he cares the most about; and they happen to be the two who disagree most with what the serial predator is doing. There must be a way for them to understand the things he is doing. They should know he is doing it for them and all good law-abiding peaceful people. He sometimes thought how heart-wrenching it would be for his mother to see his picture plastered on TV stations around the country as the media vilified him. These thoughts kept him sharp and several steps ahead of the investigators. The last thing he wants is to get caught and have to deal with all the negativity that would rain down. For him, getting caught is not an option. He reached for Monica's hand and squeezed it gently.

"I love you, Moni," were the words he spoke as he lifted her hand to his lips and kissed it.

In front of the VCU building, Briscoe leaned over and gave Monica a deep wet kiss goodbye as they embraced tightly. He got out of her BMW and walked to the building's entrance, rang the door bell and stood in front of the camera/intercom display. After a brief pause there was a buzz as the lock released. He pulled the door open and entered a dimly lit foyer that used the limited sunlight that peeked through two narrow slits of glass in main door. He walked down the corridor toward the squad room, where the detective's desks are located.

In the squad bay, he was greeted by Detective Sutton, who directed him to a desk near the center of the room. The rows of desks were partially partitioned by partitions at desktop height. They gave far less privacy than the typical cubicle. On Sutton's row, three desks that backed up to three more desks and across the aisle was the same set up. The entire squad bay consisted of thirty-six desks arranged neatly in rows. It had a *Hill Street Blues* flavor but with a modern day Fortune 500 office appeal. The supervisors had offices at the ends of the bay and along the corridor that Briscoe walked to get to the squad bay.

"Hey Officer Briscoe, good morning, have a seat right here. I'll get the keys to the vehicle you will be signing for," Sutton said as he extended his hand.

"Good morning," Briscoe said shaking his hand.

"Help yourself to a cup of coffee. I'll be right back," he pointed to a table with a coffee maker, cups, and condiments.

He disappeared around the end of the row of desks. The only other people in the office were two midnight shift detectives. They did not pay much attention to Briscoe but focused on their computer screens and the work laid out in front of them. Briscoe looked on Sutton's desk to see if there was any useful information pertaining to the serial predator. One thing jumped out at him; a list titled "Personnel Files" that contained his name. He wondered what it was about and why his name was on the list.

He took a look around to ensure the other detectives were not watching him and Sutton was not on his way back. He moved the list aside and looked to see if anything else on the desk would further explain the list. There was nothing useful. He put the list back in place and sat back wondering. He did notice that the other names on the list were those of the officers on the task force, but why would Sutton look into their personnel files? What was he looking for? He wondered if the psychological profile came back stating the killer could possibly be a cop and if the VCU detectives were looking at the personnel files of all the officers to see if they could find a match. His imagination was working overtime. He was running every possible scenario and an thinking of an appropriate response.

"Man you got one of the nicer rides," the sound of Sutton's voice startled Briscoe back to the present. "We tried to get nondescript vehicles that would blend in and not draw any attention. We had the windows tinted dark enough that someone would have to strain to see who was inside. You got a Pontiac Grand Am. It's maneuverable, somewhat sporty but not enough to make people gawk at it, and its compact enough for you to get in and out of tight places. I hope the legroom is sufficient for you. If not we'll swap you out something bigger."

"Okay, that's cool, thanks," Briscoe said.

He was not concerned with the vehicle, but with the list on Sutton's desk. *If only there was some way to turn the conversation to the list on his desk.* He thought about just asking, *What the hell, Sutton knows that cops are the nosiest people in the world, and just about anybody would have looked on his desk.* He is going to have to navigate this one with caution.

"Are there any new leads on the predator?" he caught Sutton's gaze and held it as he studied his body language to gauge if his physical stance would match his verbal response.

"Naw, nothing new right now, but we do have some leads that we are following," Sutton wanted to keep him motivated but he couldn't give details.

"Are there any that I can help you with? I know a lot of street people in some of the areas where the predator struck. I can talk to people and see what I can gather for you," he was fishing at this point and wanted to encourage Sutton to release some more details of the case such as potential witnesses or evidence that they did not disclose during the briefing they gave earlier in the week.

"Hey man, that's great. I'll keep you up on anything that I might need you to look into. But the main focus we need from you guys is surveillance on the targets we gave you. We believe it's only a matter of time before our boy hits one of them,"

No matter how bad he may want the additional help, he knows Whitehead does not like information going out to anyone, not even the Chief.

"Sanford told me you are a good worker and hard charger. He said you know a lot of the people on your beat and you have a good rapport with them."

"I try to do the best I can for them. I think they trust and confide in me in return," Briscoe's persona was modest.

But, in this case, he was trying to get Sutton to open up to him. Even though the homicide detectives said they disclosed everything they had on the case, Briscoe knew they always hold something back. He figured now would be a good time to ask about the psychological profile.

"So what was the outcome of the psychological profile Detective Whitehead mentioned in the briefing?"

"We don't know yet. The FBI is coming by in a few days to present it to us," he said this with less enthusiasm than Briscoe would have anticipated.

Sutton didn't buy into the whole profile thing, but his partner did, so he went along with it.

"I guess it could be useful in some ways, but I won't stake the investigation on it," his deference to Whitehead was evident in his support of the FBI profile, but his personal feelings were they could do without it.

"Once you get the results, will you guys give us a lead on what we should be looking out for?" Briscoe hoped that was the plan; he also hoped the profile was the direct opposite of him.

"That's Whitehead's call, but I don't see any reason he wouldn't want to disseminate it down to you guys," he honestly couldn't think of a reason why Whitehead would not want to inform the detail.

Briscoe was confident Sutton shared everything possible with him and that he had nothing to worry about. He was still curious about the list on Sutton's desk, but there was no way he was going to bring it up and give Sutton cause to wonder. He will just have to trust that the list is something routine.

"Cool. I'll keep my ears open and let you know if anything blows my way,"

Briscoe wanted to sound eager about helping to catch the serial predator. He thought, *How ironic. I am looking for me.* If there wasn't so much at stake, he would probably laugh.

22

The final day of counter-surveillance training went well. Afterwards Briscoe, Karen, and other members of the teams went out for drinks. They went to the FOP lodge on 4th Street where they could unwind and talk freely. Karen was wearing a pair of Levis jeans that gripped the voluptuous contour of the lower half of her hour glass frame. Her tan blouse was reminiscent of a camisole with its tight fit and lingerie appeal. Briscoe stared at her throughout the training today; *Daaaaammn, that girl is so fine!* He could not stop the visions of his body wrapped around hers that danced around his mind. It didn't help that Seth and Mathis continued to point out how hot she was. It seemed as though she knew that she got Briscoe's attention. He occasionally looked at her and caught her watching him. All she would do is smile that gorgeous super-model smile of hers and wink.

It was Karen's idea to go for drinks at the FOP following training. Briscoe declined at first but since the rest of the crew was going, he decided to tag along. Secretly, he wanted to be there with her. He had a strong desire to be near her. He knows she would love nothing more than to ply him with alcohol and jump his bones. But with the others being there he is in no danger of that happening. Besides, Officer Kewon Staley, one of the officers on Karen's team, was all over her. He was feeling her out and trying with everything he had to book her. She does not seem interested, but since when has that stopped a dude from trying to hit? Staley seems like he would be her type, in the physical sense, he is six-feet-one-1-inch tall, sports a lean athletic build and has a pretty boy exterior. But Karen is used to guys hitting on her and has made up her mind that Briscoe is the one for her. Even if she did get with Staley, she would not let Briscoe know.

The mood was light; everyone was exhaling and looking eagerly to their new assignment. Karen sat next to Briscoe in the booth overlooking 4th street. Downtown was very much alive with cars jostling for position and people milling around carefree, enjoying the weekend. They had errands to run, family and friends to see, and the all important shopping to do that most weekends are made of. Staley sat directly across from Karen while Seth sat across from Briscoe and Mathis pulled up a chair.

After the first round of drinks and a lot of laughter, Karen placed her hand on Briscoe's knee under the table. He continued as though he didn't realize her hand was there. Her touch tingled as it sent instant heat to his loins. He could not believe she was making a move like that with all the guys sitting there. She moved her hand to the inside of his knee and stroked up and down his inner thigh. He could not move or do anything to let the others know what Karen was doing. As she erotically massaged his thigh, his penis got hard and began to press violently against his pants begging for a piece of Karen. He looked at her and she smiled slyly as she continued to feel her way up his thigh. Briscoe could not follow the conversation at the table for the sensation his body felt. It seemed the room went dim and he and Karen were the only ones there. The desire to exchange body fluids with her wracked his being. He wants to feel the fullness of this woman who is touching him in such a way that he cannot concentrate on the other people. Just as he was about to stop her hand from its exploration, Karen reached up higher and felt the thickness of his manhood. When she felt the rock hardness of his pleasure stick, she looked into his eyes begging for a taste of his treat. Her penetrating eyes sent a rush over him that almost made him explode in his pants. For fear someone would realize what they were doing, Briscoe put his hand on her and gently squeezed, stopping her sensual stroke. He gently moved her hand from his penis to the seat, where he held it tightly while they continued to socialize with the others. *Whew, that was hot and so dangerously close.* Briscoe didn't want to lose control, but Karen was the one who took him there. Once the arousal in his pants settled down, Briscoe said his farewells and departed.

He is a vibrant young man with desires and a very healthy sex drive, but he cannot allow his world to become complicated by Karen. However, he thought, *Oh My God!! That shit felt great.* He spent hours thinking about Karen and not many of those thoughts were bad. If he isn't careful, he is going to lay that girl down.

The sun set and the rulers of the darkness are about to take to the streets and do their unlawful bidding. Tonight they will have company. Briscoe is going to pay a couple of Brick's people a visit and it ain't nothing nice. Judgment day is upon them and the reaper is coming to collect. The few drinks Briscoe had relaxed him, gave him a feeling of confidence and comfort in his mission. He began to wonder about what he was doing and if it was having an impact. Or was it just punishment for the offenders. Either way, justice prevails.

His thoughts moved to Red Abernathy and Ant Lakeland. They must be comfortable in their existence and are feeling nearly untouchable since they were released. They have no idea their world is about to come crashing down upon them in the worst way.

Briscoe cruised to the block on Montello Avenue where Ant and Red sold their poison. He was in the Pontiac Sutton issued him earlier in the day and nobody seemed to give him a second look. There was Red leaning on a fence with a smug expression that screamed, *I'm better than everyone else and nobody better fuck with me!* Briscoe wanted to stop the car, run up, slap the piss out of him, and continue slapping until his head came off his shoulders. The sight of Red free on the street sent a tinge of rage through Briscoe's body. It made him want to strike with fury and vengeance. He plans to take Red off that corner for good.

There wasn't very much activity on the street for a Saturday night where Red plied his trade. An elderly woman sat on her porch directly across the street from where Red sold his poison and watched all the activity that took place. She did not seem threatened by him, but she was disgusted by what he was doing; but, like so many others, she did nothing to stand up against it. There was also a scattering of young children playing outside in the moonlight that offset the darkness. Briscoe took this all in as he moved through the block.

He turned the corner and drove into the alley on the east side of the street. It was a place where people were used to strange vehicles parking; mostly with prostitutes inside servicing their tricks, so he was confident he would not draw attention. Briscoe's plan was to get into Red's house a block away on Trinidad Avenue and wait his arrival. He took a close look around and noted his surroundings before exiting the rental car that will be his office for the next few weeks. He was not wearing the customary black attire he usually sports when he go out to do his work; instead, he was wearing a pair of blue jeans and a beige Polo shirt. He pulled his baseball cap low over his face just above his eyes in an attempt to conceal his face, grabbed his backpack, and walked the length of the alley toward the rear of Red's house, where he lives with his mother and twenty-one year old sister.

Briscoe had gathered enough information to think there was a high probability of nobody being home. Red's mother goes to Laurel every Saturday night to play bingo with her girlfriends and his sister spends most weekends with her boyfriend someplace other than the house on Trinidad. He hoped they would not deviate from the norm. Just to be sure, Briscoe walked past the rear of the house checking it from top to bottom, looking for any sign of inhabitants. As he walked past he checked for signs of a dog and the actions of neighbors. The alley was clear except for a few dogs that barked as he passed by yards on his way to the mouth of the alley to go around front. While walking along the street he looked for anybody sitting on their porch, a common pastime for people in this community. A hot summer night draws them outside like moths to a flame.

There were a few people out, some sitting quietly on the porch, while others were in small groups making boisterous conversation. Briscoe studied the front of Red's home as he passed by and was relatively certain there was nobody inside. He looked around at the people outside but did not want to appear interested in anything, because he did not want any attention focused on him. He passed Red's house and hastened his pace. There was an entrance to the alley four houses down from Reds' but Briscoe decided not to turn into the alley. With all the people out on the street he felt cutting through the alley would get the attention of somebody and they may possibly remember his description once the investigators start to question folks. He decided to go down to Neal Street, double back through the alley, and quickly make his way back to the rear of the house.

As he approached the house, he donned his leather gloves and reached for the gate. He made his way quickly to the rear of the house and walked down the steps that led to the basement entrance. Now he was completely shielded from view and could take his time quietly breaking into the house. The door to the basement was wood and glass. The wood was rotted and the paint was nothing but specks. Briscoe wondered if there was a lead poisoning hazard there. He guessed the house was one hundred or more years old and was not well kept. The door was flimsy and would be easy to force open, but stealth was the order of business right now. The locks are rusty and the cob webs are an indication the entrance has not been used in a long time. Briscoe wasn't sure what to expect on the other side, but based on the condition of the yard he had an idea of the clutter and filth that awaited him. He took a rubber suction device from his bag and stuck it to the glass; using a metal rolling blade, he cut a large circle around the suction device. He steadied himself and pushed hard inward on the glass causing it to separate where it was cut. He carefully pulled the piece out and sat it quietly on the ground. He reached inside and turned the knob on the dead bolt lock, then reached down and released the knob lock and turned . . . voila! He's in.

It was obvious that the basement was only used for storage. There was junk everywhere. Old toys, electronic devices, clothes, books, tools, you name it. Briscoe could not use his flashlight or turn on the lights because of the people out on the street. Street lights shone through the curtain-less windows and provided sufficient light for what he planned. He moved quietly up the steps listening closely to every sound. He thought back to when he was in Liberia advising the government as a member of a Special Forces A team and how his other senses were heightened when he had to eliminate someone due to conditions.

Walking up the steps reminded him of the time he was inside a rebel enclave and tasked with clearing a two story bungalow with a team of Liberian soldiers. As the point man on the raid reached the top of the steps, he twisted the knob and pushed the door open. A rebel, standing on the other side with a Kalashnikov PKC, opened fire ripping the soldiers face completely off.

Briscoe did not want that to happen to him so he leaned into the door and listened closely before turning the knob. He cracked the door slightly looking to see what he could in the dim glow provided by the street lights. He pulled his Sig from his bag and wrapped his hand comfortably around it. He stood straight up and steadied himself as he moved with grace and purpose into the room scanning for any movement. There was none and he advanced forward and checked the entire downstairs. On this level, the house was basically unkempt and just slightly less cluttered than the basement.

How the fuck do people live like this? he wondered as he went up stairs to clear that area. The neatest place in the house was Red's sister's room. Although small, the room was neatly organized and her bed was made with frilly lace pillows and stuffed animals. She had pictures of herself and several friends, male and female at various events adorning her walls, nightstand, and dresser. The same could not be said about Red. His room was a mess. Instead of a bed with a frame, there was a mattress set on the floor with a crumpled sheet that didn't appear to fit. On the walls were a few Jet magazine beauties and a poster of Tupac. Roaches ran rampant and the room actually smelled of urine. Briscoe put the gun back into the bag, backed out of the room and went downstairs to prepare for Reds arrival.

He was sure Red would return to the house because he made frequent trips to use the bathroom and retrieve product when he ran low. It was only a matter of time before he comes home. The only thing that could throw a monkey wrench into what he planned is if the mother or sister came home before Red. He hoped that fate was on his side tonight. Briscoe knew his plan was simple and would be executed without a problem. However, the waiting was the part that requires much discipline. He has had long hours waiting and has learned to be patient, but it was never easy.

He sat on the couch in the living room, careful not to disturb anything, facing the door with his silenced weapon on his lap. He is able to see out of the front window through the sheer curtains, but as long as no light is on inside no one can see him. He decided he would close the curtains before Red comes home because he cannot risk being seen if Red turns on the light before he can engage him.

After sitting for twenty minutes, Briscoe closed the curtains to allow his eyes to adjust to the darkness so he would be 100 percent ready for Red. Another thirty minutes passed when Briscoe heard keys jingling at the door. He picked up the gun and stood off to the side so once the door opened the person would have to walk a few feet into the open before he could be seen. Judging by the rapping and husky voice, it had to be a male, and the only male expected was Red.

The door closed and a click was heard as Red engaged the lock. When he stepped forward he never looked in Briscoe's direction. He felt an explosion of pain that ripped through his thigh that felt like his leg was ripped off above the knee. He shrilled as he fell to the floor clutching the spot where the hollow point +p+ round tore through his flesh. The burning pain brought tears to eyes and his nose started to run. Just as he was trying to make sense of what just happened to him Briscoe stepped into view holding the P245 at his side.

"No, please no!" Red pleaded.

Briscoe leveled the gun directly in his face, "Stop crying and let me see your hands," he ordered.

Red held his hands out above his head as he lay on his back, "I don't have anything."

Briscoe bent down and patted his waist area and pockets for a weapon. He dragged the lanky nineteen year old across the chipped and dull hardwood floor into the living room where he had a little more room to work with.

"What have I done to you?" Red begged. "Please don't hurt me, I didn't do anything to you man. What did I do?"

"You are a killer and killers can't be allowed to walk free," Briscoe stood up and kicked Red as hard as he could in the leg he shot him in.

"Oww!" he screamed. The pain was coursing through his body like a mighty rushing river, but the fear was more overpowering.

"Do you remember me?" Briscoe asked turning his baseball cap around backward exposing his face.

"No, I don't know you from anywhere," Red was afraid if he said yes his assailant would not let him live for fear he would be able to identify him. His small mind has not yet processed that this whole thing is about his death . . . and nothing else.

"I think you do remember, because you saw me lots of times working your neighborhood. Now it's time for me to work you," even though the room was dark, Briscoe could see the fear emblazoned on Red's freckled face.

"Please sir, I'm just a kid, I'll never do anything again, I promise," he was now crying like a child.

"You should have thought of that before you decided to run with Brick and do his killing. Now it's your turn," Briscoe crashed down on Red's face with his elbow smashing him in the mouth displacing teeth. His screams and cries were almost infantile. His nose was running with snot that mingled with the blood from his mouth. He was a weak man for nineteen and for a minute Briscoe found it hard to believe he was the one who beat another young man to death.

"I'll change, I promise. I don't want to die. Please sir, I'll be good and give my life to God. Please sir, please. I'm just a boy," he begged and cried through his busted mouth.

"You're not a boy, you are a man! Now die like one," Briscoe yelled as he punched him with so much force in the eye it swelled shut immediately. Briscoe put the gun in the bag and commenced beating Red to death with his hands. There was blood everywhere; on Briscoe's pants, shirt, shoes, and even his face and arms. The fury he unleashed on Red was vicious to say the least. He slammed, his head on the floor so many times he could hear his brain sloshing around in his skull. When it was all over, Red suffered crushed ribs, a broken pelvis, a skull fractured in multiple places, and a face turned to ground sausage. Briscoe did all this damage with rage and the force of his two hands. He stood up and looked down at the heap that was once Red and nearly lost his lunch. He turned away and choked back the vomit that welled up inside. It was as if he was outside of his body during the entire beating. He nearly blacked out.

Briscoe has never lost himself before and this disturbed him. Red's pleading was echoing in his head as he stood above his body trying to get his legs beneath him. *Oh my God, what have I done?* He went to the bathroom and grabbed a towel from the shower rack and wiped the blood from his face and arms. He checked to be sure he didn't track blood under his shoes, then checked around the room to ensure he didn't drop anything incriminating. He rolled the towel and placed it in his backpack. Thoughts were racing through his mind, but he could not entertain them right now. He must get out of this house and get to safety. Allowing himself to second guess at this point would cause him to be careless and that could be the only clue Whitehead needs to discover him.

He went out the house the same way he entered. Back in the car, he drove out of the alley and headed straight home. Red's pleading echoed in his mind like a thousand bats squealing in a dank cave.

"He was promising to give his life to God and I stamped that life right out of him," Briscoe talked out loud, choked back tears and wondered if he had done the right thing. For the first time he questioned his actions.

Strangely, he thought about how Red's mother will feel when she walks into that cluttered living room and finds her baby, lifeless and misshapen lying in his own blood. The drive home seemed like it took forever, his upset stomach and pounding head did not help shorten the ride. Somewhere in the midst of the beating Briscoe blacked out, because the last thing he remembers before coming back to his senses was Red offering his life to God. *What if God wanted him to stop beating Red and allow the boy to serve Him?* Red sounded like a child who just needed chastising, not like the cold-blooded killer Briscoe went there to punish and remove from the roster of life.

"God please don't punish me for this. Please forgive me," he cried out.

He arrived at home and parked in front of his house because his Charger occupied the driveway. He looked around but did not see Monica's car anywhere. Good he thought, the last thing he needs right now is company. He stripped out of his clothes and placed everything; including the belt and shoes he wore, in a plastic trash bag along with the towel he used to wipe Red's blood from his face. He placed the bag under his bed and then climbed into the shower where he stood with the water beating off his head and cascading down his face. He stood like that for a long time. He had to adjust the hot water twice because it started to run cold. He struggled with the images in his mind, trying to shake the feeling that he killed a child. He told himself that Red was a man and deserved everything he got; however, that was a part of the battle being waged inside between his heart and mind.

23

"Thank you for coming Deborah, but I would have been more than happy to come to you," Whitehead used his most professional speech, although he was beaming like a schoolboy with a secret crush on the prettiest girl in class.

"Oh no it's my pleasure Jamie," Agent Bell was also smiling from ear to ear showing Whitehead all thirty-two.

They sat at the conference table in the same small conference room where he and Sutton briefed her on the case a couple of short weeks ago.

"Can I get you something to drink?" he offered.

"No thanks I had a Starbucks coffee on the way over. I'm good for now," she pulled a folder from her bag and emptied the contents on the table.

"I have an interesting profile of the killer. It isn't as close as I would like it to be, but based on the people killed and the methods used, I'm confident that we are in the ballpark."

"I know this isn't an exact science, but I believe in you and I will take anything I can get that is the least bit helpful," he looked into her eyes and she held his gaze. The part about believing in her touched something inside of her. She couldn't stop herself from smiling. The sexual tension was building and they were just getting started.

"I'll start by saying that the killer is not your run of the mill street thug. He has had formal training in the art of killing. Whether it came from the military, law enforcement, or special personal security training is beyond me, but he was definitely not self taught," she pointed at the crime scene photos as she spoke. "Look at the well placed shots when he killed multiple persons at one scene. His movements are precise with and without the gun."

"That is one of the theories I concluded myself," Whitehead interjected.

"As I delved into his psyche I came up with a few options. None of them stuck out any further than the others. That is why I said I am not as close as I would like to be. So, I will give you all the options and with the great work that you do, I'm sure you can make it work," she could feel her body heat up as she spoke. There was a tingling sensation that rose between her legs and Whitehead sitting so close to her looking into her eyes as she spoke intensified the sensation.

"That is so kind of you Deborah; I'll do my best with what you give me," his heart was thumping and he could sense a bead of sweat start to form on his forehead. Wow, the tension between them is so great.

Agent Bell has thought about Whitehead since the day she met him. She was tempted to ask him out for drinks or dinner, but the professional side of her would not allow her to do it.

She talked to her best girlfriend about it and she said, "Go for it girl, you're not getting any younger, fuck all that professional shit, get that man!"

Now she is back in his presence and feeling him like crazy. Throughout the discussion of the serial predator, she was thinking how sexy Whitehead was and how good he smelled. The aroma of the Calvin Klein, his favorite cologne, was nearly intoxicating her. She thought how awkward it would be if she asked him out and he turned her down. The embarrassment would be too much to bear. She was feeling him and could sense he was feeling her. At least she hoped there was a vibe she was picking up.

"The killer is a champion for justice," she continued. "He has witnessed a lot of injustice and has reached a point where he is taking matters into his own hands. He is may be a person who was the victim of a violent crime, but I consider that theory pretty weak based on his training and skill. Even if I were to consider that he was victimized at an early age, it is still a weak theory. He possibly witnessed someone close to him suffer violence and then watched the perpetrator walk free. That is a very strong possibility, one you should give a lot of attention."

Whitehead nodded his acknowledgement.

She continued, "He is also a person who has a strong sense of right and wrong, but not in the biblical sense. He does believe in God, but he is not driven by religion. I would venture to say he probably only attends church on special occasions. He has few friends, yet he is liked by many. He does not let his guard down to allow new people into his life easily. Socially, he is as normal as you and I, but he has strong opinions about justice and they are clearly what drives him. His occupation could be in any field; however, based on the crime scenes I would venture to say he is probably in law enforcement."

"Wait a minute," Whitehead interrupted. "Are you saying this killer is a cop?"

"It is very possible. While studying the crime scenes I noted a lack of evidence. This guy even thought of the simple things that most people would never think of. Only somebody familiar with crime scenes would know the types of evidence the police would collect. The use of the victim's cell phone to call the police to report the murders and then the timing and terminology used during the calls. He knew just how to stretch the city's resources and he knew what to say to get the police into or out of an area."

She gave Whitehead a sympathetic look, because as she spoke she saw the disappointment on his face and his shoulders slump.

He looked incredulously into her soft brown eyes, "Damn, I hope not."

"I'm sorry sweetie, but it is what it is," she couldn't believe she said sweetie. *Damn that slipped!* She looked away too embarrassed to look into his eyes.

"I know it is Deborah. It's just hard to swallow the thought of a cop out there doing this," he liked that she called him sweetie.

"Another point to note," she continued, "the killer is a black man."

"How do you surmise that?" Whitehead had the same theory.

"He moves in and out of the black community barely noticed. Even though the killings are done at night, people would remember seeing a white man or one of a different ethnic group, and they would be more likely to report that."

"I had that same theory, thanks for helping me validate my assumption," he wanted to reach out and hold her hand, and tell her how much he has thought about her since they met.

"See, great minds think alike," she winked at him.

It was heating up in the conference room, and they both could feel the sensation in their most private regions.

"I'll take this profile and work it into my investigation. There are more police agencies in the area than I can name off the top of my head. It will be a daunting task to find out where our man is working, but I am dead set on finding him," the look in Whitehead's eyes sent a shiver down Agent Bell's spine.

She wanted to fall into his strong arms and for the first time in her life be submissive to a man.

They went over the entire profile in great detail. Three hours had passed since she came into VCU and it was nearing lunch time when they finished.

"I appreciate all you have done for us; the department owes you a debt of gratitude. I guess I could start paying that debt by treating you to lunch," Whitehead appeared confident on the outside but he was sweating inside.

"Thank you, but . . ."

"But what?" he interrupted. "Come on it will be nice to share lunch with a refined beauty such as you. Please don't make me eat with Sutton today, he chews like a cow."

His pleading sparkling eyes were too much for Agent Bell to deny.

"Okay, let me call the office and check my messages," she was giddy inside and wondered if he could see her excitement.

She stepped into the hallway for privacy and dialed her girlfriend, "Girl, I'm going to lunch with that fine hunk of man."

"That's what I'm talkin' bout. Do the damn thing girl. Go enjoy yourself and be happy; you deserve it."

"I will. I just had to tell you. I think he is feeling me as much I'm feeling him. I'll call you later and tell you all about it."

Agent Bell was nervous, excited, and self-conscious all at the same time. *What if he discovers he does not want to be with her after all? What if she is too opinionated or overbearing for his taste?* She has not been on a date in more than two years, and even though this doesn't classify as a date, she sure does hope it develops into one. The last man she dated made her feel as though she was struggling with him for dominance in the relationship. He told her that she was never going to find a man who would want to be with a control freak like her. The words he spoke have stuck in her mind. Deep down she knew she was not a control freak; she was simply a woman who was not going to accept just anything to be with a man.

"Have fun and forget about all that professional shit! Get that man Debbie!"

They have been best friends since the first grade when she moved next door to Agent Bell in the Kentland neighborhood of Landover, Maryland. She has been her dedicated and trusted friend through thick and thin, and there was nobody else in the world who she let her hair down with and became the sista girl that she was inside.

"I'm all over it girlfriend. I want this brother like no other. I'll get you up when I get back to the office," she hung up and composed herself before going back into the conference room.

"Everything okay at the office?" Whitehead wanted so badly to have lunch with her.

"Sure, everything is great. I'm ready to go," she smiled from inside out. They walked out of the conference room turning off the lights behind them.

24

Danielson grabbed his mail from his assigned cubby hole on the wall behind Patricia the receptionist, "Good morning Patricia. How was your weekend?"

"Very nice," she said. "How was yours?"

"Not bad, I just stayed in mostly and did yard work and whatever else my wife needed done," he wasn't complaining, but he thought he could have enjoyed his weekend differently.

Patricia was warm and friendly to all her coworkers. She is a married mother of three, living in Lanham, Maryland. She is only thirty but carries herself much older. She is very spiritual and heavily involved in her church. Her smooth cocoa butter complexion and voluptuous shape gets a lot of attention from men. It seems like a twinkle and a smile is always in her eyes. When men come into the office on business they are always drawn to her. Whether the man is a cop, attorney, witness, or offender, they never fail to crack on her. Her commitment to her husband is strong and she always shoots them down in the nicest way. *Hell, it's a wonder they all don't notice the huge platinum ice that is chilling her finger...oh yeah, I forgot, when has that ever stopped a dude?*

"I'll be in all morning. I have a deposition scheduled for 1:00 p.m. My wife is coming by to take me to lunch, so basically I'm here all day if you need me," since he is the head of the section, he likes to keep Patricia apprised of his schedule.

"Okay, sounds good Phil," Patricia smiled warmly and waved goodbye as he walked down the corridor toward his office.

Danielson entered his plush office leaving the door open. He sat behind the mahogany desk in front of the ceiling to floor length window and flipped through the small stack of envelopes. He stopped when he reached the one handwritten in red ink. He wondered who would address an envelope with red ink. Probably some battered woman wanting to drop an anonymous tip about her abuser hoping it would get him off her back without knowing who dimed him out.

Danielson opened the letter and began to read: *Mr. Danielson, I know what you have been doing. I am watching you when you don't think you are being watched. The disgusting things that you like to do with children will not remain your little secret.* His heart sped up like he just finished a one hundred yard dash. Sweat beaded on his forehead and his hands shook to the point he had to concentrate to continue reading the letter. *Oh my God, who sent this?* His mind was racing out of control as he hurried to the door and peered out into the hallway to see if anyone was there. He quickly closed the door and went back to his seat. He turned around to look out the window. He studied the building across the street from where he sat, as if someone was looking in watching as he read the letter. Paranoia was already setting in. He could not stop the thoughts from invading his mind, *Who knows what I've been doing? Which child are they talking about? Do they know about all of them, or just one? What do they mean they are watching? Am I being followed? Oh Lord what am I going to do?* He wondered how he would be able to go on with his day. Should he try to find out who the writer of the letter is or should he do as instructed and stop? He was faced with a dilemma that meant his freedom—possibly his life. He knows that prison is not an option for him because of the many people he has sent there over the years. It will not be a comfortable or safe place for him to exist. He spent nearly half an hour sitting at the desk thinking about his situation and feeling helpless that his fate was in the hands of a stranger. When the phone rang it startled him back to reality.

He composed himself then answered, "Phillip Danielson."

"Good morning my love," the soft voice on the other end of the connection sent a chill up his spine while the butterflies churned in his stomach.

"Hi Sasha," he was apprehensive because he was afraid she received a letter and knew about his extramarital activities.

"What's the matter hubby, aren't you happy to hear from your special lady?" she could sense something was on his mind when she heard the tremble in his voice.

They have been married for five years now. She knew him well enough to know when he was distracted.

"Oh it's nothing honey just a case that I'm working on," he lied.

"Well, don't let it get you too preoccupied that you forget about our lunch date," she teased. "I love spending time with my hunk of burning love during the work day. It makes me feel like I'm a teenager playing hooky from school to sneak off with my boyfriend."

He wished he could cancel the date with Sasha, but he knew her heart was set on it. They rarely got to meet for lunch in the city. Sasha works in Northern Virginia as an executive with Microsystems Technology. She is a tall statuesque beauty of east European decent. Her long blonde hair accentuates her high cheek bones, deep dimples, and full lips. She loves to wear shades of lipstick that draws attention to her bodacious soup coolers. Unlike the collagen ho's of the 1990s, her full lips are natural with the same sensual appeal as Sade. She rocks a very nice tan throughout the summer months and God knows she can use it. She has the curvy shape of a sister, complete with the banging onion, but the pale skin of a Ukrainian, her motherland. It's a wonder that Danielson would cheat on an intelligent, beautiful, and curvaceous woman like her. And to do it with underage girls would baffle many. Now his worst nightmare is descending on him like a London fog and he does not know what to do.

"I wouldn't miss lunch with my best girl for anything in the world," he strained to sound upbeat and excited.

"Great, I'll be there to pick you up at eleven thirty and we can walk to your favorite spot and eat outside. I can hardly wait. I love you Phil."

Strangely, hearing those words ripped at his heart and made him feel terrible.

"I love you too Sasha; I'll be waiting with bells on."

He hung up the phone, stared blankly at the letter and let the flood gates open allowing the tears to fall freely from his eyes onto the paper.

25

Briscoe was standing in the bathroom looking at his image in the mirror mulling over his destiny. When he started this thing he was sure of what he was doing and what he wanted to accomplish. Red really freaked him out. He never before lost himself to the point that his rage blacked out his senses. This was not supposed to be about him. It's about the people who cannot help themselves. It's about justice for all. It's about holding the wicked in check. *What has he done? Did he defy God? Was he supposed to let Red live to serve God?* No way, he wasn't going to do anything but run and tell that Briscoe broke into his home and tried to kill him. *Or was he going to give his life to God and never utter a word about the encounter with the powerful stranger in his living room?* Only God knows and Briscoe has to come to grips with that. *Either get on with his work, or fold and give the streets back to the evil doers. What is it going to be?*

Briscoe was trying to answer these burning questions that pierced his soul. He is about to get out on the street for his first night of the detail. His initial plans were to work on taking down Ant. But since killing Red he has been a wreck. He has barely slept, and on Sunday he even went to church. When the preacher announced altar call, Briscoe went up and knelt before the congregation. His mother was shocked that he went forth. First off, he rarely attended services, and secondly he never went up to pray. She planned to call him later to make sure everything was alright. Briscoe remained on his knees begging for forgiveness for twenty minutes. The pastor got down on his knees and prayed with him. He thought he was praying for salvation and asking Jesus into his heart. If the pastor knew what he was seeking, it would have rocked his robe right off his chubby body. Briscoe rose to his feet and thanked the preacher and returned to his seat. His eyes were red from the tears that he choked back as hard as he could. He did not want to cry in front of a bunch of people who he considered strangers.

Regardless of what he is feeling at the moment, he knows that Ant has to be dealt with. There are so many more that must be taken off the streets. Despite the intractable task, he must stay committed.

Hell, that punk ass Red wasn't going to give his life to anything but those fucking streets anyway. I did the right thing, he reasoned as he washed his face and looked into his irresolute eyes.

Briscoe left his house and headed toward Georgetown to relieve Seth. When he got into Northwest D.C. he picked up the department-issued cell phone and dialed Seth's number.

"Hey Seth, I'm inbound baby boy. What's the dealio?"

"Just waiting on you playa."

"Is he up to anything?" Briscoe knew his assignment.

Sherman Edwards was in no danger, but Seth didn't know that.

"He is in the house right now. I followed that chump all around the globe this afternoon. He came home about an hour ago with some fly-ass ghetto superstar from Southeast. I figure he'll be in for the night knocking that down. At least I would," he laughed.

"Sounds good to me. Hang in the block until I pull in so I can get your parking spot."

Briscoe planned to stay there for a couple of hours and then shoot across town and start working surveillance on some of Brick's crew.

During the two hours Briscoe sat there, he thought about how other men had begged for their lives and he didn't bat an eye or feel anything for them. Why is it different with Red? He reasoned that it might have something to do with his loss of control. He felt that all the other killings he did in the streets of D.C. and abroad in the countries he operated were strictly business. He was detached from their suffering. He was merely the vessel used to send them on their way to judgment. If he had he not lost control with Red he might not have felt the way he was feeling. He decided to stay focused on his mission and not let his anger take control. The hatred he felt when he saw Red leaning on the fence was overpowering. He has come to grips with the fact that he would not have stopped at anything to punish him, even if it meant killing his family had they come home unexpectedly. Beating him to death with his hands was the ultimate rush. The orgasmic feeling that accompanied it was frightening. Briscoe could not comprehend the emotions while they were happening. But now he can see it clearly and take steps not to let it happen again. He spent a few minutes in prayer before pulling away from the curb and heading toward Montello Avenue.

Briscoe knew the mood on the street would be sullen because Red's crew is hurt by the violent loss of their brother in crime. It is funny how the brotherhood of the street works. They claim they would die for one another, but as soon as they are actually faced with that situation, they choose themselves. If one of them goes to prison, the others will not make the trip upstate to pay them a visit, nor will they accept the collect calls their homey makes to them. He is all but forgotten. The only time this is different is when the ringleader is the one behind bars, because he will attempt to run his operation from prison for as long as he can. Their loyalty is limited to their personal desires and needs. Red would have found that out if he would was convicted of Kenneth Johnsons' murder and sentenced to years in prison. But he had to find out the hard way. Now it's too late for him to be reformed. His destiny has been signed, sealed, and delivered.

Briscoe came to grips with killing Red; however, he could not stop his thoughts. He knew how the scenario played out when his mother walked in the door and discovered the crumpled heap on her living room floor that was once her love and joy. She nursed him, nurtured him, and protected him from harm, and somewhere along the way, he became his own man. He ignored her warnings of the negative influences in life, and how he would end up dead or in jail. The agony she experienced when she looked down at her son's carcass was something that no parent should ever have to endure. It is an unnatural thing for a parent to bury a child, and in some way Briscoe felt sorry for his mother; but he knew that the universe was a place of checks and balances. Red was the cause of another mother's anguish, and now the universe has balanced the scale and given that bad Karma back to him; tit for tat.

There were only a handful of people outside on Montello and they appeared to be peacefully talking amongst themselves. He drove around to Red's house where someone set up a street shrine. There was a picture of a young Red taped to a large oak tree that was in between the street and the sidewalk directly in front of the family home. There were stuffed toy animals, empty champagne bottles, sympathy cards, and a large poster board with messages of 'RIP', 'We are going to miss you', and all sorts of well wishes for the afterlife. Briscoe wondered what made them think that evil piece of shit was going to eternal rest in heaven. He also was perplexed as to why they would use a picture of the man when he was in the 7th grade. Perhaps that is the last picture anybody took of him, but he speculated it is probably the way his mother wants to remember him. That is probably the last time she had any control over him.

There were a few candles burning despite it being past midnight. The candles were in self contained jars and were not a true fire hazard. Briscoe thought about blowing them out, but he figured that would not be a wise move. Perhaps someone just lit them and is sitting right now watching. *Oh well, I've done my job, and Red has paid restitution for the wickedness he has done to others. I can feel good knowing that I have rid the community of someone that lived to cause it pain.*

He turned his attention to, Antoine "Ant" Lakeland and what he has planned for him. He thought it would have be fitting to kill him and Red together since they started their life of crime together and took Johnson's life together. It's only a matter of time now.

His personal cell phone rang. It actually startled him because he did not expect that anyone would call him at this hour.

"Hello," he said guardedly not recognizing the phone number.

"Hey sexy, what are you doing?" Karen's soft voice sounded like she was lying in bed stroking her clit with one hand and her supple nipples with the other.

Briscoe felt an immediate rise in his jeans. His heart skipped a beat and he paused for a moment, and then responded, "I'm working."

"I know; me too."

"I thought you were doing the day-work portion for your team." He was not expecting her to be on the street; especially since they talked and she told him she was working days.

"We changed it around because I want to be home with my daughter during the day . . . and you too," she added.

He played the last part of her comment off, "I'm sure your daughter appreciates that."

"What about you?" she was not going to let him off the hook that easily.

"What about me?" he knew exactly what she meant.

"Will you appreciate spending the time with me?" after feeling his dick in the lodge she was even more determined to have him.

"I can't do that Karen. Should we be having this conversation on a government issued phone?"

He did not want to have to answer to anybody down the road about an inappropriate conversation on Karen's issued phone.

"Do you want me to call you back on my cell phone?"

"I don't know Karen, you are bad for me. You know I have a

girlfriend who I am in love with. Why do you insist on getting me in trouble?"

He is getting weak for her. The closer she gets, the more he wants to give in and taste her goodies.

"I can't help it Antonio, I want you so bad. Judging from what I felt at the table, you want me too," she whispered in the phone. "Pleeeaase, just come to my place in the morning and hold me for a little while. I want you so bad I can taste you."

The heat had risen so high inside of him that his dick was fully erect and begging to be released from its denim prison.

"Karen, I can't," he did not sound convincing and she could sense his desire as it came oozing through the phone.

"Pleeeaase," she begged in a low, seductive whimper.

His penis was pounding and his heart was fluttering.

What the hell am I going to do? This woman is hot as a firecracker and she is burning for my love. A lot of guys would kill to have her on their tip, but I have somebody who I want to spend the rest of my life with. Nothing good could come out of messing with Karen. He tried hard to convince himself not to entertain what she was saying. But the truth is he has thought about her constantly since Saturday night at the lodge. The way her hand massaged his man-muscle danced around his thoughts and he wondered just how good she could make him feel if he gave himself to her without limitations.

"Antonio, pleeeaase, don't leave me all alone. I need you to hold me baby. You know you want me too. Don't deny us baby," she was pushing his buttons and she knew it was working.

His silence spoke volumes. She knew that if he was not interested, when she first started touching him in the lodge he would have stopped her. Since he didn't, she knows it is only a matter of time before she has him . . . and that long, thick dick.

He changed the subject, "Where are you now Karen?"

"I'm on 18th Street in Northeast."

Holy shit, she is around the corner from me. He looked around as if she was somewhere watching him.

"What are you doing on 18th?"

"My assignment is over here waiting in his truck for some white bitch to come out of a house," she sounded annoyed that she had to follow him over to the neighborhood.

Briscoe figured he was at Janice's house and Christine was the white woman who went inside. It must be time for a re-up of product he speculated. Since Karen is in the area, he'd better get back across town. If she saw him over there he would have a lot of explaining to do. He could tell her that his assignment was over there somewhere, but the questions would intensify and he didn't want the hassle. He wished Karen never saw the car he was issued, but it was too late for that now.

"Where are you?" she asked.

"I'm in Georgetown. It looks like my man is in for the night," he lied.

"So, are you going to come over in the morning? I'll make breakfast; pleeeeaase," she was persistent, and armed with a renewed sense that he would give in she was not giving up as easily as she has in the past.

"I'll call you when I get off to let you know, okay?" he wasn't really planning to call her; he just wanted to get her off the phone.

"Ahight," she said in a ghetto sistah way, "Antonio, please don't stand me up. You are better than that. I don't want to cry or eat alone," she added that for good measure.

"Good night Karen. Stay safe."

He flipped his cell phone closed, turned the corner onto Penn Street and drove to West Virginia Avenue where he decided to go left and get the hell out of Northeast. *Damn that Karen is going to make me jeopardize my relationship with Monica. I know I'm not married to her, but I made a commitment to be forever faithful and true. If I give into Karen, how could I ever face Monica and be the man that she knows me to be? How could I even deal with Karen on a professional level once we engage in sex? She will find some way to let Monica know I betrayed her. Then where does that leave me?* he was conflicted but the desire for Karen was bubbling inside of his testicles and raging to be released inside of her. He will have to keep his distance because so much is at stake.

26

"Man, that profile has me spooked," Whitehead has spent the entire day and last night thinking about it. "I have to follow the leads provided, but I'm hoping it isn't a cop. Now we have to be more guarded than ever with our investigation."

"Deep down, what do you think?" Sutton knew his gut told him it was a cop. *Who else would select the victims and then know how to get them the way they did?*

"I think we are looking for a very clever predator who happens to have a lot of insight into police work. I'm hoping he just watches a lot of CSI, but I think the truth is he was once a real life cop," it was out there now and Whitehead has to work it. "Before we go outside, let's check our house and see who might fit the profile and then work our way from there."

"I'm tracking. So how should we proceed?" Sutton asked.

"We can start with the victims. Let's get the criminal history of all the victims, then check out every officer who was involved in any way with every case involving them. Then see which officers come up most often and start with them." Whitehead felt the investigative spark ignite inside of him. "Also, I need you to get back with that shem and get a much better description. I know she can do better than what she did, and she was digging you so use that to your advantage," he said grinning.

"I can do that," Sutton knew Whitehead thinks it's funny that Tanisha likes him, but he really doesn't care because he thinks she is hot. He has to remind himself that she is a chick with a dick . . . but damn, she's fine.

"Alright partner, let's start shaking some trees and see what falls to the ground," Whitehead was pumped up and ready for the hunt.

"Hi Miss Goodall, this is Detective Sutton of the Metropolitan Police Department."

"Yes," Tanisha said warily.

"I'm the detective who came out to your house and interviewed you after your ordeal," he chose his words carefully attempting to gain her trust.

"Yes sir, I remember you."

"How is my handkerchief doing?" he laughed lightly, hoping to break the ice, and make sure she knew it was him, the nice one, not Whitehead.

"I've been taking good care of it," she giggled.

"That's great. It sounds like you are doing better. How have you been?" he was genuinely concerned.

"I'm doing okay, just taking each day as it comes to me," she felt instantly comfortable with him. She couldn't put her finger on it, but there was something about him that made her want to trust him.

"I was actually supposed to call you a while ago to do a follow up interview, but I wanted to give you time. I felt like you would call me whenever you were ready. Well, I have to follow up for the record, but I was wondering if you weren't busy, maybe we could get together and maybe have a drink or something?" he stepped out there with it to see where she was.

"I'm not sure that I want to waste your time. I told you everything I knew," she was interested in Sutton.

But she was not sure that a cop, a man like him, would be interested in a girl like her. She thought about the treatment that people like her suffered at the hands of bigoted cops and the thought of one wanting to be with her gave rise to caution.

"I don't think you would be wasting my time. We could just talk. If you feel like talking about that night, cool. If not, don't sweat it," he would have to take his time with her and alleviate her fears before he could gain her confidence.

"Well, I guess a drink couldn't hurt," she was still apprehensive, but more curious about Sutton.

"Cool. Can you meet me eight tonight at Romanoff bar on Pennsylvania Avenue. It's not far from your house?" he wanted to make it convenient for her.

He also wanted to go where there wouldn't be a large crowd. A Tuesday night at Romanoff should have very few people.

"Yes, I'm free tonight and I'll be there," even though she didn't know exactly what to expect, she was excited about seeing him.

"I'm meeting with Tanisha tonight at eight," Sutton braced himself for the ribbing Whitehead was sure to send his way.

"That's good," he said nonchalantly.

"What, no jokes?" Sutton smiled.

"I've been going through the case files of the victims and have compiled a list of officers who were involved. I have the names of thirty-three officers. I was just separating them into categories. I'm going to prioritize them according to multiple victims from the highest to the lowest number. So if one officer appears in five victim's history and another officer appears in three histories, the first would be a higher priority. Once we check this group of officers thoroughly, we will move to the others on the list. I hope this bears fruit, because beyond this I'm grasping at straws.

"When I speak with Tanisha tonight I hope she will give us something more substantial to work with."

"It would help a lot if we could eliminate some of them because of race, height, or something your girl gives us that is unique," Whitehead looked up from his work with a glimmer of hope in his eyes.

"She sounded a lot more relaxed this time. I think if I take my time I will be able to get her to recall more detail. I think she is starting to trust me."

Sutton had a way with victim's families. He had a talent for comforting those dealing with grief, and was the best cop Whitehead knew at coaxing information out of witnesses.

"That's alright partner. Do your thing. I know if she has something inside you are the one to get it out of her," Whitehead admired that skill in his partner, but he couldn't miss the wide open shot. "And if you don't get any information out of her, you get that thing out of her," Whitehead laughed from his gut.

"Oh. I see you got jokes," Sutton smiled and walked away.

Romanoff Bar is a small joint; some would call it a hole in the wall. It's a place frequented by a regular blue collar crowd who meet daily to wash away their hectic day, and drown a few of their problems. The entire place is not much bigger than the basement of a house. Sutton noted there were two pool tables prominently put in the center of the room. No one was playing at either table. There were five tables lined against one wall and four on the other. The bar was long and curved around on one end. Sutton counted twelve stools, but there were only three people sitting at the bar. For the place that was so small, they still had a parquet dance floor off to the left of the bar and a small boxed area that was elevated above the floor reminiscent of a stage. He figured it was probably where the DJ set up on nights when there was dancing, or perhaps they had live music. Even though the area appeared too small for a band, he thought about how small the stage is at Blues Alley; and big name acts perform live there.

He ordered a Long Island Iced Tea and chose a table against the wall facing the door. He wanted to see Tanisha when she arrived. He had no choice but to invite her out to a public place, *How else is he going to gain her trust and get her to see that he is his own man and not ashamed of being seen with a girl like her?* The truth is he chose Romanoffs' because he didn't want to run the risk of being seen by anybody he knows. How could he explain being out for a drink with a transsexual? *Well fuck it if somebody sees me,* he thought, *the case is more important than what small minded people thought.* Even though he reasoned with himself, he was not completely comfortable meeting with her in public. The truth is, he did worry what others thought. He finished his drink within five minutes and was at the bar ordering another. The alcohol was starting to work on him as he felt himself loosen up and relax. The bartender was sliding his drink across the bar just as an exaggeratedly soft voice spoke from close behind him,

"That looks good."

He spun around and looked into the eyes of a stunning beauty. *Fuck it that she has a dick, she is Goddamn gorgeous.* The green eye shadow, the professionally laid make up, and impeccable hairdo screamed class and elegance. She was far from a chicken head or one of those Trannies you find on the street corners trying to make a buck off of some cheating husband who is confused about his sexuality. The two-piece business suit she wore with the skirt that was a couple of inches above the knee, showed just enough of her thick smooth thighs to keep a man guessing, while all the time remaining respectful. To be six feet tall and a man, she has softer edges and more femininity than many women. Her stomach is flat and her breasts are a banging 38D. Sutton stared into her gorgeous face with his mouth agape and could not find any sign of a man. He could not detect an Adam's apple, a five o'clock shadow, or any other indicators that were normally associated with transsexuals. *Daaammn!* is what ran through his mind.

He finally spoke as he extended his hand, "Hi Miss Goodall. I'm glad you came. What would you like to drink?"

"Call me Tanisha. I'll have an apple martini if you don't mind."

"Not at all," he turned to the bartender who was equally

enchanted by the beauty of Tanisha.

He was listening and started mixing the drink before Sutton could say anything. The three other men in the bar were staring at Tanisha as if she was a piece of meat and they have not eaten in weeks. If only they knew that she has a piece of meat, they would stop gawking.

"I have a table over by the window," Sutton motioned.

The bartender handed him Tanisha's drink and they walked over and took a seat.

"So how was work today?" Sutton asked.

"It was work, you know same ole same," she sipped the drink.

"I know what you mean, if it was fun it wouldn't be work," he smiled. "You work at Club Odyssey right?"

"I only do that part-time on some weekends. My regular job, the one that pays the bills is with the D.C. Department of health. I'm a program manager for the HIV/AIDS awareness program."

"That sounds important."

"It is," she enjoyed talking about her job and was very proud of her accomplishments. "So many people are infected with the disease and walk around ignorantly infecting others. I wish my agency's budget was larger, because we need to go on an educational campaign larger than the one launched against the tobacco industry."

"It is a tragedy for anybody to die needlessly because they were not properly educated on the dangers of a killer disease they can avoid," his empathy and understanding was warmly received.

"Detective you are different from most other cops."

"Call me Jake. And how am I different?" he was feeling the effects of the Long Island Iced Teas and was warming up nicely to Tanisha.

"You seem to care about people from the heart. Most cops are hard on people and don't display any care for them. Your friend wasn't too nice to me when you were at my house, but you were very sweet," she felt something inside for Sutton but wasn't quite sure what it was.

She didn't even know if he would be interested in a transsexual, however, she felt he wasn't completely against the possibility.

"I understand what you're saying but most cops really do care about people. It's just that they have to cope. They couldn't wear their hearts on their sleeves or breakdown and cry with every victim. Besides them being a wreck, the people we serve would lose all respect and confidence in them. Trust me, more cops go home at night and cry, or drink themselves to sleep, than you could imagine. It really is a stressful job and more so emotionally," his eyes were fixed on hers as he spoke and it seemed as though she watched his mouth the entire time.

He could feel the tension-mixed apprehension depart her shapely body as she relaxed in her seat and took a sip of the apple martini. Throughout the conversation, her eyes stayed fixed on Sutton and she hung on every word he spoke. The men at the bar had positioned themselves to get a better look at her and they would periodically steal glances. Sutton wondered if they had any idea she was really a he. The bar tender would lean in closer and speak low enough that only the men at the bar could hear him and then they would exchange dap and laugh. He figured the men were talking testosterone filled rhetoric about what they would do sexually to Tanisha. But once they found that surprise in her panties, they would probably be the ones getting done. The thought of them making out with her not knowing the hot chick has a dick, made him want to bust out in laughter.

"I guess you're right. You know more of them than I do, and since you are one you would know the best way to do the job."

"Yeah but I can't say that about all of them. You are right, some of them are assholes I can't argue with you on that point," they shared a laugh.

Sutton ordered another round of drinks and they both loosened up and talked about more personal issues. Tanisha spoke about her beginnings and how she had always felt that she was a woman trapped in a man's body. She told Sutton that as a little boy around seven years old she was more in tune with the girls. She played with dolls, jumped rope, and played hopscotch.

"Can I ask you a really personal question?" Sutton wasn't sure if it would be appropriate to ask, but his curiosity coupled with the alcohol made him ask.

"Sure anything," she braced herself.

"Do you still have a penis or did you have it removed," he diverted his eyes from hers.

"I'm still holding and it's fully functional," she smiled.

"Are you planning to get rid of it?"

"I don't know," she mused and continued, "I get pleasure from it and I have to admit I'm a little afraid of what it would be like without it. That would be major surgery and no telling what could happen. For now I'm content with the way things are."

Sutton had many more questions about Tanisha and the lifestyle she leads, but he didn't want to jump completely into that and lose sight of what he was really there for. He is a single man with no children or steady girlfriend; however, he does date often. He thinks Tanisha is smoking hot, and if she were a real girl he would have pounced on her the first time he laid eyes on her. No matter how hot she looks, she is still a man and he is not down with that kind of thing, no pun intended.

"So, could you be with a girl like me?" Tanisha brought the question from way downtown and knocked him off balance.

After nearly choking on his drink he said, "I have never been with a girl like you. Neither have I ever met one as beautiful as you. The possibility has never been presented to me. I can't say for sure, but anything is possible."

He wanted to keep all communications and trust open between them, but, in his mind, he thought, *Hell no! There is no way I'm playing with a dick.*

"I guess that's something a girl could look forward to," she touched his hand.

It sent a shiver through his bones making him feel uncomfortable. It was a struggle reminding himself that Tanisha was not a real girl. He decided to steer the conversation to the night she encountered the serial predator.

"I thought a lot about you since the day I met you. I wondered how you were adjusting since your ordeal," he said in his most sincere voice.

"Wow. That is so sweet of you to say. I thought about you also," she looked longingly into his eyes.

He held her gaze until something stirred inside of him and then he looked away.

"You must have really been scared," he said.

"I was terrified. After he left, I laid there thinking about my life and all that I wanted to do with it. I really thought he was coming back to kill me, even though he said he wouldn't as long as . . ." she stopped short of finishing.

"As long as what?" he locked onto her eyes and let his soul plead with hers.

"I'm just so afraid. He was so serious."

"You don't have to be afraid, I'll protect you. I won't let anything happen to you," he reached over and rested his hand on top of hers.

She sighed heavily; with fear clearly etched onto her face she said, "I trust you, but what if he finds out I talked to you and comes back to kill me like he said he would?"

"You won't have to worry about that. We would never mention to anybody that you gave us any information. You would never have to testify in court or anything formal. We just need a lead to narrow him down and then get him off the street."

He was telling the truth because any information obtained while under the influence of alcohol could be considered tainted and inadmissible in open court. He really only wanted a better description to help them better focus their search.

"Okay, I'll tell you whatever you want to know. Go ahead, and I'll do my best to recall it," she swallowed hard and then took a long pull on her drink to steady her nerves.

"Don't worry baby, I promise to protect you," he rubbed the hand that he was still holding on top of the table. "For starters, what color was he?"

"I can't be sure because he had on the mask, but I think he was black; at least he sounded black,"

"How tall was he?"

"He must be about six two or six three because he was taller than me. I didn't have on shoes and he did, but I'm guessing about that size."

"How is he built? You know fat, skinny," he did not write anything down.; he planned to try and commit it to memory.

"He was built like a football player or something. He had muscles and felt very strong," she reflected.

"How much do you think he weighed?"

"Around 220 pounds."

"Did he say anything about why he was there?"

"Yes. He said Damon had to pay a debt."

"Yeah, I remember you said that before. What kind of debt? Did he say who Damon owed?"

"He said his debt was for all the victims he left behind." She asked, "is the killer the same guy who is doing the serial killings?"

"Yes he is. We have an idea on where to find him, but we need as much detailed information that we can get from you because you are the only witness who has ever come in close proximity to him. He obviously is not interested in hurting people who are not criminals. So I don't think you will have to worry about him coming back for you."

"I wish I would have told you all this when I first met you, but I was just too scared. I want to help, I just don't want to die doing it," she was genuine.

"That's okay, at least this way I got to see you again," he smiled widely. "

He felt good about the information she provided. Now he has a really good description of the predator minus the face. Now they can eliminate a lot of suspects based on the physical description Tanisha provided. He was feeling the excitement and could hardly wait to pass the information on to his partner. It was a great idea coming out to the bar with Tanisha. Whitehead knew she was holding back, and he also knew she had feelings for was feeling (well understood in this way by readers of urban novels) Sutton.

"Do you want to come back to my place for a nightcap in private?" she came straight with it, bringing the high heat that caused him to choke on his drink and almost knocked him out of his chair.

"I wish I could. But I have to run past the office and put a couple of things in order," he fabricated that story on the fly.

She might be a gorgeous sexy tranny, but she is still a chick with a dick. No amount of sexiness is going to make Sutton swing that way.

"Well maybe next time," she was outwardly disappointed.

27

"Antonio you treat me like some shit," Karen complained.

"No I don't. I told you I wasn't coming over," Briscoe countered.

"You said you would call me in the morning; and you didn't," she stated with a tinge of anger.

"Are you mad at me Karen?"

"No. I'm just hurt and very disappointed."

"I apologize if you thought I was coming over. I told you I couldn't because I'm afraid of what might happen between us," he has to be clear with Karen.

"I told you I just wanted to eat breakfast and I wanted a hug, that's all," she said in the tiniest voice she could muster.

"I told you I am committed to my girlfriend."

"Yeah yeah, but you're not married to her yet," she always pointed out that fact.

"I've told you Karen, I want to marry her some day. I don't want to mess up what we have established. All messing around with you would do is complicate my life. How are we supposed to work together after that?"

"Just like we are working right now. I'm a grown-ass woman who handles her business. I'm not some young trick who gets all emotional and twisted over some dick. I know how to keep things in perspective," she hoped her words sank in.

"And what perspective is that?" he asked.

"You can lay me down and fuck this pussy any way you want. I won't cause any problems between the two of you. All I want is to be with you," she said.

But in her mind she figured if he made love to her once, he would want it again and again until finally he was hers alone.

"I'm sure I could Karen, but that wouldn't help my situation with my fiancée."

Technically, Monica is not his fiancée, but she didn't have to know that.

"Fuck her. She don't have anything that I don't and she could never make you feel the way I can," her blood was starting to boil.

He could feel the hostility oozing through the phone, "Okay Karen, this is getting a little out of hand. You are upset, so I think we should talk later."

"There you go running like a little bitch. Your scared ass is pussy-whipped, that's all," whatever sweetness she had left in her vacated with that last comment.

"See Karen, when you do things like this it reassures me that I've done the right thing by not giving into temptation," he was ready to hang up but she would not let go of the conversation.

"Do things like what? Point out that you're whipped? Get a little disappointed because you stood me up? I guess your perfect girlfriend wouldn't do that. I don't understand why you can't see that I am the best thing for you. I would treat you like a king and give you all of me in a way that I know she doesn't."

His mind flashed back to the lodge when Karen played with his dick beneath the table. He could feel his soldier chub up a little as he listened to her speak. He allowed his hand to fall onto the shaft that was starting to thicken and rubbed it a little while listening to her voice. Karen is a real brick house with a tremendous amount of sex appeal. He knows that being alone with her was a guaranteed trip straight into her panties. There is no way he could stop himself.

He stopped touching his package and said, "I have to go Karen. You are too much for me right now. Aren't you following your boy?" he was referring to Brick.

"Yes I'm sitting outside his house right now. You can keep talking; all you're doing is watching your dude in Georgetown. I'm not distracting you that much."

"I have some other stuff to do and I have to make a couple of calls," he wanted her off the phone.

"What other stuff?"

"Come on Karen I have things to do. So I'm gonna have to say goodbye," he was firm.

"Okay, but if you get a chance later call me so we can talk a little more, okay?" she asked.

"I'll do that if I can," he had no intention of calling her again.

"So I'll talk to you later then. Have a good night Boo. Stay safe," she hung up before he could respond.

He thought for a minute she was going to say *I love you*. He turned the ringer off on his phone, put his binoculars into the case, and stepped outside of the car. He was back in Northeast DC waiting to introduce Ant to his fate.

The entire time he was talking to Karen he was watching Ant Lakeland and two of his homies sell their product on the street corner. Briscoe was familiar with all of them because they were members of Brick's crew. He had planned to come through tonight to dispatch Ant and maybe one of the other members of his crew. Even though there are three of them, he is prepared to send them all to the upper room.

The block was quiet and they were the only people out on the street. Briscoe walked the two blocks to where they were standing. He was dressed in all black clothing with a black baseball cap pulled low over his head. His silenced .45 was tucked away in the holster attached to his belt in the small of his back. This time it was there, just in case; he hoped it would not be necessary to use it, because tucked under both sleeves of his long sleeve tee were two razor sharp stilettos.

He surveyed the area on his approach. His muscles tensed the closer he got. His mind was racing through his plan of attack and with every footstep, his senses were heightened. His focus narrowed and he shook off the effects of tunnel vision as he breathed deeply and exhaled to prepare himself for his task at hand. The sound of Red's squealing voice echoed in his head, *Please sir, I'm gonna give my life to God.* He could not allow Red to haunt him at this crucial moment. He shook his head and could feel sweat bead up on his forehead. Adrenaline was flowing through his veins and butterflies were dancing around in his nervous stomach. He could see Red's face swollen, bloody, and disfigured. It stared up at him pleading to let him have a second chance. Briscoe blinked hard twice to clear the images from his head. He was now less than a block away from his targets. His palms were sweating to the point that he had to readjust the knives to wipe them dry. The closer he got the faster his heart beat. The faster his heart beat, the slower he walked. He sensed his own hesitation.

He was second-guessing himself. *How could this be?* He thought he worked everything out and came to grips with his purpose. *This can't be happening.* He took a very deep exaggerated breath and exhaled slowly and completely as he steadied himself to attack. He was now within forty yards of the crew. It was time to man up and put in work.

"God forgive me if I am wrong," he said aloud. He produced

the knives from beneath his sleeves cuffing them along is arms, concealed from view. He plans to walk directly up to them and stab, jab, and slash his way through flesh and cartilage. He can now see their faces clearly from the glow of the street lights. They looked in his direction studying his approach. They tensed because they cannot see his face and he is wearing all black clothing walking the streets alone this late at night. The three of them stared at him without looking away. They kept their eyes on him from the moment they noticed him from about forty yards away.

Briscoe wasn't sure if they were armed, but it didn't matter to him because he was prepared to deal with whatever they threw his way. He is now twenty yards away and blinks hard one last time hoping to clear the images and the doubt. *You're doing the right thing; stop doubting. You are on the side of righteousness,* he told himself.

When he opened his eyes three police cars pulled up to the men with the spot lights glaring directly on them lighting up the corner. The men were no longer concerned about Briscoe. Their full and undivided attention went to the officers who descended on them.

Briscoe abruptly turned left, walked between two parked cars, crossed the street, and hastened back down the street toward his vehicle. His heart was beating so hard he thought he could hear it. The sweat was now rolling off his forehead and he could feel his shirt sticking to his drenched body. The temperature outside was a manageable eighty degrees, which is hot for a summer night, but he reasoned that the perspiration was the result of his increased heart rate and blood pressure.

Get a hold of yourself Briscoe, he thought. He fought the urge to look back over his shoulder as he walked as fast as he could without appearing as though he was trying to get away from something. He did not want to raise any suspicion in the cops who he used to work with nightly on this very shift. He is in the precinct that he is assigned to. The officers who pulled up on Ant and the others are his coworkers and he knows them all. How in the world would he explain to them what he is doing over there after midnight walking down the street with two knives dressed like an assassin?

He reached the vehicle, unlocked the door with the keyless remote and slid into the driver's seat. He put the key in the ignition and turned it quickly forward and then back again to turn off the dome light. He did not want to start the car and turn on the lights yet. He decided to stay put until the cops are finished with the three young men that he has plans for.

He pulled the binoculars from its case and focused in on the crew members and the cops. He tuned his police radio to the Fifth Precinct zone and monitored the officers on the scene of Montello Avenue. Boy was that close. He was just seconds away from dishing out the pain. He could have been locked in a confrontation with his peers.

Looking through the binoculars, he could see that the officers searched Ant and his boys and then sat them down on the curb. He listened as they ran the crew members information through the dispatcher for outstanding warrants. When the dispatcher gave a return that none were wanted the officers spent a few more minutes on the scene and then Briscoe watched as the three huck-a-bucks walked away. The officers remained on the corner talking a few moments longer before they dispersed and went back into service.

Briscoe sat until the last car was out of the block and then he started the car and pulled away from the curb. *Damn, somebody must have called a complaint in on the three of them. That was as close as I could come without getting caught.* He was reeling from the near encounter.

On the drive back to Georgetown, where his assignment resides, he thought about everything that transpired. His near-miss has him rattled, but not nearly as much as his hesitation and second-guessing. *Is there something wrong? Is he losing his edge? Why is he now feeling the way he does, and seeing the images that invaded his mind's eye?* He doesn't believe his confidence is shaken, because he was prepared to do them all in once he reached them. However, the physical changes his body experienced has given him cause for alarm. He reasoned that maybe he should stop his mission for awhile. *But what would that accomplish? The bad guys will only increase their unchecked activity and they will go unpunished.* What he is doing is too important for him to stop right now. He is on the brink of weakening Brick Jackson's crew to the point that they will be vulnerable and exposed. Then he could take Brick down to the ground and put him in it. However, before any of that can take place he must determine what has caused him to second-guess himself.

He pulled into Edwards block to find his car gone. He figured Edwards went out after he left for Northeast. It's no big deal; if he does not return before morning he will tell Mathis, his relief, the target went outside of the city further than the prescribed fifty miles, and he returned to his residence as instructed. For the remainder of the night he devised a plan for taking down Ant and the rest of his buddies. He also thought about the conversation he had with Karen earlier. He found himself thinking more about Karen lately than in the past. She looks better and better to him; and the things she says and does are starting to wear him down.

He has not seen Monica in a few days. She was busy with a government audit that has consumed all her time. He knows how important her organization is to her, so he gives her all the support and space she needs to be successful. They speak on the phone daily, but it's not the same as being there together. He thought that he better see her soon, because he needed to unload some of the tension that has built over the past week. After tonight, he needed to bust off in the worst way. There is no way he will take a call from Karen tonight or in the morning, because knowing his girlfriend is inaccessible he might give in and break her off a little of what she is seeking. His best bet is to go to the gym in the morning and then go home and beat his dick like it stole something from him.

Mathis collected the information for his morning report and Briscoe drove off. He had his gym gear in the car and headed straight for his workout. He needed to burn off the energy boiling inside and clear his mind of all doubts. He lifted weights damn near to muscle failure, then did cardio exercises on the bike and treadmill. At one point, he looked out the corner of his eye to notice that a tall, attractive woman was staring at him. She looked familiar to him, as if he had seen her somewhere before. They made eye contact and she smiled widely. She is a stunning redbone with light green eyes. He thought, *I know her from somewhere.*

Just as he was walking on the treadmill, cooling down after a long fast run, the long tall redbone approached.

She smiled and said, "You look like you are running from something."

Briscoe smiled back and said, "Nah, I was just trying to challenge myself."

"You don't look like you need too much challenging. You're in great shape," her eyes glistened.

"Thank you. You look pretty damn good yourself," he couldn't believe how flirtatious he came across. But he couldn't help himself; this woman was stunning.

"You don't remember me do you?" she asked, searching his eyes.

He studied her face, gazed at her eyes; they both smiled at the same time.

"Okay, help me," he said.

"I'm a friend of your sister Alicia. I was at her cookout at your parent's house."

"Oh yeah, I remember you. You were dressed a lot differently then and your hair was different," he knew that sounded lame but he was so enamored with her at the cookout.

"Well I try not to wear Prada to the gym," she giggled.

"I know that sounded lame. I mean you look great now like you did then. It's just that you look different," he was laying it on thick, even though he knows his father warned him about this woman.

"I didn't get to introduce myself at the cookout. My name is Vanessa," she extended her hand.

He shook her hand while still walking on the treadmill, "I'm Antonio."

"I know," her eyes told the entire story, "I asked Alicia all about you."

"Oh boy, that can't be good," he laughed.

"Oh no, it was all good; except the part about the girlfriend," she said abruptly.

He didn't know exactly how to respond to that, so he changed the subject, "I come here all the time. I never saw you here before."

"I come mostly in the evening, but I had the day off today and wanted to get it in early because I have an engagement this evening."

"You live near Alicia right?" he seemed to state it more than ask.

"Yeah, I live in the building across from hers. What about you; where do you live?"

"Capitol Heights," he replied.

"Alone or with your girlfriend?" she asked.

"I live alone. How about you; do you live alone?"

"I live alone and I am alone. I don't have anybody," she offered.

"That has to be your choice," he stated and then continued, "a cutie like you either wants to be alone, or you are a real scary woman who's hard to deal with."

"I don't know. It might be a little of both," they shared a laugh.

Briscoe was sensing a connection. He had to admit he wanted to know her better. There is some kind of an attraction between them and her being easy on the peepers does not do anything to weaken the attraction. He caught himself looking down at her frame every time she turned her head. Once she caught his gaze as it lowered to her ample breasts. The look she gave him said, *I want you just as bad as you want me.*

He stopped the treadmill and stepped off. She had remained there talking the entire time. They stepped aside and continued until Briscoe started walking toward the locker rooms.

"Would you like to get a cup of coffee?" she asked.

"Sure," he didn't even give it a thought. "I'll grab a shower."

"We can stop by my place first and then go to Starbucks," she offered, "You can shower there if you like; I didn't bring a change of clothing to the gym"

"Okay, that sounds like a plan. Let me grab my stuff from the locker," he said.

"I'll meet you out front," she was gushing.

He knew the right thing to do was to decline the invitation and stay away from Vanessa. Instead he thought, *Fuck it! I want to know this intriguing lady.* He knew he did not plan to cheat on Monica, but he did want to get to know Vanessa and spend some time with her. He convinced himself that nothing would happen between them except good coffee and great conversation. He enjoyed the friendship of women, even if they were platonic relationships. He spends time with women on the job and he has no problem keeping them at bay while keeping his commitment to Monica. So Vanessa should be no different.

They met in front of the gym and walked to her silver Lexus GX470 SUV. His Pontiac was parked a few spaces away. He agreed to follow her home where they would shower and then go to breakfast at the IHOP in Forestville instead of Starbucks. Once he was in his vehicle, he removed his cell phone from the console and called Monica.

"Hello," she sounded rushed.

"Good morning sunshine," he beamed.

"Hey baby; how are you?" she asked more as a reflex than a true concern.

"I'm good. I'm just leaving the gym."

"I wish I could say the same. I'm swamped. I've been in the office since six this morning," she didn't have time for small talk, but didn't want to cut him off.

"Do you have any help? Maybe you should hire a temp to help you through this process," he suggested.

"I can handle my business. It takes a little more time, but I don't need a temp. I've been doing this long enough and well enough by myself. My staff is good and we will have no problems with this," she replied sharply.

"I apologize if I upset you, Moni. I only suggested because you sound overworked. I was just concerned about you," his disappointment with her annoyance of him could not be hidden.

"I appreciate that Antonio, but I can do this. I have a lot to do; I'll have to call you later," she did not acknowledge his disappointment because she was too busy to deal with him.

He will have to understand that she is under pressure to do well. The result of the audit could mean future revenue or future losses. That is more important right now than entertaining his suggestions.

"Okay; I love you Moni. Have a good day."

She hung up without reciprocating his affection. He looked at the phone before flipping it closed, as if it could provide some answer to her irritation with him. Sometimes he cram to understand women and their moods. All he did was suggest she hire a temp to help ease the burden of the audit. She has been working on her books and business policies for the past week in preparation. The audit is in a few days and he will be glad when it's over. He wants her full attention again.

He followed Vanessa into the gated apartment complex she shared with his little sister. He looked around for Alicia's car and was happy not to see it; he did not want to explain to her that he was just going to have breakfast with Vanessa. His sister liked Monica and would immediately think something was going on between him and Vanessa. He did not want to hear all that right now. He is a big boy who knows how to keep things in perspective and his Johnson in his pants.

Vanessa parked in a spot marked with a number and the word RESERVED. She directed him to one marked VISITOR. She waited outside her vehicle while he parked, grabbed his bag and locked the doors. They walked to her building where she used a key to open the door. The building was clean and brightly lit with a vaulted glass front that provided abundant sunlight throughout the stairwell. They climbed two flights of stairs to apartment 303, a lavishly decorated, spacious apartment. The carpet was so impeccably clean that Briscoe paused at the door wondering if he should remove is shoes before entering. There was a white leather sofa with a matching chaise lounge. You could look through the glass coffee table at the shag throw rug underneath. She had a forty-two-inch plasma screen TV in the corner adjacent to the lounge. A Bose stereo system was on what appeared to be a glass and stone wall unit along with a variety of fine sculptures and other artistic pieces. The room looked like something out of Apartment Living Magazine.

"You have a very nice place," he complimented.

"Thank you. Its home for now; I'm hoping to buy a house someday soon," she beamed.

Briscoe had no idea what she did for a living, but based upon what she drives and the way her apartment looks, he was sure it paid well.

She emerged from the kitchen carrying two, sixteen ounce bottles of cherry flavored Gatorade. She handed him one and opened the other. She raised hers in a toast before he could take a sip,

"Here's to new friends—and new beginnings."

Briscoe touched her bottle with his and nearly swallowed the entire bottle in one long gulp.

"You must be really thirsty. I guess it's all that running and lifting I saw you doing," she said.

"So how long did you watch me before I noticed you in the gym?" he asked bluntly.

"I was in there for about forty-five minutes before I came over to talk to you. I saw you when I first got there. I don't know if I would say watched you, but a sister was checking you out."

"I see," he was definitely flattered that she was attracted to him, because for some reason the feeling was mutual.

It wasn't just her supermodel features and scorching hot body; he figured it had something to do with her laidback personality.

"How do you know Alicia?" he asked.

"From here. We met when I moved into the complex. Your sister is so cool, we just seemed to click from the first time we met out front."

"Kind of like us huh?" he smiled.

"Well, not quite the same," she said coyly.

He smiled at her and thought how sexy and devilish her green eyes looked at that moment. She was no doubt a cutie with mad sex appeal.

"What do you do for a living?" he inquired.

"I'm a CPA with a large firm in downtown DC."

"I work in DC, but not downtown. Where is your firm?"

"On 9th Street Northwest. It's J. Weatherly and Associates."

Monica works downtown on 10th Street, but he is sure the two don't know each other outside of the cookout. Monica would never be a friend to Vanessa. And if she knew he was there right now, there would be hell to pay for Briscoe.

"I never heard of them, but I come downtown periodically; I can stop in and see you sometimes, if that's cool with you?" He can't help himself; he really likes this lady.

"That would be great. I would enjoy that," she sounded hopeful, "but what about your girlfriend; would she approve?"

Oh boy, the dreaded girlfriend question. How should he answer that? What is it that he wants from Vanessa? Does he want to have sex with her or just be friends? He was conflicted at the moment. On one hand, he want to be totally dedicated to Monica, but on the other, he want to taste the essence of Vanessa and get to know her better. It is never a good idea to start something up while you are already in the middle of a situation. You cannot give your all to the other relationship and it will likely fail because of that. He understood all of that, yet he still had a strong desire for this mysterious green-eyed doll who stumbled across his path.

"I think you already know the answer to that," he said raising an eyebrow.

"I'm sure she would scratch out my eyes if she knew that you were here talking to me right now," she said as she walked to the stereo.

"I guess we both have a good reason not to mention it to her," he laughed nervously.

The unmistakable sound of Pamela Williams and her saxophone flowed from the crystal clear Bose speakers and filled the room.

"Don't tell me you are a jazz lover," Briscoe said enthusiastically.

"My entire life," she said. "I have a collection from traditional to fusion to contemporary. I have all the greats and some of the original divas."

"I do too; Pamela Williams is one of my favorites. You can hear the Grover influence in her music," he kicked some of his jazz knowledge to her.

"Yeah no wonder, since she is from Philadelphia. I've heard her say he was her idol," she had to let Briscoe know that she was up on jazz and could hang with the big dogs when it came to knowing the artists backgrounds.

"Do you do the concerts and festivals?" he asked.

"Sure nuff; I don't miss any of them if I can help it."

"I've probably seen you at some of the festivals and didn't even know it was you," he had to laugh at that comment.

He knew he would have zeroed in on this hottie no matter where he saw her.

"You have a love for the music, but I can't get your sister to a concert. I tell her jazz is where she would meet a nice well-established man, but she says the music is boring."

"I've gotta have a talk with her; bad mouthing my music," they slapped a high five and laughed.

"I guess we should get cleaned up and head to IHOP before its lunch time," she was enjoying the time with him and wished it could be a little different. They were mad vibing and she could feel the sensation moving through her being.

"I'll get you a towel and let you go first."

"Thank you. Normally I would say ladies first, but I smell worse than you," he sniffed his underarms.

She pinched her nose closed and fanned the air, "Yeah you're right," they laughed.

She went to the linen closet at the end of the hallway just outside of the bathroom and retrieved a towel and wash cloth set. He followed her down the hall with his gym bag in hand. She handed him the items and, just as he turned to step into the bathroom, she smacked him on the ass like athletes do.

"Enjoy the shower," she said smiling unabashed for touching his butt.

Truth be told, he enjoyed the feel of her hand smacking his ass. They gelled as if they have known each other for years. He smiled widely and stepped into the bathroom. *That chick is something special. I knew it was something about her when I first laid eyes on her.* He considered how far he wanted to go with her. The thought of Monica never crossed his mind; in fact, she only crossed his mind when Vanessa brought her up. He loves Monica and never plans to cheat on her, but there is something that is pulling him to Vanessa like a tractor-beam pulling in the Starship Enterprise. *What if this is the woman he is supposed to spend the rest of his life with? Could it be so, or is he allowing the little head to take over and do the thinking?* He was feeling so tense after his ordeal last night, he could just be vulnerable. Maybe instead of the gym, he should have gone to Monica's office, locked the door, and jumped her bones. That always soothes him when he is as discombobulated as he was last night.

He started the shower and then stripped out of his gym clothes, allowing them to lie in a heap on the floor next to the toilet. He let the water beat off his head for a while before reaching for a bottle of Vanessa's Vidal Sassoon shampoo that sat on the caddy that hung from the shower head. He squeezed some into his hands and massaged it into his hair and scalp. He had his eyes closed when he felt a hand gently caress his butt. He was slightly startled, but not completely surprised.

With his eyes still shut, he said playfully, "Who's there?"

"A lady who thinks you are too sexy to be without," her voice was low and seductive. "I came in to do your back, in case you miss a spot."

She swirled soap onto his back slowly.

"Why don't you get in and we can be done twice as fast," he invited, as he rinsed the shampoo from his hair and opened his eyes.

To his surprise, she was naked, standing in the tub directly behind him holding a bar of soap. His eyes widened as his dick thickened. She was truly a sculptured being. Her body was magnificent, and looked better naked than he imagined. His eyes soaked up every inch of her body from the top of her neatly cropped do, to the bottom of her professionally painted toenails. She was so strikingly beautiful that he could hardly believe she was in the shower with him. The lust burned white hot in his loins. The blood flooded to his penis and brought it to full attention. Vanessa's eyes locked onto his soldier and the most devilish grin crossed her lips as she licked them in anticipation of the pleasure she was sure to receive from it.

"Somebody seems excited to see me," she said with erotic susurration.

He stood fully facing her with the water running down his back.

She rubbed the bar of soap onto his chest and then handed him the bar. She used her hands to gently lather his chest, abs, and let's not forget the thick rod that extended from the fully loaded balls attached to his muscular body. She massaged the soap into his chest, swirling it around his nipples while stroking his massive cock at the same time. Engulfed in pleasure, he closed his eyes and moaned,

"Oh Vanessa."

The attraction he had to Vanessa was strong, and the magnetism between them could not be denied. He was never so enamored with a woman in his life. The desire for her was more than he could control, so he gave in without a struggle as the images of her body titillated his mind and wracked his body with incredible anticipation.

"You like that huh?" she whispered in his ear.

"Oh yeah," he managed through gasps.

"You wanna put this big, thick dick deep inside of my wet kitty?" she whispered seductively in his ear while stroking his ever hardening love muscle.

"Oh yes, I want to feel it so bad," the words mixed with air from his erratic breathing.

She sensed the pleasure he was experiencing and touched his body in places he did not know were sensual. She introduced him to erogenous zones that he never knew could bring such delight.

He stood holding the soap engulfed in ecstasy, completely enchanted by the beauty standing before him. He rubbed soap on her perfectly shaped breasts, then over her chiseled abs, and along her arms. As he massaged the soap onto her shoulders and neck, their eyes locked and the powerful yearning for one another drew their lips together in fervent passion. Her lips were soft and moist. Her tongue was sweet with passionate delight. The fullness of her body pressed against his was the best thing he has ever felt. He could not recall if his penis had ever been so hard . . . or his desire for another so strong.

The touching, the kissing, the imagery, it was all too much to bear, "I want you now!" he cried out.

"Oh yes, I want you too. Take me," she submitted, and pulled him closer turning sideways and guiding both of them under the stream of the water.

When most of the soap rinsed from their still embracing bodies, she turned the water off. She guided him out of the tub and held his hand as she led him to her bedroom. She turned into his arms and kissed him passionately while her hands roamed his well developed body. She could feel him convulse as she teased his nipples, anus, and other very sensitive places. Her hands continued to do things to his body that surprised and pleased him like never before. She used her tongue to accentuate the pleasure he was feeling, by licking parts of his anatomy. She pulled him onto the bed and continued to give him pleasure.

He tried to touch her beautiful breasts, but she moved his hand and said, "No baby; this is for you. I want you to relax and enjoy everything I'm giving you. I am so turned on watching you feel what I'm doing. Relax."

He complied with her demands and laid back in pure unbridled elation. His thoughts were on nothing but the moment, and that moment was filled with Vanessa and her nearly six-foot statuesque anatomy. He pre-ejaculated while she manipulated his balls with one hand and touched an even more private part with the other. The whole while her mouth found parts of him a delectable treat. He felt like two people were touching him. The stimulation was coming from everywhere.

"I want this big stick in my pussy," she whispered seductively in his ear and then reached in the top drawer of her night stand and retrieved a magnum size condom.

Sitting straddled on top of him, she held it up, "I knew this would fit you, the first time I saw you."

She tore the condom from the package and placed it inside of her mouth. She slid down to his pulsating erection and worked the condom onto it while giving him pleasure in the process. He has never had that happen before and he struggled not to bust off before she got it completely on his rock hardness. Vanessa knew how bad he wanted to release the bubbling tide, but there was more she wanted to give him. She wanted to blow his mind, because she wanted him to come back again and again, so she planned to make him cum again and again.

Once the condom was on, she licked and sucked his balls like they were a double scoop of chocolate ice cream. His body shivered from the electricity of her erotica.

"Please baby please," he begged for her to let him inside.

"You want my tight pussy don't cha?" she teased.

"Oh yes baby, yes please," he was jonesing bad.

"Okay," she said in between licks on his throbbing cock and

meaty balls.

She then slid her tongue into his asshole and rimmed him in a way he never experienced. He exploded in the condom as his body convulsed and he grabbed her hair and pulled to steady himself. She snatched the condom off and licked and sucked the cum that dripped from his penis. She tried to suck all the cum out of his dick as he continued to release. Her fingers were in his ass, on his nipples, and all over his body. He could not help but feel like there were two women in the bed with him.

"Oh my fucking god! I have never felt that before. I have never lost it like that before," he was reeling with pleasure, as he relaxed his muscles and laid back, breathing heavily.

"Does that feel good baby?" she asked while massaging his balls, and gently stroking his still hard cock.

"Oh yes it does. Everything you do feels fucking amazing," he could not put his elation into words.

"Relax baby. Just lay back; close your eyes and think about me," she spoke softly like an angel, "I want you to feel good. This was for you Antonio, because I think you are a special man and I'm digging the hell out of you."

Her words echoed in his mind as he lay in a stranger's bed without a care in the world. He thought about how awesome she made him feel and how easily he could get used to making love to her. If she could make him feel this good without putting his dick inside of her, she will surely rock his world with her juicy pussy. The thought of how her pussy must feel on the inside danced around his mind and kept his dick from going down. It was still hard and she continued to stroke it and lick on his nipples while telling him to relax and enjoy. Somewhere in the middle of the feeling and the relaxation, he drifted off into slumber.

28

Sutton was sitting in a fairly plush high-back leather swivel chair facing Whitehead. He bought the chair from Staples for nearly two hundred dollars. He decided his comfort and long term good posture meant more to him than spending his own money on a piece of office furniture that remained at a government office. He reasoned that he spends more of his life sitting in that chair than any other piece of furniture. Whitehead came to his desk to discuss the list of officers and the strategy they would use to follow up with them.

"Here it is partner," he referred to the list, "I dropped a few of them off of the original list of thirty-three based on the description you got from Tanisha last night."

"How many are left?" Sutton asked.

"Eight," he said. "Two of our detail officers are on the list. One of them is connected to four victims and the other is connected to three. Some of the victims were from the same area, so a working officer would come into contact with many criminals just by doing his job. He would have arrested several of our victims, so I don't want to jump to any conclusions."

"Eight is a manageable number," Sutton stated.

"Yes it is. It wouldn't have been possible if the witness didn't come clean and give you that information. I would not have been able to eliminate anybody right off the top. By getting rid of the white officers, the ones under six feet, and the extremely overweight, I was able to narrow it down," he was very happy with the cooperation Tanisha gave to the investigation.

"So what's the plan?" Sutton was eager to get started.

"The person with the most connections is Officer Kevin Tyson of the 6th Precinct. He is connected to seven victims. Tyson is a former Marine who fought in the war in Afghanistan. He was decorated for heroism and he is a close fit to the physical description," Whitehead said.

"Should we roll him up and see what he has to say?" Sutton asked.

"I don't know if we want to tip our hand," Whitehead contemplated. "If we let the suspect know we are looking for a cop, he will probably fall back and we might blow our chance to catch him."

"So, how do you propose we investigate all of them without making any aware they are a suspect?" Sutton had an idea, but he had to defer it for now.

"We can start by checking where they might have been at the time of the killings. At the same time, we can check their backgrounds more thoroughly. Deborah will assist us with that. She gave me a commitment to help with detailed background checks and she will psychoanalyze them if need be."

Whitehead planned to cover all bases.

"That's nice of her. You must have shown her an extra special time," Sutton raised an eyebrow as he smiled slyly.

"Yeah right; don't get me started on your special lady," Whitehouse grinned. "But seriously, she really does want to help, and I plan to take advantage of her expertise."

They decided to split the list in half, taking four people each and working them till they are either eliminated as suspects or determined to be the elusive serial killer who has plagued the criminal underbelly of the Greater Metropolitan area.

"I'll take Tyson and the top three on the list, which includes the two from the detail. We will keep this just between the two of us and Deborah for now. I haven't told the Captain or any of the detectives on the detail about the results of the profile. I told the Captain to let the Chief know we are still waiting for the FBI. Let's work it a little before we involve anyone else. At least we should clear this list of eight first."

Whitehead wanted to protect the integrity of this lead. He felt the only way to do that was to involve as few people as possible.

"What should we tell the Chief and the others? They are bound to start asking since they know we were awaiting the results."

"We can concoct something that is similar to the truth, but we will omit the information about the killer being a cop."

"Do you want to work our story now, or wait until they start to press us?"

Whitehead thought for a few long seconds, "Let's just wait until they press us; then we can do a quick brainstorm to come up with something to give them."

Sutton agreed and then turned his attention to the list of suspects. He recognized a few of the names as officers he worked with on other homicide cases. He was aware they were working officers and would likely be involved in all aspects of police work. That would include the glamorous and the less appealing jobs. He reminded himself to keep an open mind and be sure to take an objective approach resisting all temptation to jump to conclusions.

Whitehead knew they had their work cut out and was newly rejuvenated after his night with Deborah. He did not disclose to his partner that he spent the night digging in Agent Bell's guts. He could not resist the sister agent and, quite frankly, did not want to resist her. They clicked, and the way he felt was, if two grown folks want to spend intimate time together, whose business was it? She was a quasi-part of his investigation, and not one who would be detrimental. So, in his mind, no harm-no foul. The loving put him in a great mood. Since he has not had sex or any form of intimacy in the past eight months, it shined from within. He wanted to tell Sutton, and he will in due time; but right now, it's just between him and Agent Bell. He did wonder if Sutton could tell that he got some, especially after the comment about showing her an extra special time.

"I have the personnel files of the people already on the team. I was checking them to see who might be best suited for a permanent uniform position over here in VCU. That was the job the Captain talked about for four uniformed officers. I thought we might find them in the detail. I was going to check them out and then approach the ones I thought were the most qualified. We have to post it, but we would already know who was going to be a good fit," Sutton said as he handed the files of the two detail officers to Whitehead.

"Thanks Jake, I'll get on this right away. I'll have to do some serious background checking on these four and then check on their personal activities. I want to get to the bottom of this as quickly as possible. But I have to be thorough, and very careful not to do anything that would denigrate an honest hardworking officer," his sincerity was heartfelt.

"You got skills, partner. I know you will do the right thing to bring this investigation to an accurate conclusion," Sutton encouraged.

"I'm glad you have confidence in me. I can use all the positive energy I can get," he said as he rose and headed for his desk to start the all-important job of investigating other cops.

He dropped the two personnel jackets on his desk and sat down. He picked up the telephone and dialed Agent Bell's cell phone.

"Agent Bell," the lady's voice was professional and strong.

"Good morning sunshine," he whispered in the phone.

"Hi Jamie; how are you sweetie?" her voice turned from professional to bubbly.

"I'm good, how bout you?"

"Oh, just thinking about how wonderful last night was. I can't get you off my mind. I have your scent on me and I'm feeling you all day long," she felt as giddy as a school girl.

"Me too," he whispered with a wide grin on his face.

"Will I see you tonight?" she came straight out with it.

She had strong feelings for him and, even though she did not want to come off as clingy, she decided to let him know that she was feeling for him and wanted to spend as much time with him as possible.

"I sure hope so, because I don't want to ever sleep alone again if I can help it."

That was music to her ears. She was thinking the exact same thing. She told her girlfriend she was not going to let Whitehead slip through her fingers. She felt like he was the one. She slept with him much sooner than she has ever done with any other man in her life. The chemistry was there and they were gelling. So she let the natural thing happen, and it felt wonderful to both of them.

"I'm so glad to hear that Jamie, because I feel the same way. I like you a lot, and I hope you like me also," she knew that was a little forward, but she had to put it out there.

Now she held her breath hoping it didn't scare him off.

"I like you more than I can express in words right now. But over time I think my actions will speak volumes that my words never will be able to express," damn that sounded good to him. He didn't know he had it in him.

"Good, because I've been alone longer than I care to be. I hope that doesn't make me sound desperate," she laughed.

"No baby, it makes you sound human," he had a way of making a woman feel comfortable.

"What are you doing right now?" she asked.

"I'm looking into the officers from the list Sutton and I compiled. Why, what's up?"

"I was wondering what a sister had to do to get you out of the office for a little while,"

"I really have to jump into this. I was calling to give you the names of the eight officers who I want you to check out and do the comparisons to the profile from their backgrounds and all. But I guess we could discuss that in person," he was always happy to talk to her, and seeing her was even nicer.

"Go ahead and give me the names now, keep doing what you're doing, and then meet me for lunch. How does that sound?" she asked.

"It sounds like a plan to me," he lifted the paper from the desk and rattled off the names. They talked about his approach to the investigation of the officers and how she could help tie some pieces together. Their conversation remained pretty much on the topic of the serial predator and a strategy for capturing him. They said their goodbyes and hung up.

Whitehead opened and closely scrutinized Officer Tyson's file. He noted that Tyson never served in the military nor did he seem to have the correct build. He stands about five-feet-ten-inches and is listed at 160 pounds. He is skinny as a rail and probably lacks the strength and skills necessary to inflict the damage that was done to some of the victims. The only reason they kept him on the list was because he had more contact with the victims than any other officer. Besides, witnesses and victims often get the description wrong because they are usually under stress. Something like *Is he going to kill me* is running through their minds, not *I should remember exactly what he looks like so I can tell the police.* Either way, Tyson was going to be checked out.

Whitehead scribbled notes onto a piece of paper. He created a timeline of the twenty-one deaths that are attributed to the serial predator, complete with time of death, day of week, and weather conditions. He was familiar with every case and could vividly recall the details of the crime scenes. He checked the 6th Precinct patrol logs to see if Tyson was working at the times of each victim's death. If he could account for Tyson's whereabouts during even one of the homicides, he would have to rule him out as the predator. Most of the killings were done late night after midnight, but a few were done earlier in the night. Tyson works the third watch from 3:00 p.m. to 11:00 p.m. and he was never on duty during the homicides. As it stands on the initial inspection, Tyson was not accounted for by the police department at the time of any of the homicides. It is going to require a check on his personal life to determine if he was somewhere that could be verified. Otherwise, Whitehead will have to sit down with him and discuss his whereabouts. He did not want to do that if he could investigate him from afar. News travels fast through the grapevine in the police department. As soon as he talks with Tyson, no matter what he says about not mentioning anything to anybody, the word would fly around faster than the speed of light. Sometimes a rumor would start up in the grapevine, and the command staff would swear it was only a rumor and attempt to quash it before the force would allow any negativity to fester. One hundred percent of the time, a part, if not all of the rumor would prove to be true. The grapevine has power and many officers believe what they hear. Whitehead did not want any part of his investigation to end up on the grapevine, especially the fact that police officers are being looked at as suspects. He would never get any cooperation. He was sure to be met by the blue brick wall of silence.

Whitehead checked into Tyson's off duty activities. He wanted to know if he was involved in any clubs, associations, or other things that would occupy his time after work. He did note that Tyson was married with a three year old daughter. One of the characteristics of the profile was that the killer was likely single and unattached from a serious relationship. He would not be someone who had to answer to anyone about his whereabouts. A married man would definitely have to do that unless he has a super open relationship. Whitehead thought about his marriage and how his wife was so jealous and possessive that he could hardly take a shit without giving her details of how long it would take and when he would return from the bathroom. The predator moved about doing his deeds at various times of the night. Surely he had to do some prep and casing of his victims, which would take time. He figured it was highly unlikely, but not impossible for a married man to get that kind of time away from home without causing a big problem.

He decided he would go by the 6th Precinct during roll call and meet Tyson. He will go to the Precinct and speak with the officers, giving them a bogus update on the investigation and ask them to talk to the people on their beats about recalling anything about the nights of the killings in their precinct. He will engage Tyson in a conversation about the seven victims he was involved with. He will interrogate Tyson without him being aware it's happening. He decided to do the same thing with all the suspect officers. He knew he would have to be very careful, because cops have a knack for sniffing things out. One slip and they will know immediately what

Detective Whitehead and VCU were up to.

He called the 6th Precinct and made arrangements with the Deputy Precinct Commander to come by at 3:00 p.m. and talk with the roll call and a few officers. Once that was in place he went down the list to the next name.

Antonio Lawrence Briscoe of the Fifth Precinct currently assigned to the serial predator task force. Whitehead read as he looked into Briscoe's file. He noted some striking similarities in the predator profile and Briscoe's file. He placed a star next to his name on the list. As he checked patrol logs, he noted that Briscoe was on duty working during some of the homicides, which wasn't the case for Tyson. He would have ruled Tyson out as a suspect if he were at work during any of them that were committed outside of his patrol precinct, but he could not do the same for Briscoe. It appears that Briscoe was on duty working at the time of death for a few of the homicides in his precinct. Could he have killed them while on duty without anybody missing him? Would he have been able to commit murder in his uniform without being doused in blood? These are questions he would have to answer. However, he reasoned that Briscoe was the right build with a military background, was not married, and based on his appearance and military record alone; he is an exact fit to the profile. Although a thorough investigation of all the officers on the list was necessary, something in his seasoned gut spoke to him about Briscoe.

29

Wow; what the hell happened? Briscoe blinked, adjusting his eyes to the dark room lit only by the street light shining through the half open blinds. As his eyes traversed the room, soft peach colored walls, a pink comforter and frilly pillows embraced him with warmth that he could not explain. The feel of a stuffed toy monkey made of velvet and the softest material he could ever recall touching, made him smile. He pulled the monkey close and smelled the unmistakable scent of Vanessa, the woman who rocked him out of his socks and sent him off on a love rocket to cloud nine. His body was still reeling from the pleasure she induced. On the dresser adjacent to the bed and directly beside the door was a slamming Glamour Shots photograph of Vanessa. It looked like her hair was blowing in the wind and her cleavage was standing up and begging for the attention they deserve.

He once again could not believe how gorgeous she was. How could such a hottie be alone? He could not fathom a reason why she would choose to not have a man; because there was no doubt in his mind that dudes wanted to get next to her.

He laid thinking about what they did together from the shower to the bed and it forced a wide smile across his face. He moved his hands across his body, touching some of the places Vanessa touched earlier. His dick rose as his mind wandered. He touched his manhood and thought *Oh my God she felt so damn good.* He looked at the small LCD clock and realized it was after 8:00 p.m. He had slept peacefully for a long time. He could not recall the last time he slept so long without interruption. How could he sleep so soundly in a stranger's bed? There must be something about Vanessa that makes him comfortable enough to let his guard down and relax like he did. She took complete control of him and put him to sleep after he shot a load like he never has. They never did get breakfast or coffee.

As that thought crossed his mind so did a mild hunger pang in his empty stomach. He wondered if Vanessa was in the apartment or if she was still out. He remembered that she said she had an appointment later in the day. Perhaps she is still out. He listened trying to discern the stillness of the bedroom and the outside noises.

With the door closed, he could not tell if anyone was in the apartment or if he was completely alone. He looked at his gym bag resting on the antique padded foot locker at the foot of the bed. He got dressed and decided to venture into the apartment to see if Vanessa was there.

He stepped into the hallway and could hear voices in the living room. The soft lighting and faint sound of up tempo jazz relaxed him a bit as he made his way toward the voices. Just as he stepped into view, his eyes fell upon his sister, sitting with her back toward him.

He stopped in his tracks and back-peddled out of view. He quickly hurried back to the bedroom and shut the door.

"Oh shit!" he exclaimed in a whisper. *What the hell am I going to do now?* His mind was racing a hundred miles an hour. *Alicia is in the other room. He can't face her right now. What would he say? What will she think of him?* He knows she will tell their parents and then he'll have to deal with that drama. *Damn! How can he explain this to Alicia? How can he explain this to anybody? What about Monica?*

This was the first time he thought of her since their phone conversation on his way to Vanessa's house. *How could he do Monica like this?* He suddenly felt a heavy weight rest on his chest. His breathing labored and he started to sweat.

What the hell is the matter with me? He could not understand why he was having emotional issues. He has never experienced the feelings and thoughts that he has lately. It all started after he killed Red.

"Lord, why am I feeling like this? I am so sorry for doing anything to displease you. I only wanted to do your will. Please help me God," he pleaded softly.

He heard footsteps in the hallway and he looked intently at the door. The doorknob turned slowly and his mouth became dry and his pulse accelerated. The door creaked slowly open bathing the room in soft jazz and dim lighting from the outer room. Vanessa emerged with a bright smile on her face.

"Hey beautiful," she said as she embraced him and placed a soft kiss on his lips.

He melted, and felt instantly secure in her embrace. How could this woman have such a hold on him? He did not know, but damn it felt good.

"I see my sister is here," he said as flatly as he could, not wanting to show how panicked he actually was.

"Yeah, she came over a little while ago. We've been chillin, listening to some jazz and talking. I'm working on her. Before you know it she will love our music," she said smiling, recalling their earlier conversation.

She knew Briscoe was concerned about Alicia knowing he was there, but she kept him on the hook.

"Does she know I'm here?"

"What . . . you don't want her to know?" She knew he didn't, but she wanted to keep things real, and wanted him to come straight with it and not beat around the bush.

"Well, she knows my girlfriend and I know how Alicia likes to run her mouth." He actually didn't know how to tell her that he was afraid for his parents to know he messed around on Monica.

"Don't worry about it boo; I didn't tell her anything. She doesn't even know that I have company."

He breathed a sigh of relief so loud Vanessa could hear it.

"So it's like that huh?"

"Oh no Vanessa," he pleaded, "I just don't want to hurt anybody. I like you and right now I'm so confused. But I made a commitment to my girlfriend and I don't want to hurt her."

"What about me? Do you worry about hurting me?" she was not in danger of being hurt; she was just keeping him on the hook.

She likes him a lot and really wants to be with him, but she knows she cannot get him by threatening to tell his woman or using any of those weak-ass ghetto mama tricks. She could feel the connection, sensed his vibe, and knew that dude would be back to dive deep down inside of her wetness. She was going to get him through the loving that his body would not be able to deny. She planned to make him feel like it was something as important as the air he breathes. Something he could not live without.

"I like you Vanessa and I was attracted to you the first time I laid eyes on you. I would never hurt you and I would never hurt her either. I hope you can understand," he didn't know any other way to phrase it.

Although he has cheated on Monica and feels like shit for doing it, he still wanted to be with Vanessa. This was all new to him. He has spent his life liking and loving only one woman at a time and has never thought to see another while involved in a relationship.

"Don't worry about it Antonio, I'm good. I know you have a woman, but I'm a keeping-it-real type of sister. I want you brother man and I'm woman enough to let you know that. I'm also woman enough to be respectful. But in the meantime, don't feel stressed. We can just kick it, okay?"

He wasn't completely sure how to answer so he nodded. He wanted to go home and get ready for work and, hopefully, clear his mind.

"I have to get home so I can get ready for work," he said, hinting to her to get rid of Alicia.

"Okay boo. Let me get rid of your sister first," she leaned in and slowly licked his lips as she gently rubbed his chest. She stepped out of the room closing the door behind her.

Briscoe stood momentarily frozen in place. He could still feel her soft tongue glide across his lips. The comfort he felt with Vanessa was more than he could comprehend. It was though he wanted her more than he wanted Monica. He sat down on the bed and looked out of the bedroom window that faced the parking lot and Alicia's building. He was grateful that Alicia's apartment was on the backside of the building and she did not have a view of the parking lot. This was one time he was happy to be driving the rental car.

Vanessa came back into the room to let him know Alicia was gone and he could leave. He embraced her and spent a few moments kissing and touching before he left.

On the ride home, he did not turn on the radio or listen to music. Instead, he rode in silence thinking about the direction his life was heading. He would have never cheated on Monica in the past. What caused him to desire Vanessa so badly and allowed him to put himself in a position to do what he did. Karen is always on his jock offering up the pussy with no strings, but he resists and makes completely sure not to put himself in a position where he will give in to her. Vanessa on the other hand was a whole different animal. He was captivated by her from the start. Now he can see why Monica was so pissed when they left the cookout. She sensed something, some mutual attraction, or animal magnetism of sorts. But why not stand down and not allow himself in a position to do what he did? Perhaps it has something to do with Red.

He looked down at his cell phone that was left in the car and realized there were a few voice messages. He dialed the voice mail to listen to the new messages.

"B, holla at me when you get a minute. Peace," Sanford left the message early in the afternoon. Briscoe decided he would call him on the way to work in a couple of hours.

"Hey Antonio, I'm sorry if I came down hard on you last night. I just wanted you to know how I feel about you, and how I think we would be very good together. I understand about your feelings for your girlfriend and I'll respect that. But somehow, someway, I am going to have you, and I plan to rock your world. So think on that for a minute. Peace baby boy," Karen was jumping off the chain.

He moved to the next message.

"Antonio I'm sorry," her voice was sweet and caring, "I know I was short with you earlier. I was feeling pressure from the audit and I shouldn't have taken it out on you. I love you baby. I promise to make it up to you tonight," the latter part of the message was cloaked in seductive overtones.

Now he felt bad . . . really bad, for the first time today. He got his swerve on while his woman thought about how she treated him. She was planning to make up for what she perceived to be ill treatment of her man. If that message saddened him, the next one put a real damper on his mood and a spike through his cheating heart.

"I'm really sorry baby. Please call me back. Don't make me beg. I promise not to treat you like that again. Pleeeeaaasssee forgive me," she begged.

That message was received at 5:00 p.m. The next message was received just thirty minutes ago.

"Where are you Antonio? I said I'm sorry. Why are you making me beg? Please call me or come home," she sounded sad and panicked.

How could he face her after what he did? He looked at the number and dreaded that she called from his house. He has to go home and face her. Where could he tell her he has been? Could he say he was in the gym? He had a moment of anxiety as he smelled himself, thinking that Vanessa's scent was etched in his skin. He wished he could take a shower before seeing Monica. The drive home seemed too short and when he pulled into his block and drove up to where Monica's BMW was parked behind his car in the driveway, he continued to drive past.

"Fuck it," he exclaimed, hitting the steering wheel with his fist. He decided to wear what he had on and not worry about changing or shaving. There was no way he could face her tonight. Tears welled in his eyes, and he choked them back before they could stream down his face.

30

Karen White followed Brick onto 18th Street to the house he visited weekly. She knew they were slinging dope from the location and figured he was resupplying them. Every time he goes to the house he sits outside while the white girl, Christine, goes in with a big bag bulging from the sides and then returns with the bag looking half empty.

She watched as Christine walked to the door and knocked. Janice let her in and Karen directed her attention to Brick and the rest of the block. She couldn't quite put her finger on it, but something seemed different about the street. It was just after midnight and there was practically no one out; for a summer night that was unheard of. There always seemed to be a carnival atmosphere on this street, but tonight it was eerily quiet.

Brick climbed out of his truck and stood at the rear talking to two young guys who approached soon after he parked. They were members of his crew and they seemed to be up to something. They were dressed in all dark clothing wearing baseball caps low over their eyes. An uneasy feeling came over Karen as she continued to focus her attention on the group of men. She was parked on the opposite side of the street about a half block away, positioned to see them through her side view mirror or looking over her shoulder. The men looked around occasionally and seemed to be planning something. Karen wondered if they were planning to do something to the occupants of the house or if they were about to set up somebody on the street. She knew if something went down she would have to call for assistance if it was serious. She thought about keeping her cover and decided she would not do anything except make the call.

Her body was twisted to the left and she was looking over her shoulder at the men when all of a sudden the front passenger window of her rental car exploded into hundreds of little pieces. Startled, she turned and looked down the barrel of a .44 caliber chrome-plated handgun. The fear was emblazoned on her face and her entire life raced before her stunned brown eyes.

"Put your hands up bitch!" the bandit ordered.

Just as she raised her hands, her side window shattered, sending glass fragments into her face, hair, and lap. She screamed.

"Shut the fuck up before I blow your head off," the bandit said.

"Don't shoot. I'm a cop," she said, strangely hoping that would scare them off.

"Get her out of the car," the bandit with the gun instructed the one who broke the window on her side. The young men who were talking to Brick were now at her car door dragging her out of the vehicle and forcing her into the back of a beat up blue Dodge Caravan.

She pleaded with them to not hurt her as they shouted obscenities, punched, and kicked her. They duct-taped her hands behind her back and put her on the floor of the minivan where one of the men kept his foot on her back. She was not much of a religious person, but she prayed, begging God to save her life. She was nearly in tears, but she had to hold it together and think of a way to get out of this situation. This is one time she wished she had her gun on her and not in her purse. What a mistake to leave the gun in her purse, especially when she was on duty watching a violent felon in a less than stable neighborhood. She wondered how stupid that was. The fear was trying to grip her, but she struggled in her mind to stay positive and strong. The fear of the unknown and having her fate in the hands of a bunch of young thugs was not the easiest thing to get over. She recited the Twenty-third Psalm in her mind, *Yea though I walk through the shadow of death, I shall fear no evil . . .*

They arrived at a wooded area near Suitland Road in Maryland. The men shut the vehicle off and dragged Karen about fifty yards into the woods to a small clearing and threw her to the ground. The area was illuminated by the moon with just enough light to see shapes. Karen could see that Brick was there leading the attack. The other three men were not familiar to her. They were Ant Lakeland, Jamal Sutherland, and Kwame Kirk. Jamal and Kwame were the ones who did most of the killing for Brick. They are two bad brothers who haven't got one good bone in their bodies. They are enforcers who are loyal to Brick and have killed about eight people between them. They live in the Trinidad neighborhood like the rest. They have been running with Brick's crew for many years. Now they are in the woods with Karen about to put in work.

"Why are you following me?" Brick pulled her up by the hair.

She gasped and winced from the pain Brick caused. She

struggled to stay composed and not let them see her cry. She knew she had to tell them something.

"I'm not following you," she lied, hopefully convincing enough.

"I've seen your ass in three different places and I watched you pull up there right after I did. For the past two days every time I step out I look for you, because I know your ass was following me. Now, what the fuck are you up to?" he gripped her throat and squeezed.

She struggled to breathe and tears pooled in her eyes. Through a clenched windpipe she said, "Okay, okay."

He released his grip, and she coughed vigorously trying to gain composure and get some much needed air. "I'm a cop assigned to watch you because they think the serial killer is going to try to kill you," she decided to tell him the truth, hoping that would get him to release her.

"You crazy bitch, ain't nobody killing shit over here. I know damn well ya'll ain't worried about me being hurt," he said.

"I am supposed to follow you and if the killer goes after you I am supposed to stop him," she prayed he would see her as a protector.

He didn't. Instead he slapped her face.

"Ho, I don't need you to do shit for me. I can handle my own business. All you done is get yourself fucked up. You should'a been more careful," he looked at his boys and said, "Ya'll handle this, I'm out."

He walked from the clearing and got into his truck and headed back to 18th Street to pick up Christine.

Ant looked at Karen, "You are a thick bitch," he said feeling on her breasts.

She shuddered and shrank from his touch. "Please let me go. Nothing will be said, and you guys can go on like nothing ever happened," she tried to reason.

"Is that right?" Kwame said rubbing on her shapely behind.

"She is a fine bitch. Too bad she five oh," Jamal put his hands between her legs touching her most private parts through her jeans.

Panic gripped her and the realization of what they were going to do rushed through her mind. She lost her composure and the tears flowed as she begged them not to do what they were planning.

"You know you want to feel this big dick up in you," Kwame pulled her close, putting his leg between hers, letting her feel his hardening dick against her thigh.

With her hands duct taped behind her back, she could not easily fight back. She tried to pull away but they surrounded her on three sides. They touched her body in very intimate places all at the same time.

"Please don't do this. Please, I'm begging you. I have a daughter," her sobs were louder and the tears started to cloud her vision.

"Bitch don't nobody care about your fuckin daughter," Ant snapped, "You know what? Shut the fuck up. I don't wanna hear your mouth. I should put my dick in there anyway."

Karen continued to beg. Kwame put his palm over her mouth and squeezed her cheeks together.

"Shut the fuck up skank!" he yelled. "Hold this bitch," he said as he reached down and unbuckled her pants.

She knew what was going down if she didn't do something. So she steadied herself and kicked Kwame, who was standing directly in front of her, as hard as she could in his scrotum. He fell to the ground coiling and holding his family jewels. She jerked away from the other two and ran. By the time they reacted, Karen had a few steps on them and made it into thicker woods.

The sound coming from Kwame was that of utter pain. She kicked him so hard it felt like his nuts were lodged in his stomach. The others ran after Karen.

"Stop you bitch. I'm gonna fuck your ass up. Come back here," Jamal and Ant spit insults and threats as they searched the woods for Karen.

She continued to run as fast as she could with her hands bound behind her back. She could see streetlights through the patch of trees in front of her. She was moving quickly. Just a few more feet and she'll be in the open and could get some help. Her heart was racing faster than her feet could ever move; the darkness was giving way to light, and her heart was filling with hope. Out of nowhere, a dead tree that was still attached to its stump reached up from the darkness and tripped her. She was hurled to the ground with such force that it knocked the wind out of her. Thick foliage and underbrush scratched her face causing several lacerations. She struggled to get her breath and get back on her feet. Just as she made it to her knees, Jamal and Ant pounced on her.

"Mothafucker, you gonna pay for that shit."

Ant punched her several times in the face. Blood spewed

from her nose and mouth. They grabbed her as she struggled. They were trying to drag her back to the clearing, but she struggled and screamed as loud as she could.

"Shut the fuck up," Jamal punched her several times in the stomach.

Her screams muffled with each blow, but rose louder after each time she caught her breath. Ant tried to put his hand over her mouth and she bit down hard on it, puncturing the skin causing instant anguish. She did not release the bite until he punched her three times in the head, causing her to nearly lose consciousness.

They were struggling with her when Kwame made his way from the clearing. He ran up to the three of them and kicked Karen with the bottom of his foot in the middle of her chest. She slipped from Jamal and Ant's grip falling hard to the ground. Kwame stomped twice on her chest and twice he kicked her in her delicate vaginal area. Her screams were very weak and barely audible now. She could feel herself slipping into darkness. Her body told her the end was near, but her heart and mind said continue to fight, that's your only chance. She refused to give up and kicked back from the ground and struggled against them.

Jamal and Ant got her to her feet but her struggling and screaming was gaining new momentum, so Kwame reached into his pants and pulled out the .44. He leveled the weapon and pulled the trigger. The slug hit her in the chest with such force it knocked her from their grasp. She hit the ground unrestrained with nothing but the hard forest floor to break her fall. She was motionless, as an eerie quietness fell over them. Dogs could be heard barking in the night. You could hear automobiles driving along Suitland Road.

They looked at each other and Ant said, "Let's get the fuck out of here. She dead, let's go."

Kwame looked down and fired two more rounds from the powerful weapon into the crumpled heap of Karen.

"What the fuck you doing nigga?" Ant yelled, "She dead, what you try'na do let mothafuckers know we over here? Let's go."

They ran from the woods and jumped into the Dodge and sped away. They were silent until they made it across the DC line.

Then they laughed, "Man that was some funny shit when that broad kicked you in the junk," Jamal said to Kwame, "I bet that shit hurt like a mothafucker."

"Oh ya'll got jokes. Her ass ain't kickin' shit now. Man that shit ain't funny, it hurt."

Kwame was still upset. He rubbed his groin while the others laughed and made light of what they did to Karen.

Ant's phone rang, "What up?" he answered

"Is it done?" Brick asked.

"Yeah man, she sleepy. We on our way back," he said feeling good about doing something for Brick.

"Cool. I'll holla tomorrow," Brick said, hanging up before Ant could respond.

He knew that he fucked way up killing a cop. He thought she was following him for a rival, he had no idea she was a cop until she said something. In fact, the windows on her car were tinted so dark, he didn't know it was a woman. By the time he stepped to her the way he did, he had no choice but to kill her.

"He cool?" Jamal asked.

"Yeah dog, it's all peace. He sound relieved," Ant said, "Let's go to Eddies and get sumpin to eat. I'm starving."

Eddies is one of those landmark greasy spoon eateries that perpetuate the high blood pressure and other diet related illnesses that plague distressed neighborhoods.

"Me too," added Jamal.

"Ahight then," Kwame said turning the van right onto Minnesota Avenue heading toward Eddie's carryout.

Residents of the homes that bordered the wooded area could hear screaming. Most of them turned a deaf ear because they were used to boisterous people in the area. But when they heard the gunshots they knew something more sinister was afoot. Several of the residents called the police. Once the 911 operator received multiple calls for gunshots in one location she sent the troops. The sirens were audible in the distance and one inquisitive (not wanting to say nosey) resident ventured from his home and walked toward the spot where he saw the three bandits run from the woods. Just as he reached the spot, the first police car sped up on the scene. The officer jumped from his vehicle with his weapon drawn and ordered the man to put his hands up and get on the ground. The man explained that he heard the gunshots and saw the three men run out of the woods. Other units arrived and the man was checked for weapons and held while the other officers checked the woods. When the first officer reached Karen he radioed that there was a black female suffering from what appeared to be multiple gunshot wounds. He called for the Board, a detective, and crime scene assistance. The officer could not detect a pulse, so he established a crime scene and requested Homicide. The resident was questioned extensively on the scene by the officers, who broadcast a lookout for the three black males operating a blue Dodge Caravan. The resident was not able to give a tag number, but he was able to give the color and the fact that there were three assailants. The officers on scene were not one hundred percent sure the man was not the suspect. They went along as though he was a witness, but did reserve some skepticism.

When the paramedics arrived they checked Karen, and to everyone's surprise, they detected a faint pulse. They administered CPR and worked to stop the bleeding. Pressure dressings were applied to the gaping wound in her chest and the ones to her abdomen, and right thigh. An IV drip was established and they worked to minimize the damage done by the high powered weapon. Once she was stabilized, she was flown by Maryland State Police helicopter, to Washington Hospital Center's MedStar Trauma Center. She had no identification and the Prince Georges County Police listed her as a Jane Doe.

"Hey Karen, I'm here to relieve you, but I don't see you. Where are you?"

Officer Staley was eager to see her. He stopped on the way to relieve her and purchased two cups of coffee and scones from Dunkin Donuts. He figured he would sit with her for a few minutes, actually hoping to get closer.

"Well, I'm here. I see our boy's truck out here in front of his house. Is he somewhere else? Is that where you are? Holla back, I need to know what's happening."

He thought perhaps she had something to do and left early. But she would have called him or answered her phone when he called. She knows he has to turn in the morning report and would need her input from over night. He left her a total of five messages. He decided to watch his assignment and hope she would call him back soon.

Her rental car remained on 18th Street untouched, with the windows broken and glass on the street. Her purse was on the floor behind the passenger seat, the key was in the ignition, and the radio was on at a low volume. It was a wonder that nobody came along and stole it. Probably because people thought it was a stolen car dumped in the neighborhood, a common practice. The sun had risen in the sky and the rush hour traffic was in full swing when the call was made to investigate the auto parked on 18th Street with busted windows.

Officer Jones received the call and responded. When he arrived the first thing he did was run the tag with the dispatcher. She told him it was a rental car listed to Enterprise Car Rental and was not reported stolen. He checked the console and the glove compartment for the rental agreement. To his surprise the car was leased to the Metropolitan Police Department.

That's odd, he thought, *Why would a vehicle leased to the police department be sitting here like this.* The bells and whistles were ringing in his head. He stopped in his tracks and backed out of the vehicle. He then radioed for Crime Scene Search and a supervisor to meet him on the scene. Once he had the ball in motion, he put on a pair of latex gloves and opened the back passenger door and started a visual inspection of the vehicle. He saw the brown Coach handbag sitting partially open on the floor. He picked it up and gently dumped the contents onto the seat. One of the first things to fall out was a department-issued Glock 19 handgun.

"What the fuck?" he said carefully picking up the weapon by the barrel and setting it aside on the seat.

He continued to dump the contents until he came across a lady's wallet. He opened the flap of the wallet and his heart skipped a beat when he saw the driver's license inside.

"Oh my god," he reached up and depressed the radio microphone clipped to his lapel, "I need the supervisor who's en route to 18th Street to step it up."

"I'm about a block out, I'll be there in one minute," Sergeant Hughes advised.

Jones continued to look through the contents and found Karen's ID folder with her badge. It appeared that all the contents of her purse were intact. That included nearly two hundred dollars cash.

"What's the matter Jones?" Sergeant Hughes asked still seated in his cruiser, noting the concerned look on Jones' face.

"It's this," he said handing him Karen's ID folder, "Something happened to her."

"Where did you get this," Hughes asked.

"From her purse in that car," he motioned toward the rental car. "I have her weapon also."

Sergeant Hughes pulled the patrol car forward a few feet and tried to exit so fast he forgot to remove his seatbelt. His heart sped up and his mind raced. *What took place here? I know Karen, and that isn't her car. Something bad happened to her. She would never leave her gun and badge behind. And what the hell was she doing in this neighborhood?* He had to compose himself and make sure the scene is processed. More importantly, he had to find out where Karen is.

"What did the scene look like when you rolled up?" he asked Jones.

"Just like this. The glass was strewn across the ground, the key in the ignition with the radio on. The only thing I did was open the passenger door and go into the glove box to look for a rental agreement. When I found out the vehicle was leased to the police department I . . ."

"The police department?" Hughes interrupted.

"Yes sir, the police department. I thought that was strange, so I called for crime scene search and you."

"Okay, we will check with the Central Command Center and find out which branch had the vehicle and I'll try to call Karen at home. In the meantime, contact all the hospitals in the city to see if she was admitted. We will treat this somewhat like a missing person, but under suspicious circumstances. I'll make all the notifications to the Watch Commander and everybody up the chain," he added. "I'll have a couple of units come over and report to you. Have them canvass the wooded area around the Arboretum without alarming anyone. Let them know not to broadcast over the radio that we are looking for Karen under these suspicious conditions. If I don't reach her, we will elevate the lookout and have every cop on the East Coast looking for her," his eyes locked with Jones, and the concern was etched within.

Sergeant Hughes removed his cell phone from his shirt pocket as he walked to his car and dialed Karen's home phone which he had stored in his phone.

There was no answer. He left a message, and then dialed the Watch Commander. He explained everything and the commander concurred with his handling of the situation. He contacted the Command Center and found out the car was leased to VCU. He learned that Karen was conducting surveillance on a suspect and was working outside of the customary parameters of the department. He explained that she was missing and described the scene. He gave his cell number to the officer in the Command Center and requested that he have someone from VCU give him a call.

Moments later he received a call from Detective Sutton, "Sergeant Hughes, this is Detective Sutton. I understand you found a rental car that was assigned to our branch?"

"Yes and inside we found Officer Karen White's purse with her badge and weapon. The windows were smashed and there is no sign of White," Sergeant Hughes explained.

"What about her police radio? She should have had that with her," Sutton advised.

"I didn't see the radio, but I can check with the officer on the scene. Nobody has heard from her, and calls to her house are unanswered. Her cell phone is in the car with her other belongings. A unit is on the way to her house to see if she is inside. We are handling this as a missing person right now, but I'm sure you can understand our urgency."

"I do. I will check with her relief and see what he can tell me. I can come out there and assist with the investigation if you all need the help," Sutton was busy enough with his own homicide investigations, but this is an officer who is on his serial predator task force and he had a strange feeling that her disappearance was connected to the case.

"I will have the officer recover the vehicle. After Crime Scene Search finishes processing it, I will have it towed to the station. If there is anything you can offer it would be appreciated. We just want to find her as quickly as possible," Sergeant Hughes said.

He had to check his emotions in order to do what he knew had to be done; good police work.

Karen lay motionless with tubes coming from different parts of her body. The sound of ventilators, respirators, and the beeping of monitors filled the room she occupied in the intensive care wing. The Prince Georges County Police Detective assigned to the case came to the hospital to check her condition and to give instructions to the uniformed officer who was on guard outside her room. The detective wanted to be called the moment she wakes. He also wanted to be notified if anybody tried to see her and he wanted that person detained until he arrived on scene. The uniform officer was a Maryland officer and since they were in Washington, DC, the detective decided to go to MPD for assistance with guarding the unidentified female gunshot victim. He contacted his dispatcher and asked her to request assistance from MPD.

The precinct that services the hospital is the 5th Precinct, the one where Karen is assigned. When the request was broadcast over the police radio, Sergeant Hughes monitored and immediately headed for the hospital. He did not know it was Karen for sure, but he had to see for himself. Besides, as the shift supervisor it was his responsibility to assign the officers for that detail and make sure they are properly relieved.

He arrived at the hospital and pulled up in front. He normally would have parked in a space, but he had no time to look for a spot. He thought, *I'm the police, I'll park this thing on the moon if I want.* He hurried into the hospital and nearly ran the distance down the long corridor and around the corner to the ICU. He walked up to where the detective and two PG County Uniformed Officers were standing. The detective extended his hand and made introductions for him and the officers.

The detective explained the crime that took place over night in their jurisdiction, and told how bad off the victim was and that she was a Jane Doe. He requested assistance from Sergeant Hughes with guarding her because of the jurisdictional issues. He knew that anybody coming in would have to be detained and his officers did not have the authority to detain anyone in Washington, DC. Sergeant Hughes pledged the support and then stepped into the room to look at the female victim.

He choked up immediately and fought the tears back that tried to escape from his sad eyes. He could not believe that beautiful and lively Karen White was so near death she had to have artificial assistance to remain in this realm of existence.

"Oh my god, this is fucking unbelievable. Who the fuck did this?" his angry words surprised the detective who looked dumbfounded.

"We don't have a clue right now," the detective said, wondering why the police sergeant would be so upset over seeing a gunshot victim.

"Karen who did this to you," Sergeant Hughes said touching her arm. "Fight it baby, you can make it. Just hang on."

She showed no sign of being inside of the shell that was the lively Karen he knows.

A look of surprise crossed the detective's face, "So you know her," he said.

"She is a police officer assigned to my precinct," we discovered her car this morning on 18th Street. We just started looking for her. It looks like she was abducted."

"We found her without any ID in a wooded area in the county. Her hands were bound behind her back. It looks like the crime began in DC. Do you want me to meet with your investigator to turn everything over to them right now?" the detective was aware that the case would be turned over to MPD because it started in the city and culminated in Maryland.

That would make it a DC case. He was not happy to turn the case over, but he was relieved that they identified the victim and he did not have to be responsible for a case that was sure to have high ranking scrutiny.

"I'll have to call my supervisor and inform them of the situation. They will assign someone. Do you have time to hang on while I do that?"

Sergeant Hughes was still struggling with the idea of Karen's condition. He had to look away, focusing his attention on the detective standing next to the bed. He refused to turn his head toward the bed again. He did not like the image he saw or the way it ripped him up inside.

He stepped into the hallway and called the Watch Commander. Somehow; well, you know how the grapevine sends information at the speed of light, all the officers on shift knew she was in the hospital fighting for her life. Text messages and phone calls flew out to the officers who were not on shift at the time until everybody was informed and most of the ones on duty had responded to the hospital to see her. Whenever a cop is injured or killed in the line of duty it has a reverberating affect on all. The reverberation is that of their individual souls asking why and thinking damn that could have been me.

31

Briscoe had managed to avoid Monica all night. When he arrived home he knew she would be at work. She is still dealing with the audit, so there was no danger of her being at the house when he arrived. He spent his entire shift reflecting on his relationship with Monica and his strong attraction to Vanessa. He had always been sure that Monica was the right woman for him and there could not be another as wonderful as what he had in her. But along comes Vanessa and knocks his whole game out of whack. Even if he is attracted and completely turned out by her, he cannot allow that to influence his relationship with Monica. He could never do Monica so wrong as to cheat on her, while she is feeling for him and trying to move their relationship to a loving lifetime together. He knew he had to face her soon. He could not avoid her much longer. He was going to have to man up and make a decision. Either drop any notion of ever seeing Vanessa again or end it with Monica. He couldn't have both. I know some men would have both, and hell, maybe another one or two on the side. But Briscoe is not that kind of guy. He has to be committed to just one and that is the only way he will ever be. He thought about how Monica has neglected him lately and had seemed short with him the last time they talked. He knew she was under a lot of pressure and would never treat him like that intentionally. She even called him several times to apologize. She really loves him and he loves her. But Vanessa awakened something in him that he has never experienced. He did not know if that was admiration, love, or pure, unadulterated lust. Perhaps it is the latter; but either way, it awakened something inside of him that he could not ignore.

He got home in the morning and went directly asleep. He did not go to the gym because the only clothes he had were the ones from the day before. He really didn't want to run the risk of bumping into Vanessa. She gave him her phone number before he left her apartment, but he did not give her his number. Surprisingly, she didn't ask him for it. He couldn't tell if she was a confident black woman, or a cool, calculating sister girl who knew how to play a man into her trap.

He turned the ringers off on all his phones and slept until his body decided it had enough rest. He woke in the early evening hours and lay in the bed staring at the ceiling overhead. Now his thoughts travelled all over the place. He thought about his mother and father and how they've had a successful marriage for nearly thirty-five years and how they seemed to be in love. He thought about church and some of the people who attended and their relationships. He couldn't make a rash decision based off the past twenty-four hours, but he wouldn't want to proceed with Monica if he could not be faithful to her. There was far too much to consider. His stomach grumbled and his head felt light. He wondered if it was from hunger or the conflicting thoughts pounding on the inside of the delicate lining of his brain. He decided to get up, shower, and go to his parent's home before Monica gets off work and comes to his house. He was sure she called and left messages. If he doesn't respond to her soon, she will know something took place.

He thought how is it that he can keep the secret of his predator activity, but cannot keep his guilty cheating feelings in check. He reasoned that perhaps he feels righteous in his mission to bring justice to those that do others harm, but he feels like he is victimizing Monica if he sleeps with Vanessa.

His mind drifted back to when he first started taking out the garbage from the streets he took an oath to protect. It all started when he testified in a trial that involved a street thug and a pregnant single mother of three. He knew that he had a strong commitment to justice, but after the mockery he and the victims endured at that trial, he went on a cleansing spree like no other. He decided at that point the criminal justice system was more an injustice system, best suited for the ones who spend most of their lives manipulating it. He was not going to let that thug get away with the atrocity he committed. So, he took matters into his own hands.

Essence Simpson lived in a modest three bedroom apartment with her three children. She worked as a CPA for the IRS. She was college-educated and seemed to be moving upward. That education was courtesy of her mother and grandmother who supported her and helped with the children while she attended school. She had her first child, a son, when she was eighteen, right before graduation from high school.

Her only drawback was her attraction to bad boys. She was only twenty-eight years old, but had children by two deadbeat dudes who she could barely get to spend time with their kids, let alone pay child support. She made enough money to provide the kids with a quality lifestyle, so she really didn't trip over the money; she just wanted the kids to have a father in their lives. They would occasionally spend weekends away with their fathers or their grandparents, so it wasn't a total bust. The time they spent away provided her the opportunity to spend time with her new love interest.

That love she thought she found was the biggest mistake of her life. Gerald "Nookie" Cartwright was a loser. He had nothing going in his life but a long criminal history of incarcerations and deviance. He was a member of a crew that sold drugs, committed armed robberies, and whatever else they figured they could get away with. Somehow or other, Essence hooked up with him and ended up impregnated with his demon-seed. Besides him being a street thug with no long term future, he was nearly thirty and called Nookie. What the fuck kind of man is named Nookie? It's one thing to be called that when you're a teen, but goddamn, get rid of that name when your ass is half way to social security.

Nookie started dating Essence, and like all new relationships, it started out in story book fashion, with lots of attentiveness, and even understanding. But somewhere along the way, the real Nookie emerged. He soon did not like her going out without him, and he told her what to wear when they did go out, which was rarely. He found a reason to dislike all of her female friends and did everything he could to keep her away from them. He even had confrontations with some; threatening physical harm if he caught them in her apartment or out in public with her. He successfully alienated her from the world that nurtured, supported, and believed in her. That was the beginning of the abuse. It quickly moved from the psychological to the physical. He once forced her to sit in a small dark closet in her bedroom for four hours. When she tried to go to the bathroom he pulled her by the hair and told her she would use the bathroom when he felt like letting her use it. He ordered her back into the closet and kicked her so hard in the ass that her bladder released. She peed on herself right there in the middle of the bedroom, just feet away from the bathroom. He called her all sorts of derogatory names and belittled her to the point she felt worthless.

That sort of treatment went on for nearly two years with no end in sight. She would go to work and even though her closest co-workers and friends could see a change in Essence, they were powerless to get her away from Nookie.

Now don't get me completely wrong; on a few occasions she called the police and put his dumb ass in the system. After one beating that left her with a broken foot, she called the police, who promptly arrested Nookie. Well, Essence went through every phase of the Battered Woman Syndrome and on that occasion let him off the hook.

The next couple of times he did physical harm that resulted in severe injury, she tried to testify against him, but each time she relented and they continued along the abusive path toward her destiny; a path that left emotional and physical scars on her children as well.

The case that brought Briscoe into their lives was the most heinous thing that could have been done. The worst part is Nookie thought he got away with it; but he was sadly mistaken.

Last December around Christmas, the abuse came to an abrupt halt. It was the twenty-second of December and while everyone else was enjoying the festivities of the season, Essence was living a nightmare. Just after midnight, Nookie stumbled into her house drunk and high, feeling like the king of his castle, even though it wasn't his castle. Essence was still awake sitting in the living room watching a movie. Knowing that he was high, she decided not to say anything to cause an argument. He grunted something incoherently, and she just continued to watch the movie as if she did not hear him.

"Bitch, what the fuck is wrong with you?" he slurred angrily, making his way to where she was seated on the sofa.

"Excuse me?" she said softly.

The lump in her throat and the quiver in her voice indicated to him that she was nervous. He seemed to thrive on her fear. The more fear she showed, the more vicious he treated her.

"You heard what I said ho! Don't be try'na act like you mad at somebody. I'll come up in this mothafucker at anytime I feel like!" he slurred badly, but the rage was evident in his eyes.

Essence could not understand why he treated her this way. She had done nothing or showed any sign of being upset with him. It seems like all he wanted to do was take out his aggression on her.

"I know baby; I'm not upset about anything."

"I don't give a fuck if you are. I'm grown and I'll do whatever the fuck I feel like doing. Take your ass to bed! Don't be sittin' up waitin' for me to come home, like you checkin' up on what I'm doin," he hit the power button so hard on the TV he almost knocked it to the floor.

She wanted to finish watching the movie and said, "Just go to bed Nookie, I'll be in there in a few minutes. I want to watch the rest of the movie."

She turned the TV back on with the remote control.

That was a mistake, because Nookie was in no mood for reasoning. This time he hit the TV so hard he knocked it to the floor. The thirty-two-inch flat screen sputtered and went blank. Flames of hell flickered in his eyes.

"You fuckin slut," he spewed as he lunged toward her like a lion pouncing on a helpless gazelle.

His fist came down on her forehead with force and fury knocking her backward over the sofa. Her head hit the wall with such force that her delicate brain crashed into the inside of the cranium that was designed to protect it from harm. She was motionless but that didn't stop Nookie from crashing down on top of her with his knee in her stomach as he punched her repeatedly in the face. Her limp body offered no resistance to the abuse that was being leveled on her. Nookie, engulfed by his rage, did not register that she was not breathing as her head went from side to side from the hard, manly blows laid upon her once pretty face.

"Don't you ever fucking turn on a TV that I turn off," he yelled as he said each word accompanied by a blow to the face.

Nookie didn't hear the screech of the young underdeveloped male voice until after he felt the blunt force of the glass ashtray that he hit him with.

"Get off my mother," Essence's oldest son yelled while swinging the ashtray wildly striking Nookie twice more, leaving a gash in his head just above his right ear.

"Boy I'm gonna fuck your ass up,"

Nookie leaped to his feet and grabbed the small boy around the throat crushing his larynx and cutting off the oxygen to his brain. He picked the boy up and slammed him onto the broken TV that lay mangled on the floor. He began to stomp on his little frame causing internal damage and severe pain. Nookie stood to his feet and looked around at the mess he made of the two bodies crumpled on the floor. He looked up and locked eyes with Essence's five year old daughter. With her eyes as wide as silver dollars she turned and ran crying to her bedroom.

He said, "Come back here you little shit."

He started to run toward her and tripped over a chair that had fallen over during the course of his rage. His face caught the edge of the kitchen counter and everything went dark just before he crashed hard to the floor.

The commotion in the apartment was so loud the neighbors on both sides called the police. When Briscoe and the other units arrived, they found an unlocked door and a bloody scene. The two younger children were huddled in the bedroom shaking and crying.

Essence died, along with the fetus that was growing inside of her womb. Her son was left in a permanent vegetative state. The five year old girl said Nookie beat her mother and brother, but Nookie claimed they all were attacked by an unknown man who must have fled the apartment. Even though he had injuries, nothing on the crime scene supported his claim. When the case went to trial, his attorney placed enough doubt in the minds of the jury that they found him not guilty.

Briscoe was so infuriated he followed Nookie for nearly three weeks studying his daily routine and everything about him. When the time was right, he dished out the punishment that Nookie deserved. The elation he felt coursed through his body like electricity. Since that night in the park at the Potomac River, he has served up the ultimate justice to twenty-two others. He knows it is the will of God that he continue what he is doing, because the city needs to have the trash taken out.

By the time Briscoe showered and got dressed, it was after six. He was surprised Monica had not come to the house, but he was relieved she didn't. He gathered his stuff for work and left the house to visit with his parents before work. He had not been to his parent's house in a couple of weeks and figured it would be nice to see them, not to mention avoid the confrontation with Monica.

He switched on his phone and noted that he had voice messages. He braced himself before listening to them. He knew more than likely it was Monica trying to understand why he has not talked to her in two days. *Her heart must be breaking and it is all my fault*, he reasoned sadly. As he listened to the first couple of messages his heart sank. Monica pleaded and cried. She believed he was upset because of the way she spoke to him two days earlier. She vowed never to treat him that way again and begged him to talk to her.

He saved the messages and moved on to the next. The sound of despair he heard in Mathis' voice sent a chill up his spine and alerted him that something was terribly wrong before Mathis could get to his point. When he did say why he was leaving the message, Briscoe abruptly snatched the steering wheel to the right and pulled the car over into the Riverside Shopping Center and stopped alongside the Safeway Food store.

His hands trembled as he pressed the number 1 key to listen to the message again. *Oh my God, somebody shot Karen. She is lying in the hospital fighting for her life. What the fuck happened?* He fought back the urge to explode into a ferocious cry. Tears pooled in his eyes and his heart raced faster than his thoughts. He really felt like his entire world was crashing in around him. So much is going wrong and he is starting to feel as though he can no longer control his destiny.

The self-doubt was now trying to creep back into his psyche. But how could he let that happen? He has come too far to fall apart now. He has to refocus his attention, and gain control of himself or it could cost him his freedom, or worse, his life.

He did not allow himself to cry. Instead, he concentrated on Karen and put all the other concerns out of his mind for now. He will deal with Monica, Vanessa, and all the other nagging issues later. Right now Karen needs him, and he needs to know what happened to her and who he will make pay. *For trying to take her life, the fools who did it will pay with their lives.* His mind was razor sharp and his resolve was impregnable. It was time to put in work and nothing was going to stop him.

When Briscoe arrived at the hospital he met officers from the 5th precinct in the lobby who told him Karen was in grave condition, unresponsive, and hooked to life support.

"She is in really bad shape Briscoe," Officer Smith informed.

"Does anybody know what happened?" he enquired.

"She was parked on 18th Street when somebody abducted her and took her out to Maryland and shot her. The detectives are investigating, but they are not giving out a whole lot of information right now. I think they are still trying to piece it all together."

"Who is handling the investigation?" he was hoping it was at the precinct level.

"Right now it is Detective Brown. He is on the predator task force. If she doesn't make it the case will go to Homicide," Smith frowned when he said the latter part.

"She is strong; I know she will make it. I feel so bad for her daughter. No child should have to go through something like this,"

Briscoe has a weak spot in his heart for children. He does not want to see them suffer any pain. His desire to protect them is the reason he started on his mission of justice. Seeing Essence Simpson and her young son sprawled on the floor was an image that burned into his being. To see the boy remain in a permanent vegetative state while the culprit walked free was more than he could stand.

Now his fellow officer is lying in a hospital bed, the victim of some smug assholes who thinks they are going to get away with this. That was a total miscalculation on their part. He could hardly wait to leave the hospital to find the ones responsible and serve them up the worst punishment of their life.

"Are you on your way out?" he asked Smith.

"Nah, I'm on her detail. We have two officers positioned at the door to her room in the ICU. I'm on the main entrance and Scott is in the parking garage. We are pulling up any and everybody who looks suspicious," Smith said.

"Do they think the person who did this is going to come up here and try to finish the job?"

"Not sure, but I guess you can never be too careful. They kept this from the media so the only way somebody would know she is in here is if somebody close to her leaks it out,"

The thought of someone wanting to hurt Karen did not sit well with Briscoe. He could not understand why a person would want to hurt her in such a way. He knew she was a working officer who went out and made cases, but the people of the street understand the taboo associated with killing a cop and the hell that would be rained down on their neighborhood until the suspect is caught. So it just didn't add up.

"Alright Smitty, I'm going up to see her. I'll holla atcha later brother," they shook hands.

Briscoe went into the gift shop to purchase a teddy bear and a bouquet of balloons. He walked around the corner from the information desk and made his way down the long corridor that leads to the Intensive Care Unit. As he passed the courtyard he looked at the people in hospital gowns, some with IV bags on polls attached to their arms smoking cigarettes. They were enjoying a smoke and talking amongst themselves and Briscoe could not help but wonder what their ailment was. *It would be ironic if some of them were suffering from cancer. How can someone be in the hospital and still not take a more active approach to good health?* He figured if he were diagnosed with an illness he would do everything in his power to lead a healthy lifestyle aimed at never getting another disease. Well, *to each his own. They will have to deal with the consequences of their actions. By failing their bodies now, their bodies will fail them later when they need it the most.* Once he passed the picturesque window that showcased the manicured courtyard, the thought that he was being judgmental crept into his mind. It was not his place to decide that the people in the courtyard had done anything to cause their condition. He should not think of them in such a way.

"Check yourself Briscoe," he said aloud.

He reached the ICU and came face to face with Detective Whitehead. For some reason his presence shook Briscoe. A queasy feeling churned in his stomach and his heart sped up a few beats. *Why is Whitehead here? Oh my god, is she dead?* His hands trembled slightly. He wondered if his voice would also tremble when he talks.

Whitehead greeted him, "Officer Briscoe, how are you doing?" he said with his hand extended.

Briscoe had to transfer the teddy bear to his left hand with the balloons to shake Whitehead's hand. He looked Whitehead directly in the eyes with an inquisitive gaze.

"Is everything okay," he asked motioning toward Karen's room.

"Oh yeah," Whitehead said, "She is doing okay. She is a fighter. I'm just here checking up on her since she is on the task force I thought it would be the appropriate thing to do."

Briscoe was not entirely convinced that was his only motive for being at the hospital. Something in his gut told him there was more to Whitehead's presence; for some reason it made him uncomfortable.

"I'm going to go in and visit with her for a minute," he said uneasily, hoping Whitehead could not hear it in his voice.

"Go right ahead, I'll be here when you're done," he smiled like the Cheshire Cat.

Briscoe walked into the room and put the balloons on the already crowded table. It looked like a gift shop in her room. There were cards, flowers, balloons, and all kinds of stuffed animals. He placed the teddy bear beside her and then held her free hand. The other one had a tube inserted and IV liquids flowing into her body. He bowed his head and said a silent prayer. Her hand felt cold and hard, almost lifeless. She was completely still. The big flexible tube coming from her mouth looked as though it was attached to the one coming from her nose and the huge machine that seemed to be pumping air into her lungs worked together to keep her alive. The constant beeping and the whirring sounds of the various machines was nothing new to Briscoe, but this time it gave him an eerie feeling that knotted his stomach. He felt powerless to help Karen in any way. It was all up to her and the man above. She looked so small and frail lying in that condition. Just a few days ago, she was a healthy, strong stallion of a black woman begging him to make love to her. Now she is lost somewhere in the tiny defenseless shell of her beautiful body. She has not lost any weight, but the tubes, wires, and machines make her look very small and weak.

"Karen I know you can hear me," he said loudly. "I want you to stop trying to get time off work. Get up out of that bed you slacker and come back to work now. I miss you baby and I can't make it without you. Hang in there Karen. Fight this thing and come back to me. You know I'm going to be here for you right? Don't think for one minute I'm going to leave you by yourself, so don't you leave me alone."

He squeezed her hand as he spoke. He prayed that she could hear him and would come to his voice and have enough hope to survive. He remained standing with her hand in his and whispered a long prayer. Then he talked to her as if she could hear every word. He talked about every day events and other seemingly meaningless topics. The more time he spent holding her hand and talking, the higher his emotions ran. He was having an increasingly hard time controlling the flood gates of his tear ducts. It started when a single tear trickled down the side of his face. The tingly sensation it caused, as it ran slowly over his cheekbone and down under his chin, paved the way for the shower that followed. He gripped Karen's hand with both of his and cried like he has never cried before. He wanted to hold her tight and make everything better, but knew he could not. *Oh God why did this happen to her?*

His heart and soul cried out for Karen, begging God to heal her and shield her child from the pain of losing their mother in such a violent way. As he wiped away the tears and composed himself, the crying gave way to anger, and the anger will eventually give way to rage once he has the person responsible for putting Karen in that hospital bed.

"It's time for me to go to work Karen. I'll be back to see you tomorrow. Hang in there sweetie, and remember you promised me you would not leave me alone."

He bent down and kissed her forehead. When he stood up, for the first time he noticed the glass that enclosed the rooms in the ICU. He was on display the entire time and he saw Whitehead's stare. He caught a glimpse of him out of the corner of his eye, watching his every movement. *Damn, he saw me cry. I have to get myself together because that dude is here for a reason.* He prepared himself for the inevitable encounter with Whitehead, and then left the room.

"You two are close, huh?" Whitehead asked.

"Yeah; we were partners."

"How does it make you feel that somebody did that to her?" Whitehead was on a fishing expedition and he was trying to bait his catch onto the hook.

"It hurts to see her like that," Briscoe said as humbly as possible, working hard to mask his anger and his resolve to punish.

"Do you have a few minutes to talk?" Whitehead asked.

Briscoe wanted to say hell no, but knew there was a reason for Whitehead's presence at the hospital. He had a suspicion it was to see him. Besides, he could use the opportunity to get information on the investigation and any leads on who shot Karen.

"Yeah, I have some time."

"Let's go around the corner to the canteen and get a cup of coffee,"

Whitehead began walking before Briscoe agreed, "How long have you two known each other?"

"A little over four years," he said.

"This sort of thing makes you want to just go out and beat somebody to death. The person who did that to her shouldn't be allowed to live," Whitehead left that statement hanging in the air like a cloud.

Briscoe was aware that Whitehead was not just making small talk and knew to be careful with all of his comments.

"I couldn't call it. That's God's job," Briscoe countered.

"So you're not mad?" he raised an eyebrow but Briscoe could not see his expression because they were walking toward the canteen.

Come on Briscoe; think about what you are saying. He thought to himself. *I have to relax and do a better job of not sounding scripted.*

Just say what most people would say and stop being nervous. He had been in many stressful situations in life and has had training in various counter-interrogation techniques so he should be able to get past Whitehead easily.

"Hell yes I'm angry, but I believe in using the system for its intended purpose. If we go out and take matters into our own hands, we become just as bad as the person who did this to White," he caught a glimpse of Whitehead's expression from the corner of his eye but was unable to discern what he thought of that comment.

They reached the canteen; both got a cup of coffee and took up seats at a small booth in the rear corner. The booth provided some privacy but also offered a complete view of the canteen. It's something about cops needing to sit facing the entrance to an establishment. They have to always be at a heightened awareness focusing their attention on their environment all the time. It was not like there were any threats in the canteen. There was an elderly woman reading a book of inspirational spiritual quotes, sipping gingerly from a cup of tea. A group of five hospital-attired females were huddled at a table talking shop and enjoying a laugh. The only other people were the canteen staff and the occasional patron who purchased something to go. The place was relatively quiet, with the only exception being the periodic announcement over the hospital's PA system.

Whitehead intentionally sat in the chair facing the door causing Briscoe to have to choose the chair facing the window without a view. He wanted to limit the distractions and basically force Briscoe to look at him.

"So, how is everything going with your assignment?" he referred to Sherman Edwards, whom Briscoe was assigned to follow.

"Everything is going well," Briscoe said.

"You haven't seen any suspicious looking individuals or anything?" Whitehead asked.

"Nothing at all; everything has been quiet."

Briscoe knew there was a point and direction to Whitehead's conversation. He wished he would hurry up and make his position clear.

"Where were you last night?" Whitehead asked abruptly.

"I was watching Edwards. He never left Georgetown."

"When did you hear about Officer White?"

"After 6:00 p.m. when I turned on my phone."

"Are you in the habit of turning off your phone?"

Whitehead studied every facial expression and every movement of Briscoe. He knew where he was last night and it had nothing to do with what he wanted out of him.

"I turn it off most of the time so I can get uninterrupted sleep. Most people work during the day and don't always respect the fact that 10:00 a.m. for me is like 2:00 a.m. for them," Briscoe explained.

"I should do that when I have late nights and need to sleep in. But I can't because this fucking job consumes my life, and I have to be accessible twenty-four freakin' hours a day," he said with a hint of annoyance at how much of his life is spent on the job.

He thought about his new relationship with Deborah Bell and felt sad that there was a chance the job would come between them and consume the time he should spend with her.

"Man if you're not careful you will look up twenty years down the road and wonder what the hell happened to your life," Whitehead said with a distant look in his eyes. "What do you do with your personal time?" he asked Briscoe in a nonchalant manner.

"I like jazz, so I attend concerts and festivals. It helps me relax."

"Are you married? Have kids?"

"No and hell no," they shared a laugh. "I'm not ready for that yet," Briscoe said.

"What do you think about the job so far? I know you've only been on for about six years. That's about the time when the reality sets in that the criminal justice system is more of an injustice system. I know it can be frustrating. Most of us come to this profession with a sense of justice and a desire to see it served. Once we get a taste of the politics and other dirty dealings it can downright piss us off. I just wonder sometimes how young officers feel about it, because it makes me mad as hell. Especially when I build a solid case against a shit-bag killer and those butter-soft prosecutors let them off the hook," Whitehead was now studying Briscoe.

Briscoe listened intently to Whitehead and sensed a game of cat and mouse. He thought about the list on Sutton's desk with his name on it and wondered if they thought he might be the serial predator. It was evident that Whitehead was up to something.

"I enjoy my job. I like interacting with people and helping those in need. I try not to get all wrapped up in the things that I can't control. I do my job getting the offender off the street. If the prosecutors don't do theirs and keep them off the streets, I can't let that eat at me or influence the way I do my job," he thought *wow that sounds good.*

"I wish I could keep that attitude, but after all these years I get pissed," Whitehead continued, "You have a military background don't you?"

"Yes I do. Army," he decided to keep any details of his military history brief.

"What did you do in the Army?"

"I was Infantry."

"So you got a lot of special training on killing and stuff," Whitehead said grinning.

"I don't know if I would say that. I guess I got just as much training as anybody else who served in the Army," Briscoe hoped he did not have too much experience with the military to know just how much training he had.

"Oh? I was under the impression that you were some kind of special operations person. I heard that your military file was mostly classified," he looked Briscoe in the eyes as if to say, *I know most of the answers before you give them.*

"Nah, I wasn't all that. Just a grunt," Briscoe lied because he knew Whitehead would need a lot to get his file declassified and that was not likely to happen.

"So, what do you think about the predator out there preying on criminals?" Whitehead had a vibe. Even though Briscoe is giving him answers that are safe and does not display the mindset Deborah said the predator would have, his gut told him otherwise.

"I think he is a criminal who should be punished when we catch him," he used every bit of his training to keep himself from giving away his true feelings.

"I guess that's why you are on the task force," Whitehead said and then moved on to his next question, "What if the predator found the guys that shot Officer White and killed them; how would that make you feel?"

"I'm not sure. On one hand, I would be glad they are off the street. But on the other hand, I would feel like justice wasn't fully served."

Whitehead piped in, "Why's that?"

"Because Karen would not have the opportunity to confront her attacker and have closure knowing that they are in prison paying for what they did."

Briscoe knew that was a lame answer, but he had to sound as though he was all about the system and making it work. Then it dawned on him that Whitehead said guys. *So there was more than one.* Now is the time for Briscoe to flip the script and get some information from the detective.

"You said guys. There was more than one who attacked her?"

"Yes. There were at least three. A witness said shortly after he heard the gunshots he saw three men come from the woods where she was found."

"Did he give you all anything to go on? Is there a suspect or a lookout?" Briscoe perked up with the hope of getting a lead on who he was going to destroy.

"The only thing we have right now is a lookout for the vehicle they occupied," he briefed Briscoe on the entire case.

He even mentioned that she was watching Brick Jackson when she was abducted and taken to the wooded area and shot.

"We do know it wasn't a robbery because all of her belongings were left in the vehicle. They only seemed to be after her."

A thought crossed Briscoe's mind, but he was afraid to ask the question. He did not want to imagine that she endured the wickedness that flashed in his mind. His twisted expression could not disguise what he was thinking.

"I know what you're thinking. The answer is no; they did not sexually assault her. She appeared to fight back, even though her hands were tied behind her back," Whitehead said reassuringly.

Briscoe was relieved to know they did not rape Karen. She is a tough woman who would not go down easily. He didn't think she would allow herself to be raped while she was conscious. He figured she would die first and it appears the attackers planned to make it that way.

Whitehead has taken the conversation all over the place and even allowed Briscoe to ask questions. Now he was ready to turn up the heat a little and see where it takes him. He had a feeling that Briscoe was tied to the serial predator homicides, but was in no position to move forward against him. Right now it was only speculation and hunch. The last time he checked, neither of those were grounds for any type of warrant.

So he said, "I noticed you arrested a few of the victims of the predator. Do you remember any of those cases?"

A feeling passed through Briscoe's gut. Just as Whitehead had a hunch, Briscoe now had his suspicions confirmed; Whitehead is interviewing him to see if he is the predator. *That psychological profile must have told them something that makes them think I could be their man.* He needed to continue to be cool but try to bring this encounter to a close.

"I'm not sure. I don't recall all of his victims. If you give me some names, I can probably recall the cases. I don't always remember the names off hand, but I never forget the faces," Briscoe did not want to seem too organized and detail oriented.

"I don't have them all here in front of me, but I can think of one off the top of my head. Do you remember Miles Holloman?" Whitehead's gaze was burning through Briscoe's soul.

"The name sounds familiar. I think I locked him up for an assault or something like that," Briscoe put on his best disinterested persona.

"Yes, it was an assault on an elderly woman," Whitehead reminded.

"Oh, okay. I remember that. It was in the flea market on Benning Road." He wanted to distance himself from any emotions he had concerning Holloman.

He could not allow his expression to reveal his thoughts. Whitehead was staring so intently at him it took every bit of his concentration to remain steady.

"That must have pissed you off that all he got was probation," he probed.

"Nah, it didn't matter to me. Like I said, I did my part," Briscoe stuck with the position that he stated earlier.

"So watching low-life criminals get away with brutal crimes does nothing to you, huh?"

"I didn't say it does nothing to me. I'm saying it doesn't move me to a point to go out and hurt anyone," Briscoe was now sure Whitehead was fishing for something

It was now time for him to take the offensive on this exchange.

"Why are you asking me these kinds of questions? Do you think I'm the serial killer?"

The question caught Whitehead by surprise. It took him a second to compose himself.

"No. Why would you think that?"

"It seems like you are trying to link me to victims of the predator and you're asking me questions about my personal life as if I have some secret to hide," Briscoe remained calm, but firm.

He did not want to come off antagonistic, nor did he want to sit there like a lame duck.

"Since you are a member of the task force and your friend is lying in there fighting for her life, I wanted to get to know you better and provide a friendly shoulder to lean on. But you come off defensive, as though you are being attacked. Is there something you want to share with me? Do you have a guilty conscious about something?"

Whitehead is a master interrogator with a keen sense of people. He knows how to get what he wants out of a suspect.

"There is absolutely nothing I want to share, nor is there anything guilty about my conscience."

Briscoe was ready to jump up and run out of the hospital. He felt compromised. But how? He did not leave any evidence. He has been very careful. Now he is being confronted by the very person he wanted to avoid.

"I am just sitting here talking to you and you go off on a tangent with a wild accusation," Whitehead played it off just as well as Briscoe.

"I'm telling you what it feels like. If that is the case you are way off the mark. I'm out there looking for the predator every night. I have absolutely nothing to do with anything that is brewing in your mind. If I am a suspect, I would appreciate you informing me of that up front," Briscoe looked stern, as he stared defiantly into Whitehead's eyes.

"There is nothing to inform. I think you are paranoid."

Whitehead took a sip of his coffee and continued, "If you were a suspect, there would be no doubt in your mind of whether I thought you were. I would come at you hard and thorough. So whatever you do, don't get it twisted."

Briscoe did not believe anything Whitehead said. He felt he was a suspect. All he could figure is that damn psychological profile gave him something to work with. Covering his tracks now was going to be much more difficult with extra eyes watching and trying to tie him to the killings. But first things first; he had to end this conversation and get out of the hospital.

"I appreciate your concern for me detective. I thank you for coming to the hospital to visit Officer White, but I have to cut this short. I have to go to work in a few minutes," he said rising from his seat.

"I'm sorry if I offended you in any way. I assure you that was not my intention. I just wanted to get to know you better," Whitehead laid on his most sincere deportment and extended his hand.

They shook hands and Whitehead said, "I'll be around. Don't hesitate to call on me if you need me or if you would like to talk about anything. I'm always here, and can be reached twenty four seven."

"Thank you detective, I'll remember that," Briscoe said with a forced smile.

Whitehead watched him until he turned the corner out of sight. He reached into his jacket pocket, retrieved his notebook, and jotted down the content of their conversation.

Officer Tyson was a statistical match on paper, but Briscoe seemed to have the build, ability, and home situation compatible with the profile. He was calm, perceptive, and nothing he said was incriminating. However, Whitehead had a feeling there was more to Briscoe than what is on the surface.

Briscoe walked away feeling Whitehead's gaze until he turned the corner and headed out the emergency room exit. He did not want to run the risk of walking down the long corridor leading to the front of the building. He thought that would give Whitehead an opportunity to engage him in conversation again, and he just wanted to be out of his sight. He thought, *What the fuck? Is Whitehead on my ass because I made a mistake, or what?*

Finally back in his rental car, he breathed a sigh of relief. He understood that Whitehead was reaching for something, but was not one hundred percent sure that he didn't already have something on him. Somehow or other, he has to find out exactly what it is Whitehead knows and how he knows it. He immediately thought to go back and sanitize his Charger and the Pontiac he is currently using. The last thing he wanted to happen is for the crime scene technicians to find DNA evidence from one of his victims. It would be nearly impossible to explain why anything remotely associated with a victim is in his vehicle. He decided he would do it first thing in the morning.

He cannot spend his time obsessing over what Whitehead does or doesn't know. He has to move on and get to the people responsible for shooting Karen; he wanted to get to it right away.

As he drove from the hospital parking lot, he dialed Connie's number.

"Hey Officer Briscoe." She sounded happy to receive his call.

"How did you know it was me?" he asked playfully.

"Caller ID sweetie; but I felt it was you anyway," she giggled.

"What are you doing?" he asked.

"Nothin', what up?"

"Can I meet you real quick?" He needed information now.

"Yeah, where?"

"Somewhere that I can pick you up in the next ten minutes," he was pressed for time and needed to talk to her before heading to Georgetown to relieve the officer.

"I can be in back of the school in ten minutes," she offered.

"That sounds great I'll be there," he hung up and made a sharp left turn onto Michigan Avenue for the short ride to meet Connie.

Connie beat him to the back of the school. When he arrived he saw her leaning against the wall close to the door the kids use to come outside for recess. She was dressed in her hooker clothes, so he figured he caught her just before she was about to hit the street. Her too-short skirt revealed her knobby knees that were screaming for some lotion. The tank top tee shirt that held her tiny tits looked as though she had slept in it all night and spilled some of her breakfast on it. Connie did not seem to go far out of her way to fix herself up for the johns. She once said the johns buy her because of her good head, so they didn't care what she was wearing. Briscoe figured as long as it was something short and tight, the dudes would go for her.

She looked a little apprehensive when he pulled up beside her. She did not move from her spot; instead, she looked with wide eyes nervously at the Pontiac that pulled in the back of the school.

Briscoe let the tinted window down and said, "Hey Connie, get in."

"Oh shit, you scared the shit out of me," she got into the passenger seat and sighed.

"What's the matter," he asked.

"I didn't know who you were. I thought somebody was setting me up," she said.

"Oh yeah, I didn't tell you about this car. You remember the black one. Sorry about that," he apologized.

"It's okay. How you been?" she asked.

"Busy. What's been up with you?" he had to get the pleasantries out of the way quickly because he didn't have a lot of time.

"I been good. Just doin what I do," they both knew what that was.

He decided to jump into what he wanted to know. "Did you hear about the woman who was taken from 18th Street out into Maryland and shot?"

"Yeah, and I heard she was a cop too."

Briscoe knew that no matter how hard the department tried to keep what happened to Karen from the public, the street people would know about it.

"Did you hear anything about who did it?"

"They say it was Brick and them," she said levelly.

"What did they say happened?" he could feel his blood start to boil. That was the fucker she was assigned to watch.

"They said she was sittin' in the car and three of dem boys bust out her windows and dragged her out," Connie didn't seem to show a lot of emotion as she recited what she heard on the street.

"Who are the boys?" he asked.

"It was Ant and dem two he always wit," she knew they were killers, so she was afraid of the thought of them.

"Do you know their names," he inquired.

"I think it's Kwame and Jamal. They the ones do all the killin for Brick. Errbody know they kill people, and errbody scared of dem," and Connie was no exception.

But she liked Briscoe and trusted him. She also liked getting paid.

"Did you hear why they did it?" he was confident in Connie's information. He trusts what she picks up on the street and now he knows who he is going to get. But he wanted to know why they would choose Karen.

"I heard cause she was following Brick around, and he got mad," Connie was sincere when she asked, "Is she dead?"

Briscoe trusted Connie, but he was not willing to disclose Karen's condition. Connie was a talker, and that meant she would talk to other people. He was not willing to take the chance of letting the word out that she was in the hospital fighting for her life. That would place her life in serious jeopardy.

"She's dead," he lied.

A sadness came over Connie, "I'm sorry," she said looking solemnly at Briscoe.

"It's been hard on everybody. The investigators are working it. If they find out it was done in Maryland, they will get the death penalty," he added for effect. He knew they were already sentenced to death.

"I can find out more if you want me to," she offered.

"That's cool, but the detectives will be all over it soon. They are going to be arrested and prosecuted soon," he was sure Connie was not suspicious of him; but he could never be too careful, or become complacent.

"I'll let you know if I hear anything," she wanted to help him as much as she could.

"Thanks Connie," he changed the topic to his other area of interest, "What's been up with your girl Janice?" It has been a while since he checked on that situation.

"She been the same. I seen that white man over there again," she said disgustedly.

Briscoe almost lost it when she that. "What? The same one you told me about before?" he knew she meant Danielson, but couldn't believe he would continue after being warned.

"Yep, the same one," she shook her head remembering the sex act she witnessed between Danielson, Janice, and Shauna.

Briscoe felt like going straight to Danielson's house and beating him to death. He wondered what it was going to take to keep him from molesting that child. Maybe it is something he cannot be scared away from doing. Maybe the only thing that will cure him is death. On top of all he has to deal with, now he has to do something to stop this hypocrite pervert from further damaging the little girl who has already endured more than most fifty year olds.

He composed himself and asked, "How long ago was that?"

"About three days."

"Did you see them do anything this time?" he braced himself for the answer.

"No, I only saw him coming out."

"What time was it?"

"About 1:00 a.m.," she said.

He wondered how the hell the man could stay out so late and then get up and go to work early the next day. He also wondered how he could continue with his daily function as a chief prosecutor of people who were exactly like him. How does he molest a child, then turn around and send a child molester to jail? He decided he would do something about Danielson right away.

"Thanks for the info Connie. Is there anything else happening?" he was ready to get uptown to relieve his partner.

"Nah, nothin' I can think of," she paused for a few seconds recalling to insure she didn't leave anything out.

"I appreciate what you've done so far," he took forty dollars from his pocket and handed it to her.

She eagerly took the money and said, "Thanks Officer Briscoe, you always take care of a sista."

"You're the one taking care of me; I just try to show how much the department and I appreciate your help," he continued with his prevarication.

"I'll let you know if I hear anything else. Do you want me to call you?" she asked.

"Yeah, that would be okay. But I have to get going now," he spent enough time and got more than enough information to move in the right direction.

"Ah'ight den, I'll holla atchu later," Connie said pulling the door handle and pushing the door open. She looked back and with a smile said, "Where's my kiss goodbye."

Briscoe laughed, "Girl, you so crazy."

She laughed as she shut the door and walked into the darkness.

On the way uptown, Briscoe stopped at a CVS and purchased a can of white spray paint. He used the pay phone to leave messages on Danielson's office phone and his wife's office phone as well. He looked at his watch and noted that he had a few minutes to spare on his way to relieve Officer Seth. He decided to pay a visit to Philip Danielson.

Danielson lived in Georgetown, not far from Briscoe's assignment. His first warning was private, but very clear, and it did not dissuade Danielson from having contact with the girl. So this time he won't be so private.

He pulled into Danielson's block and drove down until he spotted the green Mercedes Benz. It was after 10:30 p.m. and the lights were still on in Danielson's house. He slowed and passed the car at less than five miles an hour. He also looked at the house to see that nobody was on the porch or in the window. He continued down the block looking for a parking spot, but couldn't find one.

He cursed the lack of available parking in such an exclusive part of the city. He wondered how people paid upwards of nearly a million dollars for their homes and didn't have ample parking.

He decided to pull into the alley about 500 feet from Danielson's home. He shut off the vehicle and turned off the dome light before exiting with the spray paint in hand. He quickly made his way toward Danielson's home, looking left, right, up, and down the street. He checked for any signs of people walking, running, driving, sitting on the porch or in their vehicles.

When he made it to Danielson's home, he looked at the front, including the windows. He was reasonably sure that nobody was looking out at anything. He raised the can of spray paint, which he was shaking the entire time he was walking up the street and turned toward the green Mercedes. On the passenger side of the vehicle in large bold capital letters that stretched from the rear quarter panel to the front tire, he wrote, "PERVERT." He then went to the driver's side and spray painted, "CHILD MOLESTER." When he finished the deed, he put the top back on the can and hurried back to his car. He smiled as he drove out of the alley.

Now let's see him explain that to his wife and his colleagues. Briscoe knew this would brand him like the scarlet letter. He planned to follow this up with a phone call to Danielson and his wife. If he had time, he would kill him like the other low life perverts. That will have to wait, but Danielson's days are numbered. Hopefully, he will get so much grief from others that he will be glad when Briscoe comes to put him out of his misery.

"I see you just pulled in the block yo," Seth said into the phone when he saw Briscoe turn the corner.

"Yeah man, I see you right there. You can take off," Briscoe was nearing the spot soon to be vacated. "Any news worth reporting?" he asked.

"Nah, just the same ole same with dude. I can't believe he is a notorious drug dealer, because he just seems to stay close to his crib," Seth said.

"I don't know, maybe he is reformed," Briscoe offered.

"Well whatever it is, homeboy ain't makin' no noise," Seth reported.

"I guess that's a good thing," Briscoe hoped he was reformed.

Perhaps Edwards took his drug money and used it to go legit. Briscoe never thought of Edwards as a target.

"That's always a good thing when a brother sees the light and does the right thing," Seth was pro-black. Even though he had to lock up black men, he didn't particularly derive pleasure from it.

"Alright man, have a safe trip home. I'll holla tomorrow," Briscoe was ready to end the call and work on his plan for Brick and his boys.

"You too brother; stay safe out here tonight. See ya tomorrow," he said warmly.

Alone with his thoughts, Briscoe reflected on his conversation with Whitehead. The detective all but accused him of being the predator. He felt, for some reason, Whitehead was locked in on him. The task force has been in effect for a couple of weeks and neither of the lead detectives have ever said hello, let alone held a conversation with him. Now, all of a sudden, the man wants to sit down and get to know each other better.

He pulled his cell phone from his pocket to call Detective Willis Sanford to see if there was anything he knew about the case that might shed some light on why Whitehead pressed him. Just as he flipped the phone open he received an incoming call from Monica. He looked wide eyed at the phone, and hesitated. It has been nearly three days without a word from him; he knew he could no longer avoid her. He took a deep breath and exhaled loudly.

"Hello," he said softly.

"Antonio! Where are you? What is going on?" the questions were coming one after the next, without room for him to answer. "Why haven't you called me? Are you mad at me?"

"Hi Monica," he paused.

She continued before he could answer, "What's going on Antonio? Did I do something wrong?" She was hurting and didn't understand why.

"No baby, you haven't done anything wrong. I've been dealing with the near-homicide of my co-worker," he stopped short of giving details.

"What happened? It must be serious to keep you from returning my calls for two days," she said with less compassion than he hoped.

"It's very serious. She might not make it. She was shot several times at close range. She is in a coma and on life support," he hoped this was sufficient to keep Monica from digging deeper into the truth of why he hasn't called.

"I'm sorry to hear that. How are you doing?" she softened a little.

"I'm okay; I spent time in the hospital. And I've been out trying to get information on who did it. That's why I haven't been able to call you back. It has consumed all my time," he lied as best he could.

"I understand sweetie, but I was going out of my mind. I thought you were mad at me because I was short with you the other day. It felt like you dumped me because of it. I knew you were not that type of man, but not hearing from you . . . I had to try and figure things out on my own. Just a two minute call to say you were busy would have been okay. At least that way I wouldn't have had to worry," she said

"You're right Moni. I apologize," he thought perhaps he was apologizing more for cheating and less for not calling.

"It's okay baby, just promise me you will never do something like that again, because it hurts more than you know," her heart was open for him and her love was true.

"I promise Moni," he felt much better now that he got past this situation with a convenient lie. He wants to stay with and be faithful to Monica, but he has an attraction to Vanessa that he cannot understand. It was never his intention, or his nature, to mess around with more than one woman at a time. That is especially true when he has a woman as wonderful as Monica. He will have to make sure he never sees Vanessa again; because he is not willing to give up his Monica.

"I'm glad baby boy," she sounded relieved and her tone softened and turned loving. "I think we need to get away for a while, just the two of us."

"That sounds like a good idea," he has not been on a vacation in a while. With all that has happened a vacation would be nice. But that isn't something he could do right away.

"I'm glad you think so, because I was on Chappelle's Travel Engine and saw a great travel deal to Aruba. We can get away for a five or six day trip. Go on the website at www.chappellestravelengine.com and read up on the trip," her excitement bubbled through the phone.

He knew there was no getting away before he put Brick down, but he didn't want to dampen her good mood, especially after what he has put her through the past couple of days.

"I will check it out tomorrow after I wake up."

"Thanks baby boy. I'm so glad because I really want to get away with you. I know we are gonna have some mad fun. I promise," she added that with a hint of seduction.

They talked for a while, sharing laughs, and feeling close to one another again. He felt bad about lying to Monica, but he felt worse for cheating on her. He reasoned that she did not deserve to be treated the way he has treated her and vowed to himself never to do it again. Monica was worthy of an everlasting love from a man that would respect and treat her right, and Briscoe felt he was that kind of man. They exchanged telephone kisses and hung up.

He dialed Sanford's cell.

"Oh my god; what wind blew you in my direction?" Sanford laughed.

"Hey dog, what up? How is life treating you?" Briscoe was happy to hear his friend's voice.

"You know I don't complain, but it's the same old shit just a different day," he said. "How about you, what's been up man?"

"Just hanging in here trying to deal with life as it comes at me," he said looking for the right time to bring up Whitehead.

"Yo I heard about Karen White. Damn, that shit fucked me up. Who in the world would want to hurt that cutie?" he stated it more than asked a question. "I know you were kind of tight with her; it must be fucking with your mind."

If only he knew the half of it. "Yeah, it is a hard thing to see her laying in that hospital bed fighting for her life."

"I haven't been up there yet, and to be honest, I really don't want to see her in that state. It's weird how I deal in death. I see some of the most gruesome shit, but I can't stand to see somebody I care about messed up like that."

That is not an uncommon thing with first responders. You tend to be detached from the misery of others as a means of coping, but when it is personal, it strikes deep.

"I understand that Will. Just keep her in your prayers," Briscoe said solemnly.

"No doubt," Sanford said and continued, "It's pretty late playa, what's on your mind?"

"Well, I stopped by the hospital on my way to work tonight and I guess I just needed to talk to somebody. Since I haven't hollered at you in a couple weeks, I thought I would call you now," that was partially true.

"You know I'm always here for you. I'm still in the office working on a case. I was about to shut it down for the night. Go ahead and let it rip. I'm all ears," he sat back in his chair giving Briscoe his undivided attention.

"I can't help but put myself in that hospital bed. I wonder what if that was me, or could that be me or any of us. Then I feel guilty that I wasn't there to protect her. We talk at night while watching our assignments, but I didn't talk to her last night when this apparently happened. Maybe I could have gotten to her before she was shot," he really did feel this way.

"I can dig your feelings, but the truth is you wouldn't have been able to do anything to prevent what happened. You know there would not have been enough time for you to make it from uptown to help her," he was sympathetic but wanted his boy to stop beating up on himself.

"I know you're right, but that doesn't stop me from feeling this way."

"Maybe you should try to focus on something else. I know you've prayed for Karen and your heart is there, but there is nothing else you can do right now. Everything is in God's hands, so the best thing for you to do is put your energy into something else. It will help you get over those feelings," Sanford suggested.

"That might be easier said than done," he replied.

"I didn't say it would be easy, I said you will have to try to do it."

"I will. Thanks for the advice. I knew calling you was the right thing to do," Briscoe said.

"I told you B, I'm always there when you need me," Sanford was a true friend.

"You know, when I showed up at the hospital Whitehead was there. It seemed like he was questioning me as a suspect," he paused to see if Sanford would offer an explanation.

"Are you sure? Why would you think that?" Sanford asked.

"I'm positive. He asked questions about past victims and my connection to them. He all but asked my whereabouts during all the homicides. Is there something going on with the case that would make him think I would be involved?" Briscoe hoped Sanford could give him something to work with.

"I haven't followed their case that closely, but I did hear their psychological profile of the killer came back, and they are treating it like a top secret classified government document. Whatever it says they won't share with anybody," he along with the rest of the unit wanted to get a peek at what it said.

"I wonder what makes him think I would be involved in killing anybody. Of all the people in the world, why me?"

"I don't know? But once they got that profile back they became very secretive and put a lock on their investigation like a pit bull," Sanford had no idea what their direction was on the investigation.

Briscoe was disappointed that he could get nothing concrete out of Sanford, but he confirmed that something in the profile directed Whitehead to him. "I don't know what they are looking for, but they are wasting time looking at me."

"Do you want me to check with him and let you know what it was all about?" he had no problem sticking up for his boy.

"Nah, don't sweat it. If it is something that he wants to pursue, let him. That way there won't be any doubts when he apprehends the right person. Barking up my tree is only going to leave him with a sore throat," Briscoe said.

"Well, I'll do a little snooping around and let you know if you are being paranoid," he said believing there was no way Briscoe could be a suspect.

"Alright Will, I appreciate it. Thanks for listening man, I needed to get these things off my chest."

"Anytime B, hang in there, and remember what I told you to do. It's gonna be alright," Sanford had his best interest at heart, and didn't want him worrying about Karen or anything else. He knew Briscoe was confident and strong, but stress could breakdown Hercules.

"I'll holla later; peace," Briscoe closed his cell phone and placed it in the console. He thought about what he was doing with trying to rid the city of violent offenders, and how he could not kill everybody. He did believe that he could deter some would-be victimizers by the fear of not knowing if he would get them. But then he thought about Karen, and how her being a cop did not stop the dogs from attacking and trying to kill her. Maybe they are not afraid, or they think what happened to Red won't happen to them. They are obviously not swayed by what he will do to them; or maybe they thought they would not leave a witness. Well, it sucks to be them because he is focused and ready to bring the pain. He reached into his backpack and retrieved a note pad. He pulled an ink pen from the console and started to write his plan for Brick, Ant, Kwame, Jamal, and let's not forget Phillip Danielson and Janice Russell. He looked at his watch and realized he have seven hours left on shift. That should give him plenty of time to work out the details.

32

"Oh my god," Danielson said as he walked down the steps from his home toward his car parked on the street in front of his house. He looked back over his shoulder to see if his wife, Sasha, was looking. She wasn't and he hurried to the car and jumped in so fast, had the neighbors seen him they would have thought someone was chasing him. He turned the key in the ignition and placed place the vehicle in gear so quickly it seemed simultaneous. He sped off before Sasha could look out the window and see the car. His thoughts were racing. *How did he know I saw Shauna? Is it somebody I know? What am I going to do?* He was engulfed in his thoughts and did not immediately notice the strange looks he received from other motorist and pedestrians caught in the DC rush hour. When he did notice he wanted to sink to the floor. He began to perspire and look nervously straight ahead. He would avoid eye contact at all cost. *What are these people thinking? Do they believe I am a child molester? Do they know who I am?* He could not stop the thoughts, or answer any of them.

One thing he knew; he could not go to work with his car looking like that. He had to cover up the words and then get it to a paint shop. He pulled into the parking lot of Moe's Hardware on Connecticut Avenue and ran inside. He went straight to the paint aisle and grabbed four cans of forest green spray paint. He paid for the paint and ran back to his vehicle. He drove into an alley around 13th Street in a quiet residential area. He got out and for the first time took a good look at the words on the driver's side of his car. He shook the first can of spray paint as he walked around the car shaking his head. He wondered if any of his neighbors saw the writing on the car. He drove off so fast that he didn't notice if any other cars were vandalized. Maybe there were other cars damaged also. Maybe he is just a victim of some misplaced adolescent fun. But his guilty mind made him speed off and buy paint to cover it up. He spray painted over the words, but they could still be seen beneath the green paint, which by the way, did not match the color of his vehicle. It wasn't even close. He quickly realized he needed more paint. He wished he had bought a pail of paint and a brush. He did not have time to sit and wait for the paint to dry to put on numerous coats. He spray painted heavily over the white letters, to the point the paint ran and dripped. He was out of paint and out of time. He needed to get to work because there were meetings and a court date. The judge would not understand his not showing up to prosecute a criminal. He drove out of the alley and headed toward his office.

The entire ride he felt like everyone was staring at him and knew what he had done. He was feeling anxiety like never before. He could barely keep his thoughts in order.

Once he arrived at his office building, he parked on the lowest level of the underground garage in a Visitor spot at the back of the lot. He did not park in his assigned space. He hoped to avoid any questions from coworkers.

He emerged from the elevator and met Patricia's warm smile, as he did every morning. "Good morning Phil," she said cheerfully.

"Ah, good morning," he said hesitantly with reservation.

She looked into his darting eyes and asked, "Is everything alright Phil?"

"Ah, yes. Everything is good," he hurried past. He didn't check his messages or empty his mailbox. He normally chit-chatted with Patricia and let her know what his schedule was like for the day, but today was unlike any other day.

"You seem . . ." he was gone before she could finish her sentence.

Once inside his office, Danielson shut the door and dropped his briefcase on the floor as he hurried to his desk. He booted up his computer and cursed it for taking so long to finish the start up process. He looked for the phone number to Maaco or any body shop that could offer same day service or get it painted within the next couple of days. He found a body shop in Northeast DC and called to arrange to drop the car off at eleven o'clock. He figured people would be at work and he would likely not be seen departing the garage. At least that is what he hoped.

He tried to collect his thoughts and figure out who was doing this to him. He wondered if Janice was planning to extort money from him. *Perhaps it was her friend Johnny, who she said she had not heard from in a while. Who else could it be?* His mind was going in so many directions he could not think of work or anything on his agenda. He picked up the phone and dialed Janice.

"Hello," Janice croaked groggily through the receiver.

"Janice. What are you doing?" it was more an accusation than a question.

"I'm in bed," she yawned.

"You know what I mean. Don't play with me," his tone was harsh.

"Huh?" she was baffled.

"What are you trying to do? Are you crazy?" he snarled through clinched teeth.

"What are you talking about Phil?" she was dumbfounded.

"Who have you told about us?" he said bluntly.

"Nobody; I would never say anything," she was wide awake now. "What is going on Phil?"

"Somebody wrote on my car and sent a letter to my office," he revealed. Then he asked, "Do you know anything about it?"

"Hell no! Why would you think I would have something to do with that? I have just as much to lose as you," her ire was raised.

"Well, who else knows that I come over there besides you? What about Johnny?" he asked.

"What about Johnny?" she snarled. "You know I haven't seen him in weeks."

His tone lowered, and the edge in his voice weakened, "I know, but do you think he could be the one doing this?"

"I don't know?" she said bluntly. "Why don't you ask him yourself?"

"I'm sorry Janice, but I don't know what to do. I'll be ruined if this gets out in the media. My life would be over," he realized Janice had no clue what he was going through. "I'll work it out. Sorry for bothering you. Go back to sleep and forget about it," he felt bad for speaking to her so harshly.

"It's okay Phil. Don't worry, it's probably somebody you put in jail. They are just trying to get even with you. They probably don't know anything," she hoped to comfort him and give him peace of mind because she did not want him to stop coming to her house.

He could not be easily consoled because his tormentor knows about the times he spent with Shauna. The author of the letter never asked for anything. They simply said to stay away from the girl. But when he went back again, the person knew it and left the message on his car. What could he possibly do now to stop them from going to his job, the media, or his family? He was at a loss for options.

He never thought that perhaps he should have just stayed away from the girl. He didn't know, but it was now too late for regrets, because he was on Briscoe's list and the end was drawing near.

"I'll figure it out Janice. I have to go, I'll talk to you later," he sounded frightened and defeated.

"Phil, don't let this get you down, we will get past it. I don't want you to worry about it. If they had something on you, why haven't they told anybody? They are just messing with you," she tried to reassure him.

"Okay Janice, thanks," he said detached from her words of encouragement.

He hung up the phone and stared out the window for what seemed like hours, but was actually less than ten minutes. He was jolted back to the present by the ringing phone on the desk in front of him.

"Phillip Danielson speaking," he said.

"Phil, what the fuck have you been doing at night?" her words seethed with accusation and condemnation.

Oh my god, she knows. What can I say? His heart dropped into his pants. The lump in his throat prevented him from speaking right away. He had to clear his throat and take a deep breath to steady is shaking hands. He knew he would have a tremble in his voice and hoped she wouldn't detect it.

"What are you talking about Sasha?" he finally forced the words from his mouth.

"I received a voicemail with details about things you've been doing late at night. Who is Shauna?" she waited for a response.

"I don't know a Shauna," he lied.

"Phil, she is a twelve year old girl!" she said angrily. "You know her mother Janice Russell don't you?"

His heart sank further into his stomach as he started to sweat. He knew if she was sitting in front of him, she would see that he was lying.

"I don't know her either. Where are you getting this crazy information from Sasha?"

"I told you Phil; it was left on my voicemail by a man. He gave me details and I recall that you were out late on the days he said you were with the child. Phil are you a pedophile?" she had to ask the question, because she could feel he was lying.

The question hit him like a linebacker; it took him a few seconds to recover. He did not know what the caller left, but they did give names, dates, and times. He knew that was enough to have an investigator over there digging for information and then determining that he slept with a minor. He quickly realized he needed to get Sasha off the government line.

"Sasha, we should talk about this in person," he suggested.

"We are going to talk about it Phil, and you'd better have some proof , because the caller promised to send me proof later today showing you with a twelve year old," her breaking heart could be felt through the phone.

Proof! Oh shit! In his mind he was doomed. If the guy was sending her proof, then he will send it to his job also and he is fucked if that happens.

"We can talk about everything when we get home tonight."

"I don't know if I can wait that long Phil. If the proof shows you messing with a child, I don't think I could stand to look at you again," she said with conviction.

Her words cut into him like a knife; but he stood on his lie, "I can assure you Sasha there is nothing going on with me and anybody. I would never do anything to hurt you."

"Is your car damaged?" she asked abruptly.

He must have said something to her about the writing on the car. He did not plan to tell her about the damage. He intended to have it painted before she sees it.

"No sweetheart, the car is fine."

"Why would you lie to me Phil? I saw the car as you drove off this morning. I was going to ask you about it, but then I got the voicemail. You are fucking a child aren't you?"

Things were going quickly downhill. *If he could not get his lies straight enough to get past his wife, how could he ever get past an investigator? Why didn't he just tell her the car was spray painted?* He kicked himself for panicking and not thinking things through.

"I've got to go Sasha; we will have to finish this tonight at home," he said abruptly.

"Okay Phil, I'll let you go. I'll see you and the car at home tonight," she slammed the receiver into the cradle.

He could not believe this was happening to him. He wanted to scream at the top of his lungs, but could not wrap his mind around the concept. He was dazed, and sat staring at the phone unable to focus on anything but his crumbling world. He blinked hard several times trying to focus, but the only thing that happened was the trickle of water that fell from his eyes. He cried silently at the predicament he found himself in.

As he wiped the tears from his eyes, he noticed the message light on his office phone was blinking. He picked up and dialed into the voicemail. He froze in his seat. The chill that went through his body, as he listened to the male voice, could have given him frostbite.

"Danielson I told you to stay away from that little girl. But your sick ass wouldn't listen. Now I'm coming for you. The pictures of you, that child, and her mother will be in your wife's and your boss's possession today. Oh, and don't let me forget the Washington Post. They will dig and dig until something is done about you. You are going to lose your wife, your job, your dignity, and then your freedom. Imagine what those boys are going to do with your lily-white ass in the joint. They are gonna fuck you up; then they are gonna fuck you. So prepare yourself because it is all going down today. I warned you!"

Briscoe bluffed on the part about the pictures, but Danielson had no way of knowing that. Briscoe had every intention of isolating him, and then when he was at his lowest level, he planned to put him out of his misery by cutting off his dirty dick and stuffing it in his mouth.

"I am totally screwed," Danielson said aloud as he pressed the key to delete the message. He was about to face an investigation that was sure to find that he has been messing around with Shauna, but that was just a small part. He has been having sex with children for years. He is currently seeing two other kids, one being his ten year old niece. Once this gets out the other children will come forward and ruin him.

He sat motionless as though he were paralyzed. He has been in his office for nearly an hour and has not lifted a finger to prepare for his appearance in court at 1:00 p.m. *How could he go to court? Everybody will be staring at him.* He felt as though everybody knew his secrets. The cat was out of the proverbial bag.

The intra-office phone line rang, once again bringing his thoughts back to the present. He looked at the caller ID that displayed Patricia's number.

Reluctantly he answered the phone, "Morning Pat."

"Phil, I just got a call from Jerry Weston. He wants you to report to his office right away. He sounded like it was urgent," she said curiously.

"Did he say what it was about," he asked nervously.

"No. He just said tell Phil I need to see him immediately. It is very important," she relayed.

The moment of truth was on him; he could no longer hide from his secret passion. *Was Jerry going to tell him to clean out his desk? Was he going to tell him that an investigation was underway?* The fear beat inside of his heart like a drum.

"Okay, thanks," he said sadly.

Patricia could tell something was wrong with Phil, but she did not press it. She wanted to get him to open up and let her know what troubled him, but she decided to let him have space, and hung up the phone.

After sitting for an additional ten minutes, Danielson unlocked the bottom drawer of his government issued desk and removed a 9mm Ruger Centerfire pistol and placed it in his brief case. He snatched a sheet of paper from his legal pad and wrote in large letters with a permanent black marker, "I'M SORRY."

He left the note on the center of his desk and walked out of the office closing the door behind him.

Instead of going out through the reception area to the elevator, he took the back steps down to the garage. He climbed into the driver's seat of his vehicle and started to cry out loud. He begged God for forgiveness, as he thought about the tremendous shame he brought on himself and his family. He never thought he was hurting anybody. But now he realizes he did. He prayed that his sister will forgive him once she finds out he has been having sex with her ten year old daughter since she was seven. He knew once his secrets got out, lives would be ruined; and he was to blame. His heart felt as though it weighed two tons.

With tears streaming down his face and pain and regret etched in his heart, he reached into his brief case and pulled out the Ruger. With his right hand, he placed the barrel of the semi automatic handgun to his chest at the point where his heart was beating the strongest.

He hesitated just long enough to say, "Please forgive me," and then pulled the trigger.

The firing pin struck the primer igniting the round and sending it exploding down the barrel and into his chest cavity. Tissue and blood splattered across the windshield, steering column, and console. The pain of the violent impact contorted his face as his body slammed into the seat and then lurched forward striking the steering wheel. The sound of the powerful handgun was deafening. Now there was an eerie silence broken only by his gurgling blood and gasping for air. Death was not instantaneous. He suffered severe pain while slumped over on his right side, bent over the console. The gun slipped from his grasp, but he did not have enough strength to pick it up and finish the job. He gasped for air that was increasing hard to swallow. For the next six hours, he laid semi conscious in severe pain, tormented by the evil he did, and the fear of the eternity he faced.

Being parked in the back of the deepest level of the garage and slumped over the console made it hard for anyone to see him when they departed the building for the day. A security guard, doing his rounds after 9:00 p.m., discovered Danielson's body. The media monitored the police radio and sprung into action when they heard a body was found in the underground parking garage of the U.S. Attorney's Office. They sensed it was big news. The breaking news appeared on the Ten O'Clock News. They recited the details they badgered the cops into giving; but they couldn't get the decedent's name pending notification of next of kin.

The news of Phil Danielson's apparent suicide was broadcast over every type of media outlet. His demise was the top story. The media spent the day speculating whether there was a conspiracy, cover up, or some other high level government shenanigans. The reports from the media were grainy and incomplete. Investigators did not disclose what his wife said about the phone call she received, the condition of his car, or the two word note he left on his desk. His death was an obvious suicide, so the Homicide Division closed the case. Due to the sensitive nature of Danielson's position, and the fact the government did not want the shit storm that would follow if they disclosed what drove him to commit suicide, they opted to drop it. The powers that be determined he took whatever secrets he had to his grave. If he was in fact a child molester, every person convicted directly or indirectly by him would scream for a new trial. It would cause an unnecessary ripple in the justice system; one nobody was ready to deal with.

33

Whitehead, Sutton, and Agent Bell sat in the private conference room at the back of the squad bay. Whitehead and Sutton both laid out the results of their investigations into the eight officers while Deborah listened intently. They came to the conclusion that none of them, and yet all of them, could be the killer. It was a difficult thing to decipher, considering it wasn't an exact science. But throughout it all Whitehead had a gut feeling about one of his suspect officers. He felt there was more to Briscoe than what meets the eye. He expressed his concerns to the others and told them why he had a feeling about Briscoe. It was not enough to move on him, but he wanted to get a closer look at him.

Deborah asked, "Have you had a chance to check out his whereabouts during all the murders?"

"Somewhat," he said flatly. He continued, "I can account for the times he was on duty. The times he was off are something I will have to look at if I ever have enough to question him. I talked to him the other day, but he was cool. He figured out that I was interviewing him, and pretty much got offended."

They listened as Whitehead recounted some of the reasons his gut feeling told him to take a closer look at Briscoe.

Then Sutton suggested, "Why don't we get him in here somehow. We can have Tanisha take a look at him and listen to his voice?"

"That's a damn good idea. Do you think she would do it?" Whitehead asked.

"I'm not sure. But I think it would have to be in such a way that didn't let them know she was there," Sutton knew she would be extremely reluctant.

"We could conduct a lineup and request Briscoe to participate along with the other officers on the list. They are all in the same demographic with similar enough builds. The only obstacle to that is having somebody defined as a suspect. If we tip our hand too soon, we could lose any advantage we might have," Whitehead frowned at his dilemma.

He knows the rules that pertain to self incrimination, as well as the police officer's rights. Having an illegal or unscrupulous lineup could jeopardize his case. He was not willing to travel down that road. So any thoughts of deception were out the window. He was going to do everything the right way. If he could somehow get Briscoe into the office and have Tanisha there at the same time, it would just be viewed as coincidental. If she is able to identify him as the one, then based upon that chance meeting he would have enough probable cause to get search warrants and move forward.

They tentatively decided to have Tanisha at the office and then ask Briscoe to come in and swap cell phones or something along those lines. When he comes in, they would have Tanisha sitting at Sutton's desk. Once she sees and hears Briscoe, she will either know him or not.

They felt that was a good plan. They also realized that Tanisha would never do it willingly, so they decided to not tell her. They would bring her in under false pretenses also. That was the only way to ensure an unbiased identification.

"Okay Jake, set it up baby," Whitehead said eager to move forward. "In the meantime, lets continue to follow up and investigate all other possibilities. But I have a feeling in my gut about this one."

34

When Briscoe received the news of Danielson's suicide, he had mixed emotions. On one hand, he was happy the sick puppy wouldn't molest the girl anymore. On the other hand, he wanted to see him suffer for a good long while before he departed. He surmised that justice was done, even though it was done at Danielson's own hands. A quote from the Bible came to his mind, "Justice comes from above; vengeance is mine, saith the Lord," so regardless of the earthly vessel used, the vengeance comes from above.

He had no idea Danielson would take the route he did. but it gave him an idea for Janice. With all he has been through, Briscoe never stopped thinking about the young girl being constantly abused by the men she is pimped out to by her mother. His hope was for her to be okay, with no long term damage. He knew it would take therapy to get past what has happened throughout her early childhood, but there was hope. He knew it was not too late to help her, but with each encounter with some dirty dick old man she would lose a piece of herself. *Hang in there Shauna, I'm coming.*

The plan to take down Brick weighed on his mind, but he couldn't shake the thought of Whitehead and their conversation. One thing was for sure; he had to be extra careful and watch his back like never before. There could be no mistakes. He will have to keep a close eye on the Homicide detectives and stay in close contact with his boy Sanford since he is on the inside. If he is considered a suspect, then he will definitely tighten up his game. He was always careful not to leave evidence, but now, more than ever, he will have to be sure of his surroundings.

Briscoe spent the next few days visiting Karen in the hospital and casing Brick's crew. He did not want to waste any time or miss his window of opportunity. On his days off, he watched Brick's entire Montello Avenue crew day and night. He studied their patterns and behavior. There was going to be no room for error. He decided he needed to make a statement so loud and clear that it resonates across the city. There was going to have to be an end to his street sweeping someday, but he wanted to be sure it served a purpose.

He reflected on the people he has taken permanently off the

streets over the past five months since he began his mission. They were all very bad people . . . for the most part. Sure there were a few he would not have targeted individually, but their gang affiliation, and presence when he moved on his target, made their death necessary. He recalled a passage of scripture that says, "There must needs be that offences come into the world, but woe unto he who brings them." He does not regret what he has done, because he knows it was God's will for him. He was carrying out God's vengeance on those who have committed offenses that caused serious pain and suffering to others. Well, in his mind at least, that is what he has come to grips with. Now his soul is at ease.

    He got an early start Saturday morning. He packed his black backpack with his zoom lens camcorder, night vision goggles, and every essential he needed for a stakeout. He packed canned food, cold cut sandwiches, and a gallon of water. He put on his black jeans, a black tee shirt, and a black baseball cap. He packed a black hoodie, just in case. He strapped on his service weapon, but packed his trusty .45 caliber Silencer equipped Sig in the backpack. He tied the Ranger Bowie knife to his ankle and took a few steps to test for comfort and concealment. He stooped, kneeled, and sat down on the floor. The knife did not interfere with his movements or cause him any discomfort. He was now ready to put in work. Briscoe planned everything for this day, down to his alibi for Monica. He was not going to be interrupted or sidetracked.

    He left his house en route to Montello Avenue. It wasn't 5:00 a.m. yet and he was on Branch Avenue making his way with every intention of beating the sun. He stopped at a 7-Eleven to grab a newspaper and a cup of coffee. If he was going to be holed up watching all day, he should take the downtime to read up on what is going on in the world. He bought a Washington Post, a Washington Times, and a Wall Street Journal. He considered himself a liberal, but sometimes you have to get the news from all perspectives just to find the truth. Each paper puts their own slant on the news, so he figured he would just read it all and derive the truth from somewhere in the middle.

    His plan was to go to an abandoned three story row house that provides a perfect view of the corner where Brick's gang deals. He checked the house out two days prior and was pleased with the concealment it provides, while giving a panoramic view of the corner and roughly three blocks in all directions. It was the perfect location. The house was partially boarded up. There was no indication it belonged to a private citizen, but just to be sure, Briscoe checked city records and learned it was the property of the city. It was once owned by an elderly woman who passed away a few years back without heirs. The city took control and ultimately sold it at the height of the housing boom for nearly $600,000. The buyers had an adjustable rate mortgage that adjusted up to a point they could not pay. The property values plummeted as the whole mortgage industry saw record foreclosures and steep declines in property values. The entire economy was reeling from the recession that bordered on depression. Unfortunately for the owners of the property, they bought in a drug and violence infused neighborhood. President Obama's stimulus package did not come in time to save them. But it works out well in Briscoe's favor.

It was important for him to get to the house before the sun came up. He did not want to risk somebody seeing him go inside. He had to leave his car in the shopping center parking lot and walk five blocks to the house. Since the car would be parked until well after dark, he did not want to draw unnecessary attention. The longer a strange car sits in a neighborhood, the more likely people are to remember details about it. He was driving the rented Pontiac, but it could be easily traced to him.

A ragged six foot wooden fence enclosed the yard. The gate was missing, so at best the fence provided concealment, but did nothing to keep intruders out. He shimmied his way into the house through the flimsily boarded back door and worked his way upstairs. He checked every room to ensure there was nobody inside . . . you could never be too careful. He cleared the house and settled in the third floor bedroom that provided the best view. The electricity was off and the house was still dark. He used a flashlight on the lower levels because it was boarded and hidden from outside view. However, when he navigated the steps to the upper level he switched the light off. His night vision kicked in along the way and he could make out everything on the upper level. Some of the windows still had curtains on them. He decided to do some rearranging with the curtains. He moved, and made sure all the curtains in the bedroom were set to where he could look out without being seen. He closed the bedroom doors to the rooms that he would not use, because they did not offer views of the street and did not have curtains on the windows. The last thing he wanted was to be seen going to the bathroom.

Speaking of the bathroom, it was a trifling mess. The water was turned off and the bowl appeared rusted. There was urine and feces in the bowl, and the smell was acrid. The house has been vacant less than two years, but it seemed as though it was vacant much longer. The place was trashed. It was like the family only took the things of value and left everything else. There was furniture of some type in every room, along with clothing, books, and a bunch of trash on the floors. The place was a total mess.

Briscoe grabbed a folding chair and set it up in front of the window, just far enough back to have a clear view without being seen from outside. He checked and tested his camera equipment one final time. Everything was good to go. He looked at his watch; it was 5:38 a.m. The sun will be up in about an hour and then roughly five hours after that the street would be in full swing. He knew he was looking at an eighteen-to-twenty hour day in that shitty house. But to him it was all worth it. He bought the papers to occupy his time while waiting for the corner to pick up. He planned for the downtime. His phone is fully charged and he has enough food to last him the duration.

For the next few hours, he read the newspapers and even took a power nap to recharge his mental battery. He was rejuvenated and ready to capture everything about Brick's gang and their movements. When he strikes, he will do it with furious vengeance and will spare no one. With such a lofty objective, he had to be sure of their patterns.

The day went pretty much according to plan. He videotaped as much activity as possible. His main battery had 210 minutes of recording time and the spare battery offered 300 minutes. So he had to do a good job of prioritizing and capturing the things he deemed most critical. It was nearing midnight and he was down to fifteen minutes of recording time. He had the faces of all the players captured on film, along with the activity that binds them. Anything he recorded now was only icing.

His shoulders and back were tired and strained from sitting in the chair or standing for such long hours. He was ready to pack up and get out of there but debated staying a couple more hours. He really needed to take a shit, but had no intentions of doing it in that house. He has been in some deplorable conditions in the past, but there was no way he was going sit his ass on, or hover over that toilet. The thought of going home and sitting on his own toilet helped make up his mind.

He packed his equipment, collected, and bagged his trash, including the newspapers, and sanitized the area, making it looked untouched in years. The room was lighted only by the street lights. The rest of the house was pitch black. Briscoe's night vision was well intact from sitting in the dark room since sunset, but he wasn't going to chance navigating the littered house without a flashlight. He reached the top of the steps and just prior to descending he heard a noise below.

He crouched down and stepped backward, away from the staircase. He listened closely. He was able to discern voices and items being knocked over. It sounded as though someone was struggling with something heavy.

Briscoe put the small Stinger brand flashlight in his left pocket. He put on his leather gloves and donned his night vision goggles. He removed the .45 from his backpack and press checked to ensure there was one in the chamber. He placed the bag on his back and started cautiously down the steps, where he could hear two men talking,

"Hold up," one of them said.

"I got his feet, just keep going straight back," the other one said breathing heavily.

"Straight back where? I can't see shit," his voice strained from exerting energy.

"Man, just keep goin the way you goin. This mothafucka is heavy."

Briscoe was now at the bottom of the steps, where he saw the two men carrying a body. They were fifteen feet away and unaware of his presence. He recognized the two men and was surprised to see that one of them was Ant Lakeland. Serendipity has smiled upon him.

He could not see the face of the man they were carrying, but he knew it was another young black male. That alone tugged at his heart. Why must men kill one another for selfish gain? There was no doubt the body being dumped was the result of some beef that originated over the primary purpose of Ant's business. The drug game has claimed more niggas than cancer. It is a downright shame.

Right now there are two lives that Briscoe is going to claim, but he feels he is claiming them in the name of righteousness for a higher purpose. By ending their lives, others will live.

He took a quiet cautious step off the bottom step and onto the same floor the gang bangers were carrying their victim. With the grace and swiftness of a highly skilled assassin, he raised his weapon and fired two quick rounds into the chest of Ant's friend. Pwt, pwt . . . was the only audible sound from the powerful weapon. The flash lit up the room and exposed Briscoe's six-foot-two-inch silhouette to a startled, wide eyed Ant. Briscoe transitioned the night vision goggles to the top of his head and the flashlight from his pocket. He shined the light directly into Ant's eyes. He was still holding the legs of the victim he and his partner carried into the house. His partner was motionless on the floor underneath the body they carried.

"Don't move a muscle," Briscoe ordered, holding the light directly in Ant's eyes.

Ant let the legs go and raised a hand to shield his eyes from the light. Briscoe shot him in the foot.

"Oww! He screamed in pain as he bent down to grab his foot.

"Shut up before I put the next one in your mouth," Briscoe said coldly.

"What the fuck man?" Ant screamed.

"I'm not going to warn you again. If you don't lower your voice, I'm going to shoot you in the fucking face."

Something in Briscoe's tone got his attention.

"What do you want man?" Ant realized he was in trouble.

He thought about the gun tucked down in the back of his pants beneath his oversized white tee shirt, but was afraid to make a move for it.

"Who is that," Briscoe asked.

"Who is who?" Ant asked.

"The dead dude you carried in here."

"Just a dude," Ant lied.

"Well, it don't matter. You don't have to tell me, I'll find out tomorrow," Briscoe left him wondering what he meant by the comment. "Who is your boy Ant?"

The question caught him by surprise. "How do you know my name?"

"I know everything. Is that Kwame or Jamal?" he asked motioning with the gun.

"Neither; that's my cousin Mike from Maryland."

"He was your cousin Mike from Maryland," Briscoe walked to Ant and put the gun to his forehead.

"Interlock your fingers behind your head," he ordered.

Ant placed his hands behind his head and laced his fingers. Briscoe patted his dip area all the way around until he found the gun. He removed the gun and placed it in his waistband. He ran his hand up and down both of Ant's legs, checked his pockets, and made sure he was not wearing a shoulder holster.

"Get on your knees," he placed a hand on Ant's shoulder forcing him to his knees, the whole time with the gun pressed to his forehead.

From his kneeling position in front of the two bodies on the floor, which he could no longer see since the flashlight consumed his vision, he cried out, "What do you want from me? My foot hurts like shit."

"I want some answers," he decided to find out a few things before punishing him.

"Answers to what?" he said grimacing from the pain in his foot.

"Why did you shoot the female cop?"

"I ain't shoot nobody," he pleaded.

Briscoe kicked him as hard as he could in the crotch. He doubled over. Briscoe bent down and punched him in the head. He grabbed him by his dreadlocks pulling him back up on his knees.

"Now, let's try this again. The next answer better be the truth, or I'm going to shoot you in your lying mouth and be done with this."

"I didn't shoot her, Kwame did," he said.

"But I know you were there. Why did ya'll do that to her?"

"Brick told us to. He said she was following him. We didn't know she was a cop until we ran up on her," he knew there was nothing else that could save him but the truth.

"Okay, do you know if you killed her?" Briscoe wanted to make sure Karen was safe.

"Yeah, we killed her. Kwame shot her like four times," he believed she was dead.

Briscoe reared back with his gun and struck Ant as hard as he could across the mouth.

His teeth loosened. The ringing in his ears, coupled with the intense pain in his head, caused him to convulse. He doubled over on the floor where Briscoe stomped and kicked him. He backed up a few feet and aimed his next kick for his face. When Ant moved his hands Briscoe kicked him as hard as he could in the middle of his face. Blood shot everywhere as he screamed out. Briscoe shot him twice in the leg. The hot lead tore away flesh and bone as it caused searing pain.

Briscoe did not expect to encounter his targets in this way; thus, he was not completely prepared to spend the time he wanted. He could not do to him what he planned, because there was no way to stop him from screaming. Oh well, the outcome will be the same, and he will no longer be around to victimize anyone.

He aimed the gun at the center of Ant's face and squeezed the trigger. Ant's body ceased all movement. The .45 tore off half his face. It was a gruesome sight, one that Briscoe did not want to remember . . . but there was nothing he could do to stop the nightmares that are sure to follow.

For the first time he looked at the entire scene. He didn't know who the other two were, but he knew they were dead. But just to be sure, he put a bullet in the head of Ant's cousin Mike. He made a sweep around the room to make sure he didn't drop anything. Once satisfied, he peeked out the back door, where he saw a car parked in the alley. He could not see if it was occupied because the fence blocked his view, but he could hear music coming from it. He could see the back half of the car. It was a dark colored four door hoopty that he figured they used to bring the body to the house.

With the gun still in his hand, Briscoe pulled the night vision goggles over his eyes and skirted around the edge of the yard hugging the fence for concealment. He reached the fence parallel to the car and looked though the spacing and saw a man sitting behind the wheel with the engine running. He must be with Ant; but Briscoe was going to make sure.

He worked his way to the entrance and in one quick motion stepped to the driver. The weapon leveled and pointed directly in the man's face.

He said, "Put your hands on the wheel."

The man complied and, with a trembling voice, said, "Don't shoot."

"I'm not going to shoot. Why are you sitting here?" Briscoe asked.

"I'm waiting for somebody."

"You hang with Ant; are you waiting for him?" Once Briscoe saw his face, he knew he was one of the people he spent the day watching.

He videotaped this young punk selling drugs and harassing females as they walked up and down the street trying to enjoy their Saturday.

"Yeah, I'm wait'n on him," he was obviously trying to compose himself, hoping Ant's reputation would scare the gunman away.

Without saying another word, Briscoe pulled the trigger. The round impacted the middle of his forehead sending flesh, skull fragments, and brain matter everywhere. His lifeless body fell over onto the passenger seat. Briscoe reached in and turned the vehicle off. He pulled the goggles from his head and placed them in his backpack. He put on his baseball cap and pulled it low over his eyes and disappeared into the night.

35

"Jake I need you to get that Shem in here ASAP," Whitehead was reeling from the four dead bodies Briscoe left on Saturday night. "We need to get her in here and the four officers we narrowed our list to. This shit is way out of hand."

"I'll call her and do all I can to get her to come here. Once I have a commitment, I'll schedule the officers to come by to take care of some business."

Sutton had to devise a plan to get them one at a time in the same space with Tanisha. He will have to get them to speak so she can hear their voices.

"Okay Jake, try to make that happen within the next day or two."

"I will give her a call now and set it up," Jake reached for the telephone and Whitehead went to his desk to get back to the stack of work waiting there.

Jake knew it would take some convincing to get Tanisha to come to his office, but he had to make it happen. He was prepared to promise her keys to the city, even though he didn't have them to give.

He was surprised by her eagerness to come see him at the office. She was feeling him, and hoped that looking at some mug shots, as he told her, would help him, and draw him closer to the possibility of being with her.

She agreed to come in the next day at 4:00 p.m. Sutton gave the good news to Whitehead and they worked on a plan to get the four officers to come in one at a time.

"We could tell them we need to do an inspection on the rental vehicles per the Captain's request," Sutton suggested.

"I don't think that will work because they would just call to let you know they are outside. Besides, I don't think that would give enough opportunity for the witness to identify anybody."

Whitehead contemplated. He stroked his chin, reared back in his chair looking skyward and wracked his brain for a good reason to bring the officers in.

"What if we tell them we need some information on their

assignments?" Sutton said.

"Yeah, but what? Then we would have to do it with everybody on the team," Whitehead was not willing to go to that extent.

Of the four officers, two are on the team, and two aren't. They knew they had to devise two scenarios for the two groups of suspect officers.

"I got it. We can tell the two on the team that we are upgrading their cell phones to Blackberry devices. We can say we are upgrading everybody. I'll go to the radio shop and pick up two now. I'll have them come in to sign for them tomorrow while Tanisha is sitting at my desk. I will engage them in conversation and let her listen to their voices," Sutton felt this was a sound plan.

"I think that'll work," Whitehead agreed, then asked, "What about the other two? What can we do to get them in here? I don't want to blow an opportunity that we might not get again."

Sutton thought hard, but couldn't come up with anything off the top of his head. They kicked around several ideas but kept coming up with objections. Whatever they do, it must appear routine and coincidental at best, and should not give rise to suspicion.

"Here's what we can do," Whitehead started. "We could pull up a name of a bandit from their beat and make them think we are interested in information on that person. We could look to see who they arrested for a violent crime lately, then call them in pretending to need information on that person."

"They would think they are helping out with something else. Tanisha could observe them for a few minutes and listen to them speak. Getting information on somebody else is something they wouldn't need to follow up on, so they would have no idea what we did with the information," Sutton agreed and was eager to put it into action.

With the plan agreed on, Sutton contacted the officers and scheduled them fifteen minutes apart. He would get them in and out as quickly as possible.

Tanisha was running about five minutes late when she pulled into the parking lot of the Homicide Division. She parked near the back of the lot, wishing she could have been closer to the entrance since she was already late. The entrance was about forty yards away and she hurried to get inside. She started across the lot just as Briscoe turned in. His attention was immediately drawn to the statuesque beauty. There was something familiar about her.

He turned down the row where she parked and started up the next row in search of a parking space. He took a long look at Tanisha while she stood at the door waiting to be buzzed in. *She sure is a tall thick chick,* he thought. *I know her from somewhere.*

Then like a freight train it hit him hard. "Oh shit!" he blurted as he turned right and drove out of the parking lot.

It was Damon's tranny girlfriend. A tinge of anger welled inside of him. *He told her not to cooperate with the police. He told her he would be back if she did.* He was now regretting that he let her live. He was sure that night she was too terrified to say a word. *How could he make such a critical mistake?* Well, he will just have to rectify it.

There was no way he was going into the Homicide office with that tranny in there. He didn't know if it was a set up or a coincidence, but either way he was not going inside. He called Sutton to tell him he had an emergency to deal with and wouldn't be able to make it until the next day. Sutton tried to press him for details, but he played him off. He could hear the disappointment in his voice.

Briscoe drove directly to Tanisha's community. He scoped out the place, then went to the auto auction lot, where he parked before. They were closed for the day. No other cars were on the street and he needed to park somewhere inconspicuous. He settled on a street in the business district a block from the auction lot. The majority of the businesses would be open until 8:00 or 9:00 p.m. He grabbed his backpack and headed for the mobile home community.

He went to the front door and quickly jimmied the lock. He was inside quickly enough that it appeared he had a key. He locked the door and marveled that after the tranny's ordeal she did not install an alarm system. That is the first thing most people would do following an intrusion and near-death experience in their home. This time she will not have a near-death, she will have a full death.

Briscoe did not want to kill a person who has done no wrong, but he could not chance being identified. He has no idea what she has already told the detectives, but he knew she wasn't at their office on a social visit. He concluded the detectives wanted him to meet with the tranny. They were going to see if she could identify him. He cannot take a chance like that again.

He walked around looking at photographs, artwork, and collectables. He got a glimpse into the life of a transsexual woman who happened to date the wrong guy. She appeared to be a hard working person committed to a couple of causes that gave her certificates and awards for outstanding service. There were several pictures of her dressed up and on stage. He could tell that she was some type of performer or model. One thing for sure, she was hot. It blew his mind how she looked more beautiful as a woman than so many real women. Briscoe wondered if she ever dated a man without letting him know she was an illusion. He heard about people like her dating guys for a while without telling them; and then bam—out comes the Johnson. That would be enough to send any man into a rage. The more he looked around, the more he felt she wouldn't do anything like that. She was some sort of advocate for transgendered issues and it appeared she was a good person. Some doubt about what he planned to do crept into his mind. However, he quickly dismissed it and told himself that in the war on the wicked there would be collateral damage.

He convinced himself that it was her fault for associating with Damon. He would not allow his thoughts to betray his intended actions. This was the only way to ensure his survival and it was going to be done.

There was no doubt the killing would be investigated as connected to the predator case, but he planned to make it look like a burglary gone wrong. Since she lives in a different jurisdiction, he hoped they wouldn't put it together until long after she was buried. But he knew the first thing the detectives would do is run her address to see if there were previous issues. They will find she was tied up there just a few weeks ago. Nevertheless, he was going to make it look like a burglary.

He went into the master bedroom, where he dumped drawers, ransacked the closet and stuffed jewelry and small electronics into a pillow case. He went into the other bedroom and did the same. Finally, he went into the bathroom and filled the tub with warm water. He was now ready for Tanisha to step through the door. He thought about calling Monica to pass the time, but then again he did not want the cell tower to pick up his number and let investigators know he was in the vicinity at the time of the murder. He didn't know if that was paranoia or extreme caution. But either way, he knew they were looking at him and he did not want to take the slightest chance.

Thirty minutes, sitting in a stranger's home waiting on them to return, feels like three hours. His mind wandered to places he knew he shouldn't go. He thought about the awesome sex he had with

Vanessa. The thought of climbing inside of her wetness was dancing around his mind. The feeling she gave him and the intense orgasm was something he had never experienced. She rocked his world with her mouth and hands. He could just imagine how good it feels inside her vagina. He has done a good job of blocking her from his thoughts, but now with so much free time, he could not stop them.

Once the thoughts began, he started questioning his relationship with Monica. He knows in his heart Monica is the one for him—but goddamn! Vanessa was the hottest sex of his life and he didn't even get his dick wet. That is the part that has freaked him out the most.

He thought about calling Vanessa later. But what would that accomplish other than to feel the fullness of the hottest woman he has ever been with.

He shook his head and said, "Damn it dude, stop thinking about her."

The sound of music coming from the driveway saved him from Vanessa. He looked out the window and watched as Tanisha put the windows up on her new SUV and gathered her belongings.

Since Briscoe torched her Chevy Tahoe, the insurance company settled quickly, and she purchased a Chevy Suburban. For a want-to-be-bitch, she sure does drive manly vehicles. Briscoe reminded himself that even though the tranny lives as a woman, it is still a man he is dealing with. He wasn't sure if that was a psychological affirmation or a warning to stay on task.

Briscoe watched until she made it to the front door. He then went down the hall to the bedroom directly across from the bathroom and stood just to the right of the doorway out of sight. He removed the chloroform from his bag and put it on a terry cloth rag. He heard the door open and close. He listened as keys landed on the counter and bottles in the refrigerator rattled when she opened the door to retrieve a cold drink. She was humming a song as she walked down the hallway toward her bedroom. She was obviously feeling good about the time spent with Sutton.

Just as she walked past the doorway, Briscoe stepped stealthily from the room and applied a choke hold around Tanisha from behind. She struggled to free herself from his steely grip. He felt that she was stronger than she appeared. Her muscles tightened and she tried with all her strength to break free. Briscoe held on tightening his grip until she crumbled to the floor, holding onto the wall for balance. He loosened his grip just enough to place the rag over her nose and mouth.

"Relax lady. Just breath and I'll let you go," he said calmly.

When the pressure was released from her throat, she took the deepest breath she could. Instead of the oxygen she sought, her lungs filled with chloroform. She could feel herself slipping away into a peaceful slumber. The fear subsided, giving way to darkness and rest.

He felt her body relax underneath him as she slipped into unconsciousness. He rolled her onto her back and made sure she was completely under. He placed his arms under her back and legs and lifted her from the floor. He carried her to the bathtub and placed her gently inside. Her limp body, unable to support itself slid freely beneath the water. He stood above her and placed one hand on her chest and the other on her forehead submerging her beneath the water. He held her there for five minutes to be sure there were no signs of life.

He looked down and bowed his head, "Lord please forgive me for what I've done. I had no choice, and I ask that you let this soul enter into heaven. In Jesus name I pray, Amen."

That was the first time he has ever prayed for someone he killed. He felt that she didn't do anything wrong; she just posed a threat to his mission and therefore had to be taken out.

He went out of his way to not cause her unnecessary suffering. He wanted her death to be as painless as possible. It gave him peace knowing she didn't suffer. The prayer settled his spirit.

He pulled the wet gloves from his hands and placed them in the backpack. He took a towel and dried his arms, wiped up the bathroom floor, and placed it in his backpack. He put on a pair of latex gloves and went into the bedroom across the hall. He lifted the ceiling tile above the dresser and placed the pillow case with the items he collected inside and replaced the tile. He looked around the room, then checked the rest of the house to see that everything was the way he wanted it to be. He picked up her purse and dumped it on the kitchen counter allowing stuff to fall to the floor. He removed the credit cards and cash and left everything else where it fell. He went back into the bedroom and placed the credit cards and cash in the ceiling tile.

He returned to the front room and looked out the window to see if it was safe to leave. It wasn't; there were two men directly across the street standing in front of their property talking. They appeared to be in their mid forties and neighbors. They didn't look like they were in a hurry to go anywhere. In fact they were drinking beer and talking loud enough for Briscoe to hear them from inside the house.

There was still about an hour left of daylight. It looks like he was stuck until darkness falls. It was going to be a waiting game. He was going to have to go straight from there to work if he does not get out pretty soon.

He turned on the TV and light in the master bedroom to make it look as though she was chilling in her room. He went back in the living room and waited patiently for the sun to set. He had to use the bathroom, but did not want to chance one pubic hair falling to the floor and giving the detectives just enough to bury him. He wasn't sure how thorough the crime scene technicians were for the PG Police, but he wasn't going to take the chance. He will just have to hold it until he reaches his car.

He sat on the arm of the couch where he was sure not to leave an impression. He thought about Karen and how much she liked him. He thought about what her young daughter must be going through. The longer he thought, the hotter his anger burned. He could not believe Brick would try to kill a cop. He was now thinking of how long and hard he is going to torture Brick. He is going to introduce him to pain that he has never known existed. He is running out of time. He must step up and put the rest of that crew away. He decided that once he did away with Brick's operation in the community, he would chill out. The heat is turning up so he will lay low for a while. The mission was a success to him because there is a reduction in violent crime in the city. Perhaps it's because the criminals are afraid to commit crimes of violence for fear they will be next to die. Or, perhaps the people who were responsible for the majority of the violent crime are no longer walking the earth. Briscoe didn't really care which was the case, as long as good people don't have to fear violence at every turn. Yeah, after Brick is six feet under he will stop dropping bodies for a while.

He still had to deal with Janice and rescue the little girl. As bad as he wanted to chop off Janice's head, he thought about how hard it would be on the child to lose her mother so violently. He will let the social services shut that mess down. He already set that in motion with the Office of Child and Family Services— anonymously.

In the meantime, he needed to get out of Tanisha's house. *Wow, time goes by so slowly when you want to be someplace else,* he thought.

The sun finally set and twilight was on them. This was the ideal time to make his move. The eyes are still trying to adjust to the night and people were less likely to look out and remember key details of a stranger. In war, most attacks occur at dusk or dawn, right at the narrow time frame between the two conditions.

Briscoe pulled his hat low over his face and stepped from the trailer home with a purpose. He did not look in any particular direction. He kept his head down moving quickly, but not too hurriedly as though he was running from something. He did not notice anybody outside and could not be sure if anyone was looking out their window at him. He stopped in the wooded area about 200 yards from his car and took a piss that seemed to flow forever. *Wow, I almost couldn't hold that,* he thought as he released the pressure.

He made it to his car and drove off. He went home to shower and change. He had plenty of time to get uptown to relieve the officer on the bogus detail.

36

Janice was taken by surprise when the police and child protective service workers stormed into her home armed with a search warrant. They recovered three kilos of cocaine, scales, a hotplate, and all the paraphernalia necessary to manufacture and distribute crack cocaine.

Briscoe tipped off the Major Narcotics Division that a tremendous amount of weight was being dealt from her home. Following a quick investigation, to corroborate the facts, they went in to shut down the operation. Briscoe knew when he anonymously dropped the information about the drug dealing from Janice's home it would get immediate attention.

He also tipped the Child Protective Services that Janice was sexually exploiting her daughter. He knew the tip would force them to contact the police prior to making any moves on Janice. Even if it couldn't be proven, it was enough to get the girl away from Janice. Besides, the drug dealing alone was enough to remove the girl and put Janice behind bars for a long time.

He pulled Connie aside and told her to stay away from Janice's house. He let her know they were about to take it down. For her safety, she should not to go around again, even if it took a year. He also convinced her to never let anyone know she was informing for him. He told her to not even tell other police officers or investigators, because it could put her life in danger.

Janice was taken to jail and her daughter Shauna was placed temporarily with her grandmother. Janice refused to rollover on Brick or Christine. She invoked her Fifth Amendment rights and asked for an attorney.

It didn't matter what she did. The evidence against her was overwhelming and her prior record will assure her a lengthy prison sentence. The girl will grow up in a safer environment and hopefully Child Protective Service will get her the counseling she will need to overcome her past and grow into a normal, well adjusted adult.

37

The call came from Mathis in the middle of the day, awaking Briscoe from a nightmare he was happy to escape. The nightmares are becoming more like terrors. In the latest installment, he was in a Federal Prison on death row. The cold loneliness felt real enough to break him out in a sweat. Lying in his sweat dampened sheets gathering his faculties, he breathed into the phone,

"Hello."

"Briscoe, it's Mathis; sorry to wake you, but I thought you would want to know," he said sullenly.

Taking a deep breath and bracing himself Briscoe asked, "What's up?"

"Karen died today," he relayed, choking back tears of emotion.

Briscoe's heart dropped into his drawers. The heaviness and sadness that settled on his spirit left him speechless.

"Hey man, are you there?" Mathis could not tell if he was still on the phone.

"Yeah I'm here," he managed.

"She passed a little more than an hour ago. She never did come out of the coma; she just lost the battle," Mathis said sadly.

A tear rolled down Briscoe's cheek and his heart trembled beneath his aching chest. He prayed so hard for her to recover, but God did not answer his prayer the way he hoped. He still could not muster the courage to speak because he would surely breakdown and cry out loud.

"When I clear this detail today I'm going to the hospital and see if there is anything I can do for her family," Mathis said.

"I think the family support unit will take care of everything for her family," Briscoe finally spoke. "Her daughter is probably crying her eyes out right now," he added.

"I'm sure. It is going to be so hard on her," Mathis agreed.

The anger inside of Briscoe was boiling. He felt his sadness start to be replaced with rage. The longer he spoke to Mathis the more determined he became to destroy Brick and his flunkies.

"Well, I will still go by and let her mom know that I will help out in whatever way I can," Mathis restated.

"Thanks for calling man. I appreciate you letting me know," Briscoe said solemnly.

"No problem; I'll catch up with you later. Peace."

Briscoe looked at the clock on his night stand and thought about Karen laying on a cold table in the hospital. For some reason his mind flashed to her being in the funeral home and the mortician embalming her beautiful body. He felt like she was cold and all alone now.

She was once vibrant and alive; full of wonder and hope, happy to see him, even though he shunned her advances. Now she is beginning the process of decomposition. He didn't know why his thoughts were the way they were, but he couldn't shake the visions that invaded his mind.

"Fuck it!" he screamed at the top his voice and jumped out of the bed. "Those motherfuckers pay tonight."

He grabbed his backpack and dumped the contents on the bed. It was time to step out and put an end to all of them. He went into his closet and removed the floor board. He pulled up a box that was four-by-two-by-one. He carried it over and placed it on the bed beside the backpack. He dialed up the combination and lifted the lid and looked at the contents.

He has not looked in the box in years. It was his just-in-case of some real big "oh shit" moment. That moment is now. He will use its contents to punish those responsible for killing Karen. He pulled out the four M67 fragmentation grenades and gave them a quick inspection before packing two of them carefully in the padded portion of his backpack.

In another section of the box was a short stack of C4 plastic explosives. He had six, one and a quarter pound blocks, time fuses, and detonators. He carefully packed four blocks into his backpack. Then he packed the igniters and detonators in a different pocket.

He pulled the disassembled Kalashnikov AK 47 assault rifle from the box and checked every piece individually before putting it all together. He did a function-check to ensure it was ready to perform. He pulled four magazines from the box, each loaded with thirty rounds of the high powered 7.62 mm rounds for the AK and packed them in the bag.

He checked his night vision goggles to ensure they were charged and ready to go. He did the same with his .45 and all the rest of the gear. He was ready to rain down fury on the shit bags who stamped out the bright light of Karen's radiant soul.

The angel of death is going to visit the corner that Brick's gang claimed as their property. He is going to reap every wicked soul on the street. The anger was swelling inside as he prepared his equipment for his deadly encounter in a few hours.

With everything packed and ready to go, Briscoe laid back on his bed and stared at the ceiling. A tear trickled down the side of his face as images of Karen's smiling face danced around his mind. He could not shake the thoughts of the brutal assault she endured and her struggle, alone in the hospital bed, which she ultimately lost. As hard as he tried, he could not stop thinking about her pain and her child's pain. His body felt hot as though he was on fire. He was so mad he was seeing red. He thought about how old folks used to say that. He had never understood what it meant before; but at this point, he knows exactly what it means. Because there was a red tint to everything in his bedroom. He vowed that he was going to see red blood flowing from Brick's body.

"I'm going to kill his boys, then I'm going to his house and blow that motherfucker up," he said aloud.

He knew there was a detail watching Brick, but it wasn't going to be enough to save his ass. He was more determined than ever before to put an end to Brick. There would be no escaping his wrath and there would be no mercy.

He picked up the phone and dialed Monica at her office.

"Monica Turner," she said professionally.

"Hi Moni," he said sadly.

"Hey boo boo. What's the matter? You sound down," she perceived something not right for her man.

"Karen died," he continued. "She never pulled through from the shooting."

"Oh my god," she felt an instant sadness for the woman she had never met, but who she knew of through Briscoe. "Is there anything I can do?"

Briscoe was glad to hear the sympathy in Monica's voice. He wondered if she would be so sympathetic if she knew how hard Karen worked at taking him away from her.

"Nah baby, the family support people will do everything to help her daughter."

"What about you Antonio? Do you need anything? Are you going to be okay?" she understood the needs of her man.

She also understood the process of dealing with the loss of someone prematurely and in such a violent manner.

"I'll be okay Moni. I just needed to hear your voice," he could feel himself calm down as he spoke to Monica.

He was no longer seeing red. He could feel control of his emotions coming back.

"Make sure you let me know if you need anything, or you need me to do anything. Do you want me to come home right now baby?" she offered, even though she was in the middle of something important.

She did not want to make the mistake again of turning him away.

"Thanks baby, but I'm going to be okay. Don't come home now. I'm going to go to the station soon to see if I can help with anything and then I have to work tonight. Go ahead and handle your business, because I know you are probably busy. I appreciate you taking time with me. I love you Moni," he knew at that moment he made the right choice by sticking with Monica.

She felt warmth that put a smile on her face. All was well with her and her man. She was going to make sure to always be in tune with him.

"I love you too Antonio and I'm here if you need me."

They embraced and kissed through the phone. He did wish she was there to hold onto and make love to. But the way he felt, he probably would just beat her pussy till it was black and blue.

He lay back on the bed and returned to the spot on the ceiling. His thoughts once again spiraled down a path of what ifs and regrets. He even started to regret not giving in to Karen. She wanted him so bad, but he rejected her in that way because of the work relationship. He knows it was the right thing to do, but it could not stop the thoughts from running through his mind.

He shifted his thoughts to his plans for later tonight. He forced himself to go over the sequence of events and his exit strategy. He knew where they would be and when. He was prepared to end all their lives tonight. There would be no innocents tonight. If a person is there to buy crack at the time, they are going down with the rest. Their vice will cost them their life.

He never wanted to hurt anybody who had an addiction, but tonight was the final blow. Since they did not consider Karen's feelings and her precious life, he will not show any consideration tonight.

The next call he made was to his mother. He talked to her about everyday things, nothing heavy. She saw the breaking news about Karen's death. Briscoe realized that the department kept it a secret to protect Karen. Now that she is dead, they are asking the public for help with identifying the assailants. Well, they are too late. Briscoe already knows who they are, and there will never be a trial on earth for any of them.

His mother was concerned for his safety. She always felt his job was a dangerous one and worried about him on the streets at night. Now with the killing of a cop, her fears intensified. Briscoe assured her that she didn't have to worry about him because he was protected by God and nobody on the streets could harm him.

If he could have told her the people on the streets were the ones in danger, because he was the one to fear, she would feel better. But then she would wonder what he meant by the comment. He knows her deep spiritual convictions would never allow her to accept what he was doing to the killers. He had not been to his parent's home in a few weeks but wanted to know that they were doing well. He also wanted to talk to his mother before tonight. His father was at work and would not be home for a few hours. It was nice talking to his mother; she always cheered him up when he felt down. Sometimes he wondered if she knew he was down and went out of her way to make him feel better.

Even if she didn't ask him how he was feeling, her words and actions always said, "I know what you are going through, and I love you son."

He loved his parents more than anything in this world. He never wanted to disappoint them. That was his main motivation for not getting caught.

He spent thirty minutes on the phone with his mother and promised he would come for dinner on Sunday after church. She promptly reminded him to bring Monica, then she said a prayer over him before hanging up.

He had one more call to make. "Hey Will, what's happening man?"

He needed to check in with Sanford to see if there was anything he needed to know before proceeding with his plans.

"What up B," Sanford was in his office working a case.

"I just called to see what you were up to," Briscoe said.

"I was going to call you later. It must be true what they say; when you think about somebody they will call you," Sanford had planned to call him earlier but got sidetracked.

"Really? What's up?" Briscoe asked.

"Remember when you asked if you were a suspect?" he reminded.

"Yeah," Briscoe braced himself.

"Well it turns out they got the psych profile back. They think the killer might be a cop. Your name is one of a few that came up because of your military background and the amount of contact you had with the previous victims." He paused to give Briscoe a chance to digest what he was saying.

Briscoe listened, unsure what he should say at this point.

The only response that he could muster was, "Okay, and what does that mean?"

"That means that they are probably going to check out your whereabouts during all the killings and they will probably try to interview you. Hell, that is probably what Whitehead did with you in the hospital. I got all this information on the low and I need you to keep it there for me," he cautioned Briscoe.

"You won't have to worry about me repeating it to anybody," he assured. Then he asked, "Do they honestly think I could do something like that?"

"I think they are just being thorough." He trusted Briscoe completely and could never imagine him killing anybody.

"I hope they don't waste too much time looking into me and let the real killer continue to take lives." He sounded convincing.

"I'm sure they will catch a break that will point them in the right direction. But until then, just tolerate them. You know they have to play out every lead in order to make sure justice is served. And you know Whitehead; he is a real pit bull, but he is very good at what he does."

Hearing those words sent an uneasy feeling through Briscoe. He knew Whitehead was tenacious and he felt the man had a lock on him. Old school detectives went with their gut feelings at times and Briscoe knew Whitehead had a gut feeling about him. It would only be a matter of time before they would come full circle and square off.

"I hope they find this guy soon, because Whitehead made me feel uncomfortable. I have never been a suspect in anything in my life. I might have a military background, but I'm no killer." The lie just flowed seamlessly from his lips.

"Don't sweat it bro, I don't think it will be too much longer before they catch their man," Sanford wanted to reassure his boy. "You're a good cop and a good man. I've told that to Whitehead on several occasions. So I think this is just him following up on the profile. Don't worry about anything."

"I won't. Thanks for looking out Will," Briscoe knows now, if he didn't know before his conversation with Sanford.

He must strike quickly tonight and then lay low for a long while.

"Anything for you B. What's up for the weekend?" he asked.

"I have to go to my people's house for dinner on Sunday."

"Kirk Whalum is going to be at the Birchmere Saturday night. Do you and Monica want to go?" Sanford invited them to the popular restaurant music hall.

"That sounds good. I'll check with Monica, but I don't see why not." The idea sounded good to Briscoe.

He thought of it as a celebration after his final work tonight.

Sanford shifted gears in the conversation and said, "I didn't want to be the one to bring this up, but I'm sure by now you heard about White. How are you handling that? I know she was your girl."

Briscoe was hoping it didn't come up because he did not want to ride that emotional train again right now.

"Yeah, I heard already. It's a shame. I'm dealing with it right now. I'll go by later to see if there is anything I can do. But I know the family needs space and they are probably looking for answers from you guys." Briscoe referred to the Homicide division.

"You're right, because that shit was senseless to do that to her. We are rattling a bunch of cages, and eventually the guilty will fall in our hands. Then she will be able to rest in peace." Sanford wasn't the lead on her case, but he was helping out with it.

Briscoe thought to himself, *Some of the guilty have been punished, and all the rest will be buried before Karen.* He wished he could let Sanford know what he was doing and get him to join him with the cleansing. He thought about how nice it would be if there were good cops who cared about the community enough to rid it of the stalkers who prey on the innocent. But that is something that he will have to keep and take to his grave.

"Do you all have anything concrete yet?"

"Kind of. Some of the people in the neighborhood she was taken from are talking. We put the squeeze on everybody over there. It's just a matter of time now. He felt confident they would get the men they were looking for soon.

Briscoe also knew it was just a matter of time before they closed in on the bandits. He also knew it would only be a matter of hours before they all end up dead. Sanford is a true friend and Briscoe didn't want to lose that connection, so he vowed to be extra careful.

"Will, you know you can count on me for anything," he offered.

"I know that B. I'll let you know if you can help," Sanford said.

"Alright dude, I'll let you get back to work. I'll see you Saturday. Peace," he hung up and went back to the spot on the ceiling and his plans for tonight.

When he stepped from his house, it was early in the evening. He loaded his backpack with all his gear in the trunk of his Dodge Charger and started into town. He was dressed in blue jeans and a tan Polo shirt looking as leisurely as possible. Of all the days in his life, this was the one that he needed to be completely anonymous to the world. He wanted to be a forgettable figure on the landscape of the once renowned chocolate city.

It was just past the evening rush. People were settling into their homes, meeting up at restaurants, and other popular night spots to unwind from another hectic work day. The traffic was a lot thinner than it was an hour before, but there was still enough to add tension.

The sun was shining bright in the sky. Briscoe figured in about a month the days would grow noticeably shorter. The summer solstice was long past and the country was heading toward the autumnal equinox. He thought about how much he likes fall and the change in seasons. He loves the brilliant colors of the leaves changing, the cool, mild temperatures, and the serenity of early sunsets. There is so much beauty in and around the city, but some people never take the time to see it or enjoy the benefits of the labor that went into creating that beauty.

He made his way to Connecticut Avenue and parked his car on the busy thoroughfare, got out and locked the doors. He knew the car would be safe. Nobody would think twice about the Charger.

The amount of activity that saturated the avenue day and night was enough to keep any would-be thief away from the car, so he was not worried about his gear in the trunk.

He walked one block to the Metro and boarded a subway train for the Naylor Road station in Maryland. He can catch a taxi for the ten minute ride home.

Briscoe took up a seat in the rear of the middle car of a six-car train. He looked around at the people wondering where they were going, what they had done all day, and what type of life they lived. He looked at a middle aged man who was balding, with a potbelly that looked unnatural on a man his size. He was about five-feet-eight-inches tall and thin everywhere but the midsection. He was wearing a gray pin striped suit with a solid red tie. He had a worn brief case that looked as though it's been through many seasons of riding the Metro to and from Maryland. Briscoe looked at the wedding band on his finger and for some reason wondered if he was happily married; or did he just tolerate his life because he was stuck in it. Perhaps the man had a family who loves him, and he loves them dearly, and goes off to a job that he loves every day. Or he just trudged in, did his time in the trenches, and rode back home to a nagging, unfulfilling relationship. He started to think about his own situation at home. He has a woman he loves in Monica. *But how do you really know that is the person who will keep you happy and motivated the rest of your life? What if she turns out, over time, to not love him the same? What if he stops loving her, or desire something different?*

He shook himself away from those thoughts when he realized he was starting to think of Vanessa again. He looked around at other passengers and noticed many were listening to iPods, reading, on computers, and some were even able to get phone reception underground. People were secure enough in their environment to drop their guard in a public place. That was either due to their trust in the government to keep them safe from harm or their trust in God. Because it was hard for him to believe people would have that much faith in each other. If only they knew the dangers lurking around every corner and the many souls who wait in the shadows to do them harm . . . they would be more vigilant.

He reached his Metro stop and had no trouble finding a taxi for the short trip to his house. He looked around when he reached his house. He wondered if the neighbors noticed him pull up in a taxi. He tipped the driver a dollar and went quickly from the taxi to his house. With the time drawing near, he wanted to be complete in mind, body, and soul. He cooked a meal of broiled chicken and green beans from the can. He knew they weren't as healthy as fresh cut, but hey; what do you expect from a bachelor? He had minute rice for the starch and popped open a can of biscuits and heated them in the oven.

While his meal was heating, he jumped in the shower. The images of Karen being beaten and shot played vividly in his mind. The rage made his body shiver and tingle beneath the warm flow of the pulsating shower head. He squinted hard to banish the negative images and rubbed soap vigorously on his face. He had to focus on the work before him and not allow his emotions to overshadow his good judgment.

He finished his shower and wrapped the towel around his waist as he finished preparing his food. He fixed a plate, sat at his kitchen table, and enjoyed the meal. The image of Jesus and The Last Supper flashed across his mind. He thought, *Lord don't let this be my last meal.* The idea of not making it through the night was something he didn't want to consider. But, with what he had planned, that possibility was a reality.

When he finished his meal, he went into his bedroom, fell on his knees at the foot of his bed, and cried out to God. His heart opened up and he begged the Lord for forgiveness, strength, wisdom, and safety. He prayed for Karen's soul and for her family. His nose ran and tears flowed freely as he sobbed deep and loud. His body shook with every teardrop, but he did not attempt to stop himself from crying out loud. He embraced it and allowed himself to cry until he was all cried out. He remained on his knees in prayer for thirty minutes.

When he stood to his feet, he knew in his heart he was on the right path. God gave him peace and comfort that he was doing the right thing. He dressed in black jeans, black long-sleeved Under Armour tee shirt, and black baseball cap. He laced up his black boots and looked in the mirror as he holstered his service weapon. He put the .25 caliber handgun in the ankle holster and strapped the Bowie knife to his side concealing it beneath his tee shirt. The time was on him. He was ready to do God's work.

He went to the backyard and pulled his Montague CX 21-Speed Cruiser 20" folding bike from the shed and put it in the trunk of the Pontiac. Everything was set. It was time to head uptown to relieve

Officer Seth on the detail.

When Briscoe was a block out from his assignment, he called Seth, as usual, and took his parking space when he pulled out. He watched as Seth turned left at the end of the block and disappeared from sight. He looked at the front and side of his assignment's house and noticed the only light was in an upstairs room. If this guy was a ruthless, drug-dealing killer, he hid it well. Perhaps he really had taken the proceeds from his illegal former life and bought his way into a legitimate lifestyle. Since the detail began, Briscoe could only recall twice when he stayed out past midnight. Oh well, some people do change if given a chance. Briscoe reflected on that for a short minute and then shook it off. He had no time to waste. He needed to get down to work.

He exited the car and used his counter-surveillance training to make sure there was nobody following him. He opened the trunk and removed the bicycle, unfolding and snapping it into its fully functional position. He jumped on and quickly pedaled down the street. He glanced back over his shoulder to ensure nobody was following.

He went down M Street to Wisconsin Avenue. He cut across 24th to get into the block where he parked the Charger on Connecticut Avenue earlier in the evening. It was a Thursday night and the avenue was bustling with people moving to and fro. To Briscoe that area always had a carnival atmosphere. It was as though a party was happening every day of the week. The bars seemed to be working on a seven-day-a-week schedule with planned nightly intoxications and rowdiness. There were regulars who could be found in the same bars night after night. He figured that eventually a person would get tired of sitting on the same bar stool drinking the same old shit and feeling like shit the next day. But he knew there were things in life he was just never going to fully understand.

The daytime temperature for a late August day was normally in the mid-nineties, but this day was one of the nicest August days he could recall. The humidity was low and temps were in the mid-eighties. The daytime temps contributed to very pleasant night temps in the upper-sixties. He hoped the mild temperatures would keep most of the people in the neighborhood in their homes, even though it didn't do much to stop the party-goers in the Northwest community from frequenting the bars, clubs, and restaurants. He also knew the people on Connecticut Avenue were a different breed from the ones on Montello Avenue. That's where he was going to put a few down permanently.

He reached the car and took a quick walk around before opening the trunk. He removed his backpack, folded the bike, and put it inside. He quickly slid into the driver's seat and drove in the direction of his objective.

As he drove, he turned his police radio to the 5th Precinct zone and monitored the activity of on-duty units. There was nothing major happening in the precinct and there were lots of available units on the streets. Briscoe was faced with the possibility of staging a near-catastrophic decoy to buy the time to execute Brick's crew. He was prepared if it came down to that. It looks like it is coming down to that very circumstance.

He drove the Dodge into the block checking to see that all the players were on the street doing what they do. Sure as the night is long, they were hanging predictably on the corner, as boisterous as ever. Kwame and Jamal were among the six men on the corner. They were all drinking twenty-two ounce beers and holding themselves while they relayed a tale of a recent conquest. Or told a blatant lie that made them feel great. They carried on like there wasn't a care in the world, despite the recent loss of Ant, one of the main members of their crew.

Briscoe continued past and drove through the community checking the surrounding streets. All seemed calm.

There was still no major activity on the police radio. It seemed that all was calm for the police of the 5th Precinct. Time was of the essence. He knew now that he had to create his diversion and then move quickly on the corner.

He drove to Rhode Island Avenue. It was close enough to create a diversion, yet far enough away to allow him to do his thing on the corner on Montello Avenue without the cops arriving before he escapes.

He parked his vehicle on a residential section of the street and pulled the C4 from his backpack. He attached a blasting cap and ninety-second time fuse to each of the four blocks of high explosive. He drove to the business district and parked his car on 5th Street. He exited the car with one block of C4 primed and ready to go. He placed it in the cargo pocket of his pants, along with his police issued ASP collapsible baton.

Briscoe was aware that many of the businesses had surveillance cameras aimed at the street in front. He did a reconnaissance days earlier and chose the businesses that didn't have cameras. The first was Dave's Electronics on Rhode Island Avenue near 6th Street. The business did not have the steel shutters that many of the businesses used for security during the off hours. They did have the wire mesh, but the holes were big enough to put an arm through, and that was all Briscoe needed.

He walked to the front of Dave's and used his baton to break the glass. A loud audible alarm immediately sounded. This didn't startle Briscoe because he fully expected that level of security at a minimum. He pulled the pin on the igniter attached to the time fuse and made sure that smoke was coming from the fuse before dropping the block of explosives inside the store.

He turned and walked leisurely back to his car, parked a forty-second walk away. He pulled away from the curb and started down 5th Street just as heard the loud explosion of the powerful C4. He heard dispatch over the radio call for the alarm sounding. He knew it would only be a matter of seconds before the call went out for the explosion.

Making his way around the block, he watched as police cars raced to the scene of the explosion, and listened as the dispatcher requested the Fire Board. There was hustle in the precinct now and a lot of commotion on the radio. But that was just the beginning of the diversion.

Briscoe went to Hamlin Street and parked his Dodge in a residential area. Once again he exited the vehicle with his cargo pockets filled with the other three blocks of C4. He headed toward 12th Street. This was far enough from Rhode Island Avenue to give him time to drive out of the area. He knew that after this, all police resources would be stretched to the limit. He knew they would request assistance from other precincts. By that time, Briscoe planned to be back in Georgetown on his assignment.

He went to the Community Outreach Center located between 11th and 12th Streets. Starting at one end, he pulled the igniter on a block of C4, and threw it against the building. He jogged the length of the building throwing the other two blocks as he jogged. He continued to run out of the block and back to his car on Hamlin. The explosion could be heard for several blocks. There was a five-second delay between explosions. The first went off before he could make it to his vehicle.

He drove casually out of the area and back to the area where his targets were. He listened to the pandemonium on the radio and was pleased to hear that nearly all the units were pulled from the other sectors of the precinct to assist with the multiple explosions on and near Rhode Island Avenue.

He had one more thing to do, then it would be lights-out, party-over for Brick's crew. He went to the pay phone at the Exxon gas station on Benning Road and called 911. He claimed responsibility for the explosions and said the next would go off in the Metro station at Rhode Island Avenue.

The call prompted the dispatcher and police supervisors to pull all units to the area to evacuate the train station, stop all traffic, and cordon the area. The tranquil night became a hot bed of bedlam in a matter of minutes.

With the police overwhelmed still trying to figure out if they are under a terrorist attack, it was the perfect time for Briscoe to do what he came to do. But he still had to be careful and move with precision and speed. There is still a possibility that a cop was in the area and caught up on a case that he couldn't drop to help out in the other sector.

He drove down Montello Avenue and noted that the original six were now joined by two other young men. So now there were eight people on the corner, looking like they were having a block party. Aside from them, the street was clear, and Briscoe drove around in a two-block radius to ensure there were no police in the area and the streets were relatively clear.

He parked his vehicle on Florida Avenue. He attached an earpiece to his police radio and clipped the radio to his belt, beneath his shirt. He was locked into the 5th Precinct radio zone and monitoring the activity. He removed his police-issued Glock and put it under his seat. He replaced it with the silenced .45, and checked the .25 in his ankle holster. He looked over the disassembled AK in his backpack. Now he was ready and exceedingly confident.

He walked to the back of the car and pulled the bike from the trunk. Once it was unfolded and locked in position he got on and rode east toward Orren Street. He turned left, rode up four blocks, and turned left onto Owen Place. His objective was down at the end of the block still engaged in conversation and oblivious to their impending demise.

Briscoe stopped at the mouth of the alley and pulled the AK

from his backpack. He quickly assembled and loaded the powerful 7.62 mm assault rifle, and placed the extra magazines in his left cargo pocket. He put two M67 grenades in his right cargo pocket, placed his pack on his back, and strapped it tight around his waist. He mounted the bike and rode toward the eight men on the corner. The radio was still alive with activity and the units were busy evacuating the Metro station. He listened to the dispatcher inform the watch commander that calls for service were stacking up with no available units to respond. The watch commander advised the dispatcher to only voice emergencies and priority calls. That was good news to Briscoe, because he could be relatively sure that there were no cops in the immediate area.

He went halfway down the street and dismounted from the bike. He laid the bike on the ground between the sidewalk and the curb, and walked toward the men on foot. He got within fifty feet of them, reached into his pocket, and pulled out one of the fragmentation grenades. If one of the people on the corner saw him, they did not acknowledge his presence. He pulled the retainer clip and placed it in his pocket. Then he pulled the pin and placed that in his pocket also. He released the spoon, catching it in his right hand. He placed that in his pocket also to avoid leaving any evidence that could be traced back to him. The grenade has a five-second delay to detonation, so he had to throw it immediately after catching and pocketing the spoon. He dropped flat to the ground to avoid being struck by any shrapnel produced by the grenade.

The grenade landed behind the furthest person from Briscoe with a deafening sound. It set off car alarms as the explosion released the fragmented shrapnel from its tightly packed casing. The carnage was immediate and all eight of the men fell to the ground. The two closest to the grenade died instantly. The others were in varying degrees of consciousness, but they all were struck by shrapnel, and the concussion left them all disoriented.

Briscoe ran quickly to where the bodies were strewn across the ground and fired the powerful assault weapon indiscriminately, striking them in the chest, head, back, legs, and wherever else the rounds landed. When the thirty round magazine ran empty, he released it from the weapon and replaced it with a fresh mag of thirty. Once again, he fired into the bodies. There was no movement from any of them. But he did not care. He was going to fill them with enough lead to poison them. Their lifeless bodies absorbed the bullets as they tore into their flesh ripping away skin, muscle, and bone. He could hear dogs barking and saw several porch lights come on.

In one swift motion, he transitioned from the rifle to the Sig Sauer and walked between the bodies and placed one round in each head, or what was left of a head. He ran to his bike and pedaled in the direction from which he approached. He glanced at the many people who peeked from their windows and at some who boldly stepped onto their front steps. He rode the bike over one additional block before turning south toward Florida Avenue. Halfway through the block, when he was sure there was nobody around, he stopped the bike, crouched down behind the parked cars for concealment, broke down the AK47, and put it in his backpack. He kept the grenade in his cargo pocket—just in case. He didn't want to think of what that just-in-case would entail.

Calls were pouring into the 911 center and the dispatcher requested units from other precincts to respond immediately to Montello Avenue for the report of an explosion, multiple automatic weapon fire, and several men down. Briscoe knew the troops would roll in from the surrounding precincts in a matter of minutes. He pedaled as fast as he could to make it back to his vehicle before any police cars made it to the scene. He used the remote on his key ring to open his trunk when he was still fifteen yards away. He jumped off the bike and collapsed it in one swift motion. He tossed it into the open trunk and sent the backpack behind it. He closed the trunk and jumped into the front seat. He waited a few seconds before starting the vehicle. He looked around to see if anybody had followed, or if a scout car was nearing his location. He listened for the sirens in the distance and studied the block for a few more seconds. With confidence he started the vehicle and drove west on Florida Avenue. He crossed over West Virginia Avenue and was passing Gallaudet University when he heard the first unit arrive on scene. The first responding officer could barely contain his emotions when he saw the wreckage of human life splattered all over the landscape of the crew's coveted corner.

A smile tugged at the corners of Briscoe's mouth. Justice was served. He felt Karen could rest in peace now. The radio was so busy it was difficult for officers to get on and transmit information. A canvas for witnesses was being conducted and the lookout that was initially broadcast was for a male of unknown race wearing dark clothing, riding a bike, and carrying a rifle. He was glad to hear that riding the bike has paid off. He rode it from where the Pontiac is parked as a matter of speed and distance to where he parked his Dodge. But he rode it to the corner to let the witnesses see him on it. That would make the police look for a person on a bike or on foot. Without a better description, they would not know to look for a vehicle.

Briscoe monitored the radio all the way to the Northwest quadrant where he parked his Dodge. The revelry was still in effect on Connecticut Avenue and life was moving forward as usual on this very popular thoroughfare. The events he caused in Northeast have not touched one fiber of the fabric in the party-laden area where he parked. Oh well, such is life and it must go on.

He pulled his shirt off, changed into a gray Polo shirt, and removed the cargo pants, changing into a pair of light stonewashed blue jeans. He changed from boots to sneakers and put all the clothing he took off into a brown paper sack. He was careful because he still had the grenade in the pocket of the pants. He placed his .45 in the bag and reached under the seat to retrieve his Glock. He put the bag in the trunk and removed the bicycle. He locked his vehicle and rode the bike back to the Pontiac.

With his work done in the Northeast community, his next task was to destroy Brick. It has been three days since the massacre on Montello. That is what the news media has dubbed it. Due to the use of explosives and the terrorist threats Briscoe used as a diversion, the investigation has been elevated to the highest priority. It now officially involved the FBI, ATF, and Homeland Security. Even with all these top investigative agencies in the manhunt, Briscoe was not at all fearful. He was now more determined to put Brick away, then refrain from his mission for a while. The main criminal organization is all but dismantled. And the other violent criminals in the area are afraid they could be targeted by the predator. He was confident that his mission was successful to this point. He would have no problem backing off until the heat subsides.

Ring, ring . . . the BlackBerry rang, startled Briscoe, and pulled him away from his thoughts.

"Hello," he said not immediately recognizing the phone number.

"Officer Briscoe; this is Agent Bell of the FBI." She said pausing for effect.

His heart skipped a beat and he felt sweat form on his forehead. He thought how hard it would be to disguise his guilt if she was standing before him.

"Yes," he answered cautiously.

"I'm calling in reference to the serial predator case. I'm the agent who created the psychological profile. I would like to meet with you tomorrow." She deliberately did not elaborate.

She wanted to gauge his response to her statements. He looked at the time noting it was 11:30 p.m. He knew there was something up with him and the investigation. *Why would an FBI agent call him so late at night and ask to meet with him the next day? He knew he was a lot of things, but a fool was not one of them.*

She was fishing for something she didn't have. If they had anything on him, they would have run up on him and did all they needed to do to get the evidence necessary to convict him.

"That's cool," he said casually.

"So what time can I expect you?" She was a little surprised that he didn't take the defensive.

She thought about what Whitehead told her and fully expected him to question her motives and try to get an understanding of what she wanted.

"I just want to help with the case in any way I can. I'm available at your convenience. I get off from this detail at 7:00 a.m. So any time after that is fine. I don't have anything on my schedule." He played it off so well he had to stop himself from laughing, but he didn't stop himself from smiling inside.

Wow, what a cool customer, she thought. "Is nine good for you?" she asked.

"That'll work. Where do you want to meet?" he inquired.

"You can come to my office at FBI headquarters downtown," she said more as a directive than a suggestion.

"Okay, I'll be there at 9:00 a.m. sharp." He tried to sound as enthusiastic as possible.

"Thank you for your cooperation and being an accommodating officer." Agent Bell could not gauge him from the brief conversation.

She chose to use the word cooperation because she wanted him to feel some degree of discomfort.

"No problem ma'am, I'm just trying to do my part to help. I'll see you in the morning," he said.

What the fuck does he have to deal with now? They are going to try to squeeze his ass and God knows what else. He was not feeling good about an encounter with the agent. He knew it was just a matter of time before they start to check for trace evidence in his vehicle and on his person. The investigators are very slick. He knows they can employ tactics that could trip up the most seasoned criminal. He is doing a service for all those who are victimized and oppressed, *so why is the government fucking with him?* He felt himself grow angry, and tried to change his thoughts, but it was futile. The impending meeting with Agent Bell was going to dominate his thoughts for the rest of the night.

Paranoia was starting to set in. Briscoe looked around to see if somebody was watching him. He has been trained in the fine art of counter-surveillance and did not notice anybody observing him. But he needed to know for sure that he was not being watched. Once he was sure of that, he wondered if his company-issued BlackBerry was bugged. His thoughts went to the idea of his vehicle being bugged and his personal phone wiretapped. He physically shook his head trying to escape the thoughts. So many scenarios of his impending meeting with the FBI ran through his mind. Why did they want to talk to him?

He finally decided to leave Georgetown and kill Brick before the heat really picks up. A couple of days ago he spoke to Officer Staley, who was on the task force assigned to Brick. He told Briscoe that there was no replacement for Karen. He said they just did not watch him overnight because he didn't go out late at night, except to the house on 18th Street. And that was recently raided and shut down. Brick's operation had crumbled before his eyes; with the killing of his entire crew, it was time for him to join them.

Briscoe called Staley on his way to Brick's house. He steered the conversation from Karen to Brick. Staley told him that he followed Brick out of town earlier in the evening. He said once they got beyond the one hundred mile mark, he turned and came back to the city. Briscoe asked if he knew where Brick went. Staley said he followed him south on I-95 beyond Richmond, Virginia. Staley told Briscoe that Brick had family in North Carolina and he was probably going down to visit. Briscoe knew it was more than a visit. He was fleeing. Brick has to know that he is next.

The anger boiled over in Briscoe. It was to the point where he could not let Brick continue to breathe freely. There was no time like the present to pounce on his prey and put him six feet deep.

He slid open the BlackBerry and Dialed Officer Mathis number.

"Hello," the gruff male voice sounded.

"Hey Mathis, I'm sorry to call you so late. I have an emergency out of town and have to leave right now." He sounded urgent.

Mathis was sound asleep until the ringing of the phone startled him awake.

"What's going on? Is there anything you need me to do?" His concern was genuine.

"I have an aunt in Connecticut who's been suffering from a long illness. She fell down a flight of steps tonight and it looks like she is not going to make it. The problem is there is nobody there to look after her or her affairs. I'm the only one able to straighten things out. There is also a possibility of foul play, so I have to be there first thing in the morning to do my best to set things straight." The lie sounded convincing.

He knew the only thing Mathis would do was pass it on to Whitehead and Sutton. He didn't care, because by the time he tracked down Brick and removed him from existence, they will still be following dead-end leads.

"Okay man, I'll let them know in the morning. Call me if you need anything. Have a safe trip up there," Mathis said warmly.

"Thanks Mathis. I'll holla later on when I get up there," he offered.

"Just take care of yourself and lookout for your people." Mathis was a genuinely good man and really cared about what he was going through.

Briscoe sanitized his home and the Pontiac he left in the driveway. He took all the weapons and explosives from his house and put them on the rear floor of the Dodge. He grabbed the burn barrel from his back yard and put it in the trunk of the Dodge. He had to tie a string through the trunk latch to hold the trunk down for the short trip he had in mind for the disposal of the barrel.

Once he was satisfied that his house, back yard, and Pontiac were completely sanitized, he packed a bag with everything he needs to survive comfortably and enough clothing to last two weeks. He took a last look around his house before closing and locking the door.

He plans to call Monica later in the morning. By then, he should have a well-thought-out lie to tell her. He knows that the excuse he gave Staley for leaving could be easily verified. He would have to come up with something better by the time the questions start to fly. He considered his parents and what he could tell them about his absence that will not raise any red flags. Whatever he does, it has to be consistent. Oh well, he will deal with a lot of that later. Now his mind was focused on finding Brick and raining down heavily on his soul.

38

It was after 9:30 a.m. when Agent Bell called his BlackBerry. He did not answer, so she left a message asking if he forgot about their meeting. She called Whitehead, who informed her that Briscoe had an out-of-town emergency. He confided in her that he planned to pull the Pontiac Briscoe has been using into the crime lab and scour it for clues. With all the additional help, Whitehead was now able to focus on all the leads, including his hunches. The heat was turning up. He was going to find out if Briscoe was his man or not.

Just as Whitehead hung up the phone with Deborah, Sutton walked up to his desk.

"Hey partner, I just got some news from PG." He appeared perplexed.

"What's up Jake." Whitehead looked in his eyes and knew it was serious so he gave his undivided attention.

"Tanisha was found dead in her bathtub. It appears the body has been there for more than a week."

"Damn, I'm really sorry to hear that," Whitehead was genuinely disappointed about her death.

He also knew that she met all the suspect officers except Briscoe. So his suspicion level rose higher as his gut churned.

"They recovered a footprint from the flower bed," he said with hope for a good lead.

"Do you think it was our boy?" He was referring to the serial predator.

"It's hard to say until we get all the details of the case. They said on the surface it looks like a burglary gone bad, but we will have to wait and see," Sutton said.

"Well, I know you are going to stay on top of it Jake," Whitehead felt sorry for the loss of their only eyewitness. He said, "Your boy Briscoe went out of town abruptly. That tells me to look more closely at him."

"I know you have been dealing with that gut feeling for a while. But we don't have enough to obtain a search warrant or even bring him in against his will to talk. We just have to keep at it and hopefully our killer will slip up and do something careless." Sutton wanted to violate procedure and do whatever was necessary to capture the killer.

He figured that if the serial predator was the one who killed Tanisha, there is no telling who else he would kill. Killing violent criminals is one thing; killing witnesses is a whole different ballgame.

"I think the phone on your desk is ringing," Whitehead advised.

Sutton went to his desk and answered the phone. Moments later. he came back elated. "They have a video tape," he said excitedly.

"What?"

"Yes it looks like Tanisha had a hidden camera set up to video tape her bedroom and there is activity on the camera. We have a picture of our boy. Now we can put him away." He was nearly jumping for joy.

Whitehead stood up and grabbed his hat.

"What are you waiting for? Let's go and look at the tape now."

Overjoyed, Sutton turned to follow Whitehead out the door.

"Let's get our man."